The
Reluctant Matchmaker

SHOBHAN BANTWAL

KENSINGTON BOOKS
www.kensingtonbooks.com

Bantwal

KENSINGTON BOOKS are published by

Kensington Publishing Corp.
119 West 40th Street
New York, NY 10018

All Kensington titles, imprints, and distributed lines are available at special quantity discounts for bulk purchases for sales promotion, premiums, fund-raising, educational or institutional use.

Special book excerpts or customized printings can also be created to fit specific needs. For details, write or phone the office of the Kensington Special Sales Manager: Kensington Publishing Corp., 119 West 40th Street, New York, NY 10018. Attn. Special Sales Department. Phone: 1-800-221-2647.

Kensington and the K logo Reg. U.S. Pat. & TM Off.

ISBN-13: 978-0-7582-5885-4
ISBN-10: 0-7582-5885-2

First Kensington Trade Paperback Printing: July 2012
10 9 8 7 6 5 4 3 2 1

Printed in the United States of America

Acknowledgments

As always, I offer my initial prayer of thanks to Lord Ganesh, the remover of obstacles.

My heartfelt appreciation goes to my warm and supportive editor, Audrey LaFehr, who has placed her faith in me again and again. Special thanks to Martin Biro, Vida Engstrand, and Paula Reedy, consummate professionals who make my writing career a pleasure.

The friendly and dedicated editorial, production, public relations, and marketing folks at Kensington Publishing richly deserve my gratitude and praise for yet another job done well. I look forward to working with you on my future projects.

To my agent, Stephanie Lehmann: I thank you for your invaluable help and guidance at every step. I would not be here without you.

The Writers' Exchange at Barnes & Noble in Princeton, New Jersey, and the Writers' Group at the Plainsboro Public Library deserve my thanks for their insightful comments and suggestions. I offer a grateful hug to my many other friends and faithful readers, who are my cheerleading group.

And last but not least, to my super-supportive family: I am deeply grateful to have you all in my life and for putting up with my idiosyncrasies—and for loving me in spite of them.

Chapter 1

I had no clue that within the next hour my life was about to take a dramatic turn. The bizarre incident struck so unexpectedly that it left me dazed and fighting for breath. Literally.

In my mother tongue, a little-known Indian language called Konkani, this type of rare occurrence is sometimes referred to as *nasheeba khéloo*. Destiny's game.

I'd heard of epiphanies and traumas changing people's lives in a flash. I'd known one or two individuals who had either plunged into misfortune or zoomed into orbit because of a single momentous event, but I couldn't believe my experience could match or even outdo theirs to some degree.

Those kinds of outlandish things happened to others, in my opinion. Ordinary folks like me were exempt from such encounters. Or maybe not.

One minute I was striding forward, trying to maintain my best "smart marketing-public relations executive" image, and in the next I was falling on my back, arms flailing, my short skirt riding upward, providing the shocked people gathering around me an unobstructed view of my underwear.

Sheer humiliation. Well, at least I'd had the sense to wear my best panties, the ones I'd splurged on at Victoria's Secret.

It had started out as a normal day. I had strolled into my sixth-floor office in the multi-story building in Princeton Junction, New Jersey, like I did each weekday morning. Granted, I had an important meeting later that day, and I was uptight about it. I was to meet our highly respected president and CEO for the first time since I'd joined the company with the odd name of Rathnaya, Incorporated.

After my shower that morning I'd taken extra care with my hair and makeup. Then I'd silently offered my prayers before the altar. When it came to important business meetings, I didn't like leaving anything to chance.

Like my great-uncle from India always said, "Prepare yourself well for any kind of catastrophe, but always be sure to pray to Lord Ganesh. Think of the elephant-headed god as your insurance agent." It was no coincidence that my great-uncle was named Ganesh. He also happened to be an insurance agent for the Life Insurance Corporation of India.

By the time I'd gotten to the altar my mother had already finished her daily *puja*—ceremonial Hindu worship. Mom prayed every morning before breakfast. Despite being a modern woman and a medical doctor, she followed the old-fashioned custom of not eating or drinking anything before offering the day's first prayer.

She had placed a single yellow chrysanthemum on top of each of the idols of all her gods and goddesses. The oil-soaked cotton wick in the silver lamp had burned itself out.

Unfortunately I wasn't all that fervent about my Hindu faith. I went to the altar every now and then—when I needed a little extra help from above—like today.

After praying I'd felt much calmer. So what if I had to face the head of the company for the first time? I was a professional and could handle most anything. Or so I thought.

I would realize how wrong I was by the time the workday came to an end.

At precisely 8:07 A.M., our office assistant, Priyanka "Pinky" Malhotra, and I wished each other good morning as I stopped by her desk, or the administrative office as she preferred to call it.

The marketing-public relations department occupied a corner suite made up of three rooms, the first one being a main outer office with Pinky's desk, a row of file cabinets, a fax machine, a copier, and a coffeemaker. It opened out into the long main corridor, but in the back it had two doors that led to separate offices, the smaller one being mine and the larger belonging to my boss, Paul Zelnak. The only access to Paul's and my offices was through Pinky's area. She was our gatekeeper.

Locking her door conveniently locked the entire department. I appreciated the safety feature.

Pinky took one look at me and beamed, the dimple in one cheek deepening. "Meena, you look great!" She swiveled her chair around to study my outfit more carefully. "Went on another shopping spree?"

"Uh-huh."

Then her gaze lowered to my feet. "Wow, new shoes, too. Nice."

I gave her a pleased grin. I'd hoped others would love my ensemble as much as I did. After I'd spent hours in the store looking for a fall wardrobe, it would've been a letdown if someone hadn't noticed. "Thanks."

Pinky looked down at her own black pantsuit paired with a blue shell and black mid-heel pumps. "Everything I wear looks so blah. How come when you wear the exact same thing it looks all stylish and cute?"

"Aw, that's not true," I said with a dismissive gesture of my hand. If only Pinky ate a few less candy bars, she'd be attractive. She had a pretty face with sparkling dark eyes and an infectious smile. Losing a bit of weight could work wonders for her. And the slightly outdated black pantsuit could look elegant if it were paired with a coordinated scarf or jewelry.

Pinky was a good worker and a kind soul, and she had become a friend and confidant in the short while that I'd been working in the company. Besides, as a forty-year-old mother of two young boys, Pinky didn't really need to look chic. She'd bagged her man sixteen years ago, and he apparently loved her, spare tires and all.

"It *is* true, Meena," Pinky argued. "That's because you're young and thin and pretty."

I shrugged. "Thin yes, young maybe . . . but pretty? I don't know about that." And frankly, I didn't feel all that young anymore, not since my thirty-first birthday two months ago.

My parents and our extended family had dropped more than a few hints about my flagging biological clock, my soon-to-fade looks, and my shorter than average stature—my bane. The consensus was that if I didn't find a husband within a year, I was quite likely to die an old maid.

With each passing year I was supposedly inching closer to tooth loss, dementia, and osteoporosis. I'd probably lose even more inches because small women were more susceptible to bone deterioration, according to Shabari, my mother's younger sister. I called her Shabari-pachi in the Konkani tradition.

Of course, like most ethnic folks born and raised in the U.S., my siblings and I didn't speak our mother tongue, although we understood every bit. However, we managed to carry on stilted conversations in Konkani with elderly relatives during our rare trips to India.

Shabari's birthday gift to me had been a book titled *Score a Hit before Your Ovaries Quit*. It wasn't a gag gift. My aunt's sense of humor didn't extend to witty presents. I hadn't read beyond the first chapter yet, but it was a primer for women on the art of landing a man.

At this point, my aunt wasn't dropping hints; she was grabbing me by the scruff of my neck like she would a recalcitrant puppy and dragging me toward matrimony. A thirty-something, unmarried niece could diminish her own young daughters' marriage prospects. In fact, the ripple effect of one black sheep's deficient image could potentially taint the entire clan.

Pinky wiggled her eyebrows at me suggestively. "Is that suit in honor of your meeting with Prajay Nayak today?"

"No." What was Pinky thinking? That I was out to bat my eyelashes at our CEO? Besides, I was nowhere near that significant chapter in my *Score a Hit* book yet and wouldn't know how to go about flirting the right way. The book said there was a method to everything. But I had to master the subtle art of seduction first, before I ventured into practicing it.

"After all, he is your *jaathwalla*. He's a good catch, right?" Pinky meant he belonged to my Gowd Saraswat Brahmin subcaste—GSB for short. But as far as I knew, that was all the CEO and I had in common. He was a genius, a wealthy man with a corporation of his own, with all the surrounding power and trappings, while I was a nobody with an ordinary job.

To some extent Pinky was right, though. I did want to impress Mr. Nayak, but for entirely different reasons.

First of all, it was important to my career. I firmly believed in setting the right tone. And I was ambitious.

Second, since he and I both belonged to the tiny community of GSB-Americans, his family and mine had several common acquaintances. My mother had filled me in on some names. If I made a poor impression, word would spread through the gossip mill like red wine on a white sheet. I'd worked too hard to attain the image of a bright and hard-working professional to end up with a "loser" reputation.

Third, jobs like mine were rare. I wanted to keep it for a long time.

And last but not least, a dumb image would ruin my chances of finding a decent husband. Who would want a dunce for a wife, especially the cerebral Indian guys with advanced degrees and 4.0 GPAs that my parents introduced me to?

My mother on the other hand, after she'd discovered who Nayak was, and that he was single and unattached, had hinted that I should try to charm him.

"One never knows when and where fate will strike, and it is up to an individual to give it a slight nudge in the right direction," she'd declared with a hopeful edge to her voice. She had apparently heard good things about Prajay Nayak from a number of her friends. In the Konkani book of matrimonial prospects, Nayak was a superb catch.

Pinky's teasing grin tugged my wandering attention back to

her. "Who are you trying to kid?" she challenged. "Admit it; you're wearing a classy outfit to impress *him.*"

"Absolutely not," I retorted. "I went shopping the other day, and the new line of clothes looked fabulous. I tried on a few things and . . . you know the rest."

"I know it well. Your credit card suddenly grew legs."

I laughed at her apt portrayal of my shopping habits. "Am I that predictable?"

"Spoiled brat is what you are. Your mom and dad give you too much money and way too much freedom."

"Not anymore," I countered. "I've been paying for my own credit card bills and my auto insurance and gas since I started working six years ago." I pointed to my outfit. "Strictly department store. And very often deep-discount stores if my savings account starts looking anemic."

"You don't say!" mocked Pinky.

"I love discount stores. They have some really cool stuff."

"Humph."

"You don't like them?" I threw her a wide-eyed look.

"I adore them. Besides, they're the only shops I can afford." One thin, scornful eyebrow shot up as Pinky turned back to her computer. "I wasn't talking about the stores you shop at, silly; I meant the things your parents do for you. How soon we forget the free room and board."

I headed quietly back to my desk because I had no rebuttal. She was right. I was still living with my parents, Ramdas and Kaveri Shenoy, along with my younger brother, twenty-eight-year-old Mahesh, who was a medical resident at one of the nearby hospitals. He and I were the fledglings who'd left home for a few years to acquire an education and then returned to the nest as adults.

Mom loved having us around nonetheless. She'd been quite despondent when my brothers and I were at college. "So quiet and lonely without the kids," she used to moan. "Your dad and I walk around like ghosts in this house."

However, now that two out of three were back, Mom complained that Mahesh and I were sloppy, that our ever-ringing cell phones and late nights disturbed her sleep, and that our erratic eating, bathing, and sleeping habits left the kitchen and bathrooms in disarray.

Maneel, my older brother, was a successful stockbroker at thirty-three, and had his own condo a few miles from our home in Princeton. But most of the time Maneel hung around our house, so he ate with us almost every night. His state-of-the-art refrigerator held nothing but beer, soda, and a fat jar of salsa. Despite having a shiny new washer and dryer in his condo, he ended up doing his laundry at our parents' place. He saved on groceries and laundry just like Mahesh and I, but had the nerve to label the two of us "cheapskates."

It's not as if I hadn't thought about moving out of my parents' home, but rents were so obscenely high in New Jersey. And it wasn't for nothing that people denigrated New Jersey for having the highest auto insurance rates and income and property taxes in the nation. How did ordinary people manage to make a living in our state? I often wondered.

Besides, Dad and Mom lived in a big, comfortable house with a finished basement. It wasn't posh, but it was a secure home in an upscale neighborhood, and Mom was a superb cook. Mahesh and I were no fools.

Dropping my purse in my desk drawer, I strode over next door to my boss's office. It was dark.

"Paul's not in yet?" I asked Pinky with some surprise before heading toward the coffeepot that she'd already started. Sniffing the wonderful aroma, I poured myself a cup. Paul was usually here before I was.

Pinky shook her head. "I heard there's an accident on Route 1 and the traffic's a mess. He's probably stuck in that."

"But he would've called us. He has a cell phone."

"Paul's not late yet. And Jeremy already called twice to check on Paul." Pinky rolled her eyes.

Jeremy Larkin was Paul's gay partner, and at times a minor source of aggravation for Pinky and me.

I looked at my wristwatch. "If Paul doesn't show up soon, Jeremy's likely to call again."

As if on cue, the phone rang, and Pinky answered it. "Hi, Jeremy." She assured him between pauses that Paul would be fine. "Don't worry. . . . I'm sure he'll be here any minute. . . . Not answering his cell, huh? There's a traffic backup on Route 1. . . . Oh, you know about that. . . ."

I stood close enough to her desk to be able to hear most of Jeremy's words. He sounded upset. No surprise there.

Pinky lifted her gaze to the ceiling. "I'm sure Paul's not a statistic, Jeremy. . . . I'll tell him to call you the second he gets here. . . . You're welcome."

Hanging up the phone, Pinky gave a dramatic sigh. "I don't know how Paul puts up with Jeremy day after day after day."

"Paul actually likes it. He's got a doting mother, friend, partner, and lover, all rolled into one hunky package."

"Hunky yes, but more irritating than a mosquito in heat."

"I know what you mean," I said on a laugh, and took a sip of my coffee. Pinky had an amusing way with words. "But he cares deeply about Paul. It's quite touching."

"My husband cares deeply about me, too, but if he called me twice a day to ask about my blood pressure and my ovaries, I'd get annoyed."

"Hmm." Jeremy was like a mother hen around Paul. He packed a healthy lunch for Paul each day with a sandwich or salad, fresh fruit, and a little plastic pouch with herbal supplements to prevent every possible health risk, from elevated cholesterol, diabetes, and high blood pressure to an enlarged prostate and impotence.

From looking at all those pills, one would think Paul was a doddering old man, but he was only fifty and in good health. Granted, he was overweight, and he was losing hair, but he looked quite virile.

Nonetheless Pinky and I made sure Paul took all his supplements religiously. Keeping Paul in good health meant peace and quiet for the rest of us. Jeremy was forty-eight and going through a midlife crisis. As long as things were going well at home, Jeremy's calls to our office were limited to about two per day.

I disposed of my foam cup in the trash and glanced at my watch again. Paul's unexplained absence was beginning to trouble me.

Chapter 2

I returned to my desk to await Paul's arrival. Both my incoming e-mail and hard mail baskets were bulging. My day was going to be packed.

Any girl's first year in a job is challenging enough, what with attempting to be sweet but diplomatic, curious but not nosey, friendly but not sycophantic, helpful but not pushy—and all the while trying not to step on some important and sensitive toes. Combine that with the serious marketing efforts of my employer, an aggressive, high-tech company, and I had a tough job.

The business was growing despite the shaky economy, so my life was full—and then some.

I worked hard to make the company look good. I handled their marketing campaigns, press releases, newspaper and magazine ads, charitable events. I edited and published the quarterly newsletter, and I did anything and everything that involved dealing with the public or the press.

My title was marketing and public relations manager. Sometimes I felt like the janitor, because I was expected to clean up the public relations mess if someone from the company made a faux pas.

Whenever the proverbial crap hit the fan, I ran for my bucket and mop. There was never a dull moment. Nonetheless I loved my job—most of it, anyway.

Rathnaya designed and developed advanced software for

NASA, the United States Armed Forces, many federal government agencies, and some state and county governments.

Working with the Feds, the military brass, and an assortment of other bureaucrats on secret projects was a complicated job, and once in a while Rathnaya's top executives made the mistake of giving too little or too much information to the media, and the backlash had to be handled by Paul and me.

Although Paul, whose title was marketing director, was a nice guy, he was a bit on the laid-back side and tended to push things my way—especially the sticky, messy issues that he didn't want to soil his large fingers with.

That was precisely why he'd hired me, a woman with an MBA from Cornell, two years experience working for a mid-sized Jersey newspaper, and three years with a prestigious Manhattan public relations firm—until they'd laid me off when the economic crisis hit. Then there was my brief volunteer stint working on the last governor's political campaign.

For my age I had a pretty impressive work history. My job with the gubernatorial campaign hadn't amounted to much more than placing election posters in strategic locations and answering phones while I looked for a paying job. But it looked good on my resume.

I glanced at the digital clock on my desk. Paul still hadn't shown up. Our meeting was in twenty minutes. I didn't mind going to meetings without him, especially now that I'd become accustomed to this place and the various personalities. But I still disliked the thought of going to this particular meeting alone.

It would be unnerving to meet the CEO without Paul beside me. Although I was the one who did most of the routine work, Paul was the guy who had the final authority to sign off on it. Plus he was an excellent talker—he made the simplest projects sound impressively complicated. That's why he was the director and I the underling.

If Paul was sitting in traffic, he should have called by now. A horrible thought struck me. Could he be the one involved in that accident, like Jeremy feared?

Paul walked in just as I was about to share my disturbing thoughts with Pinky. "Morning, ladies," he said absently, stopping at Pinky's desk.

Heaving a sigh of relief, I raced to greet him. "Am I glad to see you! We were worried about you, Paul."

"Some guy got rear-ended by a cement truck, so I had to sit in traffic for nearly an hour," he grumbled. Most people would have been irate, but Paul was treating it like a minor inconvenience.

"Jeremy called," Pinky announced. "He's convinced you were the accident victim—a statistic."

"I had a feeling he'd be upset," said Paul as he strode toward his office, carrying the hunter-green insulated lunch bag Jeremy had packed for him. "My cell phone had to die on me today of all days."

"You have a car charger, don't you?" I asked his retreating back.

"I've been meaning to buy one . . . but haven't gotten around to it." He stuck his head back out the door. "Pinky, could you please call Jeremy and tell him I'm fine, but I can't call him right now?"

"Sure thing." Pinky was already grabbing the phone.

I made a mental note to buy Paul a cell phone charger for his car as a Christmas gift. I'd have to find out the exact make and model of his phone.

A few minutes later, having gulped down a quick cup of coffee, Paul stood at my door, portfolio in hand. "Ready to go, Meena?"

His wide body practically filled the entire doorway. The bald patch on top of his head gleamed under the fluorescent lights. What was left of his hair was combed neatly. His latest cologne, a gift from Jeremy no doubt, drifted up to meet my sensitive nostrils. Very pleasant.

"Ready as I'll ever be," I said, and grabbed my notes and pen.

CEO Nayak, who generally divided his time between the Washington, DC, area and India—either wooing customers in Washington, or meeting with his subcontractors in India, was going to address the managerial staff this morning. I'd never met him in the eight months that I'd been with the company.

I'd met his partner, Nishant "Nish" Rathod, several times. Nish was the chief financial officer. He was housed in our office, so he was a familiar figure around the place.

Nish was a decent guy—friendly, cheerful, entirely different from my image of the usual accountant type. Although a smart and disciplined man when it came to fiscal matters, he didn't seem obsessed with the bottom line like some CFOs I'd come across.

He didn't dress like an accountant either. A stocky man in his late thirties, he generally sported twill pants, colorful Indian cotton shirts, and no tie. He laughed and kidded a lot. Nish was a likeable man.

And the company name—Rathnaya. Couldn't they have found a simpler name? But the two partners' names, Rathod plus Nayak, had turned into Rathnaya, Inc.—a very strange handle that I personally thought was bad for PR. Most people referred to it as Rat-Naya.

Who knows, maybe a weird name like that worked in highly technical circles, where guys wearing pocket protectors discussed computer codes and discovered ways to build the most hacker-resistant firewalls in the universe.

My job was simply to make Rathnaya look good—outlandish name and all.

Although not nervous by nature, when I got tense, like I was at the moment, I needed to go to the bathroom. "Paul, you go on ahead," I said. "I've got to run to the ladies' room."

Paul shifted away from the door. "No problem." He flicked his cuff back and looked at his watch. "We've got about . . . four minutes. I'll wait. You run along."

Paul had come to accept my pre-meeting trips to the ladies' room with his usual calm.

Inside the restroom, after getting the essentials out of the way, I stood for a moment in front of the mirror. The auburn highlights in my shoulder-length hair gleamed. My makeup looked fresh.

The suit looked pretty good, too. It was a soft, copper-colored material with a skirt that showed about three inches of skin above the knees, creating the impression of longer legs. Every millimeter of leg was important when one stood barely five feet. The suit went well with my cream blouse and pearl earrings. I wanted to look my best for the meeting.

Irrespective of my mother's aspirations, and who or what Prajay Nayak was, first impressions were still vital.

Returning from the ladies' room, I nodded at Paul. "Let's go."

We got into the elevator and headed for the ninth floor—the penthouse. Rathnaya occupied the top four floors of the building. The second through fifth floors were taken up by a number of small businesses, while the first floor housed various doctors' offices.

"Don't look so anxious," Paul said, briefly taking in my appearance. "You look fine, prettier than usual." His hazel eyes twinkled with teasing admiration.

"Thanks, Paul. You're good for my ego." If any other fifty-year-old man had given me that look, I'd have wondered about his intentions, but Paul was overtly gay. I lifted an eyebrow at him. "Do I really look that nervous?"

"A little."

I caught him checking his own appearance in the smooth chrome wall and patting his tie. I smiled to myself. I'd often wondered how a guy like Jeremy, with his classic good looks and impeccable taste in clothes, had fallen for a plain, rotund guy like Paul. But Paul had a sense of humor and integrity, so the physique could be overlooked. Also, he handled Jeremy with infinite patience and tenderness.

That's probably what kept the fastidious Jeremy and Paul together—opposites attracting and all that. Pinky had informed me that the two men had been partners for some eighteen years—a marriage made in heaven. In some ways I envied their happy relationship.

The topic of looks reminded me of something. "Is the CEO really as tall as everyone says?" I asked Paul.

Paul nodded. "Looks more like a basketball player than a computer geek."

Well, if Nayak was really that tall, then my mother's hopes about him and me were groundless. I was a midget even by Indian standards. Besides, anything other than a professional relationship with him would be a direct conflict of interest.

Oh well. I didn't care one way or the other. As long as Nayak proved to be a good boss and I could keep my job forever and not get laid off like I did from my last one, I'd be okay. If he was half as decent a guy as Nish, then I had nothing to worry about.

As the elevator headed for the penthouse, the butterflies in my stomach fluttered more briskly. I'd heard a lot of gossip about Prajay Nayak.

Some of the younger women in the office seemed to get all starry-eyed when they talked about him. I wondered if he could be gay—like Paul. An Indian man unmarried at thirty-nine was a bit unusual.

A large corner office on the top floor was set aside for him, but I had been told he hardly ever used it. I'd seen some pictures of him from newspaper clippings and company newsletters, but it was hard to see whether he was handsome or ugly or plain. He just looked taller than most of the men in group photos.

He was considered a whiz, though. On that one point the verdict was unanimous. An engineering degree followed by a master's in computer science, both with high honors, and both from MIT, said a lot about the guy's intellect.

The entire office seemed to be in awe of the man's brains. Of course, the staff was eighty percent Indian-American, so getting a fair report on the man was a bit like asking the royal family how they felt about their reigning monarch. Apparently he was generous, too. He and Nish regularly rewarded their top salesmen with large bonuses.

But the few men who didn't care for him were unusually acerbic in their comments. That could be simple jealousy on the part of some guys in the same age group as Nayak—men who had ended up working for him instead of competing against him.

And I didn't know of a single businessman who hadn't made a few enemies along the path to success.

It was only natural for a woman like me, who weighed not an ounce over eighty-five pounds in my heaviest wool suit, to feel a bit anxious about meeting a big and powerful man. But I was ready. In fact, I told myself, I was looking forward to the meeting.

The elevator doors opened. I forged ahead, my thoughts entirely occupied with what I was going to say in the meeting and how I would handle tough questions.

In the next instant I collided with something that could have been the front end of a truck. Before I knew what hit me, my feet slid out from under me.

Chapter 3

I went down with a sickening thud. The breath left my lungs for a second. Agony ripped through my foot. "Ow!" I knew for sure that I'd broken it.

God knows how long I lay there. It felt like a lifetime, while I heard shocked gasps and people talking all at once, footsteps hurrying from various directions, making the floor beneath me vibrate. Someone said something about the police . . . ambulance . . . doctor. I was too stunned to pay close attention.

I heard a deep, male voice yell, "Can someone call nine-one-one?"

A female voice answered. "I called Dr. Murjani's office on the first floor. The doctor's on his way right now."

"Good thinking," said the male voice.

Suddenly a man's face appeared above mine. The darkest, most penetrating eyes I'd ever seen peered down at me. His nose was huge, dense eyebrows drawn in a *V* right above it. The expression looked almost ferocious.

"I'm sorry, Miss Shenoy," the man said. It was the same deep voice I'd heard a moment ago. "Are you all right?"

I wasn't all right, but I blinked at the stranger, the pain and shock rendering me speechless.

"It was all my fault," he said.

"It wasn't *all* your fault, Prajay," said Paul's voice from somewhere nearby. "Meena kept marching forward without looking."

Thanks a lot for the support, Paul. I grimaced, trying not to dwell on the pain radiating from my foot. So this was Prajay Nayak, the guy I was supposed to meet in a formal conference room, with a professional handshake.

I met him all right. In a collision.

"No, it *is* mostly my fault," insisted Nayak. "I was rushing down the hall, and the elevator opened suddenly. I couldn't stop in time."

I was afraid to move my head, but I could see a bunch of people gathered around me. I knew my legs were completely exposed—nearly all the way to my crotch. My position was only a notch above lying on an examination table at the gynecologist's office—with my feet in stirrups.

Tears began to sting my eyes, and my lips started quivering. I bit my lower lip, but I couldn't stop it from trembling. The pain in my foot was turning to agony, and the humiliation of falling on my behind in front of the CEO and every other executive and a couple dozen others was even worse. I wished I'd pass out so I wouldn't have to see and know what was happening to me.

The elevator doors behind my head whooshed open, and a man demanded, "Where's the patient?"

The doctor had arrived. Some in my riveted audience moved aside to make way for him. I'd seen Dr. Murjani in passing, since his office was located in the building. Nayak's face was replaced by the doctor's familiar, middle-aged one with its cocoa-brown skin, gold-rimmed glasses, and thinning gray hair.

He squatted beside me and placed a bag on the floor. "So, young lady, you fell on the floor?"

"Uh-huh," I whispered. Wasn't that as obvious as the mole on his cheek? Why else would anyone in his or her right mind be sprawled over the floor of an office hallway?

"Can you count my fingers?" he asked, holding up three digits. When I answered correctly, he asked me my full name, which I managed to mumble. Then he inquired if I had blurred vision or a headache. When I said no to both he pulled out a penlight from his bag and gazed closely into my eyes.

He nodded in satisfaction. "You don't seem to have a concussion. Good thing this is a heavily carpeted floor."

Good thing, I reflected with an inward groan. I could have been lying there with a fractured skull if it weren't for the lush, foot-sinker carpet.

"I want you to stay very still while I feel your neck, okay?" said the doctor.

I sniffled in response. My nose was starting to run, and the tears were sliding down my temples and onto the carpet. The onlookers had closed in again.

He inserted his fingers under the nape of my neck and moved them around. "Any pain in the back or neck?"

"No."

"Good." He moved my head to one side while he felt my shoulders and arms. With my head turned I could see a bunch of familiar people staring at me with genuine concern on their faces. "Now, where exactly does it hurt?" asked the doctor.

"M-my foot . . . right foot," I mumbled. "Can I have a tissue please?"

The doctor stuck his hand in his bag and pulled out a tissue, then dabbed my eyes and nose. "Stay still. I don't want you to move yet." Then his exploring fingers traveled down my thigh and right leg, sending a fresh wave of pain through me as he reached below the calf.

"Ouch!" I cried. "That hurts."

"Okay, okay, I see what the problem is," he said. "I'm going to examine your foot. It might hurt a little more, but I have to do it, all right?"

"Ow!" He wasn't kidding about the pain.

"Easy, young lady. Nothing's broken. It's just a bad sprain."

If this was what a sprain felt like, I wondered how a bona fide fracture would feel.

"We'll need to move her to a couch or something," ordered Dr. Murjani. "Somebody get me a couple of plastic bags filled with ice."

"I have a couch in my office," offered Prajay Nayak.

"Good," said the doctor. "I'll need help moving her there."

"I can carry her, Doctor. Is that all right?"

"Yah, sure. Go ahead."

The fierce face came back to hover over me once again. I felt huge, sturdy arms lifting me up . . . up. In the meantime my injured foot was dangling in the air and causing me horrible anguish. I groaned.

"Sorry." His face was only inches from mine now and looked contrite.

Someone lifted my foot and held it elevated, easing the pain a little. I was traveling high in the air, my eyes only a couple of feet below the ceiling while I was carried in a pair of arms that felt surprisingly safe to be in. They held me like I was a cloud. My head rested on a shoulder wide as a football field, and the fabric against my cheek was soft and fragrant with a manly scent.

For a second I closed my eyes. It reminded me of Dad's holding me in my childhood, when I needed comforting during an illness or after a terrifying nightmare.

"She needs to be seated, not lying down," instructed the doctor.

A moment later I was placed with incredible gentleness on a tan sofa with my back against the armrest and my feet stretched out in front of me. At least now my skirt wasn't riding too high, only up to mid-thigh.

One look at my right foot and I winced. The shoe had fallen off, the hose ripped at the toes. The ankle looked like it belonged on a baby elephant—fat and gray. I started to sniffle again. I'd never be able to use my right foot again. I'd likely be a cripple for the rest of my life.

"Now, now, I know it hurts, but this should make it better." The doctor put zippered sandwich bags filled with ice cubes on either side of my ankle and secured them with a stretch bandage. He was right. Although the ice was a shock to the skin, it did ease the throbbing.

"Will I be able to walk again?" I was almost afraid to ask the question. What if the answer was no? It was my right foot, too. I'd never be able to drive or walk . . . or dance.

"Of course you'll walk again," the doctor said with a short laugh.

"You're sure?"

"Didn't I tell you it's just a sprain?" He grabbed a tan and black accent pillow from somewhere and slid it under my foot.

Just a sprain? It felt like my foot had been put through a meat grinder.

"You'll need to stay off the foot for a couple of days and then take it easy for a while after that," he added. "In two days you'll be hobbling, and in a week or so you may start driving. Just don't wear any high heels for a couple of weeks."

"But high heels are the only kind of work shoes I have," I protested. I was a professional, not some elderly woman who stepped out of the house to buy groceries once a week. But at least the doctor had assured me I could walk. That was something.

"So wear sneakers for a few days," he said with a stern expression.

"But—"

He probably saw the gleam of defiance in my eyes and decided to nip it in the bud. "You want that foot to heal or not?"

"Yes," I replied on a sigh. "May I have a tissue, please?" I asked once again, trying not to give in to my urge to wipe my nose on my sleeve. The doctor handed me a wad of tissues. It was such a relief to finally blow my nose and breathe normally.

Meanwhile Nayak stood a little distance behind the doctor, brows still knotted, and my shoes dangling from his fingers. Nish and Paul stood next to him, arms folded, looking equally distressed.

With the pain beginning to ebb, I noticed something. Despite his size, Paul looked rather small next to Nayak. Nish looked miniscule.

They weren't kidding when they said Nayak was tall. And now that I was sitting up and looking at him from a different angle, he wasn't all that fierce-looking.

He wasn't scary at all. Why had I thought that when I was lying on the floor?

I also noticed the large window beside the couch, with a view of the parking lot and the street beyond. From up here the maple trees in the separator islands looked more colorful in their various shades of fall.

"I'm going to prescribe a painkiller and a muscle relaxant for you, Miss Shenoy," the doctor said, and started scribbling on a prescription pad. Then he dug through his bag and handed me a bunch of individual foil packs of pills and a business card. "Some samples—enough for today and tomorrow." He pushed two pills out of the foil with his thumb and handed them to me. "I want you to take these right now. And take one of each tonight, after dinner."

I looked at the pills and wondered if they would knock me out, make me forget the pain and humiliation of everything that had happened.

Suddenly something struck me. The doctor had made a house call of sorts. Doctors didn't usually make house calls. In the rare event they did, it had to cost a ridiculous amount. "Uh, Dr. Murjani, about your . . . fees?"

"You have insurance, don't you?" he said, his brow descending. His expression clearly said he hoped to God I had insurance.

"Of course she has insurance," Nayak's voice cut in. "All our full-time employees are covered." He shot the doctor a meaningful glance. "Don't worry, Doctor; I'll take care of whatever the cost is."

The doctor's face cleared up. "Now make sure she doesn't drive home, Mr. Nayak." He pointed a finger at me. "If any problems arise, you call my office at that number." Before grabbing his bag and exiting the room, he offered me one last word of caution: "No high heels until the foot is back to normal."

I nodded and thrust the card, prescription slip, and the remaining foil packs in my jacket pocket. "Thank you."

"You're welcome," he said with an unexpected smile. Now that his fee was assured, he seemed to be in a jovial mood. He motioned for Nayak to follow him. Nayak deposited my shoes next to the sofa, and the two men stepped outside, talking in hushed tones.

Nish, who'd stood by in total silence, stepped closer to me. "I'm sorry about what happened, Meena. But don't worry; we'll take care of everything. I'll make sure the worker's comp papers are filed properly and all that."

I managed to crack a watery smile. "Thanks."

"If there's anything I can do, call me."

Nish left after those comforting words, but Paul came to stand beside me with a bottle of water. "Here, you better take your medication right away." He glanced at my foot and offered me a sympathetic look. "Hurts something nasty, huh?"

I nodded, swallowed the meds, and gave the bottle back to him. "Thank you."

"I'm sorry, Meena," said Paul, screwing the lid back on the bottle. "You were rushing out of the elevator like an express train. Unfortunately Prajay was coming toward you at an angle. It was an accident waiting to happen." He shook his head and clucked. "I didn't see him either, until he was almost on top of you."

I blew my nose once again. "It's not your fault. I was careless." I looked at my foot wrapped in ice cubes. The pain had eased, but the ice was numbing the whole leg. "I firmly believe in fate. It was meant to happen."

"You really believe in that stuff?"

"I was destined to make a rotten impression on the boss," I assured him. "Now he's going to hate me for causing all this trouble, and my job's going to be history."

Paul laughed. "Where'd you come up with a notion like that?"

"I'm serious, Paul. This doesn't look good. You should start looking for another PR manager soon."

"Stop talking nonsense. No one's going to fire you. People don't get fired for taking a spill." Then he looked at his watch. "I doubt if we're going to have that meeting after all."

Just then Nayak walked in. "We'll have to arrange for Ms. Shenoy to be driven home," he said to Paul.

"I'll drive her home," Paul offered. "In fact, I'll have Pinky drive Meena's car to her house, and I'll bring Pinky back. No sense letting Meena's car sit here for the next several days if she's going to be out."

"I agree." Nayak looked at me thoughtfully for a second. "Let her stay in my office for a while and rest. We'll take her down to your car later."

"Good idea." Paul glanced at me. "You going to be okay?"

"I guess. But I don't want to be in Mr. Nayak's way. Maybe I can hobble downstairs with you?"

"You won't be in my way," said Nayak, cutting me off—reminding me who was boss. "I'll work in the conference room since the meeting's canceled." He inclined his head toward the door. "You go on, Paul. Call me in a couple of hours, and we'll have Miss Shenoy transported to the parking lot."

I was grateful for all that Nayak was doing, but irritation was beginning to set in. He was talking about me like I wasn't there, like I was some kind of cargo to be *transported*. Was he afraid I'd sue him?

It had to be that—fear of a lawsuit. Why else would he have carried me in here himself? Why else would he let me stay in his office and rest? Why else would he pretend to care about my welfare?

Whatever his reasons, I had no choice but to stay put. I was more helpless than a newborn puppy. Tears of self-pity started to gather in my eyes.

"Miss Shenoy, is the pain really bad?" Nayak was at my side in a flash. He glanced at my foot. "Can I do anything for you?"

I shook my head. The man looked desperate. He was terrified

of a lawsuit. "You don't have to fuss over me, Mr. Nayak. I don't plan to sue you or anything."

"That's the last thing on my mind, Miss Shenoy," he retorted, clearly insulted by my remark. "I'm more concerned about your health, believe it or not."

His eyes were still on my foot. Thank goodness my toenails were painted in a shade called Blushing Rose, to match the pink sari I'd worn as bridesmaid at my best friend Rita's wedding the previous weekend. Rita's mother had insisted that I also wear a row of fake pink pearls and matching earrings.

I'd looked like a skinny stick of bubble gum, but I'd had no choice, since Rita's parents were paying for my ensemble. Anyway, at the moment, under the circumstances, my toes looked reasonably good due to the recent pedicure, despite the tear in the hose.

"I'm sorry you had to cancel the meeting because of me," I said to Nayak, mopping my eyes. By now they probably looked like boiled lobsters.

"Don't worry about it. We can reschedule."

Now that he was standing right next to me, I took a closer look at him. His face was large and matched his overall size. His nose was long and hooked. But there was an intelligent spark in his eyes, and his mouth was wide, with a generous lower lip. The mouth was his best feature. His hair was thick and black and slightly wavy.

He wasn't a bad-looking guy, but there was something hawk-like and intense about him. I shivered at his nearness.

Perhaps discomfited by my inspection, he checked his watch. "Will you be all right here by yourself?"

I nodded. "The pills must be working, because the pain's receding. I'm feeling a little light-headed, too."

"Can I get you anything? Coffee, soda?"

Why not? How often does a girl get to be carried in the arms of a CEO and then get pampered on top of it? "Coffee would be nice, thank you," I replied with a grateful smile. "Lots of cream and one sugar."

"Got it." He strode out of his office.

For the first time I noticed the beautifully tailored pinstriped pants that draped well over his endlessly long legs, starched white shirt that stretched across his wide shoulders, and the glossy black wing-tip shoes. Nice. I was always a sucker for preppy looks. The suit jacket was on a hanger over a coatrack by his desk. It looked bigger than my dad's bulkiest winter coat.

Since I was alone now, I let my gaze wander over the office. It was a very masculine room, with large windows in the two perpendicular walls. The cappuccino vertical blinds were open. Dense ivory carpeting covered the floor.

The cherry desk and credenza were generously wide. The chair was an ergonomically designed contraption made of chrome and brown leather. It could probably be adjusted a dozen different ways to accommodate Nayak.

A row of cherry bookcases covered half a wall. They held books and binders, mostly on software and computer-related subjects. A large oil painting of an Indian rural scene dominated the wall behind the couch I sat on.

From my vantage point I could clearly see two photographs in wooden frames on the credenza. A middle-aged couple in one—most likely Nayak's parents. The other one showcased three children: two boys around ten and eight respectively, and a girl, perhaps three years old. I wondered who the kids were. A family resemblance was certainly there—the boys had the thick eyebrows and the girl had the same mouth as Nayak.

Nayak walked in with a steaming mug of coffee and napkins. I turned my attention to him, feeling a bit guilty about having stared at his family pictures. He must've guessed what I'd been up to, because he inclined his head toward the credenza. "My parents, and my niece and nephews."

"You have a nice family." I accepted the coffee and took a cautious sip. It was wonderful—rich and creamy, with a hazelnut flavor. They sure had nice coffee in the executive break room.

He smiled, the unexpectedly sunny motion softening the harsh planes of his face. "Yes, I do."

After a couple more sips of coffee had me sufficiently warmed up, my confidence grew. "Can I ask you something, Mr. Nayak?"

"Sure. And call me Prajay. We're rather informal around here. I'm sure you know that by now."

"Uh . . . Prajay, are you going to fire me for this?" I pointed to my foot.

His roar of laughter startled me. "Are you serious? It was an accident. I'm to blame for it more than you. I was so preoccupied, I wasn't paying attention to the surroundings."

"Me too, I guess."

"You're so small compared to me. You went down quick."

"Hmm." No wonder I'd felt like I'd been knocked over by a truck. "Still, it caused quite a stir . . . and you had to cancel an important meeting."

He dismissed it with a wave of his large hand. "Accidents happen, Meena. We just adjust our schedules accordingly." He looked at his wristwatch. "If you'll be okay by yourself, I think I'll go work in the conference room."

"Sure. Thanks for everything."

"Just leave the cup on the table beside you. I'll stop by in a couple of hours and take you downstairs." As he reached the door, he turned around briefly. "If you need anything, just holler. Anna, my assistant, is right outside."

"Thanks."

He picked up some folders and a laptop computer from his desk and strode out once again. I nearly chuckled when I realized I'd been nervous about meeting him. Come to think of it, he was a nice guy—a gentle giant. I'd worried unnecessarily. And he smelled really wonderful.

Besides my weakness for sharp dressers, I was also partial to men who smelled good.

Maybe it was the painkiller that was doing a number on my brain. I was beginning to feel a pleasant wooziness creeping over me. I put the empty mug of coffee on the end table, wiggled my bottom, and slid down a little so my head rested on the pillow that had been tucked behind my back.

Everything around me started to take on a hazy glow. The pain was almost gone. Those pills were fantastic.

I closed my eyes and sighed. Prajay Nayak was a sweet guy. I was beginning to like him. A lot.

Chapter 4

Dr. Murjani's painkillers were so potent that I evidently fell into a deep sleep on Prajay Nayak's couch. How much more embarrassing could it get, especially when it was supposed to be the day to make my best impression?

My nap must have been a minor coma, because when I woke up I found myself at home, in my own bed, dressed in my own pajamas. It took my brain several seconds to absorb the other details. My purse sat on the floor next to the bed. I slowly pulled myself up and sat leaning against the headboard. My head spun before settling down. My ankle was still very sore, but the pain was bearable.

So how did I get here? Was I dreaming?

I had no recollection of being carried in Prajay's arms to the elevator and then to Paul's car. What a bummer. I had been hoping to recapture that special feeling of being held like a fragile creature in a strong pair of arms, somewhat like the scene from *King Kong,* and I had wanted to sniff that amazing cologne once again.

It would have been my one chance to experience what one of my historical romance novel heroines did when the dashing hero swept her up and carried her to his private quarters after she'd had an attack of the vapors. The first time Prajay had done that, I had been in too much pain to savor the experience.

Now I'd never know the joy because I'd slept through the whole thing.

Prajay must have thought I was ungrateful. No matter how big and strong he was, it wasn't an easy task to carry a dead weight all the way to the elevator, down to the lobby, and then to a waiting car.

"You're awake," said a familiar voice from the doorway. I glanced at my mom as she approached my bed with a lap tray. "I figured you'd be up by now, and probably hungry."

She was dressed in baggy jeans and a black sweatshirt. Mom looked young when she wore those instead of a sari or a stuffy pantsuit. Taller and bigger than me, but still slim, she had a pointed chin, sparkling eyes, and dark, curly hair that she wore in a single braid. She didn't look like the mother of three grown children.

I was feeling relaxed and lethargic—probably the aftereffects of the drug. This was pleasant, getting spoiled by my mother. Only in instances of dire illness did one get this kind of royal treatment from her. Mom wasn't the fussing, hovering type. Brisk and practical was more her style—despite her being a medical doctor with a large practice.

"Thanks, Mom," I said with a grateful smile as she placed the tray over my lap and adjusted the folding flaps to fit over my thighs.

"How's your foot feeling?" She bent down to examine it with a professional frown, then nodded. "Looks much better. Thank goodness it was just a simple sprain."

"Still hurts, but not as bad as this morning." Sometimes I wished she'd give me a hug or a maternal kiss. But those gestures had stopped after I'd gone past the toddler stage.

"I keep warning you about your taste in shoes," she chided. "Those ridiculous stilts that you insist on wearing are dangerous, not to mention unhealthy for your feet."

"It had nothing to do with my stilts, Mom. I was walking out of the elevator while Prajay Nayak was rushing out of his office, and we collided. Both of us were careless. The mouse got knocked over by the elephant."

"Ah, yes. Prajay is Madhu and Nalini Nayak's son. Very tall guy, right?"

"Very."

"All their sons are exceptionally tall. I haven't seen them since they moved to Massachusetts many years ago. The older two are married, I believe. Prajay's the youngest boy."

"Boy? He's thirty-nine, Mom." Knowing my mother, she was probably calculating the age difference between Prajay and me and his average annual income. "Goodness, have I been sleeping the entire day?" I asked in an attempt to change the subject. A glance at my bedside clock told me it was nearly dinnertime.

Mom nodded. "Those muscle relaxants can knock you out. I've seen some of my patients sleep for twelve hours straight."

I stretched my arms above my head and yawned. "They're fabulous. I feel like a new person." I glanced at the tray and grinned. "Even the *batata song* and *dali thoi* smell good."

The bright yellow *dali thoi*—split pea soup seasoned with mustard seeds, chili peppers, and curry leaves—wasn't one of my big favorites, but at the moment it smelled delicious, served over a small mound of rice. *Song* was a fiery hot potato and onion curry—a staple of my people. I dug into the food eagerly—not my usual style.

Mom gave me a puzzled look after I'd eaten a couple of spoonfuls. "I've never seen you eat like this."

"I'm famished. Must be because I slept through lunch," I said with my mouth full. "So tell me, how exactly did I arrive home? Did Paul and Pinky drive me over?" I was anxious to find out. By any chance had Prajay decided to drive me home?

"Pinky called me at my office to tell me what had happened, so I canceled my appointments for the afternoon, came home, and waited for you to arrive."

"Sorry you had to cancel because of me." Mom never let her patients down, if she could help it. She must've been truly worried about me to do what she had done.

"That's okay. Things happen sometimes."

"How did you get me up here?" I chewed another mouthful of rice.

"Paul drove you home and carried you upstairs while Pinky drove your car here. Then she rode back to the office with him."

So it hadn't been Prajay who'd brought me home and carried me. I felt mildly disappointed. But what more could I expect from a stranger?

Mom was still talking. "It wasn't easy getting that suit off you and putting your pajamas on." I made some appropriate sound and continued to eat while Mom made herself comfortable at the foot of my bed. "Nice people, those two, Paul and Pinky," she remarked. She'd heard me talk about them but had never met them.

I took a sip of water to douse the *song* burning my tongue. "They're both very nice. Paul is one of the few non-Indians in the company, but he's adjusted well to the spicy food in the break rooms and the various Indian languages floating around. He's even learned a lot about our customs and religious holidays."

"Good for him." Mom seemed impressed.

"Most of the Rathnaya people are nice, except for Gargi Bansal. She's a bi . . . piece of work."

"Why? She doesn't like you?"

Mom was under the odd impression that everybody in the world liked her kids. It always came as a shock when one of us told her someone resented us. "I think she's a little jealous. She's about my age. She's been working there as a programmer for four years and is still a programmer, while I got hired as a manager right away."

"But that's because you must be smarter than she is, right?"

"Not smarter, Mom." Another one of Mom's misconceptions—that her kids were brighter than most. "She's got more brains than I do if she's a computer professional. I just happened to have the combination of marketing and public relations experience that Paul and Nish were looking for."

"I see." I wasn't sure if Mom was satisfied with my explanation, but she accepted it. "You know, I was just thinking."

Uh-oh, Mom was *thinking*. "About what?"

"Paul—he didn't look like he's gay. Didn't you say he was homosexual?"

"Yes. And he makes no bones about it."

"But he doesn't look like that."

I smiled. "Gay people don't exactly wear a label, Mom. Paul looks very manly, but he's one hundred-percent gay. He's got a boyfriend who's rather feminine and handsome."

"Feminine and handsome?" Mom snickered.

I placed the empty plate back on the tray. "Jeremy is good-looking, almost pretty, and not all that masculine. He walks with a slight swing in the hips and fusses over people like a woman."

"Really?" Mom looked at me like she'd never heard of such traits.

"Uh-huh. He prepares wholesome lunches for Paul, and makes sure he takes his prostate-health pills and herbs, and calls regularly to check on Paul." I sighed. "He drives Pinky and me nuts sometimes, but Jeremy's a sweet guy. I like him."

"So you like sweet guys?" Mom suddenly seemed very interested.

"Sure. If I could find a nurturing guy like Jeremy, I'd get married tomorrow."

"You want a *gay* husband?"

I burst into laughter. "No, I meant a nice, caring guy like Jeremy, but a straight one."

Picking up the tray, Mom started to walk toward the door. "Thank goodness."

"Thanks for bringing me dinner, Mom." With a smile I watched her back disappear. Mom was so comical at times and so naïve for a woman who'd been practicing gynecology and obstetrics for three decades.

For lack of something to do while I lay in bed, I picked up the partly read Nora Roberts novel off my nightstand and started to read, but I couldn't concentrate. I kept reliving my experience earlier.

Lord, what a day. What were the folks at the office saying? They'd stood staring at me at first, and then some of them had disappeared after the doctor had shown up.

I hadn't heard from any of them after that, not even Pinky. I hoped she'd call me at home tonight. To make sure I hadn't missed any calls, I reached into my purse and pulled out my cell phone to check my messages. No calls.

I put the phone on the nightstand. No one cared.

But that wasn't fair, was it? It was generous of Pinky and Paul to have done all they'd done. And even kinder of Prajay. I made a mental note to send e-mails to thank them.

How long would I have to lie in bed? I wondered. I'd be climbing the walls by tomorrow morning, or tomorrow evening at the latest. Unfortunately my work couldn't be done very easily from home.

A little while later I heard the grinding sound of the automatic garage door sliding open. Dad had come home from work. I heard him talk to Mom downstairs before he stopped by to check on me.

"What's this I hear about you falling in your office?" he asked with a scowl.

"One of those freak accidents," I replied, knowing full well that Mom had already given him the uncut version. Those two shared everything. There were no secrets between them as far as I knew.

"So how long are you going to be out of commission, *charda?*" He approached my bed and patted my face.

He still called me *charda*—child—after so many years. I kind of liked it, because he never used the term with my brothers. Being a girl, I was also given lots of hugs. The boys didn't qualify for those, either. They got enthusiastic slaps on the back or high fives. Being a girl gave me princess status in Dad's heart.

What I didn't get from my mother, I got from my father.

"I'm not sure, Dad," I answered. "I can't go to work for at least a day or two. I'm hoping I can get one of my coworkers to give me a ride so I can go back at least by early next week."

He bent down and peered at my foot. "You're sure it's not broken?"

"Dr. Murjani says it's only a sprain. Mom checked it out. She agrees with his diagnosis."

He straightened up. "If Kaveri says it's a sprain, then it should be okay." Dad had implicit faith in his dear wife's medical opinion.

"Actually what you're looking at is nearly half the size of what it was this morning. It looked like a bloated eggplant." I wanted to make sure I had Dad's complete sympathy.

"You want me to give you a ride to your office for a few days?" Dad was a sweet guy, especially when he got into his big, protective father mode.

"If I can't get anyone else, maybe I'll take you up on your offer." I hoped it didn't come to that. My hours were erratic and so were Dad's. It would be hard to coordinate our schedules. And we worked in opposite directions.

After giving my hair an affectionate ruffle, Dad headed out. "Let me know. And don't go gallivanting with your friends. You need to rest."

"I promise I won't gallivant, Dad," I replied wryly. I was in no shape to even hobble to the other side of my room, let alone go out on the town. I tried to wiggle my ankle. It hurt like the dickens, so I settled back against the pillows once again. Walking to the bathroom later was going to be painful.

I went back to my book for a few minutes before my cell phone rang. I eagerly snatched it up.

"Hi, Meena," said a familiar voice.

"Pinky!"

"You sound kind of . . . hyper," she said. "Is it the medication?"

"No, I'm just happy to hear from you. I was feeling a bit sorry for myself."

"How are you feeling? I mean physically."

"Much better, thanks."

"I'm so relieved. You had us worried, you know—especially when you slept through the entire ride to your house."

"Did . . . did Paul haul me from the ninth floor to his car?"

"No, Prajay did. He held you like you were an eight-pound baby instead of a grown woman."

"Oh?" So Prajay had played the gallant knight again. That pleased me. Immensely.

Pinky kept talking. "Imagine my shock this morning, when Paul called me from the ninth floor and said you were flat on your back and the doctor had been called. The whole office has been talking about it since."

"I bet. So, does everyone know what size panties I wear?"

"Instead of worrying about your foot, you're obsessing over what people think of your underwear?"

"Hey, didn't Paul tell you I was lying there with my skirt pushed all the way up to my butt?"

"Paul would never say something like that. He's worried about you." Pinky was quiet for a moment. "But Gargi told me about how your bottom was showing."

"I don't believe she was even there." I thought about it. Gargi wasn't management and wouldn't have been included in that particular meeting. "One of her gossip buddies must have told her."

"Maybe. But she seemed to know details."

"She's probably telling her exaggerated version to everyone." I should have known that woman would pounce on bad news like a bee on pollen.

"Don't worry. Most of the people were worried that something serious had happened to you."

"Thanks, Pinky. It's sweet of you to try to spare my feelings. And thanks for taking such good care of me."

"Anytime, my dear. And you know what? Prajay stopped by this afternoon to ask me if I'd heard from you."

A delicious little thrill zigzagged through my veins. "What'd you tell him?"

"I told him I'd called your mother and that you were sleeping like a baby."

"What did he say?"

"What is this, an inquisition?" Pinky mocked. "First you tell me you're not all dressed up to impress him, and now you want to know every word he said."

I grinned to myself. "He did go out of his way to be nice."

"Yes, despite the drool you left on his couch."

"I drooled on his couch?"

"Just a little. When I went upstairs to wake you up, your mouth was open and drool was sliding out one side and onto the couch."

"Oh, no! This is sounding worse and worse." I could be a guaranteed winner on *America's Most Embarrassing Videos*.

"Don't worry," clucked Pinky. "I managed to clean it up before anyone could notice, so you're safe. No stains on the couch, either. But no matter what I did, you refused to wake up. You murmured something incoherent and went back to sleep. So I just went through your purse and found your car keys myself."

"I see you even remembered to deliver my purse and shoes to my house. I owe you one, Pinky."

"Don't be silly."

"So what else did Prajay say?"

"Nothing. He seemed relieved that you were okay."

"Are you sure? When I send him a thank-you note, I want to remember every detail of what he did for me."

"I'm sure. All he did was transport you to Paul's car."

"Oh." So he'd packed me into Paul's car and thought good riddance. I couldn't admit to Pinky that I was disappointed. But then, what was I expecting? Prajay Nayak was someone I'd met briefly, under weird circumstances. Despite his vehement denial, his concern for me probably stemmed from the fear of a lawsuit. Nothing personal.

And why was I so anxious about his opinion? He had this austere face and a body like an army tank. But on the other hand, he had a gentle side to him—a softer, generous side.

He had hauled me in his arms. Twice. That counted for something. Besides, I'd never dated anyone who dressed so sharply or had such gentlemanly manners.

The two men I'd dated somewhat seriously so far had turned out to be selfish and egotistical. One of them was a medical resident I'd met three years ago. He was so full of himself because he'd made it through Harvard Medical School that he thought women had to bow to him. I'd wished him good-bye and good luck after four awkward dates. He couldn't imagine why a woman who barely reached his shoulder didn't find him irresistible.

The other guy, a Konkani accountant introduced to me by my parents, had hinted that his future wife had to be modest and obedient. Neither of those adjectives even remotely described me. I broke up with him after three dates, much to my parents' disappointment. Besides, he was a lousy kisser. He'd tried to kiss me on our third and last date, and it was like being slobbered on by a Saint Bernard. Then he'd asked me if I'd enjoyed the kiss.

Compared to those two guys, Prajay Nayak came across as a nice man with a solid brain and a kind enough heart. But then, why would he throw a glance at a little pixie like me?

So imagine my surprise when the next day a dozen flame-colored roses with his get-well card arrived for me. I tried not to get too excited, because I still suspected it was the fear of a lawsuit that had prompted the gesture.

Mom was ecstatic. In her old-fashioned mind, if a single young man sent me flowers, it was with the intention of courting me. I hated to spoil her fun, so I kept my mouth shut.

Just when I thought the surprises were over, another stunning thing happened a day later. Paul called me to find out if I was in any shape to return to work on Monday, and I said, "Yes, if either you or Pinky can give me a ride. If it's not too much . . . trouble?" I added hesitantly. It was an imposition, since they both lived some distance from my home.

"Guess what," said Paul casually. "Prajay has offered to give you a ride to the office and back for the week."

I searched my brain for a logical explanation "Why?"

"When he found out where Pinky and I lived, he offered on his own. Apparently his condo is close to your home."

"But isn't he returning to Washington soon?" My heartbeat had crept up a notch.

"Not for a few weeks. He's taking care of business in our office at the moment."

Of all times to have business in the local office. "I'm not sure,

Paul. I don't want to inconvenience Prajay further." The thought of riding with the king himself was exciting—but disquieting at the same time. Prajay still intimidated me somewhat. Besides, I'd embarrassed myself plenty already, and the possibility of adding to it was pretty high if I had a fifteen-minute commute each way for several days. "My dad can give me a ride."

"Doesn't your father work around Moorestown?"

"Yes, but my father offered, and Prajay is only trying to be kind. . . ." It was indeed a stretch for Dad.

"Look, if I were you, I'd take Prajay's offer," encouraged Paul. "Your house is right on his way, so it's not like he's going to be greatly inconvenienced. You can hobble around on your own now?"

"He doesn't need to carry me, if that's what you're asking."

"Good. I'll see you Monday, then?"

"Sure. Thanks, Paul."

When I informed Mom, she beamed. "What did I tell you? He is interested."

"No, Mom!" I snapped. "Can't you understand that any kind of personal relationship between him and me would be . . . improper?"

Mom shook her head. "If both parties are interested, it's not sexual harassment or anything. Coworkers fall in love and get married in almost every office—despite the rules."

"We're not exactly coworkers. He's my boss. He's the boss of everybody who works at Rathnaya." I realized I was yelling, venting my frustration on my mother. It wasn't her fault that I stood no chance with Prajay. I softened my tone. "I suspect he's going out of his way to be kind because he's afraid of a lawsuit."

Mom's eyes widened. "How can he think that? Respectable Konkani folks don't go around suing people." Then she turned thoughtful for a moment, and a slow smile settled over her face. "You know what? I still think fate literally threw the two of you together. Karma can be very strange at times. See, now he's sending you flowers and offering you a ride."

I took a deep breath. Mom had to be reined in. "Don't go

around thinking such things. And please, please don't say anything to anyone. This is strictly business, okay?"

"Okay." Mom nodded, but the subtle twinkle in her eye didn't diminish. My aunts would be hearing about this soon. I knew she was itching to get her hands on the phone. Nothing I could say was likely to change Mom's way of thinking. She was making big plans to get rid of me the old-fashioned way: marry me off to the first guy who showed interest.

And she was convinced Prajay's actions were a sign of interest.

Chapter 5

In a way Mom was right. Fate had taken me to a company called Rathnaya and then literally put me in the path of its CEO. To that extent I did believe in karma, but I didn't for one minute think it had happened for good reasons.

I'd never even heard of Rathnaya until a year ago, when I was desperately looking for a job. I'd come across their ad for a marketing/PR manager on the Internet and applied for the position. After two interviews I'd ended up working for Paul.

At the moment, I was sitting with Mom, Dad, and Maneel in the family room, after eating a family dinner. My injured foot was propped up on the coffee table. The swelling was down, and the pain had lessened.

Mahesh was on call this weekend, like he most often was. The poor guy worked all the time.

I observed Maneel sitting cross-legged on the carpeted floor, TV remote in hand, flicking through channels. Although I'd never say this to his face, my big brother was a nice-looking guy, with Mom's lively eyes and dark, curly hair combined with Dad's sturdy build. Maneel was popular with girls.

At five-foot-ten, he wasn't exceptionally tall, but he was muscular and lean. He was also bright and earned a lot as a stockbroker. For one so young he had quite an impressive investment portfolio. Lots of matrimonial inquiries regarding Maneel came to my parents from the families of eligible girls. Maneel had been dodging them, claiming he wasn't ready for marriage yet.

I knew for a fact that Maneel was playing the field. I'd seen him flirting with girls at restaurants and popular spots where my friends and I hung out. But we Shenoy kids had our own unwritten code of honor: I'd say nothing about Maneel's girlfriends to my parents, just like he and Mahesh, although protective of me in typical brotherly fashion, didn't discuss my business with the rest of the family.

Dad looked comfortable in the recliner, reading an engineering magazine, while Mom sat at the other end of the couch I was sitting on. Her feet were tucked underneath her hip, and a phone directory sat in her lap, cushioning a piece of notepaper on which she was writing a letter to her mother. Her reading glasses were perched on her nose.

My maternal grandmother in India, my only living grandparent, didn't have access to a computer, making e-mail communication impossible. She was also hard of hearing, so the phone wasn't an option, either. As a result, my mom continued to send her old-fashioned letters. Right now, I'd bet anything Mom was giving her a full account of my accident.

As I sat there observing my family, I clearly recalled their reaction last year, after I'd announced that I'd been offered a job at a company called Rathnaya. My brothers had scoffed and teased me to no end.

"Rat-na-ya? Is that some kooky dance club?" Maneel had asked with a sneering lift of one eyebrow.

Mahesh, the tall, skinny brother, had grinned with delight. "Mom and Dad spent all that money on your Ivy League degrees, and you are going to work for an exterminator who annihilates rats?"

Shaking with annoyance, I'd faced my brothers. "For your information, Rathnaya is one of the most successful software companies in the Northeast. Not exactly Microsoft, but it has a great reputation in its niche market."

Maneel had nodded in mock comprehension. "The niche market of the mighty Rats."

Mahesh had grinned some more. "Mighty nerds."

"Stop it, you two! Don't bug your sister." My dad had dealt the boys a stern reprimand. It was generally my father who came to my rescue in such instances. Mom believed her cherubic boys could do no wrong. She intervened only if things got out of hand.

Mahesh had made little nibbling motions with his mouth to emulate a rat. "See, even Dad used the word *bug*."

Mom had finally frowned at the boys. "Don't you two have anything better to do than tease your sister?"

"We're only trying to get a clearer understanding of Meena's new job," they'd said with innocent expressions.

"Meena has found a good job with a great company. It's owned by two nice Indian guys, so it's a reputable business," Mom had announced. In Mom's book of wisdom, anything done by an Indian was good, and if it was done by a male, it was near perfect. She belonged to the male-worshipping Indian sisterhood.

She had told me how thrilled she and Dad had been when their firstborn had turned out to be a boy. Then I'd come along, a disappointment—although Mom denied it vehemently. And then, as if to make up for my sorry birth, Mom and Dad had had another boy, one more precious male who could carry on the Shenoy name and legacy.

As if it weren't stressful enough to be sandwiched between the proverbial heir and the spare, I was the one born with a fussy personality.

Mom often mentioned that she was in labor for several hours before she gave birth to me. "For a tiny infant who weighed next to nothing, you gave me hell," she'd said. "Maneel and Mahesh were big, but quick and easy. A few major contractions, and they were out—just like that," she'd added.

"It's not my fault, is it?" I'd whined. "You and Dad planned on having kids, so you can't complain about the resulting aches and pains."

Mom's expression had softened when reminded of the plain fact that bringing children into the world was a decision made by adults. "I'm not complaining, dear. We wanted you, and we love you," she'd declared. "But you were so fussy and colicky. You just refused to eat."

"Don't forget the recurring ear infections, Mom," Maneel had prompted.

I'd been tempted to put my hands around Maneel's manly neck and squeeze. He loved adding to Mom's dramatic recollections of what an unpleasant baby I had been, although he had only been two years old at the time of my birth.

"Well, it's too bad I'm still here to make your life miserable, isn't it?" I'd snapped back.

"I didn't mean it in a bad way." Mom had added that conciliatory remark after one of those reflective walks down memory lane and my subsequent hurt reaction to her comments. On the other hand, she always seemed to carry sweet memories of my brothers' early days. "Such good babies they were. Except for the usual chicken pox and the occasional cold or flu, the boys were no problem."

"So you're saying you've forgotten the incident when Maneel drove your brand new Mercedes into the Goldmans' pool when he was fifteen," I'd said with a saccharine smile. "And what about the time Mahesh dropped out of ninth grade and ran away from home to join a rock band?"

Naturally Mom had pretended not to remember any such occasions, and Maneel and Mahesh had claimed those episodes were no more than youthful indiscretions.

"If dangerous actions as a teenager are 'youthful indiscretions,' then ear infections and alleged anorexia before the age of six are not even matters for discussion, are they?" I'd countered.

Fortunately Dad, my sole defender, had admonished the boys. Better yet, he'd clearly remembered the boys' antics. "My auto insurance didn't skyrocket and the police didn't have to conduct a search-and-rescue operation because Meena had an ear infection," he'd declared, with a final glower that shut the boys up—at least temporarily. Even Mom had quieted down for a bit.

It had been my turn to grin in triumph. I was my dad's favorite, and he almost always came to my rescue—my knight in shining armor. He'd apparently carried me in his arms and sung lullabies to me during my notorious sleepless, colicky days.

I had vivid early memories of Dad reading to me when I was a toddler and soothing me in the middle of the night when I'd gone through my many childhood illnesses. More than my mother, it had been my father who'd provided me with comfort when I'd most needed it. Even now, he fussed over me when she didn't.

But Mom freely acknowledged that I was better looking than she. That was the one concession she made. "You were a lovely baby, Meena. You're the image of my mother, the same fair complexion, big eyes, and perfect nose. You have her silky brown hair, too." However, the rueful clucking sound would follow. "I had hoped you'd grow taller than Amma, but you never grew beyond five feet."

Naturally, my brothers had grown to decent heights, but I was the midget, probably from having eschewed food in my growing years.

Well, I had to admit things weren't all that bad for me. At least Mom and Dad didn't make me feel unwanted. I was given the same privileges as the boys.

They loved me. There was no doubt about that—but that subtle difference in their approach to raising us was always present.

The boys were investments in the future, while I was more like a hothouse plant, meant to be nurtured until they could find me a decent husband and give me a reasonable sendoff by way of marriage. But that was the Indian way, so I didn't complain.

Since Dad was an engineer and Mom was an obstetrician/gynecologist with a healthy practice, I never lacked good clothes and other little luxuries. I even drove a snazzy silver Mustang on which they'd made the down payment.

But despite all his support, Dad was still very strict with me when it came to curfews and dating and such. He couldn't under-

stand my choice of career either. "Marketing and public relations? What kind of occupation is that?" he had asked with a
puzzled frown when I'd picked my courses at Cornell.

"It's the right choice for me, Dad," I'd replied with an impatient sigh.

"Such a waste of your talents. You're good at math and science."

"But I have to struggle to do well in those subjects," I'd explained. "The analytical part of my brain is no bigger than a
peanut. But my creative side works just fine, and I'd prefer to
use that."

"That's nonsense. If you tried harder you could do anything."

In Dad's mind there were only a handful of careers for sensible, middle-class folks like us: engineering, medicine, law, accounting, scientific research, and computer science. He'd been
pleased with Mahesh's choice of medicine as an occupation but
a bit upset about Maneel's undergrad in finance and then the
MBA—until Maneel had started to rake in an above-average income. Then Maneel had started to invest Dad and Mom's savings aggressively, and they were showing healthy gains.

All of a sudden, Maneel was Dad's golden boy. Dad couldn't
get enough investment advice from his smart son.

Now I was not only the little runt, but I was also the one with
a silly profession, little more than a glorified clerk. Mom of
course had dismissed me as a clone of her mother, small and reasonably bright, but not motivated, and therefore good wife-and-
mother material to some man who'd be astute enough to
recognize my potential.

Mom didn't say it in so many words, but I could see the disappointment in her eyes. Her two sisters were medical doctors
like her, also living in the U.S. and in successful practices. She
had to have had high hopes for her kids, and yet, only one child
was following in her footsteps.

But then Maneel, although not a doctor, was a cherished
male child, so he was easily forgiven. I had a feeling Mom was

secretly hoping to marry him off to a doctor so Maneel's life would become more balanced.

"Is this Nayak fellow going to offer you a ride every day or just one day?" asked my father, interrupting my thoughts and pulling me back into the moment. A young, single man offering his daughter a ride was of obvious concern.

"I'm not sure, Dad, but Paul seems to think the offer stands until I'm back on my feet. I'm hoping I'll be able to drive myself in a few days." Seeing my father's troubled look, I added, "I have a feeling Prajay Nayak is being extra nice so I won't think about suing him." I didn't want Dad worrying about what would happen to his virgin daughter—little did he know—in the hands of a young man who'd have her to himself for a few minutes in his car.

Maneel stopped playing with the remote for a moment to offer his opinion. "A lawsuit is something to think about, Meena. Just drop a hint or two that you've talked to a lawyer. Any time this Nayak guy wants to fire you or get fresh with you, you can hold that over his head."

I threw Maneel a dark look. "All you think of is money. I'm just glad to have a job. Marketing and PR positions are rare, so I'm grateful to Prajay for doing all this for me." I put on my most righteous expression. "I'd never hold a lawsuit over anyone's head—especially a guy who's going out of his way to be kind."

"PR jobs being rare is right," said Dad. "That's what happens when you choose some obscure career instead of something sensible like engineering or accounting."

Mom lent him her enthusiastic support. "Medicine is even better. Doctors never have to face layoffs as long as there are sick and pregnant people in the world."

I grimaced at Mom. "Medicine is too icky for me."

"Icky? It's the noblest profession." Mom looked thoroughly insulted.

"Nothing personal, Mom, but not all of us are cut out to work with ovaries and uteruses," I argued. "And then, on top of that, you get sued if a baby's born abnormal." My mother had been named in a lawsuit some years ago, when the parents of a malformed child had blamed her for it.

"That's enough," chided my dad, visibly embarrassed. He was uncomfortable with talk about gynecological issues. Mom refrained from discussing her work in front of my dad for that very reason.

Maneel winked at me. All three of us siblings kind of enjoyed embarrassing our prudish dad sometimes. His face looked flushed and his eyebrows wiggled when that happened.

"Loosen up, Dad," Maneel teased him. "You've been married to an obstetrician for thirty-four years."

"Yeah, Dad," I added, encouraged by Maneel's ribbing. "You and Mom had three kids together—a direct result of . . . sex."

I regretted my words the instant they left my mouth.

Mom blushed like I hadn't seen her do since she'd been presented with an unexpected award for outstanding medical service to the community some years ago. "You don't know what you're talking about."

This time Dad tossed his magazine on the floor and sprang out of the recliner. Then he simply walked away, his face looking redder than ever. The poor man was such a sweet and decent soul, and yet I had stomped all over his delicate sensibilities.

Actually, it was admirable that he and Mom were still so devoted to each other, and so much in love in their old-fashioned, arranged-marriage way. Not only did I have deep respect for their relationship, but I hoped to have something like that in my own life someday. But whenever they reminded me of my poor choice in professions, I always ended up getting defensive, and in the process, striking back at them.

However, today I'd gone too far. Could it be the result of all those painkillers I'd been swallowing?

To add to my guilt, Mom picked up her letter and followed Dad out of the room. I should have apologized to both of them, but I couldn't. It would mean alluding to the embarrassing subject of their sex life again, and that was something nobody talked about. Not in our home.

Maneel waited till Mom's back disappeared, then glared at me. "Good job, Miss Public Relations."

"You were teasing them, too."

"Nothing like your remarks."

I gave a contrite shrug. "Sorry. You know how it is when they attack my inferior choices in life."

"No sense saying sorry to me. It's them you should apologize to."

"But they went off on my job again . . . and you know how mad I get when they do that."

"I know how you feel. Didn't I get the same lectures about my career in finance until I made a few good bucks? Give them a couple more years and they'll accept it."

I looked at the clock and swung my feet to the floor. The sharp pain in my right foot made me wince. "Damn!"

Maneel looked up. "You need help going upstairs?"

I shook my head and limped to the door. "I can do it. By Monday I'm back at work anyhow. Then I'm really on my own."

Slowly I managed to make my way up the stairs, down the hall, toward my room. Everything was quiet in my parents' room, and the door was closed. A pang of guilt sliced through me. I had to think of some way to apologize.

As I hobbled to my room, my thoughts shifted to the coming week. Monday was going to be a challenge, with me traveling to get to work in Prajay's car. I wondered what kind of car he drove. Was he the sports car type, the stolid, four-door sedan type, or the big, indomitable SUV type?

I couldn't wait to find out.

Chapter 6

On Monday morning, in spite of my crass remark on Friday night, Mom and Dad were surprisingly solicitous of me. In fact, by early Sunday the whole episode seemed to have vanished.

The three of us had gone out to a nice brunch after Mom came home from delivering a set of twins. She had looked exhausted from being up most of the night with her patient, and Dad had suggested going out to eat.

Sunday evening, I'd tried to make it up to my parents by cooking my famous pasta with mushrooms and broccoli for dinner. By then I was able to hobble around and do quite a bit by myself. The pasta was a big hit along with my spicy broiled fish and tossed salad.

By seven o'clock, it seemed like I'd been completely forgiven. But then I always was, even after my worst mistakes. Mom and Dad didn't hold a grudge for long. They couldn't afford to, I suppose, after having raised three liberated and strong-willed children.

For work today, I put on a comfortable navy pantsuit. Then came the footwear—socks and sneakers. The swelling around my ankle was minimal now, but it hurt if I tried to walk normally, so I held on to the banister and gingerly made my way downstairs to have the toast and juice Mom had promised to set out for me.

"You're sure you're fit to go back to work, *charda?*" Dad

looked at me skeptically as he put his empty cup in the sink and shrugged into his jacket.

"I'm fine, Dad." I chuckled at Mom's worried frown as she rinsed the cup and placed it in the dishwasher. "Mom, stop looking like I'm going to be drafted into the military and shipped off to war. I'll be sitting in an office chair all day, and I'm getting chauffeured by my boss."

Mentioning the boss instantly wiped the frown off Mom's face. "So what is he like, this Prajay?"

"Nice enough," I replied and took a casual sip of my juice.

"What does that mean? Is he friendly?" Mom made this impatient gesture with her hand. "Does he have a sense of humor? Is he smart?"

"Mom, I spoke all of four sentences to the man." I put the glass down. "I was in agony at the time."

"Of course you were."

"Later I was under the influence of strong painkillers, so I can't really answer your questions."

"Hmm. Guess you'll have a chance to get to know him better now."

"Mom, you have to understand something: He's a big man, a giant, and I'm a little mouse. The twain shall never meet."

Mom took off her apron and smoothed her pants and tunic top. "One never knows. Stranger things have happened." Having made her final comment, she picked up her purse and walked out of the kitchen.

Dad shot me an amused look and patted my face. "Have a nice day, *charda,* and don't strain yourself." He turned around as he reached the door. "Call me if you need a ride home after work."

I finished my breakfast and settled down to wait for Prajay to show up. Once again the nervous fluttering started in my belly. Our first encounter had been the most dramatic kind. Our brief conversation had occurred after he'd placed me on the couch in his office, and that had been rather strange, too.

I had sent Prajay directions to our house by e-mail the previous day and hoped they were clear enough. I waited in the family room, my purse beside me, watching the clock ticking away. At 7:52 A.M., I began to wonder if Prajay had forgotten about me.

However, some ten minutes later I heard a car pull into the driveway and looked out the window with relief. And I couldn't help frowning. A red Toyota Camry with faded bumpers and a dent in the fender came to a stop outside our door.

A rich man like Prajay drove *that?* My idea of a little sports car or a sturdy Jeep, or even a Hummer, disappeared in that instant. But then he was an Indian, and we *desis* were a stingy bunch. He probably poured all his profits back into the company and enjoyed no luxuries.

Oh well. I lifted my purse and stood up, then let the right leg get used to the weight for a second before I proceeded to the foyer to open the door. The doorbell was already ringing.

Prajay Nayak stood on the porch. "Good morning," he said very politely in that deep voice of his.

He looked more disturbing than ever. Without my high heels my eyes were on a level with his chest. He wore a dark gray suit with a cream shirt and a maroon tie with gray splashes. I raised my eyes all the way up to make contact with his. *Jack and the Beanstalk* came to mind. He wore dark glasses, so I couldn't see his eyes.

"Good morning," I replied in a voice that sounded a little hoarse. Now that I was facing him, the flutter in my belly climbed up. "I—I hope the directions were okay?"

"Fine. Sorry, I'm running a little late, but I had to borrow a friend's car."

"Oh."

"So you'd be more comfortable," he explained.

"You didn't have to do that."

"Getting in and out of my car would be rough for you," he said.

"That's very kind of you." That explained the Toyota. The poor man had been forced to drive a beat-up old sedan because of me. So exactly what car did he normally drive?

Despite his dark glasses I could tell he was looking at my sneakers. "How's the ankle?"

"Not too bad, thank you," I said in a more normal voice. Now that the ice was broken, I felt much more at ease.

"You're sure you're ready to return to work?"

"Oh, yes," I replied cheerfully. I was more than ready to get back into my routine. "I just have to set the burglar alarm and lock the door."

"You go ahead and set the alarm, and I'll get the door," he offered and took the keys from me. He waited outside while I punched in the code, then stepped out. In one quick motion he locked the door and handed the keys back to me. "Want me to carry your purse?"

"Thanks, but I can manage." A mental image of Prajay carrying a small navy handbag with a gold clasp made me smile inwardly.

He opened the car's passenger door, then gently helped me in before proceeding to his own side. I felt like an invalid and wondered if this was the way he treated his grandmother.

Prajay's legs seemed awkwardly folded at the knees as he settled himself behind the wheel and started to back out of the driveway. "This is a nice house, Meena," he remarked.

"Thanks." Now that I was so closely packed inside the confines of the car with him, my awkwardness returned. He seemed to fill the entire space. "I'm sorry you had to give up your car just for me," I said after a long silence. We'd already reached the stop sign a block from our house.

"It's no problem. Besides, my friend was happy to make the exchange." He grinned at me, the gesture both unexpected and attractive. "If I don't watch out he'll want to keep my Corvette indefinitely."

"You have a Corvette?" I couldn't help smiling. His grin was infectious. "What color?"

"Nothing exciting. It's gray, more like silver."

"Are you kidding? I love silver cars. Mine's a silver Mustang." It would have been nice to go for a ride with this man in his Corvette. Instead he was stuck driving me in an old Toyota. But he had grinned, and it was still very pleasant sitting beside him and hearing his nice voice.

He merged into the heavy rush-hour traffic on Route 1. Seconds later we came to a stop at a red light. "Looks like we have something in common, then. We both like sporty silver cars."

"Um-hmm." I glanced at him, while his long fingers beat a tattoo on the steering wheel, waiting for the light to turn green. A little impatient, I decided, watching those fingers with their blunt tips and short nails. Wanting things to happen in a hurry wasn't a bad trait. It was the mark of a quick brain. "Thanks for the flowers," I remembered to say. "They're lovely. You didn't have to, you know."

"You're welcome. It's standard practice at Rathnaya when an employee is ill."

Oh well, so much for my thinking that he'd personally arranged for the flowers. That effectively shut me up. What was I thinking, dreaming up all these romantic possibilities? I was worse than my mom. Prajay was just being a nice guy and a polite boss, while I was casting him in the hero's role. I forced my gaze back to the road and kept it there all the way to the office. Good thing it was only a short drive.

When he pulled into his reserved spot right by the front of the building, once again he went around the car to open my door and assist me in alighting. He opened the door to the building for me and then walked extra slowly through the lobby to keep pace with my awkward shuffle toward the elevators.

A few of Rathnaya's staff were arriving at the same time. Prajay and I got some curious looks. I could practically hear the rumor mill buzzing: *Prajay Nayak drove Meena Shenoy to work. You think something's going on between those two? They belong to the same caste and all, nah?*

Inside the elevator, we were surrounded by a bunch of people. I smiled and nodded at the ones I knew.

On the sixth floor, Prajay got off with me and made sure he delivered me safely into Pinky's custody. Then he said to me, "I might be late leaving the office this evening. Hope that's okay?" When I nodded, he hurried out the door and disappeared.

I hadn't even said a proper thank-you and he was gone. I sighed.

Pinky's amused comment brought me back to reality. "Must be nice being chauffeured by the boss."

"Kind of awkward."

Pinky gave a sly smile. "How's the foot?"

"Much better. And I'm almost off the painkillers. I only need one at night so I can sleep."

Paul ended his phone call and came out of his office to greet me with a welcoming hug. "How're you feeling, kid?"

"Almost back to normal, thank you."

"Prajay make it to your house okay?"

"Yes. He had to borrow a friend's Toyota so I wouldn't have to wiggle in and out of his Corvette."

Paul's eyebrows flew up. "Very thoughtful of him."

I agreed and opened the door to my office. It looked like Pinky had tried to neaten up my messy desk without actually disturbing my paperwork. I smiled at her obvious efforts.

Although I'd been out less than three working days it felt like weeks. It hadn't been fun being cooped up in the house, wondering what people were saying about my accident—mainly speculating over Gargi's loose comments.

Once I sat down at my desk it was easy to get into the swing of things. I'd been working on two press releases the previous week, which I managed to complete and put on Paul's desk for his review. Then there were some letters to be drafted, to be sent to the governor's office, the appropriate state senator and assemblymen, and some local politicians, about the company's latest acquisition. The politicians would be happy to hear that the move would create more jobs in the state. Later, Paul and I worked on our latest ad for *NJ BIZ* magazine.

I attended one minor meeting late in the afternoon. By the end of the day my ankle was beginning to ache. I'd probably been putting too much weight on it as I'd limped back and forth several times to the ladies' room, the conference room, and the copier.

When Paul and Pinky got ready to leave for the day, they both looked at me with concern.

"You going to be okay until Prajay shows up?" asked Paul.

I smiled brightly. "Of course I will. Go on home, you guys." If Paul didn't get home on time, Jeremy was likely to call.

"Want me to stay with you?" offered Pinky, but I noticed her eyeing the clock.

"Don't be silly." I waved her away. "Your kids are waiting for you."

After Paul and Pinky left, I browsed a bit on the Internet, going to various sites to look at our competitors' ads. I always liked to see what others were doing to boost their business.

I didn't have to wait too long for Prajay. He called a few minutes before he showed up, giving me time to brush my hair and freshen my lipstick. "Sorry to have made you wait, but I had a few things to finish up," he explained.

"It's nothing," I said and stepped out. "I should be the one to apologize for being in your way."

"It's no problem, Meena. My condo is close to your home." Once again Prajay helped me into the car with all the grace he could muster. I stumbled a little while climbing in, but managed to get the seat belt fastened.

Going home was much easier than the ride in to work, but the trip was longer because it was dark outside and the evening traffic was heavy. I could converse more freely, now that I knew he was easy to talk to.

While stopped at a traffic light, Prajay turned to me. "So, how do you like working for Rathnaya?"

"I like it a lot. It's different from anything I've done in the past."

"Paul tells me you're very efficient."

I knew Paul thought highly of me because he'd told me so. Nonetheless my cheeks warmed. "Paul's a kind man."

"He may be kind, but he's a tough manager. He didn't have

nice things to say about the last person working in your position."

"I heard." Pinky had filled me in on the lazy young man who'd been goofing off and doing a lousy job overall. Apparently Paul had tried to give him the benefit of the doubt for nearly six months, but the guy had blown it time and again, and ended up getting fired.

"I'm glad to have someone good on board this time," said Prajay as the light changed and we started to move once again. "We can use all the help we can get in the PR area, especially with a name like Rathnaya." He must have heard me chuckle, because he briefly turned to smile at me. "I told Nishant nobody would take us seriously with a silly name like that."

"Nishant's the one who decided on the odd name?"

"His father did. Some astrologer advised him that the name should have exactly so many consonants and syllables in a certain pattern."

"You're kidding!"

"It's supposed to bring good luck, according to Nishant's father."

I pondered it for a second. "Well, looks like the astrologer was right. The company's been growing steadily since you started it twelve years ago. You've acquired two companies, are in the process of buying up a third one, expanded your public sector presence, and have taken on more subcontractors."

Prajay gave a satisfied nod. "You've been doing your homework."

"I had to, before I interviewed with Paul and Nishant."

"No wonder they were impressed." He turned the car onto my street. "Nice work on the press release about our acquisition . . . and on the new ad campaign."

I didn't know he'd already seen the new ads. "Thanks," I replied, feeling ridiculously pleased. I was beginning to like this guy more and more. His fierce face was starting to look rather attractive, too—even the nose didn't look all that big. When he smiled and his features softened, he looked . . . nice.

I was almost sorry when he pulled into our driveway. I had enjoyed the ride immensely. When he walked me to my front door and opened it for me, I asked him if he'd like to come in for a cup of tea or a soda, but he thanked me politely and declined, citing more work to do at home. "I'll pick you up around quarter of eight tomorrow," he said and strode back to his car.

"Thank you, Prajay." I stood at the door and watched him drive away.

Such a pleasant giant, I thought.

Chapter 7

I rode back and forth with Prajay for a total of five days, before I felt sure I could drive myself. It was with regret that I told him I was well enough to do it on my own. I wished I could prolong the rides indefinitely, but then he'd catch on to my lie, especially since I had begun to walk more normally.

The rides together had been especially delightful because we had talked about a lot of things, the business, our respective hobbies, our favorite movies, music, and just about everything. As we'd discussed various individuals from our Konkani community, we'd discovered that we knew some of the same people, especially since he had spent part of his childhood in New Jersey.

Best of all, Prajay and I had laughed a lot. I'd not only come to respect him and his capacity for hard work and his keen business sense, but I also genuinely appreciated him as a person. I didn't know when he was planning to return to Washington, but I hoped it wouldn't be anytime soon. I wanted to get to know him better.

During the following week, I didn't see Prajay at all, much to my disappointment. I knew he was in the building because I'd seen his Corvette parked in his reserved spot. Each day that week, I had put on one of my most impressive outfits, hoping to run into him. I had even lingered in the break room on the ninth floor to chat with a few people who I was friendly with, but there had been no sign of Prajay. It was as if he were hiding in some deep, dark cave.

I heard from Paul that Prajay and Nishant were neck-deep in negotiations with the Jersey-based software company they were about to acquire. That explained his absence despite being in the building. When I left for home every evening, the Corvette was still in the parking lot. I told myself that he was just another nice guy. And my boss. Nothing more.

By Friday night I was convinced that I'd probably never see him again.

On Saturday evening Shabari-pachi and her family decided to join us for a potluck dinner. The two families often did that, pooled whatever they had in their respective refrigerators and threw together an informal meal. It often ended up being an odd medley of leftovers, but it was fun to have my aunt and uncle, cousins, and both my brothers to lounge around with.

My cousins, Amrita and Lalita, were twenty-five and twenty-three respectively, and we got along well. When we were growing up we used to fight like alley cats, but as adults the three of us were like sisters—still arguing furiously at times, but basically close.

Amrita was a final year medical student, and Lalita was in graduate school, studying for a master's in bioengineering.

Shabari-pachi, who strongly resembled my mother, swooped down on me like a vulture just as we were finishing our dinner. My hopes of having a satisfying family get-together dissolved when I noticed her curious expression. "I hear Prajay Nayak is your boss . . . and he's sending you flowers?"

"They were a standard 'get well' bouquet ordered by his secretary," I said, trying to keep my voice even.

"But Kaveri tells me they were expensive roses. *Desis* are stingy about things like flowers. If he sends roses it has to mean something."

"They were nothing special."

"But I understand he's been driving you to work and all that." She winked at me, trying to be subtle. But she didn't have a subtle bone in her body.

I sent my mom a blistering look across the table as I ate the last bite of the chicken with spinach curry on my plate. She'd blabbed to the whole world. "Prajay Nayak merely offered me a ride for a few days because my ankle was sprained and his condo isn't too far from here. Since then I haven't seen him."

"What's this I hear about you falling at his feet?" teased my cousin Amrita with a wicked smirk. Tall and shapely, with long silky hair and a killer smile, she knew exactly how to yank my chain.

"I fell on my rear end and made a fool of myself," I said blandly.

Mahesh joined in the conversation with gusto. "Fell flawlessly, so she could show him her legs, just like in the movies."

"Watch it, Mahesh," I warned.

Maneel, not to be outdone, threw in his contribution to the tease-fest. "Then she conveniently decides to use the poor, unsuspecting guy to chauffeur her for several days. Very clever, slightly devious," he said with a mock impressed look.

To make matters worse, Guru-bappa, my uncle, whose full name was Gurunath, started snickering. "Did the trick work?"

Mom sighed. "I wish."

"Tsk-tsk," clucked Shabari-pachi. "You should have made the most of the situation, Meena. Why didn't you pretend to limp for a few more weeks?"

"I dislike deceit." My jaw clenched hard.

"It's not deceit," Shabari countered. "You would have had a chance to use some of the hints in that book I gave you for your birthday."

I frowned at my aunt. "All the hints in the world wouldn't do me any good with this guy. He's built like a monolith. He's not for me."

Shabari-pachi's eyes took on a familiar, calculating gleam. "Then maybe he's suitable for our Amrita." Her gaze shifted to her own firstborn.

I grinned when I caught Amrita's expression of cross impatience. The spotlight had landed on her. "Mom, stop trying to fix me up. I told you I'm too busy to look at potential husbands."

"Nonsense. Kaveri, Madhuri, and I went through grueling residencies after we were married, and still managed to have kids. If we could juggle homes, husbands, kids, *and* demanding careers, I'm sure you can find the time to meet the right boy," declared Shabari-pachi with the imperious air of a queen.

The rest of the conversation went on in the same vein, with talk shifting from Prajay Nayak to other eligible young men, then gradually to my brother Maneel. The sneaky devil suddenly got up, claimed he had work to do, and pushed his chair in.

Every time my family brought up the subject of *his* marriage, Maneel did a vanishing act. I had a suspicion he was seeing someone and wanted to keep it a secret from my parents. One of these days I'd have to pry it out of him. It wouldn't be easy, but I had my ways.

Maneel made a quiet escape out the front door. Everyone laughed when Amrita made a face and said, "He-Man turns to Jell-O-Man when it's his turn."

I agreed. It was nice to be the teaser instead of the teased for a change.

Meanwhile Lalita, perhaps to avoid the topic of marriage, excused herself from the table and went to the family room. A bit more introverted than her sister and my brothers and I, she preferred to do things by herself. She resembled Amrita to some degree but was slimmer and even prettier than she.

Fortunately Shabari-pachi and her family left soon after the table was cleared and the dishes washed and put away. I'd had enough of my aunt's third degree. I loved her dearly, but her interference in my life was a nuisance.

It was the Indian way. Playing matchmaker was every Indian woman's prerogative; my mother and my aunts chose to exercise it freely.

On Monday, just as I was winding up for the day and getting ready to shut down my computer, I received a surprise e-mail from Prajay: *Meena, I need to discuss something personal and confidential with you. I'd appreciate it if you don't mention it to anyone. Please stop by my office after work if you can spare the time. Thanks. PN.*

I read it once again to make sure I'd understood it correctly. There was no mistaking the intent: after work; personal and confidential; needed to see me in person; in secret.

A slow tingle of anticipation started to hum along my skin. It sounded mysteriously delicious.

Maybe he was interested in me after all. He hadn't indicated it by a single word or sign. Had he been worried about sexual harassment and personnel policies and such? He seemed very proper in his behavior. So what had happened all of a sudden to make him come forward like this? Maybe it was time for him to return to DC and he wanted to find out how I felt about him before he left.

Whatever it was, it looked promising. I sent him a response: *I'll stop by today after my two colleagues leave. Is that okay with you?*

His reply was instant: *Sounds good. Thanks.*

I couldn't wait for Paul and Pinky to leave. Pinky left at her usual five o'clock because of her kids, but Paul took forever to make a move. He was on the phone with Jeremy for several minutes, writing down a list of items he was supposed to pick up from the supermarket.

Since our two offices were separated by a thin wall, I could hear every word of the conversation. By the time Paul had written organic spinach and mushrooms, farm-raised tilapia, high-protein pasta, and Asian sesame dressing with no MSG, I knew exactly what the two men were having for dinner that evening.

I waited for Paul to hang up the phone. *Get it over with and get to the market already.* I cracked my knuckles once or twice.

When Paul finally put on his jacket, slung his lunch bag over his wrist, and stuck his head in my office to bid me good night, I breathed a small sigh of relief.

"You still here?" he asked with a curious expression.

"I'm meeting a friend for drinks later." I tried to sound casual. "Figured I'd go directly from work."

"Have fun." Paul took off, whistling under his breath. And why not? Jeremy was waiting to cook him a lovely gourmet meal.

I looked at the clock. Twenty minutes to six—hopefully most of the folks had gone home for the day. But then this was an IT company, and people worked the oddest hours. They pretty much made their own schedules. Well, I'd just have to work around it. This was an important issue for me . . . and Prajay. It couldn't wait.

Making a trip to the deserted ladies' room, I fixed my hair and makeup and dabbed a little perfume on my pulse points. I regretted not having worn something softly feminine and pretty. But how was I to know that Prajay would drop this bombshell on me at the end of the day, especially since I hadn't seen him or heard from him for an entire week?

This morning I'd chosen to put on a steel gray suit and a yellow shirt with silver buttons. Very professional, but hardly seductive. I was still in sneakers, too. But at least my face and hair looked fine.

I tried to practice various expressions in the mirror—just in case he said what I thought and hoped he'd say: stunned surprise, pleased astonishment, the dazed look, wide-eyed delight. Nothing looked genuine, so I gave up. I wasn't one of those females who believed in putting on airs, anyway.

Besides, he'd seen me at my worst—flushed and swollen-eyed, runny-nosed, and flat on my back, hysterical with pain.

And yet he wanted to have a very private talk with me. Maybe Mom was right about fate's throwing us together.

I locked the door leading into the main office and took the elevator to the penthouse. Now that I was headed in that direction, my heart was pounding. My hands were shaking, so I thrust them in my pockets. Perspiration began to form on my skin.

What was I getting into? All at once reality struck me with a punch similar to the collision I'd had with Prajay three weeks ago. Did I really want to see this guy socially? Was he my type? I'd probably romanticized my involvement with him only because it had happened in such a dramatic manner. Was it akin to a patient's spinning fantasies around her doctor or therapist?

If I'd met Prajay the normal way, I'd have had a brief and formal meeting with him, and that would have been the end of it. He wouldn't have carried me in his arms or driven me to work. I'd never have gotten to know him on a personal level. I wouldn't be on my way to his office now. More like sneaking in after-hours.

The elevator doors opened. I stepped out very carefully and looked both ways to avoid a repetition of my fiasco. The hallway was deserted.

Prajay's office was the closest to the elevators, so I didn't have to pass by other people's offices, thank goodness. I heard a male voice speaking somewhere at the far end of the hall on the other side. It sounded like a phone conversation. I heard the click-click of a keyboard. Ignoring all the familiar sounds, I kept moving.

Anna's desk was unoccupied. Hopefully she was gone for the day. The efficient Anna was actually Annapurna. Everyone called her Anna for short. She was a perfect executive secretary—friendly and professional, yet very discreet—but I had the feeling Prajay didn't want even her involved in whatever he was about to reveal to me.

Prajay's door was wide open, and he was sitting at his desk, studying his computer screen with a slight frown. He looked totally absorbed. He seemed to be an intense man, highly focused on his work, and yet he seemed so easygoing on a personal level.

I observed him in silence for a moment. His shirt today was a light olive with a coordinated tie and gold cufflinks. It looked good on him. His dress habits were a complete contrast to those of his friend and partner, Nishant.

From what I'd gathered about the two men, Nishant was the shrewd money manager, while Prajay was the wheeler-dealer as well as the technical brain behind the business. They made an impressive team.

Prajay obviously hadn't heard my approaching footsteps, so I knocked on the door.

He looked up. The frown vanished. "Hi, Meena."

"Hi." Overcome by nervousness, I hesitated on the threshold.

"Please come in," he said. As I stepped inside, he motioned to me to take one of the guest chairs across from his desk. Then he did something that made my pulse take a disturbing leap. He strode toward the door and shut it before turning to me. "Thanks so much for coming."

"No problem." I sat down and wiped my damp palms on my skirt.

He actually seemed to blush. "I'm a little embarrassed."

A tiny warning bell went off in my brain. What was I doing in this man's office? Alone. After-hours. I looked at the closed door and a wave of panic hit me. I barely knew him. Five days of riding in a car with a man to and from the office didn't amount to knowing what went on in his mind. He could be a weirdo, for all I knew. Maybe that's why he was still single at thirty-nine?

Good Lord, what if he tried anything funny? I was too tiny to defend myself against a man his size. Nonetheless another part of my brain wanted him to touch me. How could I want *that* and yet be afraid of it?

But it was too late to run. I had to see this thing through somehow. Hopefully those comforting sounds I'd heard from neighboring offices meant there were others still working on this floor.

I took a deep breath. I was a grown woman with abundant confidence. I'd dated before, so I knew a little about men. I'd managed to shake off the kissie-poo Saint Bernard type and had successfully kept groping fingers at bay while at college.

No big deal. I could . . . handle this guy, too.

Chapter 8

When Prajay returned to his own chair behind the desk, my racing pulse calmed a little. See, he didn't have any intentions of attacking me or any such thing. He still looked like a gentleman. I felt foolish when I saw him get comfortable in his seat. Not a single sign of his being a predatory wolf.

So much for my fears and hopes of being ravished on the rug.

He leaned forward, braced his elbows on the desk, and clasped his hands, like he was praying. "I don't even know where to start, Meena."

It was too quiet in the room. Maybe he could hear my heartbeat. "Is this like . . . uh . . . Are you sure you want to talk about it?"

He sighed, long and loud. "I've given it considerable thought, and yes, I want to talk to you about it." He picked up a pen and twirled it between his fingers. "I'm sure the gossip about me has reached your ears a number of times."

"Gossip is part and parcel of any office. I don't pay attention to it," I informed him with a shrug.

He acknowledged my white lie with a slight smile that said he didn't believe it for one moment. "I turned thirty-nine this year, and the pressure to get married and settle down is mounting. My family is beyond dropping hints now."

"I see."

"My father lectured me on the subject last night. Again." He pretended to wince. "More like blistered my ears over the phone lines."

"Um-hmm." He was clearly struggling with the issue. Those long fingers were still twirling that pen. I knew all about parental pressure. I wondered if he had aunts and uncles like mine, people who pushed and prodded and poked and harassed. I bet he did. What Indian family didn't have its share of meddlesome relatives?

"My older brothers were married by thirty," he continued, "and they have wives and kids and homes of their own."

"So you're the odd man out?"

"That's me—the odd man. What they don't realize is that my brothers took up stable jobs after they got their degrees. A few years later they had enough savings to think of marriage and family. On the other hand, when I was that age, I was busy starting up a company. I was up to my long chin in debt."

I nodded, trying to focus on his issues rather than mine, trying not to wonder where all this was leading and how it was going to affect me. "You had no time for anything other than work."

"When I try to tell them that, they just point to other Indian businessmen my age, men who have families. They can't understand why I cannot make time for a personal life. They're worried that people might think I'm gay."

"Are you?" I was sincerely hoping he wasn't gay. Not when I found him *so* appealing.

"No. I've assured them of that." He heaved another tired sigh. "But it makes them nag even more."

Relieved, I nodded my agreement. "I know all about nagging parents."

"You?" Prajay threw me a puzzled look. "But you're so young; you have plenty of time."

"Thirty-one's not young for a woman, at least not an Indian woman." From the way my aunts and my mom carried on, I was about to start menopause any day now. But I couldn't tell Prajay that.

"You don't look thirty-one. I figured no more than twenty-four, or five, at the most," he said.

"Thanks." Now that he knew my real age, maybe he'd stop beating around the bush and ask me out. All this hemming and hawing was making me ill.

"Well, getting back to me, I've been introduced to God knows how many women. I've tried my best to get to know them—taken them out to dinner, movies, dancing . . . the whole dating scenario. But something or the other just doesn't seem right." He gave me one of those looks that said *you know what I mean?*

"I know exactly what you mean, Prajay." Been there, done that.

"Then you understand how frustrating it is—meeting all these girls and realizing not a single one is right for you." He threw the pen down and stared at something outside the window.

I was getting thoroughly impatient now. Where was all this leading? Was he saying that all those other women were unsuitable but *I* was the right one for him? If so, I wished he'd get on with it. A savvy businessman like him ought to be able to express something as simple as that.

"Well, let me get to the point, Meena," he said and picked up his pen once again.

About time. "I'm listening." The perspiration was beginning to bead on my upper lip. What was I going to say if he came right out and asked me out on a date? Sure I was impatient to hear it, but what was I to do about it? Accept? Say thanks but no thanks and get out of there? But then his male ego could get bruised from the rejection and consequently I could end up losing my job. On the other hand, dating one's boss was clearly a conflict of interest.

Damn, there was no right answer. "Exactly what is it that you're looking for, Prajay?"

"Since every woman I've met so far hasn't quite measured up to my height requirements, I've decided to do something about it."

Hallelujah! He was going to say he didn't mind my puny stature, that size had nothing to do with personality, that it was what was inside a person that mattered, that good things often come in little packages, and that he had recognized my potential the day he'd first laid eyes on me . . . and so on. I straightened my spine, put on my most receptive look, and braced myself for the truth.

"I'm planning on putting an ad in the matrimonial columns of a few newspapers and Internet matchmaking sites," he said.

"What!" I nearly jumped out of my chair. I couldn't have heard that correctly. Were those blasted painkillers still doing a number on my brain?

"I know, I know. It comes as a surprise to you, I'm sure."

Try shock. I cleared my throat. "Uh . . . yes."

"I know what you're thinking. An Indian guy with a successful business shouldn't have to resort to such desperate measures to find a wife."

"Hmm."

"But I've given it a lot of thought . . . and I think it's the best way for me."

I stared at my trembling hands. I'd been such a fool. How could I have been so blind? He hadn't shown any interest in me by word or deed, and yet I'd been fantasizing like a giddy-headed schoolgirl. All that swooning in the larger-than-life hero's arms and his falling in love with the petite heroine had gone to my head, along with Murjani's pills.

I'd never ever look at those little white disks of idiocy again. They had killed off several gray cells in my head.

Somehow I managed to look up at him. "Newspapers and Internet matchmakers?" My voice came out as an anguished whisper.

"You know what I mean, sites like Matchmaker.com, IndiaMatrimony.com, and print media like *India Overseas,* etcetera."

I nodded dumbly. Yeah, I knew all about those sites. Some of my friends had posted their profiles on those. They got dozens and dozens of hits, but the quality of respondents was preposterous—great entertainment for us.

And this guy wanted to use those same sources? Oh well, he'd have to learn his lesson the hard way. He deserved to learn it the hard way for being so naïve. And so damn blind. "In that case, what is it you want *me* to do, Prajay?"

"You're good at writing ads. I want you to create one or two good ones for me."

I turned it over in my mind for a second or two. "So you want *me* to be your campaign manager in *your* quest for the perfect bride?"

He snapped his fingers, his face brightening up. "I knew you'd get the idea in a second."

Oh yeah, eureka. I wasn't dreaming this. It was really happening. "Why didn't you ask Paul to do this for you, Prajay? He could do an outstanding job for you. And you've known him longer than me. You trust him."

He shook his head. "Paul's a good man, and I certainly trust him, but he'd never understand the concept of a matrimonial ad. If it were a *personals* ad, he'd have no problem. But you, on the other hand, belong to my community."

"That still doesn't qualify me for writing matrimonial ads for you."

"But you know how these things work. You know the inner workings of the Konkani psyche." He made an all-encompassing gesture with his right hand. "Plus, I've come to know you, as a professional. I can trust you with a confidential matter like this."

"Sure." Now that the disappointment had settled like a lead ball in my belly, I was ready to handle it in the best way I knew: like a *professional*. "What requirements did you have in mind?" I leaned forward and borrowed a notepad off his desk and a pen from his pen holder.

I was ready to do business. Damn it, I was going to be his campaign manager, his marriage consultant, his *Yenta*. His karma shaper. How ironic was that, after I'd come here with such great expectations for myself?

"Let me see," said Prajay, interrupting my thoughts. "First thing: She has to be somewhere around six feet tall. Every girl I've dated and met through my parents has been too short."

No kidding, I thought with a mental grunt. Short as in what—five feet and ten inches? He'd have to start looking amongst the women's basketball teams for anyone taller than that. "What else?"

"She has to be educated, of course . . . at least a bachelor's degree."

"Sure—you don't want an uneducated *dhuddi,*" I said, using the Konkani term for dim-witted female and making him laugh. I wrote: *at lst 6' and BD*—my version of shorthand.

"I definitely want a Hindu girl—caste and sub-caste don't matter—as long as she's cultured and forward-thinking."

"Got it," I said and scribbled some more.

"Sense of humor is a must. I can't stand a woman with no sense of humor."

"Of course. Humor is important." My list was getting longer: H—Caste no barrier—Cul & Fwd-Tkng—SOH . . .

"Beautiful, fair, innocent, virgin, and all the usual attributes, I suppose?" I asked with a cynical lift of my brow. I hoped my bitterness didn't come through in my voice, because I could taste it in my mouth.

He laughed again, the sound deep, rumbling, and filled with amusement. "I'm not good-looking, so I'm not particular about the woman's looks. Decent-looking would be nice. Attractive would be a rare bonus," he said with a humorous twist of his mouth. "And innocent virgins? Are there any left?"

I sent him a skeptical look. With a flourish I held the pen up. "Any particular profession you're looking for in this woman?"

"Hmm." Prajay looked out the window again, eyes narrowed in speculation. "I guess I'm open to anything, as long as she's not in direct competition with me." He turned his attention back to me. "It wouldn't exactly be pleasant to share my life with someone who owned a company that bid on the same jobs as mine, would it?"

"Sleeping with the enemy, you mean?"

He chuckled. "I knew you'd understand." Then his face took on a puzzled expression. "You know something? You and I think similarly in so many matters. Why do you think that is?"

Duh! We were made for each other. Don't you see that, you blind-as-a-bat goofball? It's as plain as the hooked nose on your face. But I gave him a saccharine smile. "Maybe because our upbringing was very similar?"

"You hit the nail on the head." His brow lifted a notch. "Anything else you can think of that I might have missed?"

"What about age requirements?

"Make it between, oh . . . thirty-two and thirty-nine."

Now wasn't that funny? I missed the cutoff age by a year. *One* lousy year. "How about her location, Prajay? Don't you want this woman to be within a certain distance, so you can meet and date . . . and whatever? What if she lives in Siberia or something?"

He threw his head back and roared with laughter. "I like your sense of humor."

No, you love *my sense of humor. You just haven't realized it yet.* "I'm glad. So, what'll it be? Siberia or Sudan or the South Pacific?"

Still chuckling, he said, "Northeast U.S. would be reasonable."

"Okay, Northeast it is." I rose from my seat. "Anything else, before I leave?"

"The ads have to be entirely anonymous, naturally."

"Naturally. I'll give this some thought and have something suitable written up by tomorrow morning. Is that all right?"

He came to his feet. "More than all right. I appreciate your help, Meena."

"No problem." I tore off the sheet and shoved it into my purse, then returned the notepad and pen to his desk. "You want me to e-mail this to you?"

"No, that's not a good idea. Why don't you put it in the mail to my condo address?" He handed me a piece of paper with his address on it.

He came around his desk to stand only a few feet away from me. His cologne was doing weird things to me. I was tempted to reach out and touch the crisp fabric of his shirt. That's all I could reach anyway. His face was way up there, out of my range. To be able to touch his face, I'd have to climb on top of his desk.

I took a couple of steps back, closer to the door. "I'll put it in the mail."

Now that the consulting session was over, I was dying to get out of his office. Despite its generous proportions, it was stifling. My heartbeat was still irregular, and my emotions were running amok. This was the worst work assignment I'd ever taken on in my entire life. I hated it, and yet, what choice did I have? If the CEO asked me for a favor, I couldn't very well thumb my nose at him.

As I reached for the doorknob he said, "Meena, I'd like to pay you for this."

"Don't be silly. It won't take all that long."

"I don't care how much time or effort it takes. You've already stayed past your quitting time today, and you're going to work on it at home. I expect to pay you the standard consulting fee that I pay my contractors."

"You don't have to feel obligated, Prajay. I'd do it for any . . . friend."

"Well, I'll pay you a friendly, discounted fee in that case," he said with a grin. Then he came forward and extended his hand. "Thanks again. And please, not a word about this to anyone. Not your parents or friends . . . no one, okay?"

I put my hand in his. "You have my word." My hand was shaking. Damn, but it felt good to have his enormous paw wrapped around my tiny one. "Good night, Prajay."

"Good night. Careful driving home. And take care of that ankle."

"Sure." I opened the door and stepped out. The foot felt achier than ever. Thankfully the elevator doors opened immediately. I didn't want him to see my face. I didn't want anyone to see my face. It was burning. I'd just agreed to assist the very man I wanted for myself in finding his ideal woman.

As if that weren't unpleasant enough, the elevator stopped at the eighth floor. In walked Gargi Bansal.

She looked fresh as a marigold in her brown slacks and yellow top. Her long dark hair was smooth and shiny, her makeup perfect, and her fingernails manicured. Maybe she was on her way to meet a guy. Her perfume was a bit overpowering but not unpleasant. She slanted a smile at me. "Hi, Meena. Working late today?"

"Yes." I tried to keep my voice even.

"Are you all right? You look a little flushed." She eyed my sneakers. "Your foot is okay, I hope?"

"It's healing nicely, thank you."

"So you were working on the ninth floor today," she said with a knowing smirk.

"Um-hmm." I realized my voice wobbled. I was still reacting to what had happened in Prajay's office. And Gargi Bansal was wondering what I had been doing in the penthouse after working hours.

Now that the whole office knew Prajay had carried me in his arms twice, all they needed was Gargi's help to conclude that I was having an affair with the CEO—spending my evenings on the ninth floor and going home with rosy cheeks. Great.

If it had been true, I wouldn't have cared, but it was so far from the truth it was ludicrous. Not only would my reputation be torn to shreds, but I wouldn't even get the prize at the end. I was actually helping the prize acquire his ideal wife. On top of that, I couldn't even defend myself by telling the truth to anyone. I had just sworn not to tell a soul about my secret assignment. Nice, tight corner to be hemmed into.

I turned to Gargi with my own faux smile. "A new advertising campaign. All that overtime and brainstorming for a two-line slogan."

She shrugged. "Don't know much about liberal arts type of work. I'm a programmer."

The elevator came to a stop in the lobby, and we both stepped out. Good thing I was still crawling at a tortoise's pace—it gave me an excuse to motion to Gargi not to wait for me. She rushed off. I'd bet anything she was already working on that ugly rumor about Prajay and me.

Lord, what had I got myself into?

Chapter 9

That night I sat at my home computer and wrote up several ads—different wordings to capture the essentials. I'd let Prajay decide which ones he wanted to use. I put the printed sheets in an envelope and readied them for mailing.

The next morning, I made the mistake of leaving the envelope and my purse side-by-side on the kitchen table while I ate my breakfast.

Mom's eagle eyes fell on it. "Meena, what are you mailing to your boss?" she asked with a hopeful expression. I noted her sidelong glance at my father, who was trying to drink his tea and scan the *New York Times* headlines at the same time.

"Some ideas for a future marketing campaign."

"Then why send them to his home address? Wouldn't marketing ideas be discussed in the office?" Mom was no dummy.

"This is something he's working on secretly." I got up to put my empty cup and cereal bowl in the sink. "Intellectual property and competitors," I whispered and put my finger over my lips.

Mom looked thoroughly intrigued—and pleased. "He told this only to you and nobody else?"

"Um . . . something like that."

She tapped Dad on the shoulder. "Did you hear that, Ram? The Nayak boy is telling Meena important trade secrets."

"Mom! Will you please get the thought out of your head?

There's nothing between that man and me. He's my boss. I merely *work* for him. You get that?"

"Sure, dear." Mom picked up her car keys and headed out to grab her coat from the closet, but I didn't miss the smug look on her face. Fortunately Dad got busy putting on his own jacket and seemed unaffected by Mom's remarks. But then Dad seldom revealed what was going on in that seriously analytical mind of his.

I said good-bye to him as he left for work and got ready to head out myself.

At the office, things were quiet. Until about three o'clock. When I went to the break room to buy a soda from the vending machine, I ran into Deepak Iyer, a young systems analyst and self-proclaimed expert on everything from literature to foreign policy.

Unfortunately I wasn't nimble enough to make a quick escape. He cornered me at the door. "Hey, Meena, don't run away."

"I need to get back to work," I explained with a polite smile.

"Long time no see. How're you doing?"

"Fine, thanks." I opened the tab on my soda can and took a sip.

He glanced at my sneakers. "Heard all about your mishap, *yaar,*" he said, using the Hindi word for friend. "What a horrible thing to happen in front of a bunch of people."

"You can say that again." I was trying to brush it off as a minor incident, but it was hard when someone insisted on reminding me of my humiliation.

"I'm sorry, *yaar.*" He studied me for an instant. "Looks like you're feeling okay now?"

"Feeling better and better," I said and started to head out, but he stopped me with a hand held up.

"Meena, wait. I was . . . wondering if you'd like to . . . maybe go out to dinner or for drinks this Friday?"

"My Fridays are busy, Deepak. I have such a large family; I can't believe how fast my weekends go." I smiled sweetly to take the sting out of the rejection. Deepak and I had been through this routine before. He asked nicely, and I turned down his invitation with a smile.

Deepak was a stocky guy with a South Indian accent. He used some kind of shiny gel in his hair and walked with a confident swagger. A lot of girls in our office thought he was quite the prize and shamelessly tried to attract his attention, but for some reason he'd set his sights on me.

I had a strong suspicion it was Deepak's temporary work permit visa status that made him chase after me instead of one of the other women who were in the same situation as he. And there were lots of women in the office, much more attractive than me. Being a hi-tech company, Rathnaya was filled with computer professionals recently imported from India.

Quite a few guys like Deepak asked me out. I suspected those guys wanted to woo and marry an American citizen, to guarantee their own permanent status in the country. It bothered me, this constantly having to lie and say I was too busy to go out with them.

They were all nice enough, highly educated, decent, affable, but I hadn't found a single one who was my type. I wasn't all that fussy about a guy's looks, but most of the men from India were a bit too serious for my tastes. Their sense of humor was different from that of the boys who'd been raised in the States.

Besides, they were usually looking for the sweet, modest, compliant, all-Indian woman. None of those adjectives even came close to describing me.

Meanwhile Deepak was giving me that *aw, come on, can't you make time for a hot guy like me* look. "A simple dinner shouldn't take up the entire evening, Meena. Just two coworkers getting a bite to eat isn't a big deal, right?"

I took another sip of soda and mulled it over. One had to admire his tenacity and capacity to handle rejection. I'd turned him down at least half a dozen times. He wasn't bad looking, either. In some ways he was even attractive. "Okay, I can make time for dinner."

He grinned, white teeth gleaming against his dark skin. "That's great, *yaar*. Never thought you'd agree."

"I have to give you credit for perseverance, Deepak. Maybe my accident has left me with less willpower . . . or something."

"Or something." He sounded so self-satisfied that it made me uneasy. Too late to bail out of it now. I was beginning to lose my appetite for my soda.

"So, you want me to pick you up at your house?" he asked, the grin still lingering.

"That's not necessary." It wasn't gallantry that prompted the offer but curiosity about where I lived. He was scoping out my suitability as a future wife. "I'll meet you at the restaurant. You choose the place."

His grin faded. "Okay then. How about meeting at India Jewel around six o'clock?"

"Sure." I poured the rest of my soda down the sink and tossed the can in the recyclables container. I'd smoothed his ego a bit by letting him decide. Besides, I wasn't really interested in going out with Deepak Iyer. But I was still bristling from my meeting with Prajay. The hell with him. Let the man go find his Amazon woman on the Internet or in the rain forests of Brazil for all I cared. I was an attractive woman and had plenty of men interested in me.

"All right, *yaar,* we have a date."

"Not exactly. We're just two coworkers having dinner together, remember? I'll see you on Friday then." I gave him a casual wave. Deepak seemed pleased, but his eyes narrowed on me. He seemed suspicious of my sudden and unexpected capitulation. I'd turned down his invitations often enough for him to wonder if something strange was going on.

I went back to work. If Deepak was expecting any kind of physical excitement on Friday night he was mistaken. I didn't intend to do anything with him other than eat a friendly dinner and return home.

I'd gone out on dates in my college days. I'd had my share of kissing and fondling, but I had allowed only one of them to get into my bed. And that had been a *big* mistake. During my senior year in college, two of my girlfriends and I had gone to a New

Year's Eve party and become drunk on cheap champagne. The party had continued into the early hours of the morning.

Too intoxicated to think straight, I'd let a guy named Eric talk me into accepting a ride in his car to my apartment. Eric was a hunk, and a nice guy, but one thing had led to another and we'd tumbled into bed, both of us too drunk to know right from wrong. The next morning, I'd woken up to find Eric gone. And my virginity, too.

I was twenty-one. And devastated.

I'd hated myself then. In a daze, I'd barely managed to get through the next couple of weeks. I hadn't gone home to visit my parents for several months after that. I couldn't face them. How had I managed to get into such a horrible mess?

It wasn't so much the sleeping with someone that had troubled me. It was the careless, emotionless way I'd done it. If I'd had deep feelings for the guy, I would've thought it sweet and acceptable, romantic.

I wasn't entirely sure if Eric had used any protection either. Just to be sure I hadn't contracted some terrible disease or become pregnant, I'd reluctantly gone to the campus clinic to get myself checked. Everything had turned out all right. I'd sent Lord Ganesh a tearful thank-you prayer for saving me from a terrible fate.

After that I hadn't allowed myself to get into that kind of situation ever again. I never wanted to go to bed with anyone who I wasn't totally committed to. And I'd never gotten drunk again, either. If nothing else, that affair had proved to be a good lesson in sobriety.

I'd kept away from the dating scene after that incident, until the Indian guys, heartily approved by my parents, had come along. And darn it, not a single one had proved suitable.

So here I was, after a long hiatus, attracted to the Jolly Brown Giant, who in turn was looking for a she-giant. Therefore I was going out on a date with a guy named Deepak Iyer.

At least Deepak was a smart, educated guy with a good job. I could have done worse.

I never heard anything from Prajay about receiving my envelope. But on Friday afternoon I got an e-mail: *Meena, thanks so much for the wonderful job. I posted a few ads right away and got loads of responses. I'm overwhelmed and don't have the time to sort thru them. I need more help from you. Could you please stop by after work? If not today, early next week? Thanks. PN.*

I sent Prajay a reply that I could spare a few minutes before I left for the day. I had to keep my dinner date with Deepak, but I didn't tell Prajay that.

Once again, I had to tell Paul that I was meeting a friend after work. He gave an approving smile. "Friday night date. Good."

I smiled back and waved him away, then went directly upstairs, armed with my notebook and pen. Anna was just leaving when I stepped off the elevator. She looked at me curiously. "Meena, what a surprise!"

"Hi, Anna. Is Prajay in his office? I need to go over some new ads with him," I said, talking a bit too fast and sounding breathless in the bargain.

"He's on the phone," replied Anna, shrugging into her jacket. "You can wait here if you'd like." Her brow creased. "Paul is not attending the meeting?"

"Paul had . . . plans for this evening."

"Oh." Anna pulled her purse out of her drawer and looked at me. "It's odd that Prajay didn't mention any meeting about ads to me."

I put on my most baffled expression. "He didn't? Hmm . . . must have slipped his mind."

"Must have." Her gaze shifted to my feet. "How's the ankle?"

"Much better, thanks. Can't wait to get rid of the sneakers," I replied, relieved to switch subjects. I could only lie so much with a straight face.

The sound of Prajay's voice winding up the phone conversation reached us. "Looks like he's off the phone. Why don't you go in," said Anna, and she left me standing there.

I watched her press the elevator button as I started toward Prajay's office. From her expression I could tell she was eager to know what I was doing here after-hours. And I knew that she knew I was here for reasons other than business.

But what the heck could I do? I had put myself in a tight spot. I could only hope this was the last time I'd have to meet Prajay surreptitiously. I honestly didn't know what other kind of help he wanted from me.

This time he was standing at the window, hands in his pockets, his back to me, and seemingly deep in thought. He turned around when I knocked. "Come in, Meena. Could you close the door please?" He waited till the door was shut. "I can't thank you enough for your assistance."

"You're welcome." I sat in one of the guest chairs. "What can I do for you?"

He handed me a stack of printouts of e-mail messages. "Dozens, and I haven't had a moment to glance at them. I need some serious help."

"These are your private messages, Prajay. I can't do anything with them. You'll have to find some way to deal with it." If he was looking to me to find him a bride, he was barking up the wrong tree. I had my limits.

He gave me a helpless look. "I realize that, Meena, but I really don't have the time."

"What about Anna?"

"Are you kidding? She's very efficient, but this isn't her forte. She'll think I'm insane to run an ad for a bride. She had an arranged marriage." He shot me another vulnerable puppy-dog look. "You're my campaign manager, aren't you? I'll pay you for it. I pay my consultants seventy-five dollars an hour." When I rolled my eyes, he gave me a beatific smile that tugged at my softer side. "Eighty? Please?"

"All right. What exactly do you want me to do?" What the heck—I'd come this far. Might as well go all the way. And honestly, eighty dollars an hour for a clerical task sounded too good to pass up. I'd consider it my Christmas bonus.

"Would you mind sorting through them for me? Get rid of the ridiculous replies and keep the promising ones? Pick the top two or three for my consideration."

I scowled at him. "How would I know which ones are best for you?"

"You wrote the ads, Meena. They described exactly what I wanted. I'm sure you can pick what suits me."

"You're a weird man, Prajay. How can you trust a stranger to pick the right woman for you?"

He shrugged. "That's why I'm the oddball. And I trust you to make a good choice. You've come to know me quite well by now, right?"

"Not really," I replied in a final attempt at dissuading him. But it didn't work.

"Just find someone who's at least six feet tall and has a decent education and a sense of humor."

"No kidding."

"Halfway decent in the appearance department wouldn't hurt, either."

"How would I—"

"There are pictures attached to some of those messages," he interrupted.

"Fine, I'll take a look at them tonight." I rose from the chair. "What do you want me to do with the bad ones?"

"Toss them." He inclined his head toward the cup sitting at his elbow. "Can I get you some coffee or something?"

"No, thanks, I have to go. I have a date."

"I'm sorry." He didn't look like he was sorry. "I hope I didn't delay you too much."

"Next time, could we please talk about this someplace else? My coming to your office after-hours doesn't look right."

His frown was genuinely puzzled. "But you work here."

"Look at this from the other employees' perspective. We're both young and single, and Konkanis. If they see me entering your office and meeting with you behind closed doors, what do you think their conclusion will be?"

The frown cleared. "You're right. What was I thinking?" He rose to his feet and ran to open the door. "I'm really sorry, Meena. Next time we talk about this, it will be somewhere . . . more discreet."

"I'm glad you understand." I looked around. "Can I have an envelope for this please?"

"Sure." He hurried to Anna's desk and returned with a manila envelope.

"I'll mail the best responses to your home." I slipped the papers into the envelope. This had to be both the easiest as well as the toughest assignment I'd ever taken on. And the most lucrative.

"Thanks again." He appeared a little flustered. "And . . . enjoy your date."

He extended his hand for a handshake, and I responded. A brief tingle went up my fingers and shot through my arm, then spread all over. It was the most pleasant and exciting sensation I'd felt in a very long time.

I glanced at Prajay's hand as I reclaimed my own. He thrust it in his pocket immediately, so I didn't have a chance to look at it closely. His face told me he'd felt something, too, because he looked uneasy. But he was a man, and what did men know about magnetic undercurrents and those small signs of connection between a man and a woman?

I tucked the envelope under my arm and headed out. Prajay's disinterested attitude toward my going out with another man was disturbing. He hadn't shown an iota of curiosity. He'd even wished me a pleasant date.

Well, like I'd said before, the heck with Prajay. I was going to have a good time on my date.

Chapter 10

When I arrived at the restaurant at six, there was no sign of Deepak. Being a Friday, the restaurant was crowded, so I decided to ask for a table for two right away instead of waiting in my car. When the waiter asked me if I'd like to order something to drink, I shook my head. I was going to give Deepak fifteen minutes. If he didn't show up, I'd go home.

Ten minutes later there was still no sign of him. The nerve of the guy—after he'd been asking me out for months. Was this his idea of a joke, or was it revenge for my turning him down so many times? Either way, I wasn't laughing. If and when he did show up, I'd give him a piece of my mind.

It was awkward sitting alone in a restaurant filled with Indian people who stared at me curiously. Indian women very rarely sat alone at a restaurant table, unless they were on business and were forced to eat alone. So I pretended to be the busy businesswoman alone in town and pulled out my cell phone to call Rita. Keeping the conversation at whisper level was more likely to make it sound like business, so I kept it very low. "Hey, Rita. It's me."

"Who's me?"

I wasn't sure if she was being funny. Maybe she couldn't hear me clearly.

"It's Meena. What are you doing? Where are you?"

"I'm at the grocery store, in the checkout line." She sounded like she was in a rush. "Can I call you after I get home?"

"No, you can't. I need to keep you engaged on the phone *now*."

"Why?" Her voice took on a tone of alarm. "Omigod! Are you . . . being carjacked or something?"

"No! I—"

"Should I call nine-one-one?"

"No, no, nothing like that," I assured her quickly. "I'm at a restaurant."

"Are you sure?" she whispered. "If some asshole abducted you, I'll signal the cashier to call. The police can track you if I keep you on the line."

"No, Rita. There's no asshole involved. Well, there is in a way, but . . . never mind. It's a long story. I'm waiting for my date to show up."

"You have a *date?*" Rita must have yelled loudly enough for the entire supermarket to think they were under a terrorist attack.

The sound of Rita's excited exclamation was so ear-piercing, the folks at the table next to mine must have heard it. Their glances in my direction proved it. "Rita, keep your voice down," I murmured urgently.

"Okay. So tell me, who is he?"

"Just a guy from work—an FOB." Rita knew FOB meant fresh off the boat.

"Hmm." Rita went silent. She was obviously giving my reply some serious thought. Both she and I, since we had been born and raised in the U.S., had made a pact a while ago that we'd never go out with FOBs, unless we were desperate. It wasn't like we disliked them or anything—we just felt that those men had a different outlook on life.

Rita clearly concluded I'd reached the unenviable *desperate* stage. "Is he good-looking at least?"

"Yeah. But see, there's a problem. He was supposed to meet me here at six o'clock. Now it's what?" I looked at my watch. "Thirteen minutes after six and no sign of him."

"So why are we whispering?" Rita asked, finally realizing this was a strange conversation.

"You know how embarrassing it is to sit alone in a crowded restaurant. I'm pretending to have a serious conversation with you so everyone will think I'm from out of town, here on business and forced to eat alone."

"I see." Rita was the only one in the world who'd understand my convoluted logic. Sometimes we were uncannily like twins in our thinking. Rita's sigh was loud. "Listen, I'd love to make you look like you're on important business, but I have to hang up. The cashier's bagging my stuff. Got to run."

"I understand. Give my best to Anoop."

"Sure. Call me later, okay? I want to know all about the date."

"Yeah, right." There might not even be a date. My temper was heating up. The time on my watch was 6:14 P.M. One more minute and I'd be gone. Deepak Iyer would soon be history as far as I was concerned. I'd never, ever been stood up before.

Just as I shut off the phone and stuck it back in my purse, Deepak walked in the door. He stood for a moment to survey the scene before his eyes came to rest on me. He rushed over instantly. "I'm so sorry, Meena." He pulled out a chair and sat down across from me.

I tossed him my frostiest look. "You should be."

"I would have been here nearly half an hour ago, but I got stopped by a cop." When I remained silent he added, "For careless driving."

"Can't you think of a more original excuse than that?"

He pulled out a handkerchief from his pocket and wiped the moisture off his face. "I swear it's the truth, *yaar*."

From the expression on his face and all that perspiration, I wondered if maybe, just maybe, he was telling the truth. "How serious was the violation?"

"I went through a red light."

"No kidding?"

He wiped his face once again. "That's what I get for trying to make it to the restaurant in a hurry. I wanted to get here *before* six." He pulled out a piece of paper from his breast pocket. "My ticket—in case you think I'm lying."

The thought had crossed my mind, but without touching the paper I knew what it was. He was telling the truth. Just as I was getting ready to vent my fury on him for nearly standing me up, he was sitting there like a lost little boy whose mommy was nowhere to be seen. I hate when that happens.

Besides, he got into trouble with the traffic cops because he was in a hurry to meet me. How could I resent that?

Eventually, I think it was my inherent maternal instinct that led me to break down and smile at him. "I'm sorry, Deepak. I hope it doesn't mean major points on your license."

With a groan he thrust the ticket back into his pocket. "Three points. Insurance surcharge for the next three years."

"Oh, Deepak, I'm really sorry." This time I sent him my most empathetic look. Insurance companies could be malicious when it came to such things. I knew that from experience. I was being much more cautious with my lead foot these days since my last speeding ticket.

After two whole years I still fumed about that ticket, especially since I had been doing a mere seventy-six on the turnpike when the rest of the drivers were zooming past me. I was convinced that the big, burly cop had major issues with his weight and didn't like small, thin people like me.

I could have told the cop I had my own issues, like not being able to find sophisticated clothes in my size, like my foot not quite reaching the gas pedal, like having to look at people's lower backs and butts in elevators, like having to put up with cute-but-derogatory nicknames like half-pint, squirt, twerp, and Lilliput. But I'd kept my mouth shut and hadn't argued with the officer. I had been in deep enough trouble already.

"Thanks. I can use some sympathy, *yaar*," said Deepak, looking relieved that I finally believed him. He glanced up at the waiter who'd magically appeared at our side and was pouring water into our glasses. "What would you like to drink?" Deepak asked me.

"Water's fine, thanks," I replied and accepted a menu from the waiter. "I'll reserve my appetite for dinner." I studied the menu while Deepak asked for a diet cola.

Dinner turned out to be rather pleasant, much to my amazement. My shrimp *vindaloo,* with its extra hot spices cooked in vinegar, was excellent. Deepak seemed pleased with his *mutton do pyaza.* Goat meat and onions in a fragrant brown sauce.

The *parathas,* whole wheat bread rolled out in wide circles, were hot and deliciously crisp. The cumin rice that came with our meal was excellent, too. I refused dessert, but Deepak ordered carrot *halwa*—grated carrot simmered in cream, butter, slivered almonds, and sugar, and delicately seasoned with cardamom. It looked colorful and sinfully rich.

Deepak and I talked. I mean really talked. In the end I couldn't believe I had spent well over two hours sitting there, shooting the breeze and enjoying a pleasant dinner. I realized he wasn't such a bad guy. Rather opinionated, but not bad.

He was bright. That wasn't a surprise—he was a graduate of one of the Indian Institutes of Technology, known as IITs. The popular CBS magazine show, *60 Minutes,* had portrayed the IITs of India as some of the world's most highly rated and discriminating universities.

Just getting admitted to an IIT meant Deepak was super-intelligent. He was articulate and well-spoken, too—obviously a product of one of those exclusive boarding schools in India that catered to the well-to-do.

By the time we got up to leave it was pitch dark outside, and rain was beginning to fall. We were already into October, and the chilly rain was a reminder that winter was creeping in. I shivered a little and shook Deepak's hand. "That was nice, Deepak. Thank you."

In the glow of the outdoor lights I saw the raindrops settling like diamonds over his dark hair and his eyes take on a hopeful gleam. "So . . . we can do this again sometime?"

Dining with Deepak had been more pleasant than I'd expected, but I wasn't exactly crazy about the man. On the other hand, I had to admit he had possibility. A few more years of living in the U.S., absorbing the culture, and losing that habit of saying *yaar,* could make the man acceptable.

Pulling out my car keys, I gave him a smile. "Maybe."

"Works for me, *yaar*." He grinned. "We better get out of here before we get soaked."

I got behind the wheel of my car. Brushing the moisture off my jacket and hair, I turned on the ignition. While the engine warmed, my eyes wandered over to the envelope on the front passenger seat.

I'd have to go home and sort the pages—in the privacy of my room; I couldn't risk Mom's seeing them. I could only imagine her disappointment if she found out what I was doing: literally letting the perfect man slip through my fingers—helping him do it, no less.

Driving out of the parking lot, I slowly merged into the endless traffic. Oak Tree Road in the Edison-Iselin area was always mobbed, no matter what day of the week it was.

I kept my eyes on the traffic, but my mind strayed to that envelope. I was conflicted about those responses. I was dying to see them, and yet I didn't want to know anything about them.

What if Prajay Nayak's ideal woman was buried somewhere in that stack of e-mails? Would she be a six-foot-tall model with a gorgeous body and perhaps even a fat paycheck? Even though Prajay wasn't exactly a winner in the looks category, he was growing on me. When he smiled he looked almost . . . oh, what was that word? Not handsome. Not good-looking. But . . . *striking*. That was it.

Prajay carried himself well, and the clothes he picked were just right for his build. Besides, his physique probably helped while doing business with men who wielded enormous power. There was something about large men that gave them the extra edge when dealing with other men. The alpha-male image. Even presidential candidates were judged on how tall they were and how imposing a figure they cut.

When I let myself in the house I found Mom loading the dishwasher and Dad watching TV. Dinner was obviously over. I could smell the lingering odors of spices and vegetables. I was happy to see Maneel and Mahesh were absent. I wasn't in a mood for their ribbing tonight.

Mom looked up from the sink, her hands dripping. "You're

home." Her eyes went to the clock on the wall. She was wondering why I was home so early. Not a good sign. "How was dinner?"

I noticed she was careful not to use the word *date*. I did have men friends who had no romantic ties to me whatsoever. Every so often I had a meal with one or more of them at a restaurant, and I'd made it clear to Mom that the social occasions were definitely not to be confused with dates. And if indeed they were dates, Mom and Dad didn't seem to mind.

They knew I'd dated in college, and they had no problem with that—as long as I could assure them I was doing it responsibly, meaning no sex. The poor dears still harbored the illusion that I was a virgin.

I smiled at Mom. "Dinner was quite nice. I had dinner with a FOB."

Mom put the last dish in the dishwasher and shut its door. "That's a nasty term you young people use, Meena," she chided. "It's not nice to label people like that. Your father and I are immigrants, too."

"But you guys came here more than thirty-five years ago. You're officially BHLTs."

"As in bacon, hot pepper, lettuce, and tomato?"

"Funny, Mom," I said dryly. "In your case it stands for been here long time."

Mom wiped the counter down, then dried her hands on the kitchen towel. "All that hard work for three and a half decades, and we're reduced to the level of a sandwich."

"Cheer up." I gave her arm a friendly squeeze before heading for the staircase. "BLT is my favorite sandwich, especially with hot peppers."

Seeing me going upstairs instead of joining Dad and her in the family room and perhaps noticing the large envelope held against my chest, she raised an eyebrow. "Brought work home?"

"Uh-huh. I'd better get to it before I go to bed." I kept moving before it turned into more questions and I ended up lying.

In my room, I got changed into pajamas and brushed my teeth since it was only about two hours to bedtime. Then I sat at my desk to deal with the envelope. Prajay wasn't kidding; there were dozens of messages. His ads had said he was a successful businessman. Most women went for that kind of bold, enterprising type of guy.

I started on the e-mails with the pictures attached. The respondents were so hilarious I was ready to roll on the floor. One was a woman who looked like something from a carnival freak show. She had wild hair and wilder eyes. She said she stood six feet and eight inches. And she wasn't even Indian, let alone a Hindu. She was definitely not the one. To court her, even Prajay would have to wear elevator shoes.

I put her response through the little shredder I happened to have in my room. I had bought it when I was in college so my roommate wouldn't get into my personal business. I hardly ever used it now, but tonight it would get a good workout.

Another was a female wrestler. At two hundred and ninety pounds, she was six-one. Dressed in a revealing, orangey-yellow wrestling outfit in the picture, she looked like a Halloween pumpkin. I wondered if she thought Prajay was the kind of guy who'd enjoy having a wrestler in his bed. Bedtime games could get a little rough with a woman like that. Ouch!

Several others came across as entirely hopeless cases, too. Most of them lived in India or England or even as far away as New Zealand and Hong Kong. Unfortunately the Internet allowed everyone in the world access to matchmaking sites. And there were lots of folks out there eager to have an opportunity to marry an American citizen and live in the U.S.

Every time I sent a reply to the shredder my sense of elation escalated. If Prajay couldn't find a single woman worth his attention, maybe he'd be willing to look down his honker at me and discover that good things could indeed come in small packages.

I honestly couldn't find a single viable candidate, but since I didn't want Prajay to get suspicious, I managed to pick out two who looked somewhat promising. One was a North Indian Sikh woman who lived on the West Coast. She was six feet tall, an American citizen, and had a PhD in endocrinology. She even had a nice job as a research scientist at Stanford University. I was relieved to note that she looked rather plump.

The other female was five-eleven and worked as a nurse in West Virginia. Both women were plain looking. I sent a quick prayer of thanks. So far, so good.

Going into my computer, I quickly set up a simple database and labeled it "Search for Six-foot Siren." That way I'd be able to keep all the candidates with strong potential in a single document and mail them to Prajay accordingly.

Now that I was officially his marriage consultant, I'd do a heck of job for him, dazzle him, even if it was likely to kill me, bit by tiny bit.

I wondered what the next day's responses would bring. *Let only the most unsuitable ones come to Prajay's attention, God,* I prayed.

Maybe I was going to pay dearly in my next life for wishing such negative things on someone, but I wasn't really hurting anyone. I was only helping fate along—reshaping it, just a tiny bit.

Even Mom believed that destiny needed a nudge in the right direction once in a while.

Chapter 11

Fortunately my weekend was filled with socializing, so I didn't have much time to brood. Rita and Anoop hosted their first party as Mr. and Mrs. Anoop Tandon at their townhouse on Saturday evening.

I offered to help with the preparations despite the food's being mostly catered. I went to their place early in the afternoon, and Rita and I made some finger foods and appetizers.

The guests were our group of twenty or so close friends—all young adults of mixed ethnicities, professionals in one field or another.

It was nice to see my best friend glowing. I'd always known Rita would beat me to the altar. She wasn't particularly ambitious in the career department. She'd started working for a large insurance company as an actuary after getting a degree in statistics from Boston College. She had no desire to go beyond that. Anoop was a bright and dynamic architect. He had enough ambition and drive for the both of them.

Rita and Anoop had met two years ago when their respective parents had introduced them. Rita knew instinctively from the start that he was the right guy for her. My aunt Shabari would have been proud of her for using the hooking and reeling technique with such finesse. Rita was no fool; she knew a good thing when she saw it. And Anoop was a really good guy.

Of course, Rita's success story had my mom in raptures over

how beautifully these semi-arranged relationships worked out. Then she'd thrown me that wistful-hopeful look which said: *So why can't you be a good Indian girl and settle down, too?*

But I'd never considered myself a good Indian girl. I wasn't bad, but neither was I a soft and malleable ball of putty that could be molded by my parents. Or anyone else. I was a modern woman with modern ideas. One of these days I'd find my own man. In my own way.

Rita and Anoop's party was a brilliant success. To make a good thing better, Phil Chu and Denise Landowski announced their engagement during the evening, prompting an extra round of drinks after midnight for an impromptu toast to the engaged couple. I got a little teary-eyed to see two of my friends looking so happy.

Phil was Chinese and Denise was German-Polish, and it was great to see them now ready to tie the knot after dating for three years. Surprisingly, the families on both sides were okay with their romance.

The party broke up around two o'clock. I helped Rita and Anoop clean up and went home by three, then slept until noon.

On Sunday, since Mahesh had a rare day off, Maneel rented a couple of movies. We made a bowl of spicy *masala* popcorn and watched one of the movies in the afternoon. In the evening we ordered pizza and ate it while viewing the second movie. Dad built a fire in the fireplace, and it was lovely to stretch out on the carpet with a pillow under my head.

We lazed around, except for Mom. Her beeper went off halfway through the second movie, and she was called away on an emergency. One of her patients had gone into labor. But Sunday was one of those rare occasions when everyone in the family was in a mellow mood. We did little talking, and yet the strong sense of family hung in the air.

I liked weekends like these, when both my brothers were on their best behavior and my parents were generally agreeable to any of our plans. I preferred to think of them as family bonding days, when we turned into the Cleavers.

On Monday morning, Prajay and I worked out a system for him to hand over the daily responses to me without raising questions and eyebrows. Since I'd made it clear that it was a bad idea for the two of us to be seen in each other's company, I figured we had to work on his *bride quest* discreetly. Since his responses came via e-mail, he simply forwarded all of them to my home computer.

Each evening, I reviewed them and decided which were to be printed. It was a very efficient method, using a minimal amount of paper. Weeding out the fluff wasn't as simple as I'd presumed. But I was getting paid for this, so I didn't complain.

Mom was now used to the idea of my working on some secret project that involved Rathnaya's work for the federal government. I'd thrown that in for good measure since she'd noticed my paper shreds. She no longer considered it strange when I sat behind closed doors each night and worked on my computer. I suspected she'd given up on the notion that something deliciously clandestine was going on between Prajay and me.

Meanwhile Deepak started asking me about another date. This time he was talking about a movie, too. It was tempting, but I had work to do, so I turned down his invitation. My consulting work for Prajay paid well, and I couldn't pass up that kind of money in favor of dinner and a movie.

Besides, I had a feeling Deepak was reading too much into our dinner the other day, and I didn't want to lead him on. Indian men could be a little scary that way—one harmless little date and they started thinking in terms of holy matrimony and a lifelong commitment to sharing a bed and bathtub.

By Friday night I had added five more possibilities to my database: one professor of economics at a liberal arts college in the Midwest; one government official of mixed parentage (half Indian and half Caucasian); one fashion model (didn't look like a model in her photograph); one doctor of internal medicine (she was only five-ten, but she was a medical doctor and therefore highly qualified); one electronics engineer working in the IT field.

This last one was my most feared applicant, because she was six-foot-one, thirty-three years old, slim, and attractive, an American citizen, and she was a Brahmin. Worse yet, she lived in Bethesda, Maryland—close to Washington, DC—practically next door to Prajay's permanent home.

I had a feeling Prajay would fall in love with her in an instant. She was exactly the kind of woman he was looking for. She was my worst nightmare. I was tempted to quietly delete her message. But I had a conscience—and I'd always considered myself a fair player. Besides, I wasn't even in the running. I never had been.

I fumed over the unfairness of it all. Why did I have to inherit my grandmother's midget genes? How could one woman, like this engineer, have everything a man desired? When those two eventually met, which was likely to be very soon, they'd bond like iron and magnet. They had everything in common: their unusual height; their professions; their culture; even their geographical locations. I, on the other hand, was the exact opposite in every way that counted.

It looked like I was destined to end up with someone like Deepak. And I was as mad as a disturbed hornet at Prajay. Why was the man so obsessed with finding a tall woman? What was his problem, anyway? Maybe he *was* gay, despite his statement to the contrary.

This ridiculous quest for the perfect woman could be Prajay's cover-up to keep his sexual orientation a secret. Gay men were not accepted well by the Indian community—in fact by most of the heterosexual population. Gayness would likely have an adverse effect on his business dealings, too. What stodgy military general would want to give a contract to a gay man?

Just as I was whipping myself into a furious froth over Prajay and his taste in women, my cell phone rang. It was past nine o'clock on a Friday night, and most of my friends would be out socializing. I should have been out with them, but I wasn't in the mood. The number flashing on my phone was within my calling area. It had to be a wrong number, or someone trying to sell something.

I answered the phone with brusque impatience. "Who is this?"

"Is that how you greet all your customers?" the deep voice asked.

"Prajay?" I gave my pulse a second to settle. "Sorry, I thought you were a telemarketer."

He chuckled. "Aren't you on the Do Not Call list?"

"I am. That's why it upset me that some idiot might've still managed to get past that."

"I'm the idiot you shared your cell number with. I figured this was a safer number to call than your home number."

"Definitely. My parents answer that phone most of the time." I put on my enthusiastic employee tone. "So, what can I do for you, boss?"

"Are you busy tomorrow?"

I frowned at the floor. "Why? More consulting work?"

"Yes and no. Depends on what you'd consider consulting work."

Both suspicion and intrigue scratched at my brain. "Um . . . exactly what did you have in mind?"

"Have you been to Great Adventure lately?"

Was he talking about going out together to that wonderland of wild rides and childish delights located in Jackson? I had loved going there when I was a teenager. My friends and I used to get season tickets and hang out there in the summer. After reaching full drinking age we'd lost interest in such juvenile forms of entertainment. Bars, clubs, dancing, and travel held more appeal than roller coasters and cotton candy.

"You mean the Six Flags entertainment park?" I asked.

"That's the one. How would you like to go there tomorrow?"

My heart leapt so abruptly that I almost forgot to breathe for a second. The idea of Prajay and I pressed together in the crowded seat of a roller coaster was enticing. Would he put his arm around me if I pretended to be scared? Was this a godsend or what? I couldn't have dreamt this one up if I'd sat around for a week planning a grand seduction.

But something told me it wasn't all that simple. "What's the catch, Prajay? Are we researching something for a new project?"

"We're not researching anything. But there's a small catch."

I let out a sigh. Should've known there was a fine-print clause in the contract. "I'm listening."

"My brother and his wife are coming in tonight from New York to attend a friend's wedding in Cherry Hill tomorrow. I was more or less thrust into the role of babysitter for their kids."

"You have my sympathy." I couldn't picture him babysitting.

"I don't know what to do with two kids, aged eight and four, so I thought Great Adventure would be a nice place to keep them occupied for a few hours."

"I see." I wondered why he was telling me all this.

"What do you think?"

"Brilliant thinking on your part, Uncle Prajay. But where do *I* fit in?"

"In the role of co-babysitter. Strictly on a consultant level, of course. I'll pay you at the usual rate, Meena."

"I could make the *Guinness Book of World Records* for highest paid babysitter in the universe."

"Co-babysitter," he prompted.

I didn't know whether to feel gratified or insulted by his request. Did he think I was *that* valuable or *that* greedy? Insult won over gratification. "You really think I'm that materialistic, Prajay? You honestly believe I'll take money from you to go to a park with you and your nephews?" My offended tone was not put on. I was honestly hurt by his offer of money.

At once his voice turned contrite. "I'm sorry, Meena. I was kidding, just like you were kidding when you asked if this was more consulting work."

"Apology accepted." He did sound genuinely repentant. "Tell me more about Great Adventure. I haven't been there in years."

"I haven't set foot in that place in over two decades, not since my family moved from New Jersey to Massachusetts."

"Then what made you pick Great Adventure?"

"Tomorrow's weather forecast is for unseasonably warm temperatures, and some of the guys at the office tell me it now has new attractions for very young kids."

"Sounds like fun."

"So . . . you want to go with us?"

I couldn't help smiling as I recalled the photograph on Prajay's desk, with the two young boys who looked like scaled-down copies of Prajay. Even when I had been in pain I'd thought they were quite adorable.

A trip to a kids' theme park with those two naughty tykes sounded a bit scary. But it could have been Prajay and me with our two kids in tow, couldn't it? I could even pretend it was so. How could I say no? "I'd be honored to play co-babysitter for your nephews," I said finally.

"Great. And it's one nephew and one niece. She's the four-year-old."

"The one who's in the picture on your desk?" I remembered the round, chubby face. She was cute; she had the Nayak mouth.

He chuckled again, like a proud uncle, and the sound made me feel warm and fuzzy inside. "That's the one. Her name is Riya, and her brother is Rahul."

"Nice names. I hope they're well behaved, or we could have problems at the park. Rambunctious doesn't mix well with a crowded park and dangerous rides," I cautioned.

"They're good kids. My sister-in-law Nitya is a stickler for discipline. They know they can't get too rowdy with their uncle Prajay."

"Good. What time did you have in mind?" I was already trying to think of ways to explain the situation to my mother, without her jumping to insane conclusions. She'd have me married by Monday morning and pregnant with twins by the end of the year. I guess I'd have to tell a whopper again.

"How about if we pick you up around nine-thirty?" he suggested. "We can take the kids to McDonald's for breakfast and go from there."

"I'll meet you at your house instead," I offered quickly. "And I'll bring the spreadsheet with your best matrimonial responses." It killed me to say that, but I had to.

"Oh yeah? How do the prospects look?"

"Uh . . . one or two look good. You'll see tomorrow." To lighten the mood I asked, "How do you expect to drive the four of us in your Corvette, Prajay?" Was I to sit in his lap perhaps?

"My brother and I are going to exchange vehicles. I get to drive his SUV, and he and Nitya get to go to the wedding in my car."

"Sensible plan."

"Nitya thinks she can recapture their honeymooning days when the two of them had a sports car."

"That's so romantic . . . and sweet." I could only dream of that. And try as I might to dispel the thought, the guy sitting next to me in a sports car in my fantasy was Prajay. The man was on my mind much too much. Maybe it had to do with riding with him to the office when my ankle was injured. He had grown on me like ivy on a stone wall.

Well, at least I was going to have another chance to ride with him, even if it meant having two active kids in the backseat.

When I hung up, it was with a silly grin on my face. I looked up Google Maps on my computer, typed in his home address, and got the directions.

I couldn't wait for next morning. Sleep was hard to come by, too. Images of roller coasters and ice cream cones, and of playing pretend wife to Prajay and aunt to his nephew and niece kept me awake through most of the night.

I woke up the next morning with a tired face, but a hot shower perked me up.

When Dad saw me enter the kitchen in jeans and a sweat-shirt, already showered and with my makeup on, he looked up from his newspaper with a puzzled frown. I very rarely stirred out of bed before ten on weekends.

"I'm going to Great Adventure with some friends, Dad," I said in response to that inquisitive look. "Where's Mom?"

"Emergency."

"Another rough delivery?"

"Ruptured fallopian tube or something. She left before five in the morning."

I groaned, feeling sorry for the woman with the fallopian tube mishap, and for my mother. Poor Mom—she rarely got to enjoy a full night's sleep or an entire movie. And yet she thought medicine was the most wonderful profession on earth. Now *that* was dedication.

"I'll be late coming home, Dad, so don't hold dinner for me, okay? Call me on my cell if you need to get in touch."

He put his newspaper down and gave me his full attention. "Who all are going to this theme park?"

Was my eagerness showing that much? Dad wasn't generally as perceptive as Mom. "The usual gang," I said breezily and reeled off half a dozen names. Dad was familiar with them but never remembered their last names. Nonetheless my sense of security was short-lived.

"How come you kids suddenly planned this Great Adventure trip? After you went to college you thought it was too childish."

"Recapturing our youth before the gray hairs set in, Dad." I gave him a cheeky grin.

"Hmm." He adjusted his glasses over his nose. "Stay away from those *goondas* who do drugs. And stick to the brightly lit areas."

"Don't worry, Dad, we'll be fine." I gave him a light peck on the cheek and took off. He had already returned to his *New York Times* and his cup of tea.

Had Dad actually looked pleased at the prospect of my being

away for the day? I believe he secretly looked forward to a quiet afternoon. I knew for a fact that Mom and Dad's weekend evenings were usually packed with social events involving other Indian families.

And I was eagerly looking forward to my day at the park.

Chapter 12

Despite my excitement about the day ahead, I was nervous about meeting Prajay's brother and sister-in-law. They were fellow Konkanis and likely to suspect the exact thing that Prajay and I were trying to avoid: that we were romantically involved.

They could be snobs, too. I knew nothing about Prajay's family. I couldn't turn around and go home, either, now that I'd made a commitment.

Ten minutes later I pulled into the condominium complex and parked my car in one of the unnumbered spots. I locked my car and stood for a moment to study the three modern, multistory buildings positioned in a semicircle around the spacious courtyard.

The neat, crisp landscaping had obviously been designed by a professional. Chrysanthemums in various shades and ornamental cabbage bordered the shrubbery and shady patches beneath the fall-tinted trees. Two handsome wrought iron benches lent a certain romantic charm to the scene. The sprinklers were on at the moment, making those lush patches of grass sparkle like beds of emeralds.

The compound had an aura of quiet luxury, but I didn't hear children's voices or see tricycles or any other signs typical of a family neighborhood. This appeared to be an enclave built for upwardly mobile singles and couples with no kids. I wondered if Prajay had picked it for that very reason.

I checked the numbers on the buildings and took the elevator to the third floor of the one on my right. Before I could ring the bell, the door was opened by a young boy dressed in faded jeans and a gray sweatshirt with MIT printed on the front.

The Nayak boys obviously started young in their hunt for outstanding universities. The boy's gray sneakers looked well-worn and scuffed. The kid was exceptionally tall for an eight-year-old. It was like looking at a miniature Prajay.

"Prajay-bappa, she's here!" he yelled to his uncle.

Prajay replied from somewhere inside the house. "Invite her in and ask her to sit down. I'll be right there."

I smiled at the boy. "Hi. I'm Meena. You must be Rahul?"

He didn't return the smile. Instead he continued to stand in the doorway, giving me a very cautious and thorough once-over that reminded me again of Prajay. This was probably what Prajay had done as a boy when he first met someone. He most likely still scrutinized potential customers and business associates with the same kind of attention.

Finally the boy said, "Hi. Prajay-bappa's combing my sister's hair."

I bit back the grin. Prajay combing a little girl's hair? This I had to see.

Rahul opened the door wider and let me in. "He says you should sit down."

"Thanks." I was immediately drawn into the very male living room. It was much larger than I'd expected. The condo had to have more than one bedroom and bath. It looked like Prajay's home took up a major portion of this floor.

The two couches and two matching chairs were massive, upholstered in cinnamon-colored leather. The floor was polished oak, with a cream area rug placed under the simple coffee table. No feminine touches like throw pillows or knickknacks anywhere.

The cream vertical blinds on the large picture window made the sunlight fall in golden diagonal stripes across the rug. An entertainment center containing a giant-screen TV and a stereo system took up the better part of one wall. A watercolor land-scape hung above a modern gas fireplace.

On the mantel sat several family photos. My heart warmed as soon as my eyes fell on those.

So, this was how bachelor entrepreneurs lived: basic, but sur-rounded by refined comfort. I'd probably start purring like a kitten if I were to kick off my sneakers and sink into one of those deep, deep leather couches and close my eyes.

I turned to the staring Rahul. "Does your uncle need any help with your sister?" I wondered where the kids' parents were. Why wasn't the mother combing her daughter's hair?

Just then Prajay came out, dressed in gray Dockers, a black rugby shirt, and sneakers. Even in casual clothes, he looked dis-tinguished.

A plump little girl was holding on to his hand. She wore jeans in a soft shade of pink, paired with a strawberry pullover sweater. She had on princess sneakers with neon-pink shoelaces. Her dark, wavy hair was a mess, and her lips were set in a fussy pout.

"Sorry, Meena," said Prajay, "but I have no idea how to do pigtails. When Prakash and Nitya left, Riya wanted to leave her hair down, but now she's decided she wants pigtails." He shrugged helplessly. "Unfortunately her mom and dad had to leave early."

It was a relief to know I didn't have to meet Prakash and Nitya Nayak. "Girls are known to change their minds some-times, Prajay," I explained. "It's all part of being a woman." Riya seemed to approve of my explanation, because I saw her nod, and the pout became less pronounced.

I assessed the present situation and Riya's rumpled halo of hair for a second, then held my hand out to her. "Want me to do your hair, Riya?"

Just like her brother had done a minute ago, Riya stared at me, her dark eyes traveling over every inch of me. Her hand re-mained clutching her uncle's. Riya's face still had some baby fat, but someday she'd be a pretty girl, when those Nayak limbs turned long and lithe and the flab turned to supple muscle.

"I want scrunchies in my hair," she announced. A girl who knew exactly what she wanted.

I nodded. "No problem. I like scrunchies, too, whenever I put my hair up. You got any of your own?"

"Uh-huh. Mommy packed them in my bag." I must have passed inspection, because she let go of Prajay's hand and reached for mine. "Want to see?"

"Sure." Obviously Riya was friendlier than her suspicious brother. I winked at a grateful-looking Prajay and took Riya's hand, then let her lead me down the passageway into what looked like a guest room.

Again, the room was large for a condo, with a sunburst window. A king-sized bed with a blue and white geometric-pattern bedspread claimed center stage. The headboard was washed oak. A matching dresser and mirror completed the décor. The room was carpeted in pastel blue to coordinate with the blinds.

On the dresser, I saw an open plastic sandwich bag containing scrunchies in various colors. A pink comb lay next to it. A kid-size princess suitcase lay open on the bed, with its contents spilling out. I went straight for the dresser and glanced at Riya. "Which color did you have in mind?"

"Rose pink."

A kid who knew her colors. I heartily approved. She'd be an efficient shopper someday. I dumped all the scrunchies on the dresser top and started sorting through them. "Let's see if we can find a matching pair here." Every shade of pink under the sun was there. The child seemed obsessed with pink.

I had a feeling Riya's room at home was entirely done in pink. I recalled my own childhood, when I wanted everything purple. Lord knows how many sets of clothes I had in mauve, lilac, lavender, and eggplant.

When I located two matching scrunchies I took the comb and turned Riya around so her back was facing me. Prajay and Rahul came into the room to stand with their arms crossed over their chests to observe me at work.

"You know what you two look like?" I said to the guys, keeping my eyes on my handiwork as I parted Riya's hair and smoothed the two sides. "That classic poster where a dog and a mini version of him are shown sitting side by side, watching TV together with their heads cocked to one side."

Prajay glanced at his nephew, then laughed and let his arms fall to his sides. "We Nayak men are all cut from the same mold. If it's a boy he's got to have the thick eyebrows and the extra-long legs."

They both watched me comb and secure Riya's hair into two neat, tight pigtails. I was done in less than two minutes.

"Wow, how'd you do that so quickly?" Prajay asked.

I gave a smug smile and patted Riya's head. "It's all in the fingers." To prove my point I held up my hands and wiggled them. "Magic fingers. I bet Riya has them, too."

Riya giggled with delight and imitated my gesture.

Rahul rolled his eyes at us and ran his hand over his own crew cut. "Boys go to the barber and get a proper cut." I noticed he had a missing tooth replaced by a new half-grown one.

Riya made a face at her brother. "Mommy says Daddy and you have boring hairstyles. She says boys don't know how to be creative." The way she said it, it sounded more like "quivative."

"Pigtails are *not* creative; they're for pigs," declared her brother.

Prajay stepped in deftly and put an end to the bickering before it could escalate. "All right, who's ready for a McDonald's breakfast and Looney Tunes Seaport?"

"Me," cried Riya, raising her hand. Rahul was clearly a McDonald's fan, too, because he raced out to the living room with an excited grin, his sister close on his heels.

I looked at Prajay. "Looney Tunes Seaport?"

"Rahul discovered it. Ever since I mentioned Great Adventure last night, he's been on the Internet, doing research. He was up late, making a list of what he wanted to do today. The kid's good at computers and researching stuff," said Prajay.

"Of course he is. You were probably just like that at his age."

"Not *that* bright," he assured me. "Come on, let's go." He inclined his head toward the door. "I'm hungry for a breakfast sandwich myself. What's your favorite?"

"Pancakes with butter and syrup."

"You can have a double order of pancakes," he promised.

Just then I remembered something. "Who needs to go potty before we start?" I asked the kids.

Prajay gave me an appreciative look. "Good thought. Looks like you've done this before."

"I did some babysitting as a teenager."

Riya said she needed a little help, so I went with her to the powder room while her brother went to use another bathroom. Then we all grabbed our respective jackets and headed out. Even before Prajay had the front door locked, the kids were impatiently tapping on the elevator button.

Prajay's brother's SUV was one of those humongous black vehicles. Inside, there was plenty of room for the four of us and then some. For once, there seemed to be enough space to accommodate Prajay's legs.

Breakfast wasn't as chaotic an experience as I'd expected. Prajay was right about the kids being well behaved. Although they bickered like most siblings, they were neat eaters and very hungry. They polished off every last bit of their food and beverages. Rahul surprised me by cleaning up after his sister and getting rid of the trash in the receptacle and returning the tray to its rightful place.

Unfortunately the traffic going to the park was heavy. No surprise, with the great weather. Besides, a couple of weeks from now the park would be closing for the season, and it seemed like every family with children was headed for the same destination.

The kids were getting edgy by the time we finally found a parking spot in the sea of cars and walked toward the park's main gate. It was past eleven-thirty. That still gave us nearly the whole day to frolic.

Inside the park, it somehow became an unspoken agreement that Rahul would stay close to Prajay while Riya would hang on to me. We went on family rides nonstop for the next five hours. Of course, standing in long lines to get on those rides factored into that time, but the kids were relentless, especially Rahul.

He was disappointed that we couldn't get on the grown-up

rides and the awesome roller coaster called Kingda Ka, touted as the ultimate in roller coasters, a behemoth that traveled at insane speeds. His sister didn't meet the height requirement mandated by the park and the public safety laws.

But Rahul was determined to make the most of the day. He was practically bouncing on his toes while waiting in the lines. Once in a while he threw longing looks at Kingda Ka in the distant background, clearly visible because of its altitude, its cars thundering down the ramp every few minutes with their screaming cargos of teenagers and adults.

We rode something called Blackbeard's Lost Treasure Train— a smaller roller coaster that had Riya humming with joy as the wind whipped through her hair and pulled some of it out of her pigtails. We went on cable cars, carousels, and water rides that dampened our clothes at times.

Whenever one of the rides got a little wild, Riya unconsciously huddled closer to me. I held her, enjoying the warmth of the child and the clean toddler smell of her silky hair.

Before we went on our discovery of the Rockwall, Riya and I decided we needed a trip to the girls' room. A long line had formed there, too.

Once again I was surprised at how good the little girl was about taking care of her personal needs. Other than giving some minor help and making sure that she washed her hands thoroughly, I had to do very little for her.

By the time we came out, the boys were not only done with their own trip to the men's room, but they were waiting for us with cones bursting with rich chocolate ice cream and a big plastic tray of nachos with cheese and salsa. Riya fell on the food with a whoop. That's when I realized we hadn't had any lunch. I had been having so much fun I hadn't bothered to check my watch—until now.

It was nearly five o'clock. The sun had already lost some of its punch, and the air was cooler. I felt a pang at the thought of the day coming to an end. I hadn't enjoyed an outing this much since I was about fourteen years old.

I'd learned a lot about Prajay, too. He was patient but firm, indulgent but cautious with the kids. And they seemed to adore him. Whenever one of them acted too wild, all he had to do was give him or her a stern look and the child quieted instantly.

Until now I'd only seen his business side, the one that wore smart clothes, conducted meetings, and gave orders to his employees. This Prajay was a different man, a laid-back, family-oriented *bappa* who seemed to dote on his nephew and niece. So far, I liked both the Prajays. A lot.

While Rahul and Riya climbed the Rockwall, Prajay and I sat on a bench and kept an eye on them. Prajay touched my arm lightly. "I don't know how to thank you. You've been great as my co-babysitter."

I couldn't see his eyes behind the dark glasses, but I knew they were warm with gratitude. "My pleasure, boss. The kids are great." I smiled. "Besides I'm a sucker for pancakes and chocolate ice cream."

"You're not just saying that?"

"Nope. It's one of the nicest weekend jaunts I've had in years. Even the weather's been nice." I turned my gaze to the sun. It was turning to that ripe shade of nectarine, which meant it would disappear in the next hour or so.

A pleasant kind of lethargy came over me, and I closed my eyes for a minute. The sound of the kids' excited shrieks, Latin music playing somewhere in the distance, adults chattering, the sound of rushing water in the aquatic rides area, and Prajay's warm presence beside me. My private paradise.

I wanted to grab the fleeting moment with both hands and tuck it away as a pleasant memory—for future retrieval.

Prajay interrupted my thoughts when he said, "I hope I'm not keeping you from any social engagements."

"I've nothing planned."

"No date on a Saturday night for a young and pretty girl?" Thick eyebrows rose above the rim of the sunglasses.

My pleasant mood had me telling him the truth. "I haven't dated in some time, Prajay."

"What about last week, when you had a date?"

"That was just a friendly dinner with a coworker."

He peeled off his dark glasses and looked at me speculatively. "I hear a lot of guys at work have a thing for you."

I could feel the heat creeping into my face. "Not a lot. A few guys have asked me out, but that's just . . ."

"Just what? You don't like any of them?"

I glanced at the setting sun again. "They're nice enough, but they're not my type."

"What *is* your type, Meena?"

"I can't exactly describe him. I guess I'll just know when I meet him . . . by gut instinct." I was hoping to keep my voice casual, but his close scrutiny and highly personal questions were making my voice quiver.

"Gut instinct. I wish I could say that, but I'm so damned analytical."

"I know. I can tell from the way you're going about seeking your six-foot woman."

"Dead giveaway, huh?" he said with a self-deprecating smile. He turned his head to check on the kids and stiffened.

The spell was broken.

Both the children were high up on the wall—precariously high. My heartbeat accelerated. We'd been so busy talking that we hadn't been paying much attention.

Prajay shot to his feet and approached them. "Rahul, Riya, I want you to come down now," he said to them.

"But I want to go higher," Rahul protested.

"I want you down *now*," Prajay commanded.

"Okay." I watched as the kids reluctantly made their way down. My breath came out in a sigh when they made it to a safe height.

As he reached the last step Rahul jumped down with a cry of triumph. "Yay! I went almost to the top."

Riya leaped into Prajay's outstretched arms. He hugged her and said something to her that made her put her arms around his neck and bury her face in his shoulder. Then he gave her a tender kiss on the head before putting her back on her feet.

Something painful stirred in my chest.

I didn't realize my eyes were tearing up until Riya came bouncing up to me and said, "Meena, did you get a boo-boo?"

"No, honey. Why do you ask?"

"You're crying."

"Oh, that," I said and brushed the moisture away quickly. "The sun was in my eyes."

The explanation seemed to satisfy Riya, because she immediately demanded to go on more rides. We spent another hour doing just that. When it got fully dark and the park was ablaze with lights, Riya looked tired enough to drop. But Rahul seemed to have some energy left. Frankly I was feeling like Riya. My foot was screaming, my makeup was history, and my hair was a riot.

Prajay checked his watch. "It's late. Let's get out of here."

Rahul pulled a face and whined, "Prajay-bappa, can't we stay a little longer?" When Prajay shook his head, Rahul turned his eyes on me, the conniving little devil. "Meena, can we stay longer? Please?"

Who could resist that half-grown tooth and the crew cut? I looked at Prajay. "How about one final round on the Enchanted Teacups?" That ride had the shortest line.

With some reluctance, Prajay nodded. "Okay, one last ride, and then we're going to dinner. Who wants to go to Friendly's?"

Riya, the chubby food-lover, nodded. "Can I have chicken fingers and a clown sundae?"

Prajay ruffled her hair. "Sure, baby."

By the time we had our dinner and were heading home, the kids were so exhausted they fell asleep in the back of the car in two minutes flat. Rahul was snoring like an old man.

Tired beyond belief myself, I reclined the seat and closed my eyes, trying to recapture the conversation Prajay and I had been having on the bench. He had asked me what kind of man was my type. I'd almost told him my kind of guy was exactly like him. In fact, it *was* him. Thank God, I'd found a better answer. And the thing with the kids had distracted us, so we had moved on to other things after that.

The ride home was in silence. I let Prajay assume I was sleeping.

When he parked the car, we tried to awaken the kids. Rahul climbed out groggily, but Riya was dead to the world. The poor baby looked angelic in sleep. Prajay handed me the keys to his condo and picked her up in his arms, then carried her all the way to the condo.

After I opened the front door he took Riya to the guest room and laid her on the bed. I carefully took off her sneakers and shifted her into a more comfortable position. Rahul kicked off his shoes and sank onto the bed beside his sister. We covered the sleeping kids with blankets, shut off the light, and went to the living room.

"Want anything to drink, Meena?" Prajay asked. "You look beat." He glanced at my sneakers. "I hope your ankle isn't hurting from all that walking."

"My ankle's fine. I'll just use the powder room and go home." I remembered something. "Oh, I almost forgot." Pulling out the folded spreadsheet from my purse, I handed it to him. "Here's the list of your top six respondents. I've put them in order of suitability, starting with number one at the top."

"That's very efficient. I'm glad I hired you as my consultant."

I made an appropriate sound and walked away to the powder room. When I came out, I saw Prajay sitting on the couch, studying the list. He looked up at me. "Nice work, Meena. I guess the ball's in my court now. I'll have to see about contacting some of these women."

"Sure." I pulled out my car keys from my purse. "Thanks for a wonderful day at the park."

He rose to his feet. "Are you kidding? You gave up an entire Saturday for me. I can't thank you enough." He took my hand and held it in a firm grip. "I don't even know how to start thanking you. Between this," he pointed to the sheet he'd left on the coffee table, "and today . . . you've been awesome."

"No need for thanks, Prajay." I pulled my hand back. My pulse was doing strange things. Disturbing things. "I do stuff for people I consider my friends."

"Can I take you to dinner tomorrow to thank you properly then? Not chicken fingers and clown sundaes, but a proper restaurant."

"I told you, you don't have to do anything. You already fed me breakfast and dinner today."

"I want to take you to dinner, damn it. Why can't you accept a simple gesture of gratitude, Meena?"

"I—I don't know."

"I might look big and scary, but I'm harmless. I promise I'll only treat you to a nice dinner, and then I'll give you the check I owe you for taking care of my matrimonial problems." Perhaps seeing my continued hesitation, he added, "We'll go to some out of the way restaurant where we're not likely to run into anyone we know."

I grabbed the doorknob and pulled the door open. "Fine, if that's what you want. But what about your brother and his family?"

"Prakash and Nitya will be returning here late tonight. They're planning to drive back home tomorrow afternoon." He paused. "Can you come here around five? That'll give us plenty of time to drive out a few miles and find a decent restaurant. Where would you like to go?"

"I'll let you choose. Good night." I had to get out of there. I couldn't take one more minute of his standing there making casual talk. Hadn't the family-style outing meant anything to him?

I was nothing more than the paid consultant now? He wanted to thank me. He was going to treat me to a nice dinner and then hand me a check. How was *that* for gratitude?

Just as I was about to step outside, Prajay did something unexpected that rattled me, then left me shaking. He put his huge hands on my shoulders, bent down, and placed a light kiss on my cheek. "Good night. And thank you again." Then he stepped away and gave me a mildly baffled look. "You're so little. I've carried you twice before, but just now . . . your shoulders . . . you felt as tiny as Riya."

"Tiny as Riya? Thanks a lot, Prajay." Without waiting for his response I turned and rushed out of there. Instead of waiting for the elevator, I looked around, found the door marked Stairs, and rushed through it. I raced down the steps and ran all the way to my car.

I got behind the wheel and nearly sent my fist crashing into it. He'd touched me and felt nothing, while I'd experienced an electric jolt. He'd kissed me coolly, when I'd felt the heated urge to reach up and press my lips to his. Damn, damn, damn.

I'd been harboring all these warm, womanly feelings for him, and he thought of me like he did his four-year-old niece. How devilishly absurd was that?

"Since you think I'm a toddler in pigtails, why don't you take me to Friendly's for a clown sundae dinner tomorrow night, you big, dumb, clueless gorilla?" I murmured to no one in particular. I didn't care if anyone around saw me talking to myself. I was beyond caring. Way beyond livid.

I told myself firmly to regain my composure, then put the car in gear and drove home. My head was pounding. My ankle felt worse than it had a half hour ago.

I needed the comfort of a heating pad, aspirin, and my bed.

Chapter 13

I slept for fourteen hours. Finding the last two pills prescribed by Dr. Murjani sitting on my nightstand, I had swallowed one and sunk into bed, still wearing the jeans and sweatshirt I'd been romping around in all day.

Luckily Mom and Dad had been out at some social gathering and hadn't been home to see me raging when I'd stumbled into the house the previous night. Mom would have guessed that something was wrong if she'd seen me in that condition. I had slept so soundly I didn't even know what time they'd come home. Just as well.

By the time I showered and dressed and went downstairs on Sunday, it was lunchtime. I ate vegetable soup and sandwiches made of mint-coriander chutney and sliced tomatoes with my parents. This was my usual time to show up at the table on a weekend, so there were no questions other than to ask how my trip to Great Adventure had been.

"Great," I said with every bit of enthusiasm I could muster. "The weather was fabulous."

"I heard that King Kong roller coaster is extremely scary." Mom's expression said she wondered why people would want to ride in a death machine and call it fun.

"It's Kingda Ka, and yes, it's wild," I replied, although I hadn't taken that ride. "But that's part of the fun, Mom. The thrill of it is what makes people go again and again."

"You know what some of those thrills can do to the human brain?" she pointed out. "There's only so much excitement it can take, Meena. It can do permanent damage in some cases."

I smiled benignly and ate the last of my soup. "Don't worry. I'm not brain damaged yet."

Dad threw me his most dad-like look. "Let's keep it that way, till you find a good husband."

Maybe because of the aftereffects of the previous evening, I lashed out. "Yeah, it's bad enough that I'm a not-too-bright female. God forbid you have to carry the additional burden of palming me off with no gray cells at all." I got up from the table and placed my bowl and plate in the dishwasher. This business of getting rid of me by marriage was becoming too stale. Too hurtful.

"Stop playing the martyr, Meena," retorted Mom, looking thoroughly ticked off.

"Then why do you make me feel like I'm a burden? You never say things like that to Maneel and Mahesh. Those two daredevils can do as they please, while I have to watch every little thing I do and say."

"You're not a burden, dear," Dad tried to assure me. "In our culture, it is important to make sure that a girl is kept safe and healthy until she is handed over in marriage to a suitable boy. Then it is his responsibility to keep her safe and happy."

"You make me sound like some kind of perishable commodity that needs careful refrigeration until the right customer comes along. What am I, fillet of catfish?"

Dad's eyebrows snapped together. "*Chhee*, don't talk nonsense like that. That kind of attitude does not suit a sensible, educated girl like you."

"If you think I'm sensible and educated, then treat me as such. I'm old enough to know what's good and bad for me. Trust me."

"Okay, dear, whatever you say." Mom got up from the table. "Let's discuss dinner now, shall we. What should I make for this evening's meal?"

"I'm going out with friends tonight."

"But you went out with them yesterday."

"That was Great Adventure. Tonight we're going to dinner."

Perhaps because she'd had enough arguing, Mom quietly went to the sink and rinsed the dishes. Dad picked up his cell phone and started to dial someone. I took off for my room. I could use some peace and quiet before going out this evening.

Booting up my computer, I found several forwarded messages from Prajay. More matrimonial hopefuls. Great, exactly what I needed to cheer me up—another pound of salt to rub into my wound.

I reluctantly looked at each response and found only one that looked good: a thirty-four-year-old physical therapist and divorcée. Although I had serious doubts about her suitability, I added her profile to my database and printed the updated version for Prajay.

If he wanted a divorcée, he could have one. See if I cared. It would serve him right if she came with tons of baggage . . . like a bitchy personality, three bratty kids, and an incontinent dog. A psychopathic stalker for an ex-husband would be even better.

Picking up a book, I lay down to read. I must have read no more than two pages before I fell asleep again.

When I woke up it was nearly four o'clock, so I dragged myself to the bathroom, took a hot shower, and got dressed. Assuming Prajay was planning to take me to a refined restaurant, I wore a short, black dress with elbow length sleeves and a slightly risqué neckline. Of course, all my efforts at trying to capture his attention would be in vain. But what the heck? At least I felt good about myself when I wore pretty, sexy clothes.

I put on a slightly heavier coat of makeup, my diamond earrings, and black, high-heeled sandals. To hell with my ankle. I was in no mood to pamper it.

When I rang Prajay's doorbell, he opened the door and gestured to me to go in and sit down. He was on the phone, in the midst of a conversation that sounded like business. He was dressed in black slacks, an open-neck shirt and a sports jacket.

It was nearly five minutes before he was finished with his call. All the while I sat on the couch with my knees crossed and one restless leg swinging. He put the cell phone in his pocket and hurried toward me. "Sorry, Meena. That was an emergency."

I didn't bother to make eye contact with him. "That's okay."

"Shall we start, then?" He pulled his car keys out of his pocket.

It took some maneuvering to get myself into his Corvette without letting my short dress ride up too high. The seat was so low to the ground that it felt like I was sitting on the floor. I could barely see above the dashboard. I realized why he'd borrowed his friend's Toyota to drive me when I was injured.

Just before putting the car in gear, he turned to me and smiled, a warm, pulse-raising, belly-wrenching smile. "You look very pretty this evening."

"Thanks."

"I hope that's not inappropriate to say to an employee?"

"I don't believe so," I murmured and looked out the window. He thought I was pretty, and yet he didn't see beyond the looks, that I had a sharp mind and a decent-sized heart. And that I wanted him. Why were some intelligent males so dumb when it came to women and relationships?

Probably guessing that I was in no mood for small talk, he pulled out of the parking lot and headed for the street. "Aren't you curious to know where we're going?" he asked finally.

"I'm sure you're capable of picking a perfectly nice restaurant. You're the hotshot entrepreneur who entertains bigwigs all the time."

"Do you like Thai food?"

I nodded. "Yeah."

"Good, I made reservations at a Thai restaurant."

It turned out to be a lovely restaurant, with exotic Thai décor and pretty young waitresses in traditional *pha sin,* the narrow tube skirts in jewel-tone silk, embossed with gold designs. I ordered a glass of white wine. Two sips and the alcohol improved my mood considerably. I actually felt like talking to Prajay.

"This is a nice place," I said, taking in the hand-embroidered sequin-and-bead wall hangings and the delicate glass light fixtures.

"Glad you like it." He seemed at ease as he sat with his elbows on the table and sipped his Thai beer. "I was a bit concerned that you might not like Thai food. But then you did ask me to go ahead and pick a restaurant."

"I'm glad you picked Thai. The food's delicious." I took a spoonful of the *tom yum* soup. It was fiery hot and garnished with lots of cilantro—just the way I liked it. The *pad thai* noodles, the green curry fish, the stir-fried chicken, and the basil rice were just as scrumptious. The service was impeccable.

Even our waitress was a petite and charming girl who spoke stilted English but made up for it with her disarming smile and gracious manner.

Despite my feeling a bit more relaxed, Prajay did most of the talking. He told me about his emergency—something caused by a power surge that his troubleshooter was working on at the moment.

His cell phone rang once, and he stepped outside to take the call. It was the polite thing to do, but it left me sitting alone, looking and feeling like the abandoned date.

He returned several minutes later with a relieved smile and another apology. "Sorry about that, but the problem was solved. My crew's good, or I wouldn't have been able to make it tonight."

He picked up his fork and continued to eat his now cold dinner. He talked a little more, then stopped to peer at me. "Are you feeling all right? You've been very quiet."

Took him long enough to notice, or perhaps now that his emergency situation had been successfully dealt with, he realized I'd done very little talking. When I nodded, he frowned a little. "Are you sure? You look tired, and I'm wondering if Great Adventure was a bit too much for you so soon after your injury."

"I'm fine." I changed the subject. "Did you have a chance to

contact any of those women on the list I made for you?" Why
was I doing this, torturing myself? But I had to know—had to
understand if I stood any chance with him at all.

"No, I haven't had a single minute to even look at the list you
so diligently put together."

Hopefully he'd *never* have a minute to see it. Ever. "I guess
you'll get to it one of these days." I reluctantly pulled out the
updated spreadsheet from my purse and handed it to him.
"Here, one more beanpole for your perusal."

He thrust the sheet in his jacket pocket and chuckled. "I
guess some of them do qualify as beanpoles."

"That's what you're after, aren't you, a supremely tall woman?"

The waitress interrupted us to ask if we had enjoyed our
meal, making it impossible for me to get Prajay's response.
When we told her the meal was superb, she started to clear the
table. "Dessert, tea?" she inquired with a brilliant smile.

I said no to both. Prajay didn't want anything either, so he
merely requested the check.

On the way back to his house he stumped me when he asked
if I could go over his list with him, help him analyze it. "If I
don't get to it soon, I'm afraid I never will."

"Finding the right woman for yourself is *your* job, Prajay, not
mine. It's a very personal thing."

"I need a woman's point of view."

Sure, I silently fumed, *you need someone like a sister to guide
you in the right direction.* But sisterly affection was far from
what I felt for him.

"Maybe you can tell me what women like, how best to approach them, etcetera," he said, pulling into the parking lot of
his complex.

This was getting more bizarre by the second. Now he wanted
me to be his Love Guru and show him how to go about courting
a woman. Lord help me.

Turning off the ignition, he gave me that helpless male look.
"I really could use your guidance, you know." When I hesitated
he added, "I have your check upstairs for you."

Here we go again, I thought, my temper rising once more. He'd assumed I was doing all this strictly for the money. Well, I'd let the jerk think whatever he wanted. "Fine, I'll help you."

As soon as he ushered me into his living room and switched on the lights, I turned to him. "Tell me something, Prajay. Didn't you say you've dated a fair number of women in the past? How did you deal with them? From your attitude now one would think you're a novice at this."

"I never had to *ask out* a single one of them—each was either someone I met through my family or someone I met through well-meaning friends. Somebody always arranged for us to meet somewhere, and the lady in question would show up. I even managed multiple dates with a couple of them without actually asking."

"You mean *they* were bold enough to ask you?"

"Yes. Women seem to be much more forward than I'd expected," he said with a puzzled frown, as if trying to figure that out for the first time.

"The right word is confident, not forward. So, once you met them for the second or third time . . . did you at least hold hands . . . and . . ." Once again, I was setting myself up for major grief.

He smiled. "I managed to go a lot further than handholding with a couple of them when I was a senior in college. Well . . . one of them."

If I wasn't mistaken, Prajay was blushing. So he'd slept with one of those beanpoles, had he? The sharp stab of jealousy nearly made me wince.

What was the matter with me? I hadn't even known this man when he was in college. In fact I had probably been a freshman in high school when he was sleeping with some floozy. And yet it felt like a hot poker had been thrust into my abdomen.

This was insanity—jealousy over some woman I'd never seen, never heard of until a second ago. Served me right for probing.

I went to the couch and sat down, before my legs had a chance to give way and I made a complete fool of myself. Prajay took off his jacket and tossed it on the back of a chair, then asked if I wanted anything to drink. When I shook my head, he said, "I have some excellent coffee-flavored ice cream that my sister-in-law brought from a New York dairy. Want to try some?"

"Okay, just a little bit. I'm already stuffed." I should've said no. Instead I watched him stride toward the kitchen.

A few minutes later he returned, bearing a tray with two bowls of ice cream and glasses of cold water. I took one lick of the spoon, closed my eyes, and purred. "This is fabulous."

"It's their best-selling flavor." He picked up an envelope off the coffee table and handed it to me. "Your check."

My hand shook when I accepted it. "You didn't have to, but . . . thanks anyway."

"Aren't you going to open it? Make sure I've compensated you adequately?"

"Since I wasn't looking to be compensated in the first place, I'm sure whatever is in there is more than adequate."

"Suit yourself." He took a big mouthful of ice cream. When we'd put our empty bowls back on the tray, he went to his jacket and fished out the spreadsheet from the pocket. "Let's get down to the list, shall we?"

When he returned to sit beside me, he sat much closer. Although I tried to keep my mind on the sheet of paper, my objectivity was nowhere to be found. His nearness, the warmth radiating from him, and the scent of him were driving me nuts. "What exactly do you want me to do with this, Prajay?"

"In your opinion, who would best suit my personality? Remember I told you appearance is not the most important thing to me? Hobbies, occupation, family, sense of humor, all those things carry much more weight than looks. There's a lot more to a relationship than good looks."

"I agree." God, how I agreed. Looks were the last thing anyone should consider. I'd realized that very recently. At first sight I'd thought he reminded me of a big, graceless giant. And here I was, in love with him—a mere four weeks after meeting him.

An hour after I'd laid eyes on him, I'd looked past the face, the large nose, and the eyebrows that could scare the spots off a cheetah. Now he looked wonderful to me. Right this moment, he was so close that I wanted to throw my arms around his neck and beg him to consider me as the top lady on his idiotic list.

"Excellent! So taking all that into consideration, who do you think I should contact first, lady number one or number two?" He frowned at the paper. "They're almost tied for first place."

"I put together an entire database to sort the various pros and cons. That's how I rated them, and so lady number one is still number one. From what I can see, she'd be . . . perfect for you." My voice was turning into a tormented whisper. Why couldn't I have some control over something as simple as my voice? Good thing I hadn't gone into acting. I'd make a lousy actress.

Prajay offered me a glass of water. "Here, you sound like your throat is dry."

I took a grateful sip. "I think I should leave now." I made a big deal about looking at my wristwatch. "It's late."

He took the glass from my hand, and our fingers touched. I shook at the surge of power that shot up my arm. Warm blood rushed to my neck and cheeks. Oh no, my face was probably an open book—a woman completely smitten.

He must have felt something, too, because his hand looked a little unsteady as he put the half-finished glass back on the tray. He turned to me, a look of startled discovery replacing the casual one that had been there a moment ago.

He lifted a hand to touch the side of my face. "You . . . are . . . beautiful, Meena Shenoy."

I was trembling so much, I couldn't think straight. "I . . . uh . . . thank you." Why couldn't I come up with something intelligent and cool to say? I was sitting there like a bumbling moron when I was getting exactly what I wanted—his undivided attention.

"Beautiful, smart, caring. You're a very special young lady."

His thumb caressed my cheekbone as he studied my eyes, as if searching for something.

Still tongue-tied, I let my eyelids fall. It was hard to hold his gaze and not throw myself at him. No matter what, I still had to hold on to my dignity. And thrusting myself on him was likely to make him recoil. His other hand slowly came up, and he cupped my face with both hands. His palms felt strong and hard yet tender.

I didn't know exactly what happened or how—who leaned forward first, but suddenly his lips were on mine, warm, soft, gentle for a big man. Instinctively my mouth opened for his kiss. This was what I'd wanted for the last couple of weeks. I had dressed in one of my most seductive outfits just so I could have this. And yet, I hesitated to touch him. Oh, I wanted to very much, but one wrong move could ruin the fragile moment.

Most Indian men didn't like aggressive women. So I kept my hands tightly clasped in my lap while his full mouth glided over mine, his teeth nipped at my lower lip, and his tongue played with mine.

A yearning sigh escaped from my mouth. He must have heard it, too, because his hands left my face and his arms locked around me. I was hauled against him in one quick move, taking the breath right out of my lungs.

God, this was good—better than anything I'd ever felt in my whole life.

Although his hold on me felt like a vice grip, I liked it, basked in it. His next kiss was harder, more demanding, that of a hungry male rather than a tender admirer. And all the while my mind sang: *He wants me. He wants me.*

I couldn't hold back any longer. My hands rested on his shoulders, savoring the tautness of the muscle and the soft feel of his shirt for a moment, and then my arms slid around his neck, clamping his mouth to mine. I never wanted to let go. This was a minor miracle. I'd come here to help him locate a woman who'd make him a suitable wife, and instead I was clasped in his arms, his mouth making scalding, passionate love to mine.

Even in my wildest dreams I hadn't thought it would be this wonderful. His cologne was rousing, his hair ticklish on my fingers, and his chest was hard as a rock against my pliant breasts. This felt so damn right.

Just when I thought this was heaven on earth, he abruptly loosened his hold on me, a puzzled look coming over his face once more. But this time the bafflement was not mixed with wonder and awe. It was more like an unpleasant shock.

I had done it—exactly what I didn't want to do—I'd repulsed him. Why the heck hadn't I behaved like a nice Hindu girl and held myself in check?

He took me by the shoulders and set me away from him. "I'm so sorry. I—I don't know what came over me."

All I could do was stare at him. What was he talking about? "What do you mean?" I managed to ask.

"I'm sorry for taking advantage of you. I should be shot in the head for what I just did to a sweet, innocent young lady."

So that's what this was all about. "But I'm not innocent. And I'm not all that . . . young," I protested. My voice was back to its normal pitch. Most women my age would have loved to be called sweet and innocent and young. But at the moment I hated it.

He gave a wry laugh. "Of course you are. You're young and bright and you have a big heart. When I asked for your help, you gave it to me wholeheartedly. When most people would have brought a lawsuit against me for the stupid way I knocked you to the floor a month ago, you forgave me."

"It was an accident, Prajay."

"Then right after that you plunged into the project I gave you—finding me the right bride."

"But I only did—"

"And here I am," he cut in, "taking advantage of you when I should be treating you like a lady. Like a sister."

"Sister?" I made a disgusted face. "When we were kissing a moment ago I hardly thought of you as my *brother*."

"Well . . . maybe not," he allowed.

"I couldn't imagine my brother kissing me like that!"

Prajay lifted his glass from the tray and took a sip. "Meena, I think that wine you had earlier is affecting your thinking. Just look at me, and then look at yourself. I'm easily three times your size. I'm a huge, ungainly giant, whereas you're dainty and delicate as a doll. Another minute of that kind of rough handling and I'd have broken your ribs."

"No, you wouldn't have," I argued. "I liked it. I felt a bond between us when we kissed. I know you liked it, too. I could feel the passion in you when you held me."

"So I'm a normal man with all my instincts and hormones intact." He shut his eyes briefly and pinched the bridge of his nose, chastising himself. "In a crazy moment of passion I grabbed the first female I'd been physically close to in almost a year. Combine that with a glass of strong Thai beer, and I lost control. It was . . . lust, that's all."

My shoulders slumped. Was that all it was to him? A moment of craziness brought on by a bottle of beer? While I was baring my soul to him, he was reducing our kiss to a momentary lapse in judgment. "Is that all you think it is?" I tried to keep my voice even, but it seemed like it was going to crack at any moment. The tears were very close to crashing through the flimsy walls I was trying to hold on to.

"It has to be." He took another sip of water and rose from the couch. "What else could there be between us? I'm so much older and a lot more mature than you. I'm the boss who made a move on his pretty, young employee, and what choice did she have but to put up with the indignity?"

He began to pace the length of the room, glass still in hand. "In power, physical strength, maturity, you're no match for me." He stopped pacing for a moment. "It was wrong of me to force myself on you. My sincere apologies. I promise it won't happen again."

"But you don't understand, Prajay. You didn't take advantage of me. I was a willing participant. I wanted it as much as you did. Can't you understand that?"

He shook his head. "You're too young and inexperienced to

know what you want, Meena. As the only girl between two brothers in a Konkani family, I'm sure you lead a sheltered life. You're misinterpreting this for something deep and . . . romantic."

"That's not true." It had been a huge mistake telling him that I had two brothers and old-fashioned parents. Me and my big mouth. Now all that talking had come back to bite me.

He tossed me an indulgent, paternal sort of smile. "If you're like my female cousins, you probably read those romance books. That's not real life. Believe me, I'm not the hero type. I'm a big, rough man with a cutthroat business to run. I need a big, practical woman who'll understand my ways and accept me for what I am."

It was a losing battle, I realized with a sinking heart. He had such ridiculously exaggerated notions about my supposed innocence and cloistered lifestyle on the one hand, and his own bigness and clumsiness on the other.

Nonetheless I tried to set him straight. "You're wrong, Prajay. I've dated before. I'm more experienced than you think. And I like your large, manly looks."

"Really?" He looked more mystified than ever.

"I like your gruffness. I appreciate the fact that you're a busy man with a challenging business to run. I happen to like who you are."

He set the glass down and approached me. For a moment my heart somersaulted with anticipation. Maybe I'd convinced him with my argument. He was coming back to me, to hold and kiss me again.

I was dead wrong. He ran a fatherly hand over my head. "You're sweet. You'll make some lucky man a wonderful wife. You'll make a great mom, too. You were fantastic with Rahul and Riya yesterday—so patient, so much fun. They kept talking about you this morning, especially Riya. She loved you."

"But . . . Prajay—"

"Go home, Meena—go home before you tempt me some more." His eyes were clouded with regret. "After you've had a chance to sleep on it, you'll realize the foolishness of it all."

This time the tears gathered in my eyes. "I guess I won't have a job in your company anymore?"

His response was a shaky chuckle. "Don't be silly. You're a great PR manager, and I'm sure you'll continue to do a good job for us. I consider you not just an employee, but a friend."

My response was a muffled sniffle. I couldn't talk.

"Now go home, sweetheart. It's getting late; it's not safe for you to drive home late at night." He looked at his watch. "Besides, we both have to work tomorrow."

I grabbed my purse and walked out of his house in a daze, stumbling toward the elevator, nearly blinded by my tears. Fortunately, there was no one else inside the elevator, so I could indulge in a crying fit. Outside, on the walkway leading to the parking lot, a young couple strolling toward the building gave me an odd look when I rushed past them.

In my car, I sat for several minutes, bawling like a baby. He'd even called me *sweetheart* and then tossed me out of his house. I wanted to die. I was in love with him. Crazy in love. It had crept up on me insidiously, little by little, but now it was as clear as the fat iron lamppost sitting ten feet away from my car.

I was in love with a man who didn't want me. He was obsessed with finding a woman who was the same size as him. That, coming from a man who claimed appearance was not important in a relationship? And yet, what he wanted was a six-foot woman. If that wasn't all about physical looks, then what was?

Drying my eyes, I drove home. Fortunately Dad was engrossed in watching a PBS special on TV and didn't pay attention to me when I said a breezy good night and went directly upstairs. I figured Mom was out on another emergency. In her profession, it happened practically four times a week. Tonight it was a godsend.

I found a personal check for twelve hundred dollars in the envelope Prajay had given me. Obviously he didn't want to use the office account for something so personal. But somehow the money meant nothing now, despite the generous amount. In fact, it felt like a slap in my face, like being hired to do a job and then handed a pink slip. I'd served my purpose. He had no more use for me.

But money was still money, and I decided to bank it for Christmas presents like I'd originally planned.

That night, when I said my bedtime prayers, I ranted, *"God, why couldn't you have made me a few inches taller? Why did you have to be so stingy when you made me? Were you saving up the inches for that woman in Maryland? And if you had to make me this puny and insignificant, why did you let me fall in love with one of the tallest guys you created?"*

Chapter 14

Monday was one of the worst days of my life. When I went in to work, it was hard to go about my duties knowing the man I was in love with was somewhere in the building. His car was in the parking lot, so I knew he was there.

When Pinky walked into the office a few minutes after my arrival, she studied me for a long moment. "Feeling all right?"

"Sure." I tried to be casual while I filled the coffeepot with water.

"You're earlier than usual." Pinky measured the coffee and added it to the filter, then inserted the filter into the machine and switched it on. "You look like you have a cold or something. Your eyes are red."

"My ankle was acting up again last night, and I didn't get much sleep."

"In that case you better not walk too much today. If you need any copying or errands done, let me know."

"Thanks, Pinky," I sent her a grateful smile. "Don't know what I'd do without you."

Pinky laughed it off, but she looked pleased nonetheless, reminding me that I needed to do something special for her and Paul for Christmas. They had gone out of their way in caring for me.

I would have loved to do something nice for Prajay, too, but I was mad at him. It didn't make me blind to his good qualities, but I didn't feel particularly charitable toward him either. At the moment he was breaking my heart.

Paul walked in, parked his lunch bag on his desk, and went straight for the coffee that had just about finished dripping. "Oh man, the smell of caffeine." He poured himself a cup and sniffed with his eyes closed. He looked like a man in heaven. "Thank you, ladies," he said after his first sip.

I glanced at Pinky and found her eyes glinting with suppressed amusement. We both knew Jeremy wasn't aware of Paul's habit of drinking two or three cups of coffee each day. Jeremy wanted him to drink green tea and chamomile. Paul disliked both.

The teabags packed in Paul's lunch bag were quietly stuffed in a plastic freezer bag and left on the counter in the break room. Paul probably kept hoping somebody would take them. But nobody seemed to cast a glance at them. The bag was getting fatter by the day, while Paul filled his belly with coffee.

After finishing half a cup, Paul gave me the same suspicious look Pinky had cast me earlier. "Are you okay?"

"I'm fine." To put an end to any more questions about my health, I hurried into my office and started opening the folders waiting for my attention. I made a mental note to go to the refrigerator later and get some ice cubes for my eyes.

When I did find an opportunity to go to the break room for the ice, I ran into Gargi. It would have looked too obvious if I had turned around and run back to my office, so I sauntered in. In a long, navy skirt and soft, print shirt, and her hair in waves around her shoulders, she looked attractive.

Gargi was having a soda and an animated conversation with a fellow programmer about the merits of one software package versus another. Since computer code was alien to me, I merely said hello to Gargi and her coworker, a guy I knew by face but not by name, and headed straight for the refrigerator. But I wasn't so lucky as to escape Gargi's tongue.

"Hi there, Meena," Gargi said cheerily. "Looks like your foot is back to normal? I see the high heels are back."

"Yes. Thanks for asking."

"I hear you and Deepak are an item lately, *yaar.*" Gargi's grin was sly.

It didn't escape me that she was using Deepak's favorite word with some relish. The woman was trying to bait me. I was in no mood for it.

But that didn't mean I couldn't give back in some small measure. "When Deepak and I become an item, I'll send you an e-mail, Gargi. Better yet, I'll place an announcement in the monthly newsletter. That'll save you the trouble of having to broadcast it," I added with my most tolerant smile.

Gargi's grin didn't fade. "You have such a great sense of humor, Meena."

"Oh well," I said with a shrug. Throwing some ice cubes into a paper towel, I made a beeline for the door before she could think of something else to further ruin my day.

Concentrating on work was difficult, knowing Prajay would soon make contact with the lady rated ten on his scale of desirable women. When was he going to meet her? Would they hit it off right away? Would he be proposing marriage to her soon? Would he kiss her like he'd kissed me? Would he . . .

I forced my mind back to the pile of work on my desk. Torturing myself with such thoughts was not healthy. I had a life of my own, separate from Prajay Nayak, and I had to concentrate on that. It wasn't like I was a loser in the romance department. I got my share of male admiration and invitations for dates.

Maybe *that* was the problem—I didn't accept many dates. If I had, I wouldn't have fallen so easily for Prajay. He had come into my life during a dry spell. If I'd been actively seeing someone, I wouldn't have looked in Prajay's direction at all.

That was it. I needed a more active social life. I needed to date other guys instead of pining away for a man who didn't want me.

I made a resolution: If Mom and Shabari-pachi tried to fix me up with someone, I wouldn't balk this time. I'd give it a fair chance. Who knew where it would lead? Maybe there was a nice guy out there who thought I was the perfect size and had the right personality for him.

After that pep talk to myself, I was able to get back to work and get a lot done.

The new ads I had in mind for *Computer Digest* and *PC Magazine* were a real challenge. I was on the phone with the advertising managers for a while, negotiating space, layout, and prices. Then there was that press release about the new acquisition—the one Prajay had been working on in Jersey all these weeks. That was coming to a head according to Paul, so Prajay's days in Jersey were numbered.

Soon he'd return to DC and his normal routine. And I'd still be here in Jersey.

Maybe then I could put him and the whole kissing episode behind me. Hopefully the memory would fade, and I'd be able to get back on my feet. Lots of women got rejected, and they picked themselves up and got on with their lives.

Later that day, I accepted another dinner invitation from Deepak for Saturday. A twinge of guilt poked me in the ribs because I was using Deepak to soothe my ego, but that was quickly replaced by other, more selfish thoughts. I had to show Prajay that I didn't care what he did with his life.

As I drove home from work that evening, my cell phone rang. Excitedly I answered it, despite knowing it was illegal to use a cell phone while driving. Maybe it was Prajay, wanting to tell me he'd made a mistake after all.

But I heard Maneel's voice instead. My brother almost never called me. We saw each other practically every evening at dinner. "Hey, how come you're calling me?"

"Where are you right now?" he asked, ignoring my question.

"Driving home from work."

"Good."

"I could get a ticket for using my cell, Maneel."

"Then why did you answer it?" He couldn't care less if I got a traffic ticket. "Exactly how far from home are you?"

"I'm almost at the intersection of Route 1 and Washington

Road—coming up to the light. Traffic is horrendous; it'll be a while before I make it through the light." I wondered why my brother sounded a little weird.

"You mind stopping by my place before you head home?"

"Why?"

"I have to talk to you."

"You're going to show up for dinner later, anyway. We can talk then."

"No. I need to talk to you alone." His voice sounded urgent.

"Are you all right?" I'd been hearing that question all morning, and now it was my turn to ask. Something was definitely up with Maneel. When he didn't answer my question, I prodded. "Come on, Maneel, what's going on?"

"Just get over here and I'll tell you, okay?" He paused. "Please, Meena, I need your help."

"Gosh, you sound terrible. I'll be there in a few minutes." I ended the call. My heart was beating faster. It wasn't like my brother to seek my help. We were close, but it was the kind of closeness that involved sibling rivalry, bickering, teasing, and even helping each other out when necessary. But this was different.

Maneel hadn't asked me for help in years—not since he'd made me do his English homework for ten bucks when he was a senior in high school and I was a sophomore.

If he wanted to talk to me in private, it had to be something serious. Was Maneel ill? Had he invested Dad and Mom's money in something risky and lost it all? Was it something illegal? Insider trading . . . maybe?

Oh dear, what if Maneel ended up getting arrested? Every kind of horrible scenario played itself out in my mind while I drove as fast as I possibly could in rush-hour traffic.

After I found a parking spot, I rushed upstairs to Maneel's condo. He opened the door even before I could ring the doorbell. I went right in and dropped my purse on the coffee table.

"What's up with you, Maneel?" I didn't mean to sound abrupt, but I tended to do that when I was upset. He had a day's stubble on his face, and he was wearing khaki shorts and a faded T-shirt. He clearly hadn't gone to work. Something was seriously wrong here. He loved his job and didn't miss a day unless he was ill.

"Sit down," he said. "Do you want anything to drink?"

"Now you're really beginning to scare me." I sat down on the couch. "You're never polite to me."

All I got from Maneel was a long sigh.

"When was the last time you asked me over to your house and offered me a drink?"

"I've got a problem, Mini." He ran all ten fingers through his hair.

He hadn't called me by that silly nickname in a while. My instincts were right. Maneel was in trouble. And it was something big. My brother didn't scare easily. "Are you sick? Or looking at a conviction for something illegal?"

"No . . . yes . . . no."

"Which is it? Yes or no?"

"I'm not sick, and I didn't do anything illegal—at least in the traditional sense." He gave a sardonic laugh, frightening me even more.

"What does that mean?"

"I . . . um . . . I'm in love."

I stared at him. "Love? As in romantic love?"

He nodded.

"*That's* what you wanted to tell me?" The initial shock was instantly replaced by irritation. I rose from the couch and pointed a finger at him. "You scared me to death, you idiot. When you made it sound so mysterious on the phone, I thought maybe you'd found out you had terminal cancer or that you'd lost all of Dad and Mom's savings or something."

"I can handle those things on my own, thank you," he said, giving me an annoyed frown that matched my own.

"Then why did you call me?"

"Because I need your help."

Oh, great. First Prajay, now my brother. I must have *Love*

Guru written across my forehead. And unlike Prajay, Maneel wasn't about to offer me money for consulting, either. I couldn't even handle my own love life. In fact, I'd made a fine mess of it, and all of a sudden I was the Matchmaking and Marriage Bureau of New Jersey.

"Why do you think *I* can help?" I demanded.

"Because you have a clever mind and a slick tongue. You always argue with people, and you know how to get around them."

"Thanks a lot for the left-handed compliment." This was déjà vu. Hadn't Prajay hired me because I was good with words, because I knew how to put together effective press releases and marketing campaigns? I sank back onto the couch, watched Maneel pace the length of the living room. "You're scared to talk to Mom and Dad?"

He stopped pacing and came to sit beside me. "Mom and Dad are going to be a problem, but they're not the main issue."

I sent him a suspicious scowl. "Is she . . . an older woman?

"No."

"A *much* older woman?" Perhaps with sagging breasts and grandchildren?

"I'm not that desperate, thank you." He looked thoroughly irked. "For your information, it's someone younger than me by a few years."

"Is she a divorcée, then? With kids?"

"None of those things."

Something came to mind. It was only a vague suspicion, but I thought I just might know the answer. "She's what, Caucasian, African-American?"

He shook his head. "You couldn't be more wrong."

I'd almost run out of guesses. That left only one thing. "You're in love with a guy." I'd never imagined either of my brothers could be gay. Why was homosexuality always considered something that occurred in other families, and never one's own? Paul and Jeremy were the only gay men I'd come to know well so far.

"Where'd you get *that* idea?" Maneel growled. "I am *not* in love with a man. I'm in love with a bona fide girl. She's . . . Muslim."

"Oh boy." If there was one thing Mom and Dad would have a fit about, it was if one of us dated a Muslim. It had been ingrained in my parents. It wasn't anything personal, since both Mom and Dad had Pakistani and Middle Eastern colleagues whom they liked and respected. But they didn't have any Muslim friends.

My parents had grown up in India, where they'd witnessed the effects of the bitter enmity between Pakistan and India, and how the land of Islam and the land of the Hindus clashed again and again. To this day, the fighting occurred frequently, and it escalated with each passing year. The bloody war over the border state of Kashmir continued, with no end in sight.

Mom and Dad would have a rough time coming to terms with Maneel's falling in love with a Muslim woman.

I turned to my brother with a sigh. "You fooled around with so many girls of different colors and cultures—and then you went and fell for the one that Mom and Dad would dislike the most?"

He shrugged. "It just happened."

"What were you thinking, Maneel?"

"That's the problem. I wasn't *thinking*. I didn't exactly plan to fall in love."

I knew that. I was nursing my own heartache. Little did Maneel know that I was in the same boat as him—hopelessly in love. The difference was the object of my adoration was looking for his ideal woman. And she wasn't me.

But I knew exactly what Maneel meant: Love crept up on you when you weren't looking. In a single moment it just struck you over the head, and there was nothing you could do but slip into a conscious coma.

"So, how long has this been going on?" I asked. "Is she anyone I know?"

"You wouldn't know her. Her name's Naseem Rasul. Her parents emigrated to the U.S. from Iraq."

"Like Mom and Dad came from India."

Maneel nodded. "Her father was apparently a big shot in Iraq, until he had a falling out with Saddam Hussein."

"Wouldn't that have been dangerous?" I speculated.

"They were forced to leave the country."

I thought about it for a moment. "I'm surprised they weren't . . . killed or something." Saddam Hussein had been notorious for executing anyone who wasn't totally loyal to him.

"I don't think the matter was that serious," said Maneel. "They were merely ordered to get out of Iraq and never come back." He let me absorb that. "Naseem and I met eight months ago."

"What does she do?"

"She's a lawyer. She was involved in my employer's merger with another brokerage. She works for the law firm that handled the deal."

"So how did you guys meet?"

"In the office cafeteria."

"Over wilted salad and greasy fries. How romantic," I snickered.

Maneel smiled, obviously recalling the encounter. "She noticed the fried chicken on my tray and lectured me on the ill effects of eating fried and fatty foods."

I looked at him, puzzled. "And you let her get away with it? If I'd said that to you, you'd have barked at me to mind my own damn business."

He smiled again. "But you're my bratty sister. Naseem isn't. And she's beautiful. I couldn't help staring at her all the while she stood on her soapbox and talked down at me."

My eyes narrowed on Maneel. "So what are you saying . . . that I'm ugly?"

"Touchy, touchy." He chuckled. "No, Mini, you're not ugly. You're . . . special."

"People call their mentally or physically challenged relatives special." I rose from the couch for the second time. "I'm out of here. If you think I'm going to sit here and take your insults . . ."

He grabbed my wrist and forced me back down on the couch.

"I'm kidding. Can't you take a joke? Honestly, I think you're beautiful, too." Seeing I was still bristling, he patted my head, a partly affectionate–partly condescending gesture. "You really *are* pretty. I see how some of the guys look at you. My friends often ask me to introduce you to them."

"And?"

"Frankly I don't think they're good enough for you."

"Fine." I thawed a little—reluctantly. Besides, Maneel had protected me from the bullies in high school. "So, exactly who is good enough for me?"

He studied me for a second. "No one. But if I come across a guy with promise, I'll introduce you." He started to pace again, his mood back to restless brooding. "Naseem's parents are even more old-fashioned than Mom and Dad. They'll kill her if they find out she has been dating a Hindu Brahmin."

"Can't you guys just break up and forget each other?" I couldn't see any other way unless they both chose to throw caution to the winds and possibly alienate Naseem's parents forever.

"I wish it were that simple, Mini. I'm in love with Naseem. She's pretty, she's smart . . . she's great. And she loves me."

"Can't imagine why she loves you," I murmured.

"Neither can I," he agreed, surprising me. "We want to get married, buy a house, have kids, adopt a puppy—"

"You've got a bad case of it, you poor man." I leaned forward, parked my elbows on my knees, and cupped my face in my hands. This was awful. Maneel was in love with a woman whose family probably wouldn't tolerate non-Muslims.

How were we going to handle this? As siblings, we were in this together. What affected one affected the other two. I'd never seen Maneel like this—emotional, uncertain, tense, even a little scared.

"Does Mahesh know?" I asked.

He shook his head. "You're the first to know."

"Should I feel honored?" I smiled.

"Absolutely. I haven't told another soul."

"I think we should tell Mahesh. Maybe with the two of us

supporting you, you'll have a better chance of winning over Mom and Dad first, and then convincing them to join us in facing Mr. and Mrs. Rasul."

Maneel went to the window and leaned against the frame, his arms folded across his middle, staring out at nothing in particular. I observed him standing there, a grown man facing a grown-up dilemma. This was no teenage escapade leading to a slap on the wrist, maybe even a harsh reprimand. This was a serious matter that would affect his whole life.

He was probably scared out of his wits that Naseem's parents would put an end to their relationship and he'd never be able to see her again. Maybe he was wondering if he and Naseem would be forced to elope.

My heart went out to my brother. Despite all the nasty things he'd done to me while we were growing up, he was still my brother. And he was facing a crisis. I couldn't stand to see him like this. If I could do something to help him, I'd gladly give it my all.

Silently I went up to him and slid my arm through his. "I'll help you any way I can, Maneel."

He stood still for several more seconds. I could feel the controlled tension in his arm and shoulder, the tautness of the muscles. Then he turned and hugged me. "Thanks, Mini. You're right. I should tell Mahesh."

I nodded and moved away. "Three against two now, and eventually five Shenoys against two Rasuls. Strength in numbers. When do you plan to tell Mahesh?"

"Right now." He picked up his cell phone. "I'm not sure he's home, though. He's always working." He waited till he got connected to Mahesh's voice mail. "Hey, Mahesh. This is Maneel. Give me a call. I've got something urgent to discuss with you." He pocketed the phone and turned to me. "I need a cold beer. You want anything?"

"No, I better get home. Dad and Mom will wonder why I'm late."

He went into his modern kitchenette and returned in a moment with a can of beer.

I pulled my car keys from my purse and headed toward the door. "Let me know when you're going to talk to Mahesh. I'd like to be there, so we can put our heads together and come up with a strategy."

"You sound like a true manager." He threw me a wry smile. "Appreciate the help, Mini."

"Hey, don't think this is a free service. I'm counting on your support if I happen to need it in the future."

"I know that. Even when you were this little," he said, holding his hand at waist level, "you traded favors with Mahesh and me. Don't think I've forgotten the ten dollars you charged me for doing my homework. You've always been a little deal maker."

I grinned at him. "Cheer up, and get yourself a shave and a shower, will you. If your precious Naseem sees you like this, she's likely to fall out of lust real quick." I stopped with my hand on the doorknob and watched the amused smile soften his face. "So when do I get to meet this paragon of beauty and virtue?"

"I'll introduce her to Mahesh and you whenever Mahesh is free."

"You do that." I gave him a finger waggle, stepped out, and closed the door behind me.

For a long time I sat in my car, trying to think of the best way to deal with the matter of Maneel and Naseem. Fireworks were likely to explode when all this came out in the open.

No wonder Maneel had slipped away each time someone in the family had brought up the subject of marriage. My guess had been right: The devil had been having an affair all this time. What I hadn't guessed correctly was the girlfriend's faith.

I wondered about my parents' potential reaction when Maneel got around to telling them about Naseem, especially Mom's. I knew about her dreams of finding a Konkani doctor for her firstborn son. She was anxious to see Maneel settle down. She wanted grandchildren—a couple of wholesome Shenoy boys being the preference.

If Maneel married Naseem, Mom could still have her dream of

seeing her son happily married, and there could be a bunch of grandchildren, too. But would Naseem's parents look at it the same way? What if they disowned her? Naseem could be destroyed by it, and consequently Maneel. It wasn't a pretty picture.

One thing was clear to me: If I thought my karma was bad, Maneel's was worse.

Chapter 15

I watched Mom's eyebrows settle into a deep frown at Maneel's news. Dad sat in his favorite recliner with his hands in his lap. His face was expressionless. But then Dad usually processed most information that way—a typical engineer's way.

This was Friday night. The day after Maneel had dropped the bomb on me, he and I had managed to meet for a hurried brainstorming lunch with Mahesh. We'd decided the best way to tackle Mom and Dad was head-on. The longer Maneel postponed his announcement, the worse the situation could get. Besides, on Wednesday night, Mahesh had a rare night off, so he and I had been introduced to Naseem over pizza and wine in Maneel's home.

Maneel was right: She was beautiful. Her complexion reminded me of French vanilla ice cream with a hint of caramel. She had large hazel eyes with curling lashes and a charming smile. I could see why my brother was dazzled. The nicer part was her personality. She seemed bright, outgoing—perfect for Maneel.

She'd make a nice sister-in-law, too. That was a huge plus for me.

Watching Maneel and Naseem make goo-goo eyes at each other had made me ache inside. I'd never seen my brother like this. While it was wonderful to see him looking so happy, I was jealous. He was clearly head over heels in love. Anyone could see that. Naseem seemed smitten with him, too.

Why couldn't I have at least a fraction of that with someone special?

Too bad Naseem wasn't a Hindu girl, I kept thinking all the while we were talking and chomping on pizza in Maneel's kitchen. If she were, her parents would have had an easier time accepting Maneel as a son-in-law. Or vice versa: If we were a Muslim family, things would have been simpler.

We'd all decided that Friday was a good day to have a talk with Mom and Dad, when they were usually in a relaxed, weekend mood. We had stuck to our original plan of bringing Mom and Dad around first (and we were pretty optimistic about that), and then hopefully having them join the cause, and if necessary, face the Rasuls on behalf of the kids.

It was a long shot, but Maneel was all for it. Naseem's eyes had briefly filled with tears of frustration during our conversation, but Maneel and Mahesh had managed to make her laugh with their corny jokes.

The one promising element was that both sets of parents were highly educated professionals. Naseem's father was a research chemist with a PhD and worked for a major pharmaceutical company, and her mother was a high school guidance counselor. The deep hope all four of us were clinging to was that they would be tolerant enough to realize their daughter's happiness should come above religious differences.

So here we were, Mom and Dad, my brothers and I, gathered in the family room, discussing Maneel's potential future with Naseem. We had waited until dinner was over to make sure neither one of our parents lost his or her appetite at hearing the news.

The heir and the spare sat on the couch, with Mom sandwiched between them. Her beloved boys had been clever in orchestrating the seating arrangement.

Mom glowered at Maneel. "We introduced you to so many nice girls. You couldn't choose a single one of them?"

"Sorry." Maneel shrugged.

"Shaila is a such a smart girl. And Mahima is doing a fellowship in neurology, you know."

"I know, Mom," said Maneel, clearly beginning to lose patience.

"What about Devika? She's charming."

"Mom, Shaila has a mustache that could match mine any day, and Mahima isn't interested in marriage right now—she's too busy with her fellowship. And Devika . . ." He sighed. "She's so damn charming that she charms her way into many guys' beds."

Mom's eyes opened wide. "What are you saying? That a nice Konkani girl is a . . . slut?"

On hearing Mom utter a vulgar word, Dad abruptly woke up from his self-imposed stupor. He didn't appreciate talk like that, especially not from his wife.

I nodded at Mom. "I know it's hard for you to understand, but despite being named for a goddess, Devika's not a . . . virtuous girl. Maneel wouldn't be happy with her. And I doubt that Dad and you would have liked a daughter-in-law who cheated on your son."

For Dad's sake I kept the words on a gracious level. Devika was not the average Indian-American girl. She was known in certain circles by far worse names than slut.

"Oh well, then," sniffed Mom. "Even supposing that were true," she allowed, reserving judgment, "why did you have to go and find a Muslim girl?" She held up a hand when Maneel opened his mouth. "I have a lot of respect for Islam and Muslims, but interfaith marriages are difficult. Adjustment in any marriage is hard enough."

Again Maneel tried to explain. "Mom, please try to understand. I didn't deliberately set out to find a Muslim girl. It just happened. Naseem is a terrific person. You'll like her if you meet her."

I vigorously supported Maneel's statement. "She's really nice, Mom. And gorgeous." I winked at Maneel. "She's very fair-complexioned."

"Fairer than you?" Mom asked.

"Much fairer." That would win the prize any day with Indians. Most of them, including my mother, were obsessed with light skin.

Mahesh patted Mom's hand. He was sitting on her other side on the long couch. "Naseem's a lawyer, Mom. She works for a prestigious law firm. Her parents are highly educated, like you and Dad."

Smelling a losing battle, Mom sent Dad a pleading look. "Ram, what do *you* think about all this?"

Dad shook his head. "Looks like Maneel has made up his mind."

Mom gave Dad a dismayed look. She hadn't expected that from him, I figured.

"These kids are surrounded by dating and such things," Dad rationalized. "They're bound to get silly ideas."

"Dad, falling in love and wanting to get married is not silly," I protested. How could he turn something sweet and sentimental into something frivolous?

"I guess I used the wrong word," Dad said. "I was educated in a small town in India, and I didn't learn a lot of fancy English like you. What I meant was American culture has influenced you too much."

"We were born and raised in the American culture," Maneel reminded him dryly.

"You think attraction for a pretty face and a fine figure is love," scoffed Dad. "What happens when beauty fades and you don't love this girl anymore?"

Mahesh stepped in at this point. "Dad, did *you* think of that when you married Mom? She has some gray hairs and wrinkles now, but have you stopped loving her because of that?"

Mom first frowned at Mahesh, and then her brow rose in question at Dad. I chuckled inwardly. This was quite entertaining. Mom obviously wanted to hear Dad's answer more than the rest of us did.

"Of course not!" snorted Dad. "What kind of ridiculous question is that? In our culture we don't get married so we can fall out of love at some point. We fall in love after marriage and stay in love all our lives."

At seeing Mom's expression turn to amused warmth, I snickered. "Wow, Dad, that was profound. I didn't know you could voice your sentiments quite like that."

Dad gave me his *shut your mouth, little girl* glower. I had embarrassed him. But then I hadn't realized Dad was such a romantic in his own conservative way. He'd probably never overtly expressed love to my mother in their thirty-five-plus years of marriage.

Maneel threw Dad a bland smile. "Well then, if you and Mom are still in love, why can't I say the same thing? One's wife doesn't have to be Konkani for a man to stay in love with her all his life, does she?"

"I . . . suppose not," conceded Dad. But he still didn't look convinced.

Mom patted Maneel's face. "Maybe in a few weeks you'll feel differently, *babba*," she said, using her term of endearment reserved for him. "I've heard that sometimes these love affairs fizzle out."

I turned to Mom. "Where'd you hear that?"

She made a vague gesture with her hand. "I think it was Dr. Ruth or Joyce Brothers or someone like that. I know it was some woman who's an authority on the subject of love and relationships."

"Mom, I'm serious about Naseem," interrupted Maneel, bringing our focus back to the issue in question. "I'm not going to feel differently. Face it, your son's in love with a Muslim girl and wants to marry her."

Mom rolled her eyes, something she rarely did.

"And I need you and Dad to help me face Naseem's parents," added Maneel. "They're conservative Muslims."

With a resigned sigh Mom rose to her feet. "I guess it could have been worse."

"How?" asked Dad.

"One of my colleagues recently found out his young son has been living with a middle-aged man for three years."

"Hmm," Dad grunted in agreement.

Mom glanced at Maneel. "Dad and I are going upstairs to discuss this. If you want our help in dealing with this girl's parents, we have to come up with a plan." She made her way out of the room and looked over her shoulder at Dad, her silent cue.

Dad reluctantly got up and followed her.

The three of us drew a combined breath of relief.

"Well, that wasn't so bad," I said.

"Yeah." Maneel looked like a burden had been lifted from his shoulders. "Two down, two more to go. You think they're convinced enough to give Naseem's parents a run for their money?"

I picked up the remote control for the TV. "Mom and Dad want to see you happy. They'll do whatever they can. No one's more determined than Mom when she's on a crusade."

"You think so?"

"I know so. Besides, we did a good job of convincing them that Naseem is the best thing this family has seen since baby Mahesh's birth."

Ignoring my mocking remark, Mahesh asked Maneel, "For all the hard work Meena and I did on your behalf, what do we get from you?"

Maneel sank lower into the soft couch, closed his eyes, made himself more comfortable. "Name your price."

"Dinner and a movie?" Mahesh's idea of a treat was generally modest. The poor boy was used to the pittance he was paid as an intern.

"That's too chintzy for the kind of labor we put in," I countered. "I'd say we've earned at least a Broadway show and dinner in New York City."

Maneel opened one eye and glared at me. "Should've known

you'd come up with something big and expensive." He closed his eyes again. "What the heck, I'm in a generous mood. I'll spring for a show and dinner. I'll ask Naseem to book tickets for all four of us on Mahesh's next weekend off."

I beamed at Mahesh. "That's what's called *negotiating.*"

Chapter 16

Saturday afternoon, I got a call from Prajay. Ignoring my ecstatic heart leaping like a toad, I managed to keep my conversation on an even keel. "Hi, Prajay."

"Meena, I'm hoping you've calmed down a little since last Sunday. I wanted to call you earlier in the week but—"

"What stopped you?" I asked tartly.

"I decided to give you a few days to think about what I'd said that night."

"What you'd *said*, Prajay?"

"You know exactly what I said."

"Oh, you mean that stuff about how you're old enough to be my father, and so big that one touch is likely to shatter my fragile body?"

His sigh was clearly audible. "I didn't mean it that way, Meena. And sarcasm doesn't suit a charming and refined lady like you."

"Charming and refined? This after you made it abundantly clear that you found me repulsive?" I tried hard to keep the bitterness out of my voice, but it was impossible. The emotions I had suppressed for nearly a week were churning in my gut now and threatening to erupt.

"I most certainly didn't say that."

"But you implied it."

"I suppose there's no point in arguing over it when you've made up your mind to misinterpret my words and actions. Since that's beyond my control, I just want you to know that I value our friendship very much. I think you're a smart young lady and will do well in your career. I want to thank you for all the work you do for Rathnaya. And for me personally."

The conversation was clearly leading to some sort of conclusion. It had all the signs. "Is this a way of saying good-bye, Prajay?"

"Not good-bye but so long. I'm leaving for Washington tomorrow. The negotiations here are completed, and the acquisition is going through nicely."

"Good for you." I said grudgingly.

"We'll be adding all the new company's employees on to our payroll as of next week. Nishant will take care of that. My job here is basically over."

And I'm over, too. "I see." My throat was closing up. I'd never see him again. If he happened to come back for other business-related trips, I might run into him. Maybe. There was nothing more to keep him here.

"I wanted to say a proper good-bye to you before I left," he said. "I waited a whole week to let you cool off."

"Good-bye, then."

"Not like this, Meena. Too much has happened between us for a telephone farewell. May I stop by your house this evening?" He paused. "Or if it's more convenient, can we meet somewhere?"

He was afraid to ask me over to his house. He was scared that I'd throw myself at him again. That's why he wanted to meet in a public place. I wasn't going to let him humiliate and hurt me further. "I have a date this evening."

He remained silent for a second. "I understand. Take care of yourself and stay in touch. You know my e-mail address and my phone number in the Washington office."

"Sure." The Washington office, but not his home. He wouldn't even share his home phone number for fear of being stalked by me. I swallowed the lump that felt as large and sour as a lemon in my throat. "Good luck in your quest for a six-foot bride."

" 'Bye, Meena."

As I hung up the phone, the lump grew to the size of a grape-fruit. I collapsed on my bed and cried. I'd been crying a lot lately. For years I hadn't wept in the real sense, and now I was making up for it. Love was supposed to be an uplifting emotion, a time to smile, and yet for me it had turned out to be a surefire method of turning on the waterworks.

The first day I'd met Prajay Nayak I'd cried because of phys-ical pain, and since then I'd been weeping from emotional agony.

I needed to put a stop to this sniveling at once—start behav-ing like a grown woman and a professional.

That evening I took extra care with my clothes and makeup. Deepak wasn't taking me to a restaurant quite as formal as where Prajay had taken me, but I wanted to look my best. When I went downstairs, dressed in my pearl gray dress, Mom gave me a curious look. "Going to a party?"

I shook my head, the silver chandelier earrings swinging. "I have a date." At her slight frown I quickly added, "He's a South Indian systems analyst who moved here from India some years ago."

The frown cleared. A little. "What's his name?"

"Deepak Iyer."

"Must be from Chennai. The name sounds like he's from the south." She waved at me while I got my jacket out of the closet and put it on. "Have fun."

I chuckled as I closed the door behind me and walked toward my car. This business with Maneel and Naseem had probably made it easier for me to see a South Indian man. Mom had looked almost pleased about my date, even though Deepak wasn't Konkani. In Mom's book, the very fact that I had a date was a good thing; that Deepak Iyer was a Hindu man with a good job was as close to the proverbial icing on the cake as it would get—when compared to Maneel's situation, anyway.

We met at Katmandu, a trendy waterfront restaurant along the Delaware River in Trenton. The place was mobbed, and Deepak and I had to wait for nearly twenty minutes before we were seated. With its laidback, Caribbean-island decor and eclectic cuisine, it was a popular eatery for the younger crowd.

Salsa music played in the background while waiters and waitresses dressed in skimpy, colorful outfits served the patrons. Later, they would clear the center of the floor, and there would be plenty of spirited dancing.

I ordered a strawberry daiquiri and Deepak ordered a dark beer to go with our appetizer of chips and warm artichoke dip. After a few sips of my cold and seriously sweet drink, I felt a whole lot better. Prajay Nayak was already sliding from the front toward the center of my brain. I intended to transport him to the very back and then eliminate him entirely.

Even Deepak started to look good in his Indian shirt of indigo silk and with lots of extra gel in his hair. His cologne was a bit potent, but mixed in with the scents of sizzling onions, peppers, and barbecued ribs being served at the neighboring table, it didn't smell bad at all.

While we waited for my blackened tilapia and Deepak's jerk chicken to arrive, we sipped our drinks and talked. Deepak filled me in on some of the new employees who would be joining him and his coworkers soon. He didn't seem happy about the prospect of sharing space with the newcomers.

"Bloody stupid of Nayak and Rathod to go out and buy one more company, *yaar,*" he grumbled. "We were already crowded in that building; now they're making the cubicles even smaller."

"It's all part of a growing business, Deepak," I said, scooping up some of the artichoke dip with a chip and popping it in my mouth.

"Corporate greed is what it is." He took a swig of beer and made a face. "These two guys have more money than all of us put together, and yet they go out and look for more."

"Nothing wrong with wanting to get rich—as long as they're doing it legally and honestly."

"Doing it on the workers' backs."

"Both Nishant and Prajay work long hours, and they're very hands-on in their management style. You can't accuse them of laziness while making their employees work like dogs."

"I don't know about that, Meena. At least Nishant we see every day, but the other fellow—who knows what he does in Washington to justify that kind of income?"

Despite Prajay's current number one status on my black list, I was annoyed at Deepak's assumption that Prajay was some sort of capitalist menace. "That's not a fair depiction of Prajay Nayak, you know. He works very hard and treats his employees well."

"That is a matter for debate. He keeps bagging these big contracts in Washington, and yet our salary increase was a mere three percent last year. If that's not corporate greed, then what is?"

Deepak's habit of talking with his mouth full was beginning to irritate me as much as his denigration of Prajay and Nishant. "Do I detect a hint of envy here?"

"I'm only stating a fact."

I made some quick calculations in my head and narrowed my eyes at Deepak. "Tell me something: If you had the exact same job at another New Jersey company of comparable size and reputation, would you be making more money?"

Deepak chewed on his chip and took a second or two to answer. "I don't know."

"Come on, Deepak, be honest. You make a better salary than any of your counterparts in other companies in the tri-state area. I did plenty of research on salaries and benefits before I interviewed with Rathnaya, so I know for a fact that they pay very well. Even with the three percent, we all earn a lot more than others in the industry. What other company gives such hefty bonuses to their salespeople? Last year, Prajay and Nishant gave away three new cars to their top producers."

"Wait." Deepak held up a finger to make his point. "That is for publicity purposes—photos in the newspapers and all that. Do you think it's because they care about their employees?"

I paused while our waiter placed our steaming plates of food on the table. With a polite thank-you to him, I turned my gaze back to Deepak. "Yes, I believe they care about their employees.

We get a fair number of holidays, flextime hours, and vacation and sick days, plus generous medical and dental benefits."

"All major companies give those."

"And, because our employees are nearly ninety percent Indian, we even get a day off for Diwali in addition to the traditional American holidays," I argued, referring to the Hindu festival of lights.

He chuckled. "You sound like a commercial for Rathnaya."

"I am Rathnaya's PR manager, remember?"

Deepak was a fast eater and nearly a quarter of the way into his meal while I continued talking. But he looked up now. "Those two fellows are still too damn rich for their own good. You should have sued them for the accident you suffered."

With my fork held midway between the plate and my mouth, I stared at him. "It was an *accident*. Most people don't go suing someone over an accident."

"Of course they do, if it happens at their place of work—especially if the employer himself caused it."

"It's just not right." My sense of outrage simmered. "It's not decent behavior, period."

"When that big fellow pushes someone your size and you get hurt, you should get compensated for it, don't you think?"

Suddenly I lost my appetite and put my fork down. Most of my meal was still on the plate. "Whatever gave you the idea that he pushed me?"

"Gargi Bansal told me Prajay Nayak knocked you down."

I should have known Gargi had been running around the office making up outrageous stories. "Why would he deliberately knock me down?"

Deepak threw me a meaningful smile. "I don't know. Maybe he had his eye on you? This was his way of getting to know you better?"

"That's ridiculous." I was seething, and I let Deepak know it. "You can tell Gargi Bansal that *I* was the one who was careless. *I* was the one who rushed out of the elevator like a fool and fell on my . . . Never mind." I didn't owe him any details.

"Oh, I see now: *You* fell to get *his* attention."

"That's not what I'm saying. It was an accident, pure and simple. Poor Prajay was beside himself with worry. And he's been very kind to me since the incident."

"I heard about his offering you a lift in his car. Perfect opportunity to get to know you even better?" Deepak had the gall to wink at me.

"He was being generous. And you can tell your friend Gargi to keep her nose out of other people's business."

Deepak cleaned up the last morsel on his plate and raised his brows at me. "Looks like you don't like Gargi very much."

"Very perceptive of you." I gulped my water and looked down at my plate. What a shame. The tilapia was excellent, but I was in no mood to eat it. "If you're finished eating, I'd like to leave, Deepak."

He studied my plate. "But you haven't eaten yet."

"I'm not hungry."

"No dessert or coffee either?" When I shook my head, he glanced at the dance floor, which was just being set up. "Little bit of dancing at least?"

"My ankle is still not up to it, thank you."

"All right, then." He signaled the waiter for our check and turned his attention back to me. "All the more reason why you should sue Nayak. If several weeks after your fall you're still experiencing pain, then you have a legitimate reason for a lawsuit."

"I *don't* want to sue anyone. And I *don't* want to discuss it anymore. Case closed."

"Are you angry with me or something, *yaar?*" He looked genuinely perplexed.

"I'm livid!" I gave Deepak a fuming look and turned my face toward the dance floor. Couples were already getting ready to shake their hips to some hot Caribbean music. Under ordinary circumstances I liked that sort of energetic dancing, but today I didn't want to dance, and honestly couldn't. I didn't want to injure my ankle once again, and I felt no desire to rub my body up against Deepak's.

And all this time he had had no idea that his words had enraged me. What did he think I was going to do? Smile and agree that a lawsuit was a brilliant idea and then dance with him? What a jerk.

Until now I'd thought of him as a not-too-bad sort of guy, a little grating at times, but this evening he had revealed a few other qualities. He was petty, covetous, a bit vicious. I'd seen a distinct gleam of devilish pleasure in his eyes when he'd talked about the lawsuit.

He wanted to use me to get his revenge on two decent men he envied and disliked. How could a man enjoy a good salary and then sit there calmly drinking and eating while dreaming up ways of making his employer's life miserable?

Deepak Iyer was not a nice man. Well, I was sure about one thing. I wasn't going out with him again. He and Gargi Bansal were perfectly suited to each other. Maybe they'd hook up and start their own company someday. Then they could go out and hire folks like themselves.

When our check arrived I insisted on paying for my half of the meal. I didn't want to be obligated to Deepak for anything. When he protested, I merely held up my hand. "This is the twenty-first century, Deepak. We girls do pay our way at times."

"Suit yourself," he said with a resigned shrug and accepted the cash I handed him. We waited a few more minutes while our waiter processed Deepak's credit card and then brought it back to the table for his signature.

Outside the restaurant, I said a polite good night and got into my car. I was still bristling and didn't want to make the mistake of saying anything more to antagonize Deepak Iyer. Now that I'd had a glimpse of his mean streak, I didn't want to give him a weapon for wreaking future vengeance on me.

I got the unpleasant feeling that I'd already angered him enough to make him a potential enemy.

As I observed Deepak driving away in his black Honda, I picked up my cell phone. It was a little after nine o'clock, and I didn't want to go home yet. The prospect of spending a Saturday night alone or with my parents was depressing, in case they happened to be home. I wondered if Rita and Anoop would mind my company for an hour or so.

My voice must have sounded a little forlorn because Rita said, "What's the matter?"

"Nothing," I said with a laugh. "Are you and Anoop still honeymooning or could you spare me an hour? I am at loose ends tonight and thought I'd spend some time with you."

"Of course we can spare you an hour. Are you in the mood for a movie?"

"Umm . . ." A movie didn't appeal at the moment.

"We have a Netflix DVD we haven't seen yet." Rita must have pitied my plight—a single woman alone on a Saturday night, so desperate as to beg to foist herself upon her honey-mooning friends.

"If it's all the same to you, I'd rather just hang out with you for a while and talk."

"Then come right over. We were just about to open a con-tainer of mango-pineapple ice cream."

"Sounds delicious. Save me a scoop."

I started the car and headed for Rita's house. I needed a friend tonight. My heart was aching from thinking about Prajay. He was leaving tomorrow. Gone from my life.

Chapter 17

Visiting with Rita and Anoop was a good decision. The ice cream was sheer heaven. Since I'd eaten very little at the restaurant—no thanks to Deepak Iyer—I ate two helpings.

Rita and Anoop looked like a comfortably married couple already. He was in faded jeans and a T-shirt while Rita wore baggy pajamas.

"I feel bad about encroaching on your Saturday night plans," I said to them, putting on my contrite face.

"Don't be silly. We love having you here."

"But it's your honeymoon."

Anoop smiled and squeezed Rita's shoulder. They were about the same height, so their shoulders were almost on a level. "We can't be honeymooning every minute of the day."

Rita licked the ice cream off her spoon. "If I eat like this every night, I'm likely to get as fat as a tub, and the honeymoon will be over before I know it."

"Baby, you can get as fat as you want. I'll love you just the same," said Anoop, and he smacked a kiss on Rita's head.

I grinned at their silliness. "That's what all men say, and then they change their minds when it really happens."

Anoop rose to collect the empty bowls. "Then I'll eat more and get fat, too. We'll get fat together."

Rita nodded approvingly. "That's the spirit, honey."

"He's such a sweetheart," I said as we watched him disappear into the kitchen. He was a really nice guy—average height and weight, average looks, superior brain. But he had a big heart.

"He sure is," sighed Rita. The most blissful expression came over her round face surrounded by masses of naturally curly hair. She had the look of a contented angel sitting on her very own cloud. It was a look that sent a stab of envy right through my belly.

While Anoop loaded the dishwasher, Rita looked at me and lowered her voice. "What's wrong?"

I brushed it off with a shrug. "Nothing's wrong. In fact I was on a date earlier. He turned out to be a jerk, so I got out of it as fast as I could."

"Anyone I know?"

"No. It's the same guy from work who I went out with the other day."

"Didn't I tell you not to date FOBs? They have such antiquated views on everything."

"He's modern enough, but I told him off when he suggested that I bring a lawsuit against my employer."

"What for?"

"My accident."

"Oh." Rita made a face. "Why is it that everyone in the world thinks America is one big courtroom?"

"You have to admit we have a disproportionate number of frivolous lawsuits."

"I suppose."

"But I told this guy to get lost. I wouldn't dream of suing nice guys like Prajay and Nishant. They've been good to me. Since my accident Prajay has been exceptionally kind and thoughtful."

I noticed Rita's interest perk up. "Isn't he Konkani like you?"

"Yeah."

"So, what else about him interests you?

"That's about it."

Rita had been my best friend far too long not to see through my nonchalance. "You're interested in him, aren't you?"

It was no use pretending. I took a deep breath. "I am, but—"
Just then Anoop returned to the living room and sat down. Although I'd known him for a while now, it would be embarrassing to bare my soul in front of him. I shot to my feet. "I really should be going home."

Rita gave me a stern look. "Sit down, Meena. I want to hear your story."

"There is no story. I told you everything."

Rita glanced at her husband. "Sweetie, would you mind if I talked to Meena for a bit?"

"I'll go watch TV upstairs." Anoop shot to his feet and headed for the staircase. " 'Bye, Meena. Nice seeing you again."

" 'Bye, Anoop. I'm sorry, but I promise not to keep your wife away from you for too long."

"Hey, what are friends for?"

We watched him climb the stairs. Then Rita turned to me. "Okay, I want to know everything. Something weird is going on with you."

"You have to promise not to tell anyone, okay?"

"Do you even need to ask?"

"No, but this is like . . . so embarrassing."

Rita patted the seat next to her on the couch, inviting me to sit beside her. "I even told you about the first time Anoop and I had sex and how badly it went." She tossed me a self-deprecating smile. "Now *that's* embarrassing."

Laughing, I went to sit beside her. "But it got better and better, right?" She nodded, and I went back to my story. "It all started the day I collided into Prajay Nayak and fell down. At first I thought he looked scary, with his big nose and six-and-a-half-foot body. But then he carried me in his arms to his office and hovered over me, brought me hazelnut-flavored coffee and . . . made me feel pampered."

"Hmm." Rita looked impressed.

"By the end of the hour I'd changed my mind about his looks. When he smiled, he looked rather attractive."

"Then what?"

"He let me fall asleep on the couch in his office after I took some strong painkillers. He carried me again all the way down to the parking lot and to my boss's car. Then he sent me roses the next day."

"Nice guy."

"And oh, he even borrowed someone's beat-up Toyota and drove me back and forth to work for several days. He gave up his Corvette to make me comfortable. Isn't that sweet?"

"Extraordinarily sweet. A guy doesn't give up his Corvette for anything—if he can help it."

"That's what I said. But because of it I was foolish enough to think he was interested in me."

Rita motioned to me to continue.

"Turns out I was wrong." The familiar lump was forming in my throat. "He asked me to come secretly to his office one evening after work, so I thought he wanted to ask me for a date. Stupid me—I went prancing into his office with bells on my toes."

Wide-eyed, Rita stared at me. "What did he say?"

"Wait till you hear this. You'd never guess in a million years. I'm still in shock. Not only did he *not* ask me out, he had a special project for me. He's been unsuccessful in finding the right woman despite dating a parade of women. He wanted me to help him place personal ads in newspapers and with Internet matchmaking services for the perfect woman."

"What?"

"He wants someone who's six feet tall."

Rita's mouth fell open. "Holy cow! He asked *you* to help him find her?"

"He wants her to be well-educated, too, and in a nice career, if possible. Looks don't matter, he says. If she just happens to be attractive, well, then it's a plus—according to him."

Rita wrinkled her nose. "He wants an Amazon in his bed. Yikes!"

"Not only that, he paid me to do it. He said he pays a standard fee to his consultants and since this was sort of . . . a personal consultation, he was going to pay me the same."

"The man's insane. He couldn't find his own woman? He had

to hire a pretty young employee to do his dirty work? Especially one who happened to be interested in him?"

I realized Rita hadn't quite grasped my dilemma. "But he didn't know how I felt about him. Besides, he's somewhat like my dad—very analytical and nerdy. In a classy sort of way, though," I added. "He seemed to think it was perfectly normal to go about looking for a future wife in the same manner one would seek a car or a house, or a mutual fund."

"And you did as he requested?"

"What choice did I have? When my boss asks me to do a special project for him and pays me to do it, what do I say to him? Shove it? Get lost? Or was I supposed to tell him that I was interested in him and therefore he shouldn't look any further?"

Rita started chewing on her nails like she usually did when she was thinking hard. "I guess not. But then I've never heard of anything so wacky."

"Neither had I."

"So you agreed and completed his project?"

I heaved a long sigh. "Yes. But there's more. When dozens and dozens of responses started coming in, he was overwhelmed, and he extended my responsibilities a bit. He said he had no time to look at them, so he wanted me to study them, sort them, and pick the top four or five candidates so he could contact them."

Rita groaned. "This is getting more and more bizarre. Why didn't he get his secretary to do it?"

"He didn't want anyone to know. Because my expertise is in marketing and PR, and because I'm a fellow Konkani, he thought I was the perfect individual to handle his secret project. I was sworn to secrecy. You're the only person I've confided in."

"Hmm." Rita was chewing her coral-painted nails vigorously, ruining her manicure. "I won't tell anyone."

"Wait till you hear the rest of the story. I sorted through the responses. And you should have seen some of them—outrageous. Female wrestlers, women with thyroid problems, ex-convicts, half the female population of India . . . you name it, they were there on that list. So I had quite a job sorting the better ones from the crazies." I swallowed to keep the threatening tears at bay. "I made a neat little database with seven good candidates and handed it over to him."

"He never noticed you even once?"

The tears were close to spilling over now, but I was holding on. "Last Saturday he asked me to go to Great Adventure with him and his little nephew and niece. The kids were cute, and I had the best day of my life. Prajay was fun, and we laughed a lot and . . . oh God . . ."

I sniffled, and Rita silently handed me a box of tissues.

Grabbing a tissue, I dried my eyes. "For a day I pretended we were a family—he and I and our two kids . . . you know . . . like a pretty picture book."

"How sweet!" Rita looked like she was about to cry, too. She covered us both with the fleece blanket sitting on the back of the couch—just like we used to do when we watched videos together on weekends when we were teenagers.

"Oh, Rita, I did the most stupid thing in the world."

"What?" She knew by now of course.

"By Saturday night I had fallen in love with Prajay Nayak. I was a goner. Five-foot me was madly in love with the NBA-player-type Prajay. Talk about a failure waiting to happen."

"You poor thing. No wonder you look so miserable." This time Rita did start to shed tears.

We'd read many of the same romance novels and had the same kind of foolish belief in true love. Fortunately for her, Anoop had come into her life and swept her off her feet. I, on the other hand, had not found anyone. Until now.

And he was the wrong man.

"You don't know the half of it. On Sunday he took me out to dinner at a Thai restaurant." When Rita nodded, I said, "On the way back, he invited me to go up to his townhouse."

"What preposterous project did he have for you this time?"

"He wanted me to help him analyze the spreadsheet."

"Oh puleeez!" Rita blew her nose. "The bastard made you take *his* karma in *your* hands and mold it into shape for him."

"Exactly." I realized Rita had described the situation perfectly.

"And you willingly did it, you foolish girl?"

"Not willingly." My voice was raspy from trying to suppress the tears. "Later on he offered me ice cream and then . . . and then he kissed me."

I heard Rita's sharp intake of breath. "Omigod. How was it?"

This time I burst into noisy tears. "I—I loved it. Prajay's a great kisser. And I wanted more."

"Then you should have asked for more, honey." Rita pressed yet another tissue into my hand.

"That's the problem. He backed off and apologized. He said it amounted to sexual harassment on his part because I was an innocent and sweet young employee who he should have treated with respect and that it was wrong of him to take advantage of me."

Rita blew her nose hard. It sounded like a duck quacking. "He thinks you're a sweet virgin?"

"I told him I wasn't an innocent babe and that I had dated before, but he wouldn't listen. He gave me every reason to put an end to our relationship—or whatever it is we have. He says he's too rough, too tall, too big, too old . . . and too damn everything for a woman like me."

"Oh boy." Rita shook her head sadly.

"So according to him we're entirely wrong for each other. He says I'm a lovely and smart young lady and I'll make some man a wonderful wife and some kids a great mother in the future."

Rita gave me her best-friend look. "He's right, you know. When the right guy comes along, you'll make the best wife and mother."

I was racked by sobs and couldn't stop myself. "But Prajay is the right guy, Rita. I'm in love with him. I want him and no other guy. I've had relationships before. I've known a lot of men, but I've never, ever felt like this about anyone."

Rita put her arms around me and rocked me like a baby.

"Oh, Meena, Meena, what a horrible thing to happen to you. That big, clueless giant doesn't deserve you, honey. You can do a lot better, believe me."

"But I don't want to do better." I gave Rita a teary-eyed look. "Would you want anyone else but Anoop?"

She shook her head.

"Well, there you go. I'm in love with Prajay Nayak. And if I can't have him, then I guess I'll stay single."

Rita let out a laugh that clearly said it was a stupid idea. "Don't be silly. By this time next month you will have forgotten the man. He's not worthy of you, and you'll realize that after a while."

I shook my head vigorously. "Not likely—not the way I feel. I'm hurting like mad. I feel like my life is over."

Rita smacked my hand. "Don't say that. I don't want to hear such crazy talk. If you have your heart set on the giant with the big nose, we'll figure something out."

It was my turn to laugh. "Figure what out? He's returning to Washington tomorrow. And he doesn't want me. He wants a six-foot woman who can look him in the eye—who understands his . . . bigness. He thinks any physical contact between him and me will shatter me to pieces. He believes I'm fragile because I'm small."

"He's an idiot," Rita said.

I dried my tears again and discarded the tissues in the trash can. "I always hated being tiny. Now I hate it even more."

"You may be tiny, but you're beautiful," declared Rita. "You have more heart and spirit and spunk than any six-foot dinosaur out there. And if that Nayak guy had any brains in that big head of his, he'd have realized what a prize you are. Instead he's blindly groping around for some woman who shops at the Big and Tall Men's Store. What a dunce."

"Yeah, dunce." I blew my nose and watched the balls of tissue in the trash can piling up. Rita and I had gone through half a box of tissues.

We sat huddled under the blanket for a long time, sniffling

and denigrating men for having no brains whatsoever. That's how Anoop found us nearly an hour later. He took one look at us and stopped dead. "Are you two all right?"

I immediately jumped up from the sofa. "Sorry, Anoop. I didn't mean to burden your wife with my problems."

"I . . . It's okay, Meena." He looked at his wife with deep concern. I could see he didn't really mean what he'd said to me. His eyes said he hated me for making his sweetheart cry.

"No, Anoop, I'm really sorry. I came here to chat a little and ended up making Rita my official therapist. I'll leave you two alone now."

Rita stood up and put her arms around me. "Don't worry too much, okay? Everything will be all right. You wait and see."

I gave her a faux smile. "I'm feeling better already. You make a great counselor, Rita Tandon." It felt odd to say her married name. I wasn't quite used to it yet.

"Don't be silly. I did nothing," Rita assured me.

"You did more than you realize." I patted her hand and took off.

I left them standing in the doorway of their townhouse, their arms entwined. It was a nice, warm image to carry in my mind. Maybe Rita was right. A month from now, I'd laugh about this whole business with Prajay.

But deep down I knew it wasn't going to happen. Next month, next year, next century—it wasn't likely to happen.

Chapter 18

Just when I thought the cloud following me would never give way to light, a little ray of sunshine appeared on our doorstep—in the person of my great-aunt, Chandra Kamat, otherwise known as Akka.

On a cool, sunny Saturday afternoon, Mom's youngest sister, Madhuri Bhat, arrived from Connecticut, with Akka in tow.

This old lady was my mom's paternal aunt, my grandfather's youngest sister. Everyone called her Akka. Big sister. She was a feisty, seventy-eight-year-old widow, and she wasn't very popular with my mother and her sisters.

They referred to Akka variously as the misfit, the renegade, the black sheep—all because she had disdained arranged marriage and married a man of her choice. Although he'd belonged to the right caste and community, the very fact that she had chosen *love marriage,* as those kinds of marriages are called in Indian culture, was enough to make her notorious in her day.

Evidently Akka's behavior had been judged as scandalous sixty years ago: An eighteen-year-old had disobeyed her father and married a man who fell far below the family's high expectations. Instead of marrying the rich businessman picked for her, she had insisted on marrying a poor college professor because she thought he was handsome and charming.

The marriage had been a happy one and had produced three healthy kids, and everything had been forgiven later—but never forgotten. My mom and her relatives still talked about Akka's disregard for convention. Consequently Akka was deemed a corrupting influence on the young folks in the family.

"Keep the impressionable kids away from Akka," was the general mantra amongst the family members.

Personally I was delighted to see the little old lady. She was my favorite great-aunt. She was utterly, deliciously different from my grandmother and the other elders I knew. Slim and petite, with an infectious smile, Akka still dyed her hair, wore modern glasses instead of granny spectacles, spoke good English, and giggled. She was even known to tell an off-color joke on occasion. And she loved thriller novels and Bollywood movies.

She was totally cool.

Mom cleared her throat when she saw me coming down the staircase in a rather short skirt to greet Akka, but I chose to ignore Mom. To make up for the skirt I bent down to touch Akka's feet in the traditional manner of greeting an elder.

She caught my shoulders before I reached for her feet. "*Ayyo,* there is no need to do any of those old-fashioned things, Meena." Instead she drew me into a hug.

"Hello, Akka. It's great to see you again," I said with a grin and returned the warm embrace. She smelled like she always did—of jasmine-scented talcum powder. Her hair was an unnatural black, pulled back in a bun, high on the head—quite chic. Her pale green and white-print crepe sari looked fresh with its matching green blouse and accessorized by a simple string of freshwater pearls and matching earrings.

Mom insisted on touching Akka's feet despite her protests. Akka winked at me over Mom's head. She clearly thought this was funny: the fifty-something woman acting more old-fashioned than her septuagenarian aunt. Nonetheless she patted Mom's head and murmured the expected: "*Dev baren koro.*" God bless you.

Dad knew Akka's modern ways, so he offered her a handshake. "Welcome, Akka," he said. "Hope you are enjoying your East Coast trip."

"Ramdas, you are looking good," she said with a diplomatic twinkle in her eye. "I see Kaveri is taking very good care of you." Everyone knew the gray in Dad's hair had multiplied, and he'd gained a few pounds around his middle—marks of a man on the wrong side of sixty.

The past week had been so dismal and I had cried so much that I badly needed some cheering up. I couldn't think of anyone better than Akka to put some laughter back into my life. I'd spent time with her often enough to know she was a pistol.

I helped Dad carry Akka's bulging suitcases into the house and up to the guest room. Akka always came with interesting presents for everyone in the family, hence the excessive amount of luggage.

"Where are my favorite grandnephews?" she asked, looking around for Maneel and Mahesh as she and Madhuri-pachi were ushered into the kitchen for refreshments.

"Maneel will come by later. Mahesh is working as usual," I replied.

"This medical doctor business is too much stress and hard work. *Paap*," she clucked. Poor soul. Konkanis tended to use the term liberally to express sympathy, although it was a homophone, its other meaning being sin. "Mahesh and Amrita are working all the time."

"What's so *paap* about Mahesh and Amrita?" snorted Madhuri-pachi. "They're single, living at home, and don't have to lift a finger. My sisters and I had husbands, housework, children, and a similar schedule to juggle when we were their age. We didn't have any help or anybody to say *paap*."

With a good-natured smile Akka patted Madhuri-pachi's shoulder. "I used to say that about you and your sisters all the time when you first came to America and started your residencies. I used to worry about how you young girls managed such busy lives. Now it is Mahesh and Amrita's turn."

Madhuri-pachi and Mom exchanged that wry look that often passed between the sisters. *Yeah, right, like anyone in India ever knows or cares about how hard our lives are.*

After everyone was comfortably seated, Mom asked Akka and Madhuri-pachi, "What would you like to drink? We have soda, orange juice, and iced tea."

Madhuri-pachi asked for iced tea, but Akka cheerfully replied, "Can I have my usual, please?"

Mom turned to Dad with a meaningful look. Akka's usual was scotch and club soda. My folks drank very little alcohol, and that mostly at parties, so the booze was stored in the sideboard in the formal dining room. Dad made his way there with a tight expression.

To add to Akka's long list of misdemeanors, her liking for alcohol was a definite sore spot with Mom.

"An old widow should be reading scriptures, eating vegetarian food, and knitting sweaters. Instead Akka insists on drinking liquor and eating meat," Mom grumbled once in a while. "Sometimes I wonder if she was adopted or something. She's so different from my father and their other siblings."

Akka had a taste for mutton curry—goat meat cooked in a fiery hot brown sauce, as well as grilled *tandoori* chicken, kebabs, and spicy fried fish. Although my parents and aunts and uncles had converted to non-vegetarianism for convenience after moving to the U.S., they still disapproved of elderly folks enjoying it.

Madhuri-pachi generally turned up her nose at the mention of Akka. The old lady had been at Madhuri's place for two whole weeks, and I could see my aunt was up to her dark eyeballs with Akka's shenanigans. Akka traveled to the East Coast every year for a six-week visit.

She had a married daughter, Kalpa, who lived near San Francisco, and Akka had come to live with Kalpa and her husband and their teenage son a few years ago, after she'd become a widow. Her annual visit to the East Coast was divided equally between our house and my two aunts' homes.

Mom and my aunts treated Akka's visit with the kind of enthusiasm they reserved for the annual flu season. They tolerated it with their teeth clenched and some discreet eye-rolls. Of course, as gracious Indian hostesses brought up to honor and respect elders, they showed her all the hospitality they could afford.

Both my uncles and my dad seemed to like Akka well enough, maybe because they didn't spend as much time with her as their wives did.

Akka's stay with Madhuri-pachi was now over, and Madhuri had driven her down from Connecticut like a hot brick to be dropped in Mom's lap. Besides, Thanksgiving was just a few days away, and it was convenient to have Akka spend it with her eldest niece's family. Two weeks later, Akka would be dispatched to Shabari-pachi's house in North Jersey.

Everyone would wait for the day Akka could be hugged good-bye and put on a flight to San Francisco. They'd all have a year's respite before Akka's next trip.

Last week, on hearing that Akka was coming to New Jersey for her usual stint, Mom and Shabari-pachi had groaned, "Here we go again."

Shabari had sighed. "I'm so stressed. I can't understand why all our children admire Akka so much."

"What's not to admire?" I'd asked cheerfully. "She's such fun for an old lady."

Mom had given me a bland look. "Fun in your book, because she encourages all the silly things you kids do."

"What silly things?" I'd looked at Mom with my most innocent expression, despite knowing what she was referring to. Akka thought it was okay to have boyfriends, drink alcohol—after one turned twenty-one, of course—and wear trendy clothes.

"Don't give me that wide-eyed look, young lady," Mom had warned me. "I don't want Akka filling your head with nonsense."

I'd rolled my eyes at the naïve remark. "Mom, I don't need a sweet old lady to tell me anything I don't already know."

"In that case, try not to fill *her* head with more," Mom had said. "I have enough on my mind right now with Maneel and his problems."

"Yes, Mom," I'd said obediently.

Mom had been tense ever since Maneel had told her about

Naseem. Mom, Dad, and Maneel had an appointment to meet with Naseem's parents the following weekend. Poor Mom was losing sleep. Dad was frowning more lately and had withdrawn into himself more than usual. They were both worried about Maneel's future.

Although I didn't say it aloud, I was equally worried about Maneel's future.

Dad brought Akka her scotch, and the rest of us sipped our soft drinks along with Mom's crispy fried *piyava bajay*. Onion fritters. Madhuri-pachi was going to stay overnight and then return to Connecticut the following morning. She looked like she was ready to leave now, except Mom wouldn't let her drive a long distance alone after dark.

Akka sipped her scotch and looked around. "So, what is going on with Maneel, Meena, and Mahesh? Any girlfriends, boyfriends?"

Mom winced. Dad squirmed in his seat. I nearly let the cat out of the bag about Naseem, but decided to keep my mouth shut. If Mom and Dad wanted to share the "news," it was their business. And Maneel's.

I was astonished when Mom glumly announced, "Maneel is involved with some entirely unsuitable girl." Her tone seemed to suggest Maneel had lost one lobe of his brain.

Akka sat up. "Really? Who's the girl?"

"Our Maneel is involved?" Madhuri-pachi turned to Mom with her brows raised in dismay. "But he's such a sensible boy."

"I know," said Mom. "We had so many eligible girls' parents asking about a possible *soireek*." Match. "Then he . . . does this."

I'd heard enough. "Mom, that's not fair," I said in his defense. "You're making it sound like Maneel is dating some mutant."

"That's not what I meant," Mom said weakly.

"Why don't you tell them the good part? That she's a successful lawyer and exceptionally attractive?"

"There is that," admitted Mom. "But still, she's . . . a Muslim."

Madhuri-pachi's face couldn't have been more expressive. *"Ayyo Deva!"* Oh God. "Where did he find her?"

I sent my aunt a tolerant smile. "Where a lot of nice girls can be found: in a civilized office in New York."

To my surprise, Dad jumped in to support me. "The girl works for a well-known law firm."

Akka, who'd been sipping her scotch and listening with interest for the last minute or two, beamed. "How nice. A beautiful lawyer. I knew our Maneel had good taste."

Mom and Madhuri-pachi turned twin frowns on Akka. "But she's a *Muslim,*" they said in perfect unison.

"So what?" I protested. "Mom, I thought we went over this, and you and Dad had accepted the fact that Maneel wants to marry Naseem."

"There is a difference between accepting and being resigned to the fact, Meena," explained Mom. To the others she said, "Ram and Maneel and I have an appointment with this girl's parents next weekend."

"Appointment?" Madhuri-pachi looked lost.

"You know . . . to talk about things," Mom explained. "Maneel says they are very strict and will hate the idea of their daughter's getting involved with a Hindu boy."

"This is just like that old Hindi movie," declared Akka. "I can't recall the title." She looked at Mom and Madhuri. "Don't you girls remember that story? A Muslim girl and a Brahmin boy fall in love and both the families are ready to commit suicide rather than let the children get married."

"This is real life, Akka. Please don't reduce it to the level of some silly Bollywood movie." Mom looked thoroughly irked. The old lady had been here less than an hour, and she'd already managed to annoy Mom.

Akka clucked impatiently. "But there is a brilliant solution to your problem in the way the movie ends."

This was interesting. I was getting into this like an ant crawling into a bowl of sugar. "A Bollywood answer to a real-life problem? Let's hear it, Akka."

Akka put her glass on the coffee table for a moment. "In the movie, it is the grandmother who saves the day. She reveals to the angry families that her sister had married outside their caste against everyone's wishes in her youth and she had found everlasting happiness. They all realize that if an old lady could be so happy with an inter-caste marriage, then true love is all that counts, not religion or pride."

"So how did the movie end?" I asked.

"Eventually they have a Brahmin priest and a mullah performing both religious ceremonies." Her eyes turned wistful as she picked up her glass and took another sip of scotch. "Such a nice movie that was. A classic."

Dad shook his head. "Movies generally have happy endings, Akka. We need a practical solution."

"*Arre,* I'm telling you, Ramdas, there *is* a real solution. I should go to this meeting with you. Then I can tell them how I went against my parents' wishes and married a man they thought was unsuitable. But we had a happy marriage, didn't we? He was a good man, and so handsome. Look at our children—so clever and good-looking they are—and so successful. I will bring my photos to the meeting, so they can see for themselves."

Madhuri-pachi had a smirk on her face that said she was secretly enjoying this: the fact that her eldest sister was stuck with Akka's misguided need to help the family. "Akka might have a point, Kaveri," Madhuri said to Mom. I could see right through the tongue-in-cheek remark.

Just then Maneel walked in. The hugging started all over again, with Akka pinching Maneel's cheeks and embarrassing him. "My goodness, so tall and handsome you have become in the last year. Your mummy says you have a beautiful girlfriend and all."

Maneel gave Mom a dark, disapproving frown. "Mom couldn't wait to fill you in on the gossip, huh?" he said, hugging Akka back.

"This is not gossip, *charda,*" chided Akka. "This is a family issue. Your mummy and daddy are trying to find a way to talk to your girlfriend's parents, and I'm trying to help."

"Is that right?" murmured Maneel, then he grabbed a napkin and a handful of *bajay* from the platter. He knew when to shut up and accept the inevitable. At times Akka was like a woman on speeding roller skates.

I was probably the only one who'd been seriously pondering Akka's suggestion. "I think Akka's idea sounds promising," I said after a while.

Everyone gave me a *get real* look, but I persisted. "No, really, most old-fashioned cultures tend to respect the elderly, and we don't have anyone older than Akka at the moment. Why not use that to our advantage? Why not use every trick in the book? If they get a chance to meet Akka, Naseem's family might not dismiss the whole thing as romantic foolishness on the part of two young people."

Mom put on a skeptical scowl while Maneel brightened up. "Meena may be right," he said.

After prolonged arguing over the pros and cons of Akka's presence at the important meeting, everyone eventually agreed that it might be worth trying. They had nothing to lose.

And I felt so damn pleased that *I* was the one who'd more or less persuaded Mom and Dad to accept Akka's offer.

Akka had a goofy grin on her face. I wasn't sure whether it was because she'd succeeded in convincing the family or a result of the drink she was sipping steadily. "See, I knew you all would see the wisdom of my words," she said, and finished the last of her scotch. "Now, let's discuss Thanksgiving. What are we going to cook on Thursday?"

Chapter 19

Akka was proved right. Mom didn't want to admit it. Dad was somewhat willing to acknowledge it. But Maneel seemed ecstatic. Contrary to everyone's expectations, it turned out that Akka put on a superb performance on the day of the big meeting.

Naseem's parents, Dr. and Mrs. Rasul, as expected, were stubbornly opposed to their beloved daughter's marrying outside their Sunni Muslim community. Apparently they had an engineer picked out for her: the son of an immigrant Iraqi family like themselves. But Naseem had turned him down.

As my family returned from the dreaded encounter and walked in the door, I eagerly ran down the stairs to find out Maneel's fate. Fully expecting to see long, glum faces, I was astonished to see none.

A beaming Maneel had his arm around Akka's slim shoulders. "You deserve two glasses of scotch today. In fact, I'm going to buy you a bottle of the best single malt there is."

"Oh, you silly boy, don't waste your money on me," said Akka. "Go buy something for your pretty girlfriend instead."

Mom and Dad looked a little weary, but the battle scars I'd expected were curiously absent. "Thank God, that's over," said Mom as she took off her sandals in the foyer. "I don't think I could stand any more drama for the day."

She had worn her most conservative, loose two-piece *salwar-kameez* outfit after debating whether a sari would be better. Dad had come up with the idea that a sari might overemphasize our Hindu-ness and antagonize the Rasuls even further. Apparently Naseem's mother had also worn a two-piece outfit, proving Dad's hunch was right.

"Looks like things went well," I said, hoping someone would share all the juicy details. They all seemed to be immersed in their own thoughts.

"Not at first," grumbled Dad. "That man nearly threw us out of the house. Some nerve. What the hell did he think—that we're riffraff from some primitive corner of the world?" Dad very rarely vented his anger so openly, so I was both amazed and amused. He was wearing a starched cream shirt, gray dress pants, and a coordinated sports jacket. Nobody could've mistaken him for riffraff.

"Well, we showed him, didn't we?" said Mom, sinking onto the family room couch and propping her feet up on the coffee table. "When they heard I was a medical doctor and you have a PhD in engineering, they calmed down."

"Not right away, Mom," reminded Maneel.

"There was more crying and sighing before they calmed down," corrected Akka.

"Didn't Naseem tell them anything about our family before you guys got there?" I asked, wondering why those people had thought my parents were heathens.

Maneel looked embarrassed. "She was afraid they'd refuse to see us, so she told them only seconds before we arrived. She had no time to prepare them."

"That wasn't fair to you." I was disappointed in Naseem. How could she have let Maneel and my parents face the hostile Rasuls in that fashion? But then I could also see how she'd be terrified of her parents, especially if they were the kind who'd do something rash. "So how come you guys look like everything went okay?"

"Thanks to Akka," said Maneel, grinning at the old lady. She was dressed in an old-fashioned Dharmavaram silk sari in a dull shade of ecru. A matching woolen shawl was thrown around her shoulders. Her bun was worn lower to make it appear more conservative. Instead of her modern eyeglasses she wore a pair of horn-rimmed ones she'd pulled out of somewhere. No jewelry of any kind adorned her neck or ears. The idea had been to look as stern, widow-like, and grandmotherly as possible.

"Exactly what did Akka do?"

Akka sat down on the couch next to Mom. "I just told those Rasuls about the misery I went through when my mother and father disapproved of my choice of husbands and how unhappy everyone was and how unnecessary all the fuss had been in the end."

"She did a lot more than that," chimed in Maneel. "She shed a few fake tears and told them how most parents eventually regret their selfishness if they don't look out for their children's happiness." He threw Akka another grateful look. "You were fabulous."

"Oh, it was nothing," said Akka modestly. "And let me tell you, the tears were not fake. I get very emotional when I think of those days, when I was afraid I would never see my family and that I would make my parents ill or something."

I was getting impatient with these little snippets of the episode when I wanted to hear a minute-by-minute account. "Tell me the whole thing, you guys—all the way from the start." I looked at Maneel, all dressed up in a formal blue shirt, well-pressed black slacks, and shiny black shoes. He'd had a haircut the previous day. He looked handsome, solid, professional. "Are you and Naseem getting married or not?"

"I guess we are." Maneel bent down to loosen the laces on his shoes, then took the shoes and socks off and parked his big feet on the coffee table, perpendicular to Mom's. "But it wasn't easy. Naseem's dad yelled at her and called her an infidel. Her mom bawled and hinted at committing suicide because the family would be ruined."

Dad sat in his recliner. "Such dramatics. I have never seen a grown man beat his chest so much."

Mom blew out a tired breath. "And Mrs. Rasul's wailing. I haven't seen that except in movies."

Akka was quiet all this time, probably savoring her victory, so I said to her, "Just what did you say to them, Akka? It must've been compelling."

"Not much, dear. All I told them was that I have not regretted for one minute the decision I made at eighteen."

"Good for you," I cheered on.

"It was my father and mother who regretted their resistance to accepting my husband into the family. Of course, I didn't tell the Rasuls that part," said Akka. "But when my parents died, they went feeling very remorseful about the way they had treated my husband in the beginning."

"They did?" Mom said, suddenly turning alert. Obviously this was news to her.

Akka nodded. "When my father suffered a paralytic stroke, it was my husband who served him, hand and foot." She threw a pointed look at Mom. "Where were your big-shot papa and our other brothers and sisters when our ninety-year-old father had to be bathed and fed like a baby, and needed a bedpan? None of them came forward to take in a dying old man. It was my dear husband, God bless his soul, and I, who took care of him."

Mom looked puzzled. "How come Papa didn't tell us that?"

I watched everyone's expression, intrigued by what appeared to be an ancient but rather dirty family secret coming to light. Maneel looked equally captivated. He and I exchanged a quick glance.

A wry smile crossed Akka's face. "That's because your papa was embarrassed to admit his lack of sense of duty. As the eldest son, it was *his* responsibility. But he and the others didn't want our father because he was a burden—he was bedridden and helpless. Our mother was too timid to ask any of her children for assistance, so my husband and I took both of them into our home. And my husband was only a professor, so all we had was a small, three-room house, while all the others had big houses and servants."

"I didn't know all this," whispered Mom. I could tell she was upset. The father and mother she had adored and thought of as demigods had feet of clay; they had shirked their duty toward their sick, elderly parents. And it was probably dawning on her that Akka, the aunt everybody disapproved of because of her outlandish ways, was the one who came up looking like a hero. "I'm sorry, Akka. I had no idea."

"That's okay, Kaveri," said Akka with a dismissive hand gesture. "It's not your fault. Your parents are basically good people. They regretted their mistakes. Before your papa died, he apologized to me for his behavior."

Mom looked crestfallen. Dad cleared his throat and asked everyone if they wanted some tea. When Mom and Akka nodded, he gave me the look that silently ordered me to go to the kitchen and take care of it. I reluctantly left my comfortable seat to brew tea.

I had a feeling the elders wanted to talk some more about the surprise Akka had just dropped, without Maneel and me listening in. Fortunately Maneel followed me into the kitchen and filled me in on some of the afternoon's details.

I filled the teakettle with water and placed it on the stove. "So, our renegade Akka was your savior."

He smiled. "She warned them about how they would never see their grandchildren if Naseem decided to elope with me."

I went still. "You guys weren't really . . . thinking of eloping, were you?"

"Not eloping, but Naseem and I've talked about getting married with just Mom and Dad and *our* family and friends at the ceremony. That is, if her parents really disowned her."

"So you two are really getting married?"

"Definitely. I just don't know when. Now that Naseem's parents are convinced that the wedding's going to happen with or without their blessings, her dad's going to discuss it with their *maulvi*."

I gave him a hug. "Congratulations, you big devil."

"Thanks."

I pretended to scratch my head in puzzlement. "Hard to imagine the guy who liked dressing up as Dracula for Halloween and scaring me to death, with a wife and kids."

Perhaps because he was relieved and happy that his future looked more promising, and that put him in a generous mood, he smiled indulgently. "Maybe you'll be next to get married, Meena."

I took out cups from the cabinet and placed the teabags in them. "If I can find a guy who's willing to marry a midget."

Maneel ruffled my hair, something he rarely did. "But you're a beautiful midget with a big heart."

"You're beginning to scare me, Maneel." I threw him a suspicious look. "When did you morph into a nice guy who compliments his annoying little sister?"

But he refused to take the bait. "Any man would be lucky to have you for a wife. Like I told you, lots of guys are interested in you."

"But I'm not interested in them." And because my brother sounded so sincere in his compliment, I began to choke up and had to try hard to bite back the tears. He had changed. Was this what falling in love did to a person? In Maneel's case, it had matured him so much, I could hardly recognize him.

Suddenly my brother was a grown man. And he was going to be married soon.

Chapter 20

"Meena, can you go to Washington on my behalf for a few days?" Paul stood in the doorway to my office, looking a little tired. He was usually in good spirits in the mornings, but not today.

It was the Tuesday after Thanksgiving, so I thought it was just the usual slump that comes after eating too much and watching ball games on TV all weekend long, and then getting over Monday's extra-large workload.

I looked up from my computer. "Something wrong in the DC office?"

"Nothing's wrong. Remember I was supposed to leave this evening to help with Prajay's project in Washington? Well, something's come up here that I . . . um . . . need to take care of."

"Must be serious." When he continued to avoid my eyes, I asked, "Are there problems with the company, Paul?" I'd been wondering if the latest buyout had overextended the company's finances. I wasn't a financial genius, but it didn't take brains to realize the price tag for the new acquisition had to be huge. "Are there going to be layoffs?"

I hated to think of the *L* word. I didn't want to experience it again, not when I'd finally found my niche.

Paul shook his head. "The company's fine. This is personal."

"Jeremy?" If it affected Paul this deeply, then it had to do with Jeremy.

"How'd you guess?" Paul came inside to sit in the guest chair across from my desk.

"Instinct."

"Jeremy has to go in for surgery tomorrow." Paul looked like a lost little boy, and I wanted to go around the desk and give him a comforting hug. But I didn't. Most men I knew didn't appreciate sympathetic displays of emotion.

"You don't have to tell me," I said after a few seconds of silence.

"It's okay. It's a hernia on his abdominal wall. He's had it for some years, but it didn't bother him. He was painting the family room over the weekend. Maybe from lifting the heavy paint cans or something, he started complaining of severe pain."

"Poor Jeremy."

"So he saw his doctor yesterday. He was told he needs to have surgery."

Despite the news about the surgery, a sense of relief swept over me. A hernia was pretty much routine if my limited medical knowledge could be trusted. I'd heard Mom and her sisters talking about hernias as if they were minor colds. "It's not something serious, then, thank God."

"No, it's not, but I'd like to be there . . . just in case. And you know how Jeremy is."

"I understand." If the man I loved were having hernia surgery, I'd want to be there, too. And that reminded me that the man I loved was in DC. "So you want me to take care of the Washington project?" We always called it the Washington project, although Prajay's office as well as his home happened to be in Fairfax, Virginia, a short distance outside Washington.

In all honesty, I didn't want to do it—put myself through the torture of seeing Prajay again. In the last few days I'd more or less succeeded in keeping my thoughts about him on the objective side. With each passing day the sting of rejection had become less and less painful.

A couple of days ago, I'd even responded to an e-mail from some guy Madhuri-pachi had put in touch with me. His name was Ajit Baliga, and he was a thirty-two-year-old stockbroker from Connecticut. I had no idea what he looked like or anything else, but my aunt seemed very impressed.

Ajit Baliga came across as a decent guy, born and raised in Connecticut, with an MBA from Tufts. He even seemed to have a sense of humor. I was somewhat interested in meeting him. Maybe after a few more e-mails and phone calls, we could meet face-to-face.

I'd traveled that route before, so despite my curiosity I wasn't exactly jumping with excitement at the prospect of getting together with him. If my aunt was right about his looks and personality, perhaps he was the one for me. Mom was very optimistic.

But now Paul was asking me to go to DC. It would inevitably put me in direct contact with Prajay again. Damn.

"If you don't mind doing it," said Paul, pulling me back from my troubled thoughts. "It'll only be for two or three days."

"I don't mind. But do you trust me with such an important project?" I had helped with the press releases and knew there were information packets going out to select senators' and congressmen's offices and targeted lobbyists.

The newly acquired company had come with a monopoly on software used for specialized defense applications. Rathnaya was planning on wooing the Defense Committee on Capitol Hill in addition to the Homeland Security office.

Paul and I had to work in coordination with Maryann Merlino, Prajay's Fairfax office manager, and the advertising firm recently hired by Rathnaya to produce brochures and other promotional literature.

"I'd trust you to take over my job any day, Meena," said Paul with an encouraging nod. "You worked on most of the press release kits anyway. And Prajay more or less asked me to send you there."

"He did?"

"Yes. He thinks highly of your work."

So Prajay admired my work, but not me. "That's nice to know." I stood up. "So when do you want me to leave?"

"This evening if possible. The lobbyists are getting ready to start work, but we need to give them appropriate brochures and info packages. You can easily handle that."

"Okay," I said, trying to look enthusiastic about my first real independent assignment. "You mind if I leave early to get packed, then?"

We both looked at our respective wristwatches. Paul got up from the chair. "Go home now, so you can pack and leave before rush-hour traffic gets bad. I'll have Pinky call the hotel in Virginia and tell them to change the reservation from my name to yours. I'm booked for three nights. It's the Hyatt in Fairfax, very close to the office."

A short distance from Prajay's office? I knew he owned a house somewhere in the vicinity, too. I was setting myself up for more misery. Three nights would mean I'd be returning home on Friday. Maybe I'd never have to see him.

Prajay might even set it up so I could be working exclusively with Maryann and the advertising folks. "All right, I'll finish what I'm doing and leave in about half an hour. Can you give me all the paperwork, and e-mail me the hotel information?"

"Sure, my portfolio's ready. Pinky's typing up the last-minute stuff right now. The Hyatt has directions on their Web site." He gave me a grateful smile before heading for the door. "Thanks, Meena. I know this is very last minute."

"No problem."

Pinky poked her head inside my office a while later. "So you're going to hang out in Washington for a few days?"

"Looks that way. It's actually Virginia."

"Same thing." She gave me a wink. "Go throw a line at Prajay Nayak, will you? You guys didn't have enough time to get to know each other when he was here. And this time, don't fall on your behind."

"I'm not *throwing* a line at anyone," I retorted. Least of all Prajay Nayak. Throwing a line was a slangy Indian term, *line maarna*—as in fishing. Pinky used it often, and I'd heard many of the other Indian employees use it.

"Okay, no line," she said amiably. "When're you coming back?"

"Probably Friday. So it'll be Monday before I return here." After she disappeared, I picked up the phone to inform Mom about my trip. She was with a patient, so I had to hold for several minutes before she came on the line.

"You're going to Virginia?" She sounded both excited and a little concerned. "But you'll be alone there."

I laughed. "Of course I'll be alone, Mom. It's a business trip, not a party."

"How do you plan to get there?"

"I'm driving."

Mom was silent for a prolonged moment. "I have an idea. Why don't you take Akka with you?"

"I don't need a babysitter. I was alone at college for several years, remember?"

"Not for babysitting, dear. I was thinking maybe she could do some sightseeing in Washington on her own when you're working. She's getting bored at home all day by herself."

I heaved a deep sigh. I knew exactly what Mom was up to. She was worried about my going somewhere alone, and she was tired of Akka's presence in the house. By foisting Akka on me she'd be able to solve both problems in one sneaky maneuver. "You can't expect a seventy-eight-year-old lady in a sari to go around a big city on her own, Mom," I protested.

"Don't be silly. She has traveled to Europe, Singapore, all kinds of places on her own."

"But still . . ."

"She speaks perfectly good English, and she's very smart," Mom assured me. "Buy her some tickets for guided tours around Washington and put her on a bus in the morning. I'll pay for the tickets. She'll love it."

"Mom, are you trying to get rid of Akka for a few days?"

"Of course not," Mom snapped. "Like I said, she's all alone at home, and she has nothing to do but watch those movie videos I rented for her."

"All right, I'll take her. She'll have to settle for sharing my hotel room, though." Actually, having Akka for company in the evenings would be a heck of a lot better than eating a lonely room-service dinner and watching TV.

Mom chuckled. "She grew up in a middle-class home in India with a bunch of brothers and sisters. Sharing a hotel room in America is still a luxury for her."

When I got home an hour later, I found an excited Akka at the door, all packed and raring to go. She wore a pretty coral sari with a string of matching coral beads around her neck. She said Mom had called her about the trip. She nearly yanked me inside the house. "You and I are driving to Washington, Meena. This is going to be so nice."

I gave her an indulgent smile. "It's Virginia. No need to get that excited, Akka. This isn't a vacation. I'll be working all day, so you'll be going sightseeing all by yourself."

"I don't mind, *charda*. Your mummy called Maneel and had him do some Internet research for Washington tours. You know what, that sweet boy booked online tickets for me already—for two whole days." She held up two skinny fingers. "He said it was his present to me for talking to Naseem's parents." She smiled. "So thoughtful of him, no?"

"Very," I said. Although a bit unexpected, it was nice of Maneel to have done that for Akka, and a blessing for me. Driving home, I'd been wondering how I could go about finding information on guided tours of Washington and buying tickets at the last minute for Akka.

The drive to Virginia would take at least four hours, and it would be late by the time we arrived. Before tomorrow morning I had tons to do. Paul's bulging portfolio had to be studied thoroughly before I could go to bed tonight. So Maneel's gesture solved a number of my problems.

I hastily packed a suitcase while Akka warmed up some of the previous night's leftovers for lunch. We ate, threw the dishes in the dishwasher, loaded up the car, and set out a little after two o'clock. The skies were somewhat cloudy. Rain was in the forecast for later.

Akka proved to be a good travel companion. Once or twice she got on my nerves by jabbering nonstop while I was trying to get through insane rush-hour traffic near Baltimore, but otherwise she had kept me amused and prevented me from getting drowsy at the wheel on the boring stretches of highway.

We stopped for a quick cup of coffee and a trip to the ladies' room at a rest stop. It was getting dark, and threatening clouds loomed above us as we climbed back into the car. A few minutes later the rain began to come down, a thin, cold drizzle. I was glad Akka was wearing a thick coat and a cardigan underneath.

A sari was most unsuitable for American weather, but she wasn't likely to wear anything else. At least she wasn't averse to wearing socks and sneakers. She seemed to like Reeboks.

By the time we reached the hotel in Fairfax, it was nearly seven o'clock. It was pitch dark outside and still drizzling. We dragged our suitcases inside, and while Akka waited in the lobby, I registered us at the reception desk and picked up the key card to our room.

As I turned to leave the counter, the desk clerk handed me a sealed envelope. "There's a message for you, Ms. Shenoy."

I thanked him and went over to Akka before I opened the envelope. I figured it was from Paul—some last minute information he'd forgotten to give me. The message was scribbled on the hotel's letterhead. But it was from Prajay, asking me to call him on his cell phone. His number was included.

Frowning, I wondered why he wanted me to call him. I'd figured I'd go into the office tomorrow and then worry about running into Prajay. Tonight I wanted to have a quiet dinner with Akka and later study my notes.

Akka looked at me with anxious eyes. "Problems?"

I shook my head. "I don't know. It's a note from my boss, Prajay Nayak. He wants me to call him as soon as I get in."

"So you'll call him now?"

"Let's go to our room first. I'll call him from there." I picked up my suitcase and started rolling it, letting Akka roll her own. She was an independent old woman and had made it clear that I didn't need to pamper her by pulling her suitcase when she was perfectly capable of doing it.

Our room was on the third floor and typical: two double beds separated by a nightstand, landscape prints on the wall, and dark, floral bedspreads with heavy matching curtains on the window.

The bathroom was spacious. Akka and I would do just fine. While Akka ran to the bathroom to freshen up, I pulled out my cell phone and called Prajay.

Although I was prepared to hear his voice, his deep, manly "Hello" gave me a jolt.

"P-Prajay, this is Meena." Couldn't I at least keep the stuttering to a minimum?

"Hi. You got my message."

"Yes." My equilibrium was slowly returning. I was going to keep this nice and formal. "Was there something you needed to discuss before I meet with Maryann tomorrow?"

"Yes and no," he said. "Mainly I wanted to ask if I could take you out to dinner."

"Why?" Would he have invited Paul to dinner? And he was making it clear dinner was not going to be at his house.

"You have to eat at some point, don't you? So do I. I just arrived home from work, and I'm starving."

"If you just got home, wouldn't you prefer to eat in your own kitchen and relax?"

"I hardly ever cook. Making a pot of coffee is a challenge for me."

"Well then, do whatever you usually do instead of entertaining me. I can always find a place somewhere around here."

"I'm only a couple of miles from the Hyatt. I can pick you up in a matter of minutes."

"I don't think it's a good idea, Prajay. This trip was unexpected, so I need to study Paul's notes. Besides, I'm not alone."

Prajay was quiet for a long time. "I see," he said finally, clearly drawing the wrong conclusion.

I would have liked to continue the farce, let him think I was with a man, sharing a hotel room with him. But I didn't see any point in it, not even to make Prajay jealous. In any case, he had no interest in me.

"It's my great-aunt," I explained. "She's visiting from California, and my parents thought she could take in the sights in Washington while I'm working here. You know the usual *desi* routine, trying to cram business, relatives, shopping, and sightseeing into one short trip. She and I are sharing a room and . . ." Why was I talking so much? He didn't give a damn.

"Your great-aunt? That's wonderful," said Prajay. "She's welcome to go with us, of course. We can eat at an Indian restaurant so she can have vegetarian food."

I laughed. "You don't know my great-aunt. We call her Akka. She likes meat dishes, and she loves to drink scotch and soda. She's quite . . . something."

Prajay chuckled. "How old is she?"

"Seventy-eight," I whispered when I heard the bathroom door open.

"Sounds like an interesting lady. Please extend my invitation to her. What time do you want me to pick you two up?"

Some nerve, taking Akka and me for granted. "I think we'll just go downstairs to the lobby restaurant and make it an early night, Prajay. Thanks for the invitation anyway."

Akka settled herself in the chair by the window.

"Oh, come on, Meena. Are you still angry at me? I thought you'd have gotten over it by now."

"I'm not angry, Prajay. I'm just tired. It's been a long drive, and some of it in wet weather." I noticed Akka studying me curiously.

"We'll make it a quick dinner, and then I'll drop you off at the hotel," Prajay insisted. "You can still have an early night. I'll even save you the bother of reading Paul's notes; I'll fill you in on everything while we're eating."

It was tempting to accept his invitation. I was eager to see him again, but I wanted to protect myself, too. I didn't want to go through that long crying spell a second time. I didn't want to experience that nagging ache anymore. I didn't want to feel anything for Prajay.

But then I looked at Akka, her hair combed once again and her sari perfectly pleated. I could smell her jasmine talc. She was thumbing through the hotel guide, pretending not to eavesdrop on my conversation. She'd appreciate eating at a nice Indian restaurant. Besides, Prajay was a Konkani man, and she'd probably enjoy meeting him, too.

"All right, you twisted my arm," I said to Prajay. "How about in fifteen minutes? We'll wait for you in the lobby."

"Good. See you in a bit."

When I hung up, Akka quirked a brow at me. "We are meeting someone?"

I rose from the edge of the bed and headed for the bathroom. "Prajay Nayak is picking us up. He's taking you and me to an Indian restaurant for dinner."

Akka's lips curved with joy. "That is so generous. You said his surname was Nayak. So he is a Konkani like us?"

"Uh-huh."

"Is he married?"

"No." Just before I closed the bathroom door, I noticed the look on her face. I was very familiar with that look. The wheels in Akka's head were turning faster than those on a bullet train.

I shut the door, leaned against it for a moment, and closed my eyes. I shouldn't have let Prajay talk me into going to dinner. Now that Akka knew he was single and available, she was going to put on her matchmaker's hat and torture me all evening, maybe for the rest of her visit.

But it was too late to change my mind.

Chapter 21

The minute Prajay walked into the lobby, all my resolve to keep this meeting cool and professional crumbled. My mouth turned dry when I saw those long, confident legs striding toward us. Droplets of rain clung to his trench coat and dark hair.

Damn, but the man had some strange power over me that I just couldn't shake off.

With a fixed smile I rose from the lobby's couch and held out my hand. But instead of merely taking my hand, he bent down and placed a light kiss on my cheek, making my heart thrash around like a beached fish. "Hi, Meena. Good to see you again."

Akka's eyes went round with wonder and most likely happy speculation. I doubt she'd ever seen a man and woman kiss, other than on screen. It was only a cordial peck on the cheek, but I wanted to smack Prajay's face for doing that in front of my elderly aunt. Or had he done that on purpose? If so, what was the purpose?

He shook hands politely with Akka. In turn, Akka seemed to be fascinated by him. She raised her chin all the way up to meet his eyes. "My goodness, you are so tall. Meena didn't tell me," she said.

"Didn't she?" he said, his quiet tone and eyes telling me nothing.

Without a comment I started walking toward the exit. He ran

ahead of me to hold the door for Akka and me. I came to a stop when he opened both the front and rear passenger doors of a gleaming black BMW. "What happened to your Corvette?"

"I left it at home when you said your aunt was with you. This is my other car."

"Oh." I should have known a rich man would have more than one car—another fancy one, no less. This one was obviously to wow the old folks. He probably had a few elderly aunts and uncles in his own family. Who didn't?

I let Akka occupy the front seat beside him. The interior of the car smelled of his cologne and the faintly pungent scent of the leather upholstery. Something about the profoundly male smell sent a sensual tremor through me. Some lucky six-foot woman was going to have all this someday soon.

While I sat in the backseat thinking glum thoughts, Akka happily carried on a conversation with Prajay. He politely answered her inquisitive questions about his business and his family and everything else the nosy old lady wanted to know. If she was bothering him, he didn't show it. Anyway, he deserved it. He'd insisted on taking us out despite my protests, so he'd have to put up with Akka's prying.

I didn't pay much attention to their conversation since Akka could talk to a rock if left alone with one. What caught my attention was her gasp of delight. "Oh my, you are Gopal and Pandhari Nayak's grandson? *Ayyo,* what a small world."

She turned around to address me. "Listen to this, Meena. This young man's grandparents were people I used to know back in Mangalore. Such lovely and warm people they were. What a nice coincidence, isn't it?"

"Very nice," I said, hoping my eye-roll would go unnoticed in the dark. All of us Konkanis were somehow related since we were a very small community. Why hadn't I thought of that when I'd allowed Prajay to take Akka and me out to dinner? I should've known Akka would find a friend or relative somewhere on this planet who was in some way related to Prajay.

Thank goodness the restaurant was pleasant. Since it was a weeknight, it was quiet, with few other tables occupied. The

place wasn't much different from most Indian restaurants: ethnic paintings, framed embroideries featuring a lot of beads and
sequins, classical music playing in the background, and the two
waiters dressed in cream *kurtas* that reached mid-thigh level.

When our waiter seated us and asked what we wanted to
drink, Prajay turned to Akka. "Would you like a scotch and
soda, Akka?"

So he was already calling her Akka, instead of Chandra-pachi
or Mrs. Kamat. And naturally Akka looked pleasantly astonished at his question. "How do you know I like scotch and
soda?"

"Lucky guess," he said with a smile, and nodded at the
waiter to get Akka her favorite drink.

I sent Prajay a derisive glance. The man was shamelessly
using an old lady to try and soften me up. I was still bristling at
him. Earlier, when I'd told him I wasn't angry, I hadn't been al-
together honest with him. He continued to pay attention to
Akka, who was still busy asking him about this aunt and that
uncle, and some cousin in Australia.

When the waiter turned to me, I asked for a glass of chardonnay, and Prajay ordered a merlot.

Ultimately the evening didn't turn out so bad, because the
food was excellent. Akka seemed pleased with her favorite lamb
roghan josh curry, and my shrimp *saag* was perfect, with the
spinach *saag* velvety and fragrant, and the shrimp tender and
juicy. Prajay's vinegary hot chicken *vindaloo* was equally good.
He made Akka and me taste some of it.

We were too stuffed for dessert, so Prajay and I talked about
the next day's meeting over *masala chai*. Spiced tea. Akka quietly observed us while we talked shop. I could feel her eyes on
us, summing us up. The crafty old woman was making some
quick calculations in her mind.

When the meal was over, I had to admit the idea of eating out
had been a good one. I felt warm and mellow with the wine and
food nicely settled in my stomach. And talking about tomorrow's meeting with the advertisers had eased my anger to some
extent. Work was always an effective calming agent.

It was well after nine o'clock when Prajay dropped us off at the hotel. This time I made sure I kept my distance from him while Akka and I thanked him for a wonderful meal. I wasn't going to allow him to kiss me again. Ever. It played havoc with my sense of balance. I was determined to keep our relationship on an impersonal level.

When we got into the elevator, Akka came straight to the point. "Why do you dislike him, Meena? He is such a nice fellow."

"I don't dislike him."

"Then why were you so cold and abrupt with him? Is it because he is dark-skinned and not very handsome?"

"His looks have nothing to do with it."

"He was being friendly to you, but you were sort of . . . detached."

"I like to keep my business and personal lives separate, Akka," I said, hoping my eyes wouldn't give me away. "That's the way it is in this country. You wouldn't understand that."

"Of course I understand that. But I get the feeling that you two had some kind of misunderstanding or something."

"Why would you think that?"

"Shabari told me about your falling down and hurting your leg and your boss driving you to work. She was talking about this same man, wasn't she?"

"Shabari-pachi reads too much into everything. You know how melodramatic she is, and so desperate to set me up with a Konkani guy."

By the time we got to our room, Akka had it all figured out. "Meena, in spite of your aloofness I can tell that you actually *like* Prajay."

"I don't deny he's a nice guy," I said, taking off my jacket and hanging it in the closet. I took Akka's coat and did the same.

"Also very decent and smart." Akka was studying my face closely.

"Yes, he's all that." I gave her a candid look. "Listen, if you're getting romantic ideas about him and me, you can forget them."

Akka sat on the edge of one of the beds and took off her sneakers. "He is perfect for you even though he is very much taller than you. Height does not mean anything. Fate has brought you two together so conveniently." She went quiet for a second. "He even kissed you. So why are you fighting it?"

"A peck on the cheek is an acceptable way of greeting a friend in American society. It doesn't mean anything." I should have realized she'd make a big deal out of that kiss. Tossing aside my own shoes, I stretched out on the other bed, with my street clothes still on. "Akka, if I tell you something, will you promise to keep it to yourself?"

Akka nodded. "Of course, *charda*. You don't want me to tell your mummy and daddy that you are dating Prajay Nayak? Is that it?"

"Dating Prajay? Good Lord, what am I going to do with you?" I gave a brittle laugh. "Nothing could be further from the truth. And I'll tell you what the truth is: Prajay Nayak is not the least bit interested in me. In fact, he asked me to help him find the perfect wife."

"What?" Akka stood to get changed. I watched while she pulled off her coral sari and wrapped herself in a soft, white cotton one, more suitable for sleeping in. Then she took off her coral blouse, exposing her plain white bra, before putting on a white blouse. "Is that boy stupid or what? When the perfect girl is right under his nose, he is looking elsewhere?"

"Not just looking but actively seeking. With my assistance. He asked me to help him place ads for a six-foot woman."

"He wants *what*?" Akka frowned while she loosened the bun on her head and placed the hairpins on the nightstand. Her long, waist-length hair was impressive for her age.

"You heard it right. He wants a woman who's about six feet—someone he can look in the eye. He says looks don't matter to him, and yet he wants her to be tall."

Akka started braiding her hair. "Very silly of him."

"He paid me well for helping him, though. I made a list for him from all the responses that came in. By now he must have met at least a couple of those tall women."

"So you are working not only in his company as a manager but also as his . . ."

"Consultant."

She nodded. "You are his marriage consultant, then?"

"Something like that." I turned to look at her. "You have to promise not to tell anybody, not even Mom, and certainly not my aunts. I promised Prajay not to tell anyone. This is strictly confidential."

"I won't tell anyone. Promise." Akka clucked in dismay as she retrieved her toothbrush from her toilet kit. "*Paap.*"

"Why are you pitying Prajay? He's rich; he's successful; he's got everything." I slid off the bed and opened my suitcase to look for my nightclothes. "One of these days he'll find the tall woman he wants."

Akka squeezed a glob of toothpaste onto her brush and looked at me. "I'm not pitying him; I'm pitying you."

I stopped in the middle of unpacking. "Why?"

"Because you are in love with that man."

I pulled out my pajamas from the suitcase and stared at Akka. "What are you talking about?" I should've known she'd figure it out. Not much escaped those sharp eyes and ears. I should never have let her meet Prajay. Now she'd go tell the entire family. I couldn't stand their pity. Oh, dear God, not that. I sank onto the bed again.

"I know you, Meena," said Akka as she put down her toothbrush on the dresser. She came to sit beside me. "I have known you since you were a little baby. I know your personality well. I was watching you talk to him, first on the phone, and then at the restaurant. You care about him, don't you?"

I saw no point in hiding it anymore. Akka was too perceptive to lie to. "Okay, I'm in love with him," I admitted. "But he doesn't even know I exist. To him I'm a good PR consultant. That's all I'm good for, consulting." Despite my trying hard to avoid it, my lips were trembling. Any moment now the floodgates would burst open.

Akka put her arms around me and held me close. Her special scent and the warm feel of the wrinkled skin on her neck were my undoing. The tears gushed out. "It's awful. I don't want to work for him . . . and yet I want to be near him. What am I going to do?"

"Shh, it's okay, Meena." Akka held me close while I wept all over her.

I cried for a long time, and all the while Akka remained silent, offering me strength and comfort. And tissues from the box on the nightstand. As the sobs subsided, I realized it felt good to get it out of my system, just like the other day when I'd cried with Rita.

But this was different. Akka's was the maternal comfort I needed. I could never do this with Mom; she'd never understand the concept of falling in love. For her, love happened after one got married. On the other hand, Akka understood. Although it had been a long time since she'd been in a similar situation, she had experienced it.

When I finally stopped sobbing, Akka gave me another wad of tissues to blow my nose. "If that boy is too stupid to recognize what's good for him, he deserves some crude six-foot woman with a mustache and chest hair," she declared.

Despite my crying fit, I had to smile. "Chest hair?"

"Sure," snorted Akka. "Any woman who grows that big has to have too much male hormone, and she will grow hair everywhere. If a hairy horse is what he wants, then let him have it. It will serve him right."

"That's right, a Clydesdale with fat hooves," I said and headed for the bathroom. Looking at my face in the mirror, I recoiled. My nose looked like an overripe cherry tomato. My eyelids were swollen. I decided to take a long, hot shower to clear my head.

By the time I came out, Akka was fast asleep, snoring lightly, huddled under her blanket. The toothpaste glob on her toothbrush had lost its shiny glaze. Her book of religious verses lay on the nightstand. The poor thing had probably gotten tired of waiting for me to come out of the bathroom. I'd been hogging it forever.

I decided to read the stuff Paul had put together. Sitting on the bed, with my back resting against the headboard, I scanned the notes and realized there wasn't much there I didn't already know. An hour later, I shut off the bedside light, lay down on my side, and watched Akka sleeping.

I was glad to have her with me.

Chapter 22

When I opened my eyes the next morning, I found Akka sitting beside the window, reading by the light of a floor lamp. She looked fresh as a dewdrop, bathed and dressed in a blue and white-print sari, the freshwater pearls around her neck.

She looked at me over the rim of her reading glasses. "You must have been tired. You slept well."

I pushed the covers aside, sat up, and stretched. "What time is it?"

"Five minutes after six."

"Oh no!" I shot out of bed. "What time does your tour start?"

"8:30 from Union Station." Akka looked unruffled. "Don't worry, we have plenty of time."

"No, we don't—not in rush-hour traffic. Union Station's in Washington, and we're in Virginia."

"Maneel said something about hotel pickup and I didn't have to go into Washington in the morning."

"Are you sure?"

"Let me see." Akka rummaged through her handbag and pulled out a piece of paper. "It says the shuttle bus picks up passengers in front of this hotel at 7:15 A.M."

"Right here at the hotel? That's great. But I still need to hurry." In about twenty minutes I managed to put myself together. I wore my navy suit with a pale gray blouse and navy pumps.

"*Wah,* how smart you look in your office clothes," remarked Akka. "Very executive-like." The pride and admiration in her voice made me feel all warm inside.

We went downstairs to the hotel's restaurant and opted for the buffet breakfast. It was the quickest way to fill ourselves and get Akka on that bus in time.

While Akka finished her toast, fruit, and coffee, I spoke to the concierge about the bus. He said it almost always arrived a few minutes late. I looked at my watch. Eight minutes after seven. Akka had just enough time to run to the ladies' room before boarding the bus.

The clouds and rain from the previous night had disappeared. I was happy to note that the sun was beginning to emerge. The TV weatherman had forecast a cool but sunny Wednesday. Akka wouldn't have to walk around Washington in a cold drizzle.

While we waited in the parking lot for the bus, I handed her my cell phone. "Here, I want you to keep this with you at all times."

"But *you* need it, Meena."

"I'll be in an office with plenty of phones, whereas you'll be on a bus tour."

Akka rolled her eyes. It was a comical gesture for someone like her. "I'm capable of using a pay phone, dear."

"Pay phones are a thing of the past," I reminded her. "What if you need to reach me urgently?" I didn't say it aloud, but what if she had a heart attack? What if she fell and broke her hip? In spite of all her feistiness and zest for life, she was still an old woman. Although I was grateful for her company, I didn't think it was safe to let her go into a strange city all alone. The cell phone would be my only connection to her.

She turned the phone over in her palm. "I don't know how to use this."

I took it back and showed her how to dial Maryann Merlino's office and cell numbers. Both were programmed in. It took Akka a minute or two to figure out how the phone worked, and then she slipped it into her big, black handbag.

When the bus pulled up, I breathed a sigh of relief. About half a dozen other individuals, mostly middle-aged and older, had been waiting alongside us. As two more came out of the hotel and joined them, I felt a lot better since Akka was not the only passenger from this particular hotel.

As soon as the bus's automatic doors whooshed open, I went up to the driver to ask what time the bus would return. He told me to expect it back around 6:30 P.M. Akka was going to have a long day.

"You're sure you'll be able to handle being on your feet all day?" I asked her.

"Of course. If I get tired, I'll find a place to sit down and rest. Don't worry, *charda.*"

"Okay." I pressed four twenty-dollar bills into her hand. "Buy yourself a nice lunch and a souvenir or two," I told her.

She looked at the money and frowned. "I don't need this. Kalpa has given me enough cash. And Maneel bought me the tickets."

"Shh, just take it and stop arguing," I said.

"I can't take things from young people," she grumbled.

I knew it went against her culture to take gifts from someone younger than herself, but I pushed her. "You give me gifts all the time." I thought of the expensive pistachio-colored *kurti,* a silk tunic top with silver embroidery at the neck and sleeves, she'd brought me this time. "It's not much, so don't look like I raided the bank."

She reluctantly put the money in her bag, gave me a pat on the back, and boarded the bus. I waved at her as she settled herself in a window seat. "Enjoy your day—and be careful. Hold on to your purse," I said. The motor was running, and I didn't think she heard me, so I made hand gestures to get the message across. She nodded.

Two minutes later, I watched the bus roll out of the parking lot. It was time for me to go to my meeting. I returned to our room, touched up my lipstick, grabbed my briefcase, and went outside once again to find my car.

Despite the morning traffic, it took me very little time to get to the multistory office building with the help of my GPS.

Standing beside my car, I studied the structure. It was similar to our modern brick and glass office in New Jersey. But this branch of Rathnaya was smaller because only a handful of employees and Prajay worked here. It was more of a liaison office between the government customers and Rathnaya. Most of the technical and administrative work was done in New Jersey.

On the fifth floor, the heavy twin glass doors at the far end of the hallway showed Rathnaya and its familiar logo, the letter *R* nestled inside a circle, painted black and silver. Two doors before I reached it, I spied the ladies' room, so I ducked in there.

I checked on my hair and makeup once again. I had to look my best. I had to make Prajay see what he was missing. I was being silly of course, but it was hard to convince myself that there were no feelings whatsoever on his part. He'd been warm and attentive the previous evening.

With shoulders erect, I walked up to the glass doors and strode in. I didn't find a receptionist, only rows of small offices on either side of a long, blue-carpeted aisle.

I kept reading the nameplates outside each room, looking for Maryann Merlino. Most of the offices had their doors closed or they were open but empty. It was a little before eight o'clock. So where was everybody? Then I realized I was probably too early. In my anxious state of mind I hadn't even bothered to ask what time the office opened.

I did manage to find two cubicles occupied. A couple of curious faces, both of them young Indian males, looked up from their desks as I wandered along, but no one thought to question my presence. A young *desi* on the premises was probably the norm around here.

I had talked to Maryann over the phone often enough, but had never met her. Paul had told me she was a bubbly, enthusiastic woman in her forties. She had worked for Rathnaya since the company had first started. She had been promoted from clerk to secretary to office manager.

Just then a woman who fit Maryann's description came around the corner, a coffeepot in hand. I stepped forward with a smile. "Maryann?"

She knew who I was right away. "Meena!"

"Yes."

"My, you're an early bird. I wasn't expecting you until later, or I would've been waiting for you in the lobby."

"I didn't realize the office was so easy to get to, so I started out early."

She hastened forward to greet me with a firm handshake. "We finally meet."

"Yes." I felt tiny beside her. She was probably no more than four inches taller than me, but she was big-boned. She had on a knee-length, gray wool skirt, black sweater, and mid-heel pumps.

"Let's go to my office," she said, and walked me down to a door almost at the end of the hallway. "I was just about to put on a pot of coffee."

As soon as we entered her office I said, "Sorry. Guess I'm intruding on your early morning routine?"

"Not at all. I was hoping to offer you fresh coffee." She pointed to a guest chair across from her desk. "Put your briefcase down; have a seat." She poured the water in the coffeemaker placed on a credenza by the window. "Did you have a good drive down from New Jersey last night?"

"It rained from Maryland all the way down."

"That's a shame." She paused. "So how's Paul's friend doing? I understand he's going to have surgery?"

"The surgery's today." I didn't want to elaborate on anything. I wasn't sure how much Maryann and the Washington staff knew about Paul's homosexuality and Jeremy. Luckily she didn't ask any more questions. I liked and respected Paul too much to gossip about him.

Maryann was attractive in a motherly sort of fashion: short

brown hair with blond highlights, high cheekbones, a nice complexion, and an open, no-nonsense expression. Paul had mentioned that she had two children in college.

Placing my briefcase on the floor, I took off my coat and hung it on the coatrack by the door. "Feels strange to meet for the first time, doesn't it?" I sat down. "With all our e-mails and phone conversations, I feel like we know each other rather well," I said to her.

She laughed. "Happens to me a lot. I keep in close touch with so many people from the Jersey office. Other than Paul and Nishant, and now you, I haven't met anyone else face-to-face."

I watched her measure coffee into a filter and slide it into place. She was quick and efficient. Her office was about the same size as mine, but hers was much more cheerful and welcoming, with the morning sun streaming in through the single window. A couple of plants were flourishing on the sill.

Although paperwork in piles happened to be everywhere, I had a feeling it was organized chaos. Maryann had never come across as a scatterbrain.

Family pictures covered one shelf of a bookcase. "I'm assuming they're your sons," I said, indicating a picture with two young men in baseball caps and sweatshirts. They were sitting in a boat, squinting into the light while facing the camera.

"My boys," she confirmed. "The one on the left is Jeff. He's a senior at Virginia Tech, and Jason's a sophomore at Maryland." Her eyes swept warmly over the pictures. "My guys love fishing," she said. "They take after their father. Robert, my husband, would fish every day of the year if he could. But he's got to work to pay the bills."

I looked at the shot of Maryann and a tall, ruggedly built man. "Nice-looking husband you've got."

When I saw her beaming face I realized I'd pushed the right button.

"He was a football star and engineering major when we met." Her pride in him was unmistakable. She got out the creamer and sugar jars. The hissing, sputtering coffeepot was filling up. The aroma of coffee was spreading across the room.

"Lucky you," I said. It was nice to see someone married a long time and happy with it. Reminded me of my mother and my aunts.

Minutes later we both got our coffee and settled down to business. Maryann led me to a conference room that had a large table and about a dozen chairs placed around it.

I pulled out all the paperwork from my briefcase, and we went over samples of the glossy brochures that the advertising firm had sent us a few days earlier. We were supposed to meet a graphics designer and some other man from the agency at 9:30 A.M.

Maryann looked over my text. "Good job. Hope the advertising guys like it. Honestly, I wonder why Nishant and Prajay hired an expensive agency when Paul and you do such nice work."

"We do what we can, but this is a huge project. And we've grown so much bigger with the new acquisition, we need more professional help."

"I suppose. The competition on the Hill is stiff. Lots of software companies with powerful lobbyists working for them. We're swimming alongside the whales and sharks now." She sighed. "And in Washington, they're all bloodthirsty sharks."

"Paul says we might even be doing a TV commercial at some point in the future?"

Maryann nodded. "Maybe, in the distant future. It's ridiculously expensive. For now it's some print and mostly Internet."

We heard footsteps and voices. The other employees were beginning to trickle in. Maryann introduced me to some of them, and we chatted briefly. All of them had backgrounds in computer science; all were specialists in software design and development.

I felt comfortable in this place. The people seemed nice enough.

Around nine o'clock Prajay walked in. "Good morning, ladies. I see you're already here and working hard," he said to me.

I took an unsteady breath and managed a smile. "Maryann and I are preparing for our meeting with the ad agency."

"Excellent. I'll let you two get on with it." He turned to

Maryann before exiting. "Could you please take Meena out to lunch, Maryann? I would've liked to do it myself, but I have a meeting with a congressional aide that might go past lunch."

"Sure thing, Prajay. I was going to ask Meena and the agency folks to lunch anyway. You go on and do what you have to."

He returned his gaze to me. "I enjoyed meeting your aunt. Akka is quite a lady."

"That she is. Hope she didn't get too nosey."

He grinned, making my tummy wobble. "I have a bunch of elderly women in my family, too. So she's off sightseeing this morning?" he asked.

"Uh-huh."

"The weather's better today. I'm sure she'll enjoy it." He glanced at his watch. "I better go."

I watched him walk away. I probably wouldn't see him for the next three days.

Good thing, too, I told myself and turned my attention back to Maryann. My stomach was still trembling.

Chapter 23

At precisely 9:28 A.M., the advertising folks showed up. Maryann went out to greet them and brought them into the conference room.

I shook hands with a slim, forty-ish-looking man named Jim Dressler and a thirty-something woman called Jennifer Bellows. Jennifer was the graphic designer and Jim was from the business side. Maryann and I spent hours with the duo, debating over colors, layout, paper size, text, pictures, and covers.

I was a little irritated when Jim questioned my wording a few times, but I realized it was futile arguing with a guy who'd been in the business for some twenty years. I was a novice compared to him, so I deferred to his ideas.

On the other hand, Jennifer was easier to work with. She was more open to suggestions from Maryann and me. We were adamant that the colors be subdued. We wanted little or no pinks and purples. This was a serious software company trying to impress military brass, congressmen, and senators, and we wanted that to show. Jim agreed with us. And that was a relief.

By the time we all went out to lunch at a nearby restaurant, it was past one o'clock.

The afternoon proceeded along the same lines as the morning, except Jennifer took a few photographs of some employees at work. They were a little upset that they hadn't dressed for the occasion since they had not been informed of the photo session beforehand. But Jennifer and Jim assured them they wanted the pictures to be natural—everyday life at work.

The photo session lasted nearly an hour. By the time Jim and Jennifer left around five o'clock, Maryann and I were ready for a short coffee break. We headed back to her office. Maryann and I chatted over steaming coffee.

"So Prajay took you and your aunt out to dinner last night?" Maryann had that slightly alert look that told me she, too, was making certain assumptions about my relationship with Prajay. Why did everyone presume there was something going on between him and me? Unless . . . my feelings for him were obvious.

"I'm sure his evenings are busy, so it was nice of him to offer to take us to dinner." His evenings had to be busy. Besides, he must have started to see one or two of those women on his matrimonial list. "My aunt kept him occupied with all kinds of chatter," I said absently. I didn't want anyone, especially Prajay's employees, to get the wrong idea about the previous evening.

"So she's on a sightseeing tour today."

"She lives in California. This is her first trip to Washington," I explained. "That reminds me, do you mind if I use your phone to call and check up on her?"

"Go ahead." Maryann got up and let me sit in her chair. The phone rang several times, and I was about to give up, thinking Akka had either shut it off or she was too busy to answer, when I heard her voice come on the line. "Akka?" I said. Silence, then lots of static. "Akka?" I repeated, raising my voice.

"Oh, Meena, it's you." Akka sounded relieved.

"Who did you think it was?" I had to remind myself the poor woman wasn't used to carrying a cell phone.

She laughed. "I didn't realize it was *my* phone. The lady sitting next to me told me it was ringing."

"I understand." No wonder it had taken her so long to answer. "How's the tour going?"

"Very nice. We saw some lovely monuments, and I bought postcards and souvenirs. I'll show you everything this evening."

She sounded like she was enjoying it, thank goodness. "Hope you're not too tired," I added.

"A little bit, but everywhere we went there were benches, so I could sit down and rest."

"Good. I'll see you later, then. We'll have an early dinner somewhere nearby so you can go to bed at a decent time."

"Sounds like everything's all right?" Maryann asked after I hung up the phone.

"She's having a good time."

A half hour later, I decided to call it a day.

"Take your time coming in," Maryann reminded me with a grin.

"I won't show up at the crack of dawn," I promised, shrugging into my coat. "Yesterday I didn't know you guys start a bit later than our Jersey office."

"That's because we don't have the office staff you have—the strict eight-to-fivers. All our people are techies who sometimes work late at night. We basically let them make their own hours." She got up to get her own coat. "We'll go over the budget tomorrow. We didn't have time to talk about that today."

"That and hopefully the sample brochures. Didn't Jim say he might be able to bring us the rough drafts in the afternoon?"

"Hope he can produce them that quickly." Maryann picked up her purse.

Just as we were about to walk out of the office, Prajay wandered in. He looked tired. He had loosened his tie, and his suit jacket hung over his arm. "How did it go?" he asked us.

"Fine," said Maryann. "You might be able to see the first drafts by this time tomorrow, if the advertisers are on schedule."

Prajay's brow shot up. "That soon? Did you discuss prices yet?"

"We touched on them, but we'll talk about that in detail tomorrow. Don't worry; we'll negotiate a good price."

"Good work, ladies. Thank you."

Maryann laughed. "Don't thank me. Thank Meena and Paul.

They did all the creative work. I'm only doing the peripheral stuff."

"Oh, come on, Maryann," I chided gently. "You did a lot more than that. You're being too modest." Maryann blushed with pleasure. "And don't forget budget negotiations are going to be entirely in your court."

"Heading back to the hotel?" Prajay asked me.

"Akka should be returning soon," I said. "I want to make sure I'm there when she gets off the bus." I wished both of them good night and headed out.

Naturally I wondered what Prajay was doing that evening. Was he taking the beanpole from Maryland out to dinner?

At the hotel, since I had some time to kill before Akka's return, I went upstairs to our room and changed into comfortable jeans, pullover, and sneakers. Then I booted up my laptop and checked my e-mail.

Most of the messages were unimportant. But there was one from Ajit Baliga. He wanted me to decide on a date for us to meet. Oh boy. A date.

And he'd sent an attachment: a picture of himself. That meant he was serious about this business of us getting together. I knew Madhuri-pachi had shared my pictures with him, so he must have liked what he'd seen before starting a correspondence with me.

I opened the attachment and maximized the screen to study the photo. It wasn't a handsome face, but there was something wholesome and forthright about it, and a sparkle that could be humor in his dark eyes. He had a nice smile and plenty of hair— assuming it wasn't a toupee.

Was I ready to meet a man who was serious about marriage? At thirty-two he probably was. In the past, meeting an eligible man hadn't been a big deal, but ever since I'd fallen for Prajay Nayak I was hesitant about going out with someone. No man was likely to measure up to him, literally and figuratively.

Was I seeing all these shining qualities in Prajay that weren't really there? Was I building him up to be a hero who didn't exist? All I had had was one hot kiss with him. What did I know about him? Maybe he really was a rough, sadistic man who liked to beat up on women, and maybe he was warning me about it. He could easily crush me with one hand.

But it was hard to imagine Prajay's being cruel or thoughtless. To me he still appeared to be a gentle giant.

Of course, there was that small matter of his rejecting me.

I didn't send Ajit a response. Instead I saved the message for future consideration and shut off the computer. I'd have to give the idea of meeting him face-to-face some more thought.

A few minutes later, I went down to the lobby to wait for Akka. Instead of sitting in one of the overstuffed chairs, I decided to step outside and walk around the parking lot. The air was crisp and chilly. I thrust my hands into my pockets to keep them warm. It was nearing winter. The holiday season was already being ushered in by the retailers.

Was Prajay planning on getting married in the coming year? I wondered. He'd probably be celebrating his fortieth birthday sometime in the next few months. He'd seemed eager to be hitched before he crossed that milestone.

Briskly I strode around the perimeter of the parking lot and tried to tell myself that Prajay's birthday was none of my business. And neither were his marriage plans.

I kept walking. I'd been up early, and I'd worked all day, but I wasn't a bit tired. I was restless. Walking was a good way to keep those antsy legs moving and focus my thoughts on my surroundings instead of other things.

A minute later, Akka's bus arrived. I hurried to meet her.

Chapter 24

Seeing Akka looking beat and walking more slowly than usual, I escorted her to the room and insisted she take a hot bath. Fortunately I always traveled with my aromatherapy bath kit, so I threw in some soothing ginger-hyacinth bath crystals and filled the tub.

Inhaling the fragrant steam rising from the water, I was tempted to hop in myself and forget about my aunt. But she needed it more than I.

She sent me a dubious look. "I'm not used to tub baths. Maybe I should just take a shower."

"You'll feel great after a nice hot soak," I assured her. "Your feet look swollen. Don't forget there's more walking tomorrow. The Smithsonian museums are huge."

Perhaps because she was too tired to argue, she surrendered. While she soaked in her bath, I studied the room service menu. I called the desk and placed an order for vegetable lasagna, chicken noodle soup, and a garden salad.

A half hour later, Akka came out, scrubbed clean, dressed in her white cotton sari and smelling like hyacinths. "You were right, Meena. That bath was very relaxing. I almost fell asleep in the tub."

"I ordered some dinner," I told her. "Hope you like it."

When the food arrived a little later, Akka and I sat at the small table-cum-desk to eat our meal. The soup was salty and the lasagna mediocre at best, but neither one of us complained. I had a feeling we were both recalling the previous evening's delicious meal with Prajay.

After I placed the empty dishes on the tray outside our door, Akka showed me her postcards. And she handed me a gift: a navy T-shirt with I ♥ AMERICA printed on the front.

"Akka, you weren't supposed to buy *me* a gift. I gave you money to buy yourself something." Her thoughtfulness was making me cry.

"It's a small souvenir, *charda*—just a token to thank you for bringing me with you and treating me like your own grandmother."

The tears pooled in my eyes. "But you *are* my grandmother." I hugged her tight.

She patted my back. "Don't cry over a T-shirt, you silly girl. Tomorrow I'll spend your money on something for myself," she said with a serene smile. But she hadn't fooled me. I could see her lashes glistening with moisture.

"You promise?"

"Promise." She quickly changed the subject, probably to rein in her unshed tears. "The White House is out of bounds without special passes. They could not take us there," she grumbled.

"Maybe next time around we can plan ahead so we can get passes," I consoled her, and blew my nose. "Why don't you go to bed early tonight?"

"Tell me about your day first," she said, sitting on the edge of her bed and opening a small plastic jar. She scooped out some strong-smelling ointment and starting rubbing it over her foot. "Did you get to spend any time with Prajay Nayak?"

"Two minutes at the most." I tried to sound nonchalant while I went to the table and booted up my laptop. "I worked all day with his office manager and two people from an advertising agency. We're doing a new campaign." After the computer warmed up, I opened my e-mail.

"Sounds exciting. When I was young, I longed to have a career, but women my age didn't work outside the house." Akka

wore a thoughtful frown for a minute while she massaged ointment over the other foot. Then she looked at me. "You really
have feelings for Prajay?"

"Unfortunately . . . yes."

"I have an idea."

Uh-oh. "What sort of idea?"

"You should make him jealous."

For a moment I thought she was kidding, but her expression
was dead serious. "And how do you propose I go about doing
that?" I asked with a chuckle. "He didn't care one bit when I
went out with a guy from New Jersey."

"What guy?"

"A South Indian systems analyst."

"Nice fellow?"

"At first I thought he was okay. But he turned out to be . . .
petty."

"Aha, that's the problem," said Akka, putting the lid back on
the jar and placing it on the nightstand. "That man was not true
competition. If you start dating someone who is clever and has a
good personality and character, then Prajay will get jealous."

"Akka, please, this is not like your Hindi movies. It'll never
work." I opened the saved e-mail from Ajit Baliga. On a whim I
turned to her. "You want to see a picture of the guy Madhuri-
pachi wants to set me up with, the one she was raving about?"

"The boy from Connecticut?" Akka looked intrigued. "You
have a photo of him?"

"He sent it to me today." I clicked on the attachment, and
seconds later Ajit Baliga's picture filled the screen.

Akka slid off the bed, put on her glasses, and came to stand
behind my chair. "Such a nice-looking boy he is. And so much
more handsome than your Prajay. Madhuri was right." She
smoothed the hair on top of my head. "Now *this* is the kind of
boy Prajay will be jealous about."

I turned around and squinted up at her. "You think?" I
wanted to believe her.

"Oh, yes. This boy is intelligent and educated and most important, he is from a nice Konkani family. Madhuri tells me he earns a lot of money and his parents are rich."

"Rich doesn't matter to me all that much. I just want a nice guy—someone who's easy to get along with and has a good sense of humor."

Akka leaned forward and studied Ajit's picture more closely. "You will not know what kind of a boy he is unless you meet him. And that will not happen if your only contact is through the computer."

"I guess you're right."

She went back to her bed, took off her glasses, and put them next to her foot balm. "So, why don't you at least meet him and find out?"

"Maybe I will," I said with a slow smile. Akka had a point. Despite everyone's skepticism, she'd helped in Maneel's case. And wasn't I the one who'd seen the wisdom in her supposedly inane idea? Besides, what did I have to lose? If things worked out well with Ajit, and even if I never succeeded in Akka's preposterous plan to make Prajay jealous, at least I'd be seeing an eligible guy, a man endorsed by my family.

One thing I was sure of: I had to find a husband. I couldn't sit around brooding over Prajay for the rest of my life. I certainly wanted to get married sometime in this century. And if Ajit Baliga was part of my destiny, the least I could do was meet him halfway.

Akka picked up her toilet kit off the dresser and headed for the bathroom.

I sent Ajit a reply: *How about if we meet somewhere in NYC this weekend? I'm in VA on business at the moment & will be returning to NJ on Fri.*

He must have been on his computer right then, because within minutes I received a response: *NYC sounds good. Assuming we'll both be taking a train into Penn Station, how about meeting at a restaurant nearby for lunch on Sat? Know any good places?*

Somewhere close to Penn Station was a good idea, I agreed. I thought of this cute Mexican restaurant I'd eaten at with friends a couple of times, but I couldn't remember the exact name. I did a bit of searching on Google, managed to find the name and address, and sent it to Ajit. We agreed to meet around 12:30 P.M.

I figured if things didn't go well, we could say a polite goodbye, and I could take the train back home before it got too dark. If we hit it off, well then . . .

A mild sort of excitement began to dance inside me. I'd done it; I'd taken the first small step toward making Prajay jealous. If he was seriously seeking his Amazon in a sari, then I could go hunting for my *desi* hunk in a *kurta*. Who said life was perfect?

When Akka came out of the bathroom, I gave her the news. "Guess what, I'm meeting Ajit Baliga in New York on Saturday for lunch."

"Good." Akka peeled back the bedspread and blanket and climbed onto her bed. "You took my advice."

"Only because you were so successful with Maneel."

"And I'm wise enough to know that I will be successful with you. I know something about the human mind."

"You learned psychology?"

She laughed. "I did not go beyond high school. Who needs psychology when God has given common sense? When you have lived as long as I have, you learn how people's minds work." With a wide yawn she stretched out and pulled the covers all the way up to her neck. "Remember one thing, *charda*. You should meet this fellow with an open mind. He should be treated with respect."

"Of course I'll treat him with respect. Why wouldn't I?" I was a little puzzled at Akka's choice of words.

"Although you are meeting him to make Prajay jealous, don't go to the extent of breaking that boy's heart."

"It's not like he's going to fall in love with me at first sight, Akka. We'll just meet and see if there's any chemistry between us. Things don't work like they did with you guys and your arranged matches."

"Mine was not arranged," she reminded me. "And what are

you going to do if the chemistry is good for him? What if he takes a liking to you straight away?"

"Hmm." I hadn't thought of that, but I'd gone out with men like him before. Chemistry had been sorely absent, and there had been no hard feelings on either side when we'd wished each other good-bye and happy fishing. "I'll cross that bridge if and when I get to it. Chances are slim that a guy starts to like a girl that much the first time he meets her."

"Okay. You know this dating business better than me." Before I could say anything more, she turned onto her side, facing away from me.

She'd finished saying what she wanted to say. She needed her rest.

Chapter 25

The next morning was a lot more relaxed than the previous one. When I woke up, Akka was once again dressed and ready to go. Deciding to postpone my shower for later, I put on jeans and the new T-shirt she'd bought for me and took her downstairs for breakfast.

After I saw her safely seated in the tour bus, I went back to the room for a leisurely shower. As I got dressed, I watched the news on TV. Since it failed to hold my attention, I picked up some notes from my briefcase and read them.

It was hard to concentrate. Just like the previous morning, I was itching to hop into my car and head for work. Deep down, I knew going to work meant seeing Prajay—even if was only for a few minutes.

It was nearly nine when I parked my car outside the office. Maryann was already on her second cup of coffee when I walked in. "There you are. Prajay was just asking about you."

"He was?" My heart did a joyful somersault.

"He wanted to say hi and 'bye before he left for some more meetings on the Hill." She motioned to me to help myself to coffee.

"Has he left already?" I filled my cup and sat down in the guest chair.

"You missed him by two minutes."

My spirits plunged. So much for taking extra care with my makeup and making the effort to press my suit. I didn't bother to ask what time he was expected back. That would be too obvious. Instead I looked at my watch. "Shall we wait for our guests in the conference room?"

Jim arrived some twenty minutes later. He told us Jennifer was working on the drafts and that she'd be joining us in the afternoon. The morning's session was more about prices and time frames, so the discussion was more between Jim and Maryann. I spoke only when necessary.

Around noon, instead of joining Maryann and me for lunch, Jim went back to his office to check on the status of the drafts. He promised to call us later. Maryann and I went to a nearby pizzeria to eat.

On the drive back to the office in Maryann's car, we chatted about the company's future. "Rathnaya's lucky that when other software companies tanked during the high-tech slump, it managed to survive," I said.

Maryann shook her head. "Not just luck. We were diversified. Although most of our customers are government agencies, we do different things. If space technology or defense were our only targets like some other companies, we'd have been dead a long time ago. Both those agencies have suffered deep budget cuts over the last several years."

"I'm pretty new to the company, so I don't know that much—only the more recent developments. Tell me more."

"Well, we started out with those two areas, but both Prajay and Nishant decided it was dangerous to put all our eggs in two baskets, so to speak. So they went aggressively after different agencies. Besides the Pentagon and the FBI, we've developed software for Health and Human Services, Labor, Interior, Environmental Protection, states and counties, big and small municipalities. We handle a lot of highly classified material, too."

Something struck me then. "If it's classified material, shouldn't the company be hiring only American citizens? We have so many who are green-card holders, and some even on temporary visas."

Maryann smiled as she pulled the car into a parking spot. "Not everything we do is classified. The non-citizens work strictly on the unclassified stuff. The HR department does a thorough screening before someone's hired."

"Oh." I was learning something about Rathnaya's hiring policies.

"Background checks are rigorous for the people who work on the really secret material. If they successfully pass all security tests and get hired, they have to sign a confidentiality contract. It gets complicated."

"Was I screened, too?" I asked with a grin as I unhooked my seat belt and climbed out of the passenger seat.

Maryann locked her car, and we started toward the building. "Absolutely. And you came up clean—an American citizen who recites the Pledge of Allegiance and washes behind her ears." Her grin matched mine.

As soon as we entered her office, the phone rang. It was Jim. He and Jennifer were coming over in half an hour.

The drafts had very few problems. Jennifer and her crew had obviously done a fine job within the tight deadline. In spite of that, the entire afternoon was gone in dissecting the finer points. It was well after five before Maryann and I could go back to her office and call it a day. Once again, I used her phone to check on Akka. Her bus was on the way back to Fairfax.

"The day went so fast," Maryann said, and stretched. "At least we got a lot accomplished. Now all we have to do is make sure Prajay sees the drafts. If he approves, you can take them back for Nishant's approval."

I went to stand by her window and studied the parking lot. "Do you think you're going to need me for the entire day tomorrow?" My eyes sought out a silver Corvette. I didn't see it. But then it was already dark outside.

"We should be done by midmorning, tops. You're better off leaving before lunch if you want to make it back home at a decent time."

"Good idea," I said, and moved away from the window. "I better get going." I put on my coat and picked up my briefcase. "See you around the same time tomorrow morning?"

Maryann nodded. "Thanks for everything, Meena."

"My pleasure, and thank you for making my work here so pleasant," I said, and took off.

As I got in the car and started the engine, I was grateful I'd found a spot close to the building. Large, dark parking lots in unfamiliar areas made me nervous. Then I heard a tap on my window. And nearly jumped.

Was I being carjacked? I'd heard of instances of car thefts in and around Washington. Heartbeat racing, I instantly turned my head. It was Prajay's face outside the window. Heaving a sigh of relief, I rolled down my window.

He must have noticed the alarm on my face. "Sorry. Did I scare you?"

"I thought I was getting carjacked." I laughed shakily at my jumpiness. "Not that anybody would want my car, but it's still a reliable set of wheels."

"I tried to catch your attention before you climbed in, but you didn't hear me," he said. "Can I talk to you for a minute?"

"I'll be back in the office tomorrow, Prajay. We can talk then." I wasn't sure if I could handle being alone with him.

"I know you have to meet Akka at the hotel, so I'll follow you there. We'll talk while you wait for her."

I looked at the dashboard clock. "All right." I put the car in gear and drove out.

At the hotel, we decided to have a cup of coffee in the restaurant while we waited for Akka's bus to arrive. We picked a table that overlooked the parking lot.

"What did you want to talk about, Prajay?" I was rather proud of my casual attitude. Inside I was turning to mush.

"I wanted to thank you for coming out here on short notice and working on the campaign."

"I'm only doing my job. Besides, Paul has other things to worry about, so this is the least I could do to help."

"Still, I want you to know I appreciate it."

"No problem." I looked at the parking lot once again. More vehicles were pulling in, but there was no sign of the bus. "I should really go," I said.

"Meena."

"Yes?" Why was he stalling?

"I met that lady on the list you made up for me. Her name is Archana Mukherjee."

"Oh . . . that's nice." What else could I say? I was dying to know other details. Was she pretty? Was she what he'd been dreaming about?

"She seems like a nice person. She's brilliant."

"Yeah, I know. She's an engineer. She must be smart."

He gave a self-deprecating laugh. "I feel like a dummy in her company. She's not just good in her field but she seems so well-read about everything. To be honest, I felt a bit intimidated."

"*You,* intimidated?" I remarked. "I'm sure it was only first-date awkwardness. Things will get better. And I'm sure she's pretty."

"Actually we've met twice so far. She is attractive and out-going."

There goes Akka's theory about a mustache and body hair. If she was that perfect, why was she still single? I didn't know if I could sit there any longer and listen to him going on and on about this vision of perfection. "I'm happy for you, Prajay. Looks like you've finally met your match. Hope things go well for you and your . . . uh . . . potential bride."

He was pensive for a few moments before turning the tables on me. "So how are things going with you? How is that young man you were seeing a few weeks ago? What was his name . . . Deepak something?"

"Deepak Iyer. I'm not seeing him anymore. He's . . . He's not my type."

"Sorry to hear that." He took a thoughtful sip from his cup.

"I'm about to meet someone else, though." I figured I might as well start on Akka's harebrained campaign. Prajay would walk off into the sunset with his beanpole—or rather paragon— now that I knew she was pretty. And accomplished. And out-going.

His eyebrow arched. "Anyone I might know?"

I finished the last of my coffee and put the cup down. "You might know him, since he's from New England. He's a Konkani guy from Connecticut, someone my aunt put me in touch with. His name is Ajit Baliga."

"For some reason the name rings a bell." Prajay frowned at his coffee cup. "But then, if you're seeing him, he's got to be a lot younger than me, right? So he couldn't be my classmate or even my contemporary."

"His parents live in the New Haven area. Maybe your folks know his family, since ours is such a tightly knit community."

Prajay kept staring at his cup. "I'm pretty sure I know him, or at least know *of* him. What does he do?"

"He's a stockbroker."

"A young financial whiz." He paused. "I wish you good luck."

"Thanks." I noticed his cup was empty, too. "I've got to go. The bus is here. Akka was exhausted yesterday, and I bet she'll be in worse shape today. She'll need to eat an early dinner and hit the sack."

He rose to his feet reluctantly. "All right. I can see you're impatient to get away from me. I seem to have that effect on women."

"It's not that. I'm just—"

"Relax. I was pulling your leg." He put down some money on the table, and we stepped out into the lobby. Just as I was about to say good night, he did it again: kissed me on the cheek. " 'Bye, Meena."

I lifted my head to look at him. He was smiling warmly. For a moment I was so consumed by the man that thoughts of the bus and Akka's return flew out of my mind. I continued to stare at Prajay, frozen in the moment.

Fortunately the sound of voices snapped me out of my temporary paralysis, and I turned toward the entry doors. Several people were wandering in. The bus people. I stepped back from Prajay.

An instant later, Akka walked in, carrying a plastic shopping bag in one hand, her handbag on her shoulder, looking like she'd been to the moon and back.

I rushed forward. "Hi. How was the expedition?"

Before she replied her shrewd eyes took in Prajay standing behind me. "Nice. Those museums are wonderful. I have never seen anything like that in my life." She smiled at Prajay. "I see Prajay is here, too. My own welcoming committee. I feel so important."

"Prajay was just leaving," I said quickly, before she got any ideas. "He came to . . . uh . . . thank me for covering for my boss." I was talking too fast, but it was the only way to distract Akka. She had that speculative look about her.

"I see." She started walking toward the elevator. "Why don't you two continue your discussion? I'll go upstairs and take a bath."

"I'm going with you. I'll draw an herbal bath for you just like last evening."

"No need for that, *charda*. I know how to fill a tub."

I forcefully took the shopping bag from her while I held on to my briefcase with my other hand. "Don't argue. You're too tired to even stand on your feet. Now let's go upstairs, and I'll order room service. We both need to eat and get some sleep." I marched her to the elevator. While we waited for it to show up, I turned around for a second. "Thanks for the coffee, Prajay."

Akka smiled and waved at him. When the elevator doors opened, I ushered Akka inside and hit the button for our floor. When I looked up, I saw Prajay walking out of the hotel.

"Why did you give up a chance to spend time with him, Meena?" Akka looked confused.

"Please, let's not discuss it, okay? I'm tired; you're exhausted."

"I may be exhausted, but my mind is still working. What is going on between you two?"

The elevator doors opened, and we stepped out. "All right. You want to know? I'll tell you. That idea of making him jealous? It had to be ditched even before it got off the ground."

"Why?"

"He has met a beautiful woman who's even smarter than he. She's everything he wanted, and more. So there." I glared at her.

"Oh." Akka looked a bit stunned. She obediently went inside the room when I opened the door and ordered her in.

"And guess what? She doesn't have a mustache or body hair either."

"Oh." Akka sounded like she had only one word left in her vocabulary.

I dumped her shopping bag on her bed and my briefcase on the sofa. "You know what else? When I told him I was going to meet a nice Konkani stockbroker from Connecticut, he wished me good luck." Akka remained silent. "Wished me *luck,* damn it!"

"Oh." Akka hastily discarded her coat and sneakers and headed for the bathroom. I heard the water running for a while, and then everything went quiet. She didn't come out for a long time.

Guilt began to settle around me. I'd been so nasty to her. It wasn't *her* fault that the jealousy angle hadn't worked. She was only a sweet old lady who was trying to help me. And instead of appreciating her efforts, I was treating her like the enemy.

Well, I'd make it up to her when she came out. I'd give her a big hug and order whatever she wanted from the menu.

But when she finally came out, looking frail and worn out, all she asked for was a cup of warm milk. All my coaxing to eat something did no good. She was adamant. "I'm not hungry, Meena. All I want is a cup of milk to swallow my nighttime pills with. Then I want to go to bed."

"Akka, I'm so sorry. I shouldn't have taken out my frustrations on you," I said to her. Apologizing never came easily to me, so it took some effort. "It's not your fault. It's all mine for falling in love with a big dummy."

"He's not a bad person, Meena," she said gently. "He just hasn't realized that you are the girl for him. Give him some time. Let him socialize with that tall woman for a while. Let him learn."

"He's never going to look at me as anything but an employee. Maybe as a friend, but no more than that."

"Whatever you say," she said, and settled on the bed to massage the smelly ointment into her feet. Apparently it was some kind of *ayurvedic* herbal concoction, and Akka swore by it.

"So you're not mad at me?" I asked her.

"If I got angry at my children and grandchildren for minor things, then I would be upset all my life."

I went up to her and gave her a hug. "Thank you for being so forgiving. I'll order your cup of milk now. How about a nice apple or banana to go with it? You need some nutrition."

"Okay, order me an apple."

"I'll ask for the best apple in the house," I promised her, and picked up the phone.

Chapter 26

As if to match my mood, the next morning turned out cloudy. And it was a good thing that Akka wasn't going into the city. Although I had a folding umbrella with me, Akka would have had a hard time balancing while walking around with an umbrella and that giant handbag of hers.

Despite having nothing scheduled for the morning, Akka was dressed and ready before I was out of bed. I gave her an exasperated look. "Couldn't you sleep in and enjoy at least one quiet morning?"

She glanced at me above her glasses. "I *am* enjoying a quiet morning. I'm reading my favorite verses."

Well, who could argue with that kind of enthusiasm? I yawned and dragged myself to the bathroom. A half hour later we ate our breakfast. I called Maryann to find out how long she expected our meeting to last. "If it's going to be over by mid-morning, I'd like to check out of the hotel now," I said her. She thought that was a good idea. "You mind if my aunt comes with me to the office?"

"Not at all," she replied. "She can always make herself comfortable in the break room or in my office while we conduct business."

I looked at Akka across the table. "Would you mind waiting in the office this morning while I wind up my work?"

"Whatever is convenient for you, *charda*," she replied.

"Good. That way we can check out right now and head home directly after my meeting."

A little later, I had Akka settled in the break room with a couple of Maryann's magazines and a cup of coffee. Prajay joined Maryann and me briefly to offer comments on the proofs. He seemed pleased with them and the costs negotiated by Maryann, so I was free to take a set to Nishant for his final approval.

Around midmorning I went back to the break room to get Akka. Instead of finding her sitting all by herself with a refrigerator, a microwave, and a vending machine for company, I found her surrounded by a bunch of Rathnaya's employees.

Puzzled, I stood at the door to observe what was going on. She was sitting at the head of one of the corner tables, talking. She was holding her arms above her head, palms facing out. The half-dozen individuals at her table seemed to be listening with rapt attention.

"And then, when you feel the tension easing from your lower back, you should exhale slowly, and go back to your relaxed position." Her arms dropped, and her hands gracefully descended to the table. "This you should do at least ten times at each sitting to get any benefits out of it."

She must have become aware of me standing in the doorway, because she looked at me and smiled. "Ah, there you are. Meeting is over?"

The rest of the group turned to look at me. I walked up to them, a little suspicious of what was going on. "What are you doing?" I asked Akka.

"These young people were telling me that they spend so much time on their computers that they suffer from stiff backs and legs, so I showed them some simple yoga exercises to help them relax and avoid back problems."

"No kidding." I had had no idea my great-aunt was an authority on yoga. But then she was the self-proclaimed expert on a lot of things.

One young man smiled at me. "Your auntie is a very smart lady." The others nodded, seconding his opinion.

"And so interesting," added a young woman.

"She certainly is," I agreed. I wondered what these people were doing here listening to Akka's lecture instead of working.

"We were on our midmorning break, and we discovered your aunt here," a bespectacled man explained, probably because he saw my censorious expression.

Just then Prajay and Maryann walked in, bringing the impromptu yoga class to an abrupt end. The men and women quickly returned to their offices with their coffee and sodas. Prajay watched their hasty exit and turned to me with raised brows.

"Akka was lecturing your employees on how to overcome the ills of a sedentary profession," I explained.

"How *does* one overcome that? I'm curious myself."

"Yoga and meditation. You see, yoga is good for the body," said Akka, "while meditation is excellent for the mind and soul."

Prajay looked impressed. "I can see that the art of consulting runs in the family." He threw Akka a quizzical glance. "Maybe I should hire you as a consultant to teach yoga to all my employees."

Was it my imagination, or was there a hint of sarcasm in his words?

Akka didn't appear to notice any cynicism. She looked sufficiently pleased, but pretended modesty. "Oh, don't be silly. I know a little, and I practice it for my own health, that's all. I heard one of them complaining of back pain from sitting for many hours, so I volunteered to show him some stretching exercises followed by meditation. The others were interested, so they stayed to see my demonstration."

Maryann looked intrigued. "Maybe you should teach my husband and me some of that. My husband has a chronic back problem."

"I would be happy to teach you," Akka promised her before turning to me. "Are we leaving soon?"

"Yes. If you want to use the ladies' room, you might want to do it now," I said to her, then watched her make her way out of the break room. Maryann went after her to show her the way to the restroom. I could almost bet Akka was going to express her hope of returning someday to teach yoga to Maryann.

Prajay and I were left alone.

"So, what big weekend plans do you have?" he asked.

I started walking toward the door. "I told you I'm meeting Ajit Baliga." Prajay was right behind me as I went to Maryann's office to retrieve our coats and my briefcase.

"That's right. It slipped my mind."

Was he doing this on purpose—reminding me that he didn't give a damn about my private life? I didn't want to wait another second for Akka and Maryann to return, so I made a beeline for the hallway where the ladies' room was located. They came out just then, making it easy for me to help Akka into her coat and escort her to the elevator. Maryann and Prajay stayed with us while we waited for the elevator.

I shook hands with Maryann first. "Thank you so much for everything, Maryann. It was great meeting you. It's been an interesting couple of days."

Maryann smiled. "Interesting as in hectic, you mean?"

"I like hectic," I assured her. "A busy day goes faster."

Akka said fond good-byes to the two of them, by clasping their hands in both of hers and thanking them profusely for their hospitality.

"I'll walk you ladies to your car," Prajay offered.

"No need for that, thank you." I took Akka's arm to steer her away before she could encourage him.

Prajay shook his head. "It's no trouble at all."

"I'm sure you have enough work piled on your desk," I countered with icy politeness.

He glanced at me warily, then gave in by shaking my hand. "All right, then. Have a safe trip home."

With both relief and regret gnawing at me, I drove toward the highway. Akka looked a bit glum, too. I had a feeling she was experiencing a letdown after a busy couple of days. I glanced at her. "So, did you enjoy your short trip to Washington?"

"Yes, very much." She patted my arm. "Thank you, *charda*.

Most young people don't like to take on the responsibility of old people."

"It was nice having you with me." I sent her an appreciative smile. "Besides, you're not like the other elders in the family. I tend to forget that you're one of *them*."

Akka chuckled. "Don't tell your mother that. She will not invite me to your house anymore. She thinks I'm a bad influence on all the children."

"That's what makes you different. You're a hell of a lot more fun."

By the time we got onto the highway Akka was fast asleep, reminding me that despite her young and modern ways, she was still an old lady.

I put the car on cruise control and started to plan my meeting with Ajit Baliga for the next day.

Chapter 27

Despite having done the blind-date thing before, I was a little tense about meeting Ajit. Thrusting my gloved hands deep into my coat pockets, I walked out of the train station and toward the restaurant.

The temperatures had dropped drastically since the previous day's rain, and the wind was brisk. It whipped my hair about my face, ruining the carefully washed and blow-dried look I'd accomplished.

At least it wasn't raining. A skinny man dressed in a Santa suit and fake white beard stood outside a grocery store, ringing a bell for donations.

Pedestrians were aplenty, but like me, most seemed to be in a hurry to get out of the cold and to their destinations, so they mostly ignored poor Santa. Besides, it was way too early in the season to think about Christmas. The appetizing aroma of Chinese food wafted toward me from somewhere. It reminded me I hadn't eaten breakfast.

Looking at my watch, I realized I had about five minutes to spare before my appointed time. I hoped I could duck into the ladies' room and fix my hair before I faced my date.

When I had told Mom and Dad that I was meeting Ajit that afternoon, Mom had given me an approving nod. "I have a good feeling about this boy. Try to refrain from expressing those strong feminist opinions of yours, at least the first time you meet," she'd warned me. I think she secretly believed this was my last chance before the first gray hairs started to pop up.

Dad was more casual about it. "Be careful in the city," was his terse advice.

Akka was the only one who knew what was going on. She winked at me before I left. I was depressed about her leaving for Shabari-pachi's house the next day. Her two weeks at our house were now over, and my mom was to drive her to my aunt's place. Although she had visited us like clockwork every year, this was the first time Akka and I had become really close.

As I approached the restaurant, I knew I'd lost my chance to fix my hair. A man wearing a brown leather jacket stood outside the building, hands in his jacket pockets, absently watching the traffic. Perhaps to keep himself warm, or from impatience, he was rocking on his heels. I was pretty sure it was my date. The wind was ruffling his short, dark hair.

He must have heard the click of my high-heeled boots, because he turned to face me and stopped rocking.

It was him.

I approached him with a smile and a toss of my head to get the hair out of my eyes. "Hi. Are you early or am I late?" With my three-inch heels I could look him in the eye without having to lift my chin too high. He was an average-sized man.

He pulled his right hand out of his pocket and held it out. "I'm early. Didn't want to take a chance on being late and making a lousy first impression," he said with a grin.

Good sense of humor, I thought as I shook his hand.

He inclined his head toward the restaurant. "Shall we go in?" Opening the door, he ushered me in and shut it behind us.

"Oh, good, it's warm in here." I took off my gloves and put them in my coat pocket.

"And smells great. The aroma of *chimichangas* was driving me crazy while I stood outside," he told me.

While we waited to be seated, I looked around. The place wasn't very crowded, perhaps because of the blustery weather. Only half a dozen tables were occupied, mostly by young couples. An older man who appeared to be the owner approached us and led us to a table, telling us that a waitress would be with us in a minute.

"Are *chimichangas* your favorite Mexican food?" I asked Ajit. I slung my coat on the back of my chair while Ajit did the same with his.

"I like anything as long as it's spicy enough to strip a layer off the roof of my mouth," he replied, waiting for me to get seated. As he pulled out his own chair and sat down, I took a quick inventory. He wore a thick, gray sweatshirt and jeans. His hands were square, with a dusting of dark hair on the backs and wrists.

He looked like a clean-cut, wholesome Indian man—everything Madhuri-pachi had said he was.

"In that case, we're at the right place. They make some killer hot food here." I combed my fingers through my tangled tresses and patted them into place, hoping the effort made me look somewhat presentable.

On the other hand, I noticed Ajit hadn't bothered to do anything with his hair. It looked windblown, but he didn't seem to care. I rather liked that in a man, the lack of vanity. I couldn't stand men who constantly fussed with their hair and clothes—a feminine trait.

That's what I liked about Prajay: He was always well-groomed, but never fidgeted with his hair or his tie or buttons. I tried to shake off the thought. I had to put an end to that kind of wistfulness. Prajay was probably having a courtship weekend with his date.

A young waitress approached us, thankfully dragging my thoughts away from Prajay. She came with a couple of menus and a basket of nacho chips and a bowl of salsa. "Can I get you anything to drink?" she said, glancing at us with the usual polite ennui that comes with seeing hundreds of customers every week.

As the waitress hurried off to fetch our drinks, we studied our menus. It gave us both a chance to let certain facts about each other register. It was typical: meet, greet, assess, and deliberate. Both Ajit and I would more or less make up our minds within the next twenty minutes whether this initial meeting would go somewhere or not.

So far, so good, I concluded. He seemed nice enough and was decent looking. Whether there'd be any spark of chemistry between us was yet to be seen.

"I think I'll have the taco salad," I said, finally looking up from my menu. I'd known I wanted the taco salad even before I'd walked into the restaurant.

"Is that all you're going to eat?" Ajit dug into the chips and salsa. "No wonder you're so slim."

"You haven't seen the size of their salad," I told him, thinking he was on the slim side himself. "I bet I won't even finish half of it." His shoulders were narrow compared to Prajay's.

Oops, I was having silly thoughts again.

The waitress came back with our drinks. "Ready to order?" After taking our orders for my salad and Ajit's *chimichangas,* she disappeared.

Now that the preliminaries of food and drink were out of the way, it was time to get down to the basics of getting to know each other. "So, how was your trip to Washington?" Ajit reached for another nacho chip. In fact, he had already made a dent in the mound of chips.

"Very productive." I took a sip of my refreshing sangria. "My work isn't all that exciting, so tell me about yours."

He laughed. "You think *my* work is exciting? I buy and sell stocks and bonds." He took a swallow of his beer. "I'm glued to a computer and a phone all day. Some days, I work ten to twelve hours, and others less than six. It all depends."

"Madhuri-pachi says you're very successful; you must be doing something right."

"I live comfortably." He was no fool. He went back to eating chips, hinting that was as far as he'd go in revealing his financial status. "Your *pachi* tells me the same about you. I've heard a lot of good things." His tone was light, teasing.

"Madhuri-pachi is a bit prejudiced when it comes to her family. In her book, we're all wildly successful and good-looking."

"She was right about your looks. You're even prettier in person than you are in your pictures."

My cheeks warmed. "Exactly how many pictures of me did my aunt share with you?"

"Oh, six or seven . . . or eight." Maybe because I rolled my eyes, he added with a chuckle, "Actually I saw two. And they were nice."

"Had she mentioned to you how short I am?" Konkani boys were usually obsessed with tall girls. I didn't want him to get the wrong impression because of my high heels.

"She did say you were petite."

"Petite is a polite term for midget."

"That's okay, Meena. I'm not exactly a tall guy myself, so I have no problem meeting a petite girl." He grinned in between sips of beer. "In fact, I like petite women."

Well, this was a first. It was refreshing to come across a guy who didn't have grand notions about his own height. Right then and there I sort of made up my mind that Ajit Baliga was an all-right guy. But I was still waiting for the elusive spark. "So, have you dated many petite girls?"

He stared at me. "Didn't your aunt tell you?"

Uh-oh. "Tell me what?"

"That I used to be engaged to someone?"

"No . . . she didn't." I should've known Madhuri-pachi would conceal something significant like an ex-fiancée from me.

"I'm sorry. I was under the impression you knew." He was silent for a moment. "Does that mean you don't want to continue with this lunch?"

"Don't be silly. I have nothing against past relationships." I didn't want to tell him that I'd dated a few guys myself, even if I hadn't been engaged to any. "This is America. Dating is something guys and girls are expected to do."

He nodded his relief. "Glad to hear that. For a moment I thought you'd get up and walk out."

Our food arrived just then, giving me an opportunity to get my thoughts together for a suitable response. The combined scents of cumin, hot peppers, onions, and tomatoes made my mouth water. The taco shell looked fresh and crisp. Ajit's *chimichangas* looked wonderful, too, with curls of smoke rising from the dish.

I glanced at Ajit. "Why did you think I'd walk out?"

"Your aunt tells me your parents are very old-fashioned, so naturally I thought—"

"—that I was a conservative little fuddy-duddy?"

"Not quite like that." His expression told me that's exactly what he'd assumed.

I laughed. "That's okay. Madhuri-pachi is right about my parents, but my brothers and I are hardly like that. My brother . . ." I wasn't sure if Maneel would appreciate my discussing his affairs with a total stranger. Moreover, Mom and Dad wouldn't approve of my telling such stories to a potential groom. It would automatically render me ineligible in the eyes of most Konkani men.

"What about your brother?" Ajit pressed, leaving me no choice but to tell.

Oh, what the heck, everyone would learn soon enough about Maneel and Naseem anyway. "My older brother, Maneel, who's a stockbroker like you, is more or less engaged to a Muslim girl."

"Really? Your aunt didn't tell me that either."

"I know why," I said blandly. "She wouldn't want you to reject the idea of meeting me because my brother's about to marry a Muslim girl."

Ajit looked amused. "Just like she didn't tell you I was engaged once."

I gave a mock groan. "Aunts can be so sly and manipulative."

Now that we'd laughed about how absurd it was that Madhuri had deliberately withheld information, a level of comfort began to settle over us. As we ate, we chatted about our hobbies and favorite movies and music. Ajit's food started to disappear at a brisk pace. The guy had a hearty appetite.

Between bites I cocked an eyebrow at Ajit. "Can I ask you something personal?"

He paused. "I'll try to answer."

"Why aren't you engaged anymore?"

"She didn't want to marry me after all. She was in love with a classmate of hers and started seeing me only because her parents wanted it."

"You mean they forced it on her like they do with some girls in India?" I was beginning to feel full, so I pushed my half-eaten salad aside.

"I don't think they forced her as such. I believe they tried to convince her it was better to marry a Konkani rather than a Polish guy."

"She didn't have *anything* to say about it?" What American-bred young woman in her right mind would agree to being manipulated like that?

Ajit finished his food and wiped his mouth with a napkin. "Not in the beginning. We saw each other for about five months. It was expected that we'd get engaged, so I proposed, and she accepted. One day, she just flat out told me it would never work between us because she was still in love with her Polish boyfriend."

"Oh, wow. Must have been rough." I could only imagine.

"At least she was honest." Why was he defending her?

"But not in the beginning," I pointed out. "Was she still seeing him while you guys were dating?"

"I believe she was sincerely trying to forget him to make her parents happy. But then . . ." Ajit shrugged. "Who knows? She might have stayed in touch with him on some level."

I felt sorry for Ajit. I wondered if he had loved this girl. And who *was* she? I'd have to ask Madhuri-pachi. "I'm sorry it didn't work out, Ajit," I said.

He made a face. "Better to know before than *after* we'd been married."

"Were you . . . uh . . . did you love her?"

"I don't know if it was love. I liked her a lot, and we got

along well, so naturally I was furious when she broke up with me." He paused for a moment. "Everyone in the community knew about us. She was pretty and bright and a lot of fun. But I always felt like she was holding something back from me. I didn't know what it was then, but it made sense afterward. She was in love with someone else."

"So, did she marry the boyfriend?"

Ajit nodded. "Soon after we split up. I understand she's expecting a baby in the spring." He spoke in detached terms, but I could see a lingering something in his dark brown eyes. Was it sadness? Regret?

"How do you feel about it?"

"It's been over two years. I wish her well," he said, assuring me he was fully recovered from whatever feelings he'd had for the other woman.

I admired Ajit's ability to forgive and forget. Most men wouldn't be quite so generous where their egos were concerned. He really had to be a decent person to have done that.

However, despite my sympathy for Ajit, I felt a certain camaraderie with his nameless fiancée. When a girl fell in love, she fell hard. No matter whom I ended up marrying, a part of my heart would stay with Prajay. It was silly to assume that now, but at the moment, it was the truth. Not even a devastatingly good-looking and charming man could come close to Prajay.

Our waitress came back a second time to check on our progress and, seeing we had finished eating, asked if I'd like to take my leftover salad home, to which I shook my head. Ajit asked me if I'd like to share a fried ice cream if he ordered one.

"Okay. Maybe a little," I said, wanting to make him feel better. My sympathetic vibes and the maternal instinct to soothe a bruised ego were still humming. Poor, poor Ajit. Although he hadn't been deeply in love and he looked none the worse for the episode, his heart had been damaged a little.

The fried ice cream was excellent, so I ate nearly half of it, surprising both Ajit and myself. We had coffee with it, too. Whether it was the beer that warmed him up or something in my attitude, I couldn't say, but he seemed to open up to me some more. I learned that he had been working for the same company for six years. He owned a house in an upscale part of Connecticut, and he drove a Jaguar. Not bad for a thirty-two-year-old.

Since it was too windy and cold to take a walk outside, we lingered over coffee. Our lunch date went over two hours—closer to three. Since it wasn't crowded and we ordered more refills of coffee, the management didn't seem to want to shoo us out.

And Ajit Baliga seemed to become more appealing. Of course, it could have been a combination of the sangria, the good food, and the rich dessert that was making me more accepting of a man who wasn't Prajay. Whatever it was, it was a good feeling.

When I asked if I could split the bill the waitress handed him, Ajit flatly refused. "I never let a lady pay," he assured me.

And that was fine with me. I thanked him for an enjoyable lunch.

It had been a fun date. I'd liked the sense of comfort I'd felt with Ajit. It was different from what I had felt with the other Konkani guys I'd gone out with. This man didn't seem full of himself.

I wondered how *he* felt about our meeting. He'd been pleasant and talkative and attentive, but he hadn't mentioned whether he was having a good time. Oh well, if nothing ever came of this, at least it had been a perfectly pleasant afternoon with a pleasant guy.

Outside the restaurant, Ajit smiled at me warmly. "Thanks for suggesting this place. The food was excellent."

"Spicy enough for you?"

"Oh, yes." He thrust his hands in his pockets and looked around, as if at a loss for words.

I stood awkwardly, with the wind wreaking havoc on my hair once again. "Thanks for a nice lunch, Ajit."

"So . . . um . . . you want to do this again sometime?" he said finally, breaking a long silence.

"I'd like that. Call me." I pulled out one of my business cards and a pen from my purse and wrote my cell number on the back of it for him. Then we started walking back in the direction of the station.

The wind was worse now, and thick black clouds were beginning to gather directly above us. "Looks like it might start raining any minute. Let's get a cab," he said.

We flagged down a cab, hopped in, and settled in the seat, grateful for the warmth, all the way to Penn Station.

My train was earlier than his, so he saw me safely to mine. "I'll call you soon," he said.

"Okay," I said with a wave.

Ajit Baliga had potential. But why hadn't I felt anything other than warm skin against mine when Ajit had shaken my hand? Why had I been comparing him to Prajay in every way possible? Why had I kept recalling the meals I'd had with Prajay sitting across the table from me?

As the train started to move, Akka's warning started to bug me. What if Ajit had felt something for me?

Chapter 28

It was a relief to see Paul back in the office on Monday morning, looking like his normal laid-back self. His expression said Jeremy's surgery had gone well. But the lunch bag was conspicuously absent.

I followed him into his office. "I gather Jeremy's on the mend?"

"Yes, thanks. He's home now and kicking up a fuss, but he's doing fine."

"I bet *he* doesn't think he's doing fine."

Paul threw me a wry look before taking off his coat. "How'd you guess? He thinks he's going to die unless some minor miracle saves him."

"So how come you left him alone at home?"

"I didn't. Old Mrs. McMillan next door offered to keep an eye on him." Paul chuckled as he started walking toward the coffee machine. "Jeremy dislikes old Gertie McMillan because she's tough as a drill sergeant."

"Was it a good idea to leave them together, then?"

Paul shrugged. "I might find one of them dead by the time I get home this evening." But his sly smile said he was enjoying the thought of leaving Jeremy in the hands of some crusty old dragon.

During the next hour I filled Paul in on what had happened at my meetings in Washington. He seemed pleased with the progress.

I promised I'd write up a report for him later and show him all the literature I'd brought with me.

It wasn't a big surprise that Ajit called that night, asking if we could meet again the following Saturday. His expression when we'd parted had made it clear he'd be calling soon.

I had nothing else planned, so I agreed. For our second date, Ajit decided to drive down to New Jersey so we could go to Atlantic City, in which case it was inevitable that he'd meet my parents. I wasn't particularly happy about the idea, but in our culture the parents got involved on some level rather early in the process, so I decided to go along with the idea.

Later, when I told Mom that Ajit and I were meeting for the second time, she looked delighted enough to put her cooking on hold. Apparently this was more important than getting dinner on the table. "So you guys hit it off right away?"

"I wouldn't call it hitting it off, but he seems like a nice guy."

"Yes, but—"

"Mom," I interrupted her. "Don't go buying wedding saris or *vajra kuttuk*." Diamond cluster earrings—typically given to a Konkani bride by her parents. "We're just meeting as friends."

Mom's smile didn't falter. "Okay, but can I at least tell Madhuri?"

"No. Madhuri-pachi is going to call Ajit's mother, and they're both going to start picking out wedding invitations. I don't want that. It stresses me out."

With a resigned sigh Mom went back to the stove. Watching her look so disappointed, I placed a hand on her arm. "Hey, if anything promising develops, you'll be the first to know. Right now we're just getting to know each other."

Without warning she turned and kissed me on the forehead. Mom wasn't the hugging and kissing type. The gesture left me staring at her.

It was 10:15 A.M., Saturday. I was dressed and ready for Ajit to arrive, while Mom made brunch and Dad pretended to watch television in the family room. We were all a bit on edge, for different reasons.

"Have fun in AC, dear," Mom said, giving me an encouraging look. "You need any cash?"

"I have enough, thanks." Even though I had a job now, once in a while Mom and Dad still asked if I needed money. "I've set a gambling limit of fifty dollars for myself."

"Good idea. It's easy to go bankrupt in those casinos." Mom gave a vigorous stir to the pot of mixed vegetable *sookke,* a curry made with chopped potatoes and a variety of vegetables, cooked with a hot and spicy coconut-based sauce. The steam that arose from the pot smelled wonderful.

I went into the powder room and checked myself in the mirror. My makeup and hair looked fine. I had on simple black slacks and a red turtleneck sweater. I felt no excitement about the trip to AC. My parents seemed way more excited than I was.

This was my second date with a nice guy, a decent-looking and successful man who I happened to like a lot. And he seemed to like me, too. So why wasn't there a tingling in my bloodstream?

Hearing a car outside, I went to the family room window to take a peek. Dad gave me a curious look. Noticing Ajit's black Jaguar coming to a stop outside, I turned around and announced, "He's here."

Dad got to his feet and smoothed his jeans and sweater. Mom took off her apron and patted her hair in place. Boy, this was scary—both my parents behaving like they were about to meet a celebrity. I prayed they wouldn't get too friendly. I didn't want Ajit to get the wrong impression.

"Hope I'm not late," he said with a sunny smile when I opened the door and invited him in. He wore gray Dockers and the same leather jacket he'd been wearing the previous weekend. The chilly breeze brought in a whiff of his cologne. It smelled pleasantly masculine.

"Not at all," I assured him and shut the door. "Come meet my parents."

After I made the introductions and everyone had shaken hands, Mom escorted him to the family room. "Would you like to have some brunch before you guys leave, Ajit?" she asked him. Dad smiled widely, seconding her invitation.

Uh-oh, they were treating him like a privileged son-in-law already.

Perhaps a little flustered by the attention from my parents, Ajit raised his brow at me. "Do we have time for it?"

I shook my head. "It's a long ride to AC. Why don't we grab lunch there?"

Mom flashed her most charming smile. "Ajit, do you like mixed vegetable *sookke?* We're having that and fresh *chappatis,*" she said, referring to the thinly rolled whole-wheat flatbread that's typical of our cuisine.

"So that's what smells so good," said Ajit. "I love *sookke* . . . but . . ." He glanced at me again.

I got the feeling he was hungry after his long drive from Connecticut, and Mom's *sookke* was generally a big hit with most guests. I gave in. "All right."

Without a moment's hesitation Mom swept into the kitchen to set the table. Dad marched right behind her, supposedly to help, making me chuckle inwardly. Dad helping in the kitchen was a rarity in our home. He was clearly trying to give Ajit and me some privacy. In fact, I had a sneaking suspicion Mom had planned on inviting Ajit to brunch all along. She'd cooked an awful lot of food.

Ajit slipped off his jacket, and I noticed he had on a tan pullover sweater. The combination of sweater and Dockers looked rather nice and preppy. But he wasn't a refined dresser like Prajay. "Hope I didn't ruin your plans by agreeing to eat here," he whispered.

"No. You'll make my mom's day. You know how moms are."

"Sure." He sniffed appreciatively. "It smells great."

Brunch went off beautifully, with Mom at her most attentive and Dad at his most talkative. As I'd expected, Ajit had an appetite, so he ate loads of Mom's food, pleasing her immensely. He even gave Dad some useful tips on investing.

When we finally got into Ajit's car and pulled out of the drive-way, I noticed Mom and Dad waving at us with smug looks on their faces. I settled back in the passenger seat, praying Mom wouldn't run to the phone and tell Madhuri-pachi to start planning a bridal shower.

But I had to admit the trip to Atlantic City was pleasant. It was warmer than the previous Saturday, and the highways were not too crowded. We drove directly to Caesars Casino because I was familiar with it. I lost my fifty bucks within the first half hour at the slot machines, but I found Ajit was a savvy black-jack player, and he won nearly eight hundred dollars. To celebrate, we went into the bar for drinks.

"Let's take a stroll along the boardwalk before the sun goes down," he suggested, so we buttoned up, put on our gloves, and went for a stroll on the nearly deserted boardwalk. The breeze coming off the ocean was chilly. But the leisurely walk felt good.

We spoke little, enjoying the vista of endless ocean and sea-gulls. Every once in a while we saw a jogger or two and a few people like us trying to get some fresh air. We walked about a mile and then returned to Caesars.

We scanned the menu posted on an easel outside the restau-rant just inside the lobby, with its domed ceiling made to look like a Mediterranean night sky, complete with twinkling stars and faux moonlight. We decided to eat right there and save our-selves the bother of finding another restaurant.

All through the meal, Ajit told me funny anecdotes about his college days and his colleagues at his present job, making me re-alize that Ajit did indeed have a great sense of humor. He kept me entertained and made me laugh several times.

It was late by the time we finished eating, so we decided to go home instead of back to the casino. Ajit had a long drive back to Connecticut.

When we got on to the expressway, Ajit took his hand off the wheel and reached for mine. "You're awfully quiet. Is every-thing all right?"

"I'm just tired. I'm not much into exercise, so the long walk did it for me." I was very aware of his warm, hard hand curled around mine, but I didn't feel the same flutter I'd experienced when Prajay had touched me. I sincerely wished I could feel something, especially since Ajit was trying so hard to be pleasant.

About an hour into our drive I asked Ajit if we could go to a rest stop. We used the restrooms and picked up some coffee at the Starbucks inside the building. Once inside the car, Ajit turned on the ignition but didn't pull out of the parking spot right away.

I had this odd feeling that things between us were changing. I could sense something coming. Call it feminine intuition.

Ajit turned to me and touched my cheek. "I enjoyed the day. You're great to hang out with, Meena." His eyes were warm, and his voice sounded just a bit husky. Or was I imagining it?

"Thanks. You're not so bad yourself," I said. And I meant it. He was a very likeable guy.

"So you want to meet up with me next weekend?" His hand stayed on my face.

"Can't. Next weekend is our company's holiday party."

He removed his hand. "Maybe the weekend after?"

"Maybe." I wondered if it was too early in our relationship to invite him to our office party. All the employees had been encouraged to bring a guest. All the married people were bringing their spouses, and many others were bringing a significant other. I decided to ask him anyway. "Would you like to come to the party with me?"

His expression brightened. "I'd like that. But wouldn't I be crashing the party?"

"Uh-uh. They encourage everyone to bring a date . . . or whomever."

"Sounds like fun."

I took a sip of my coffee, wondering if I'd started something I shouldn't have. "Should I RSVP for two, then?"

"Sure. Thanks." That warm look flashed in his eyes again.

Akka's words of caution were beginning to beat a rhythmic rat-a-tat-tat in my brain. Nonetheless, we drove the rest of the way companionably, chatting. Not surprisingly, we found we knew a few people in common.

By the time he walked me to my door, I realized I was dead tired and ready for bed, so I didn't bother inviting him inside. This time when he bid me good-bye, he didn't shake hands; he kissed me on the cheek. It was a friendly kiss, nothing more. "Good night. I'll see you next week."

"I'll let you know the time and dress code for the party." I let myself in and deactivated the alarm, then waited while Ajit pulled out of the driveway before closing the door.

Taking a peek in the garage, I noticed Dad's car was missing. It meant Mom and Dad weren't home. I was grateful. I didn't want to see the look of optimism on their faces . . . not yet. Although I'd had a good time, I wasn't sure what I felt for Ajit Baliga.

The bad thing was my feelings for Prajay were still the same. If anything, they seemed more enhanced now, more painful. It was this deep pit inside my chest, which felt so empty and dark, it had no chance of ever brightening up.

Pinky reminded me about the holiday party first thing Monday morning. "What are you wearing for the party on Saturday?"

"What does everyone else usually wear? Formal, semi-formal?"

"Most of the women wear either *salwar-kameez,* or *chania-choli,* or dresses. The men wear what they always wear around here: slacks and casual shirts."

"Is the party a lot of fun or is it the usual forced office humor and lots of booze?"

"The party's always fantastic. Nishant and Prajay are big spenders."

I sipped my first cup of coffee and watched Pinky boot up her computer.

"With so many Indians in this place, I would've thought they'd have a Diwali party instead of Christmas," I said, referring to the Hindu festival of lights, which usually falls in late October or November.

"This is actually a combination. In fact, many of the folks here refer to it as Chri-wali."

"Christmas-Diwali." It made sense, since the two holidays fell so close to each other, and the basic traditions of decorating with lights and exchanging gifts were somewhat similar.

"There'll be dancing, and a DJ who plays both *Bhangra* and rock, so put on your dancing shoes," Pinky advised. "And think about bringing a boyfriend if you have one. Everyone is encouraged to bring a significant other." She gave me a meaningful look—just short of prying.

I pretended not to notice. "Maybe I will." I was glad Ajit wanted to come. It would be nice to have a guy by my side when I faced Prajay—especially if Prajay's date was going to be there.

If Prajay was planning to invite her—and he most likely would—this would be my chance to check her out. The woman I'd helped him connect with.

Chapter 29

On the day of the party, I went through my closet a couple of times, trying to decide what to wear. It was a tough choice. I wanted to look pretty and sexy and seductive enough for Prajay to notice me, but not so provocative that Ajit got the wrong idea.

It was too late to go shopping for a new outfit.

I sort of liked my plum *chania-choli* outfit. Its ankle-length, silver-beaded skirt and short blouse with a slightly risqué neckline and no sleeves was very flattering. The *chunni* was a gauzy boa that floated around the neck and shoulders. Very ethnic— and it made me look taller. But then I thought the cream silk dress with a short, above-the-knee hemline was nice, too—a bit more formal.

Both the ensembles looked good with my complexion and long, dark hair. I held each one against me and looked in the mirror, then gave up trying to make a choice for the moment and placed them on the bed. I started doing my face, hoping inspiration would strike while I worked in the foundation. I'd never had this kind of dilemma before. I usually picked one outfit, threw it on, and I was done.

The doorbell rang downstairs, and I heard one of my parents get the door. I heard voices. A minute later I heard footsteps in the hallway outside my room and then a knock on my door. I glanced at the bedside clock. Was I was running late? Was that

Ajit at my door? But then Mom and Dad would never have sent him upstairs to my bedroom.

"Who is it?" I asked.

"Meena, can I come in?" It was my cousin Amrita's voice.

"Sure. Door is unlocked."

She walked in, glanced at me and then at the clothes spread out on the bed. "Getting ready to go somewhere fancy?" she asked, one eyebrow lifted. She was wearing tight jeans and a pink sweatshirt that made her cheeks look like roses. She was such a pretty girl and so tall. I wished I had that kind of height. Some girls had all the luck.

"The office holiday party," I replied, picking up a tube of mascara. "I can't decide what to wear."

"Maybe I can help?" She held up the two outfits, studied them.

"Maybe you can." While I brushed the mascara over my lashes, I saw her eyeing the *chania-choli* a little longer than the dress. "You like that?"

"It's more sophisticated and kind of sexy." She threw me a sly grin. "Are you like . . . um . . . going for the siren image or the little cupcake? What does Prajay Nayak like?"

I tossed her a frown. "How should *I* know? And what do I care what Prajay likes? I'm going to the party with Ajit Baliga."

"Oh. I thought you had the hots for your boss."

"Where'd you get that silly idea?" I hoped my scowl looked genuine. Of course I had the hots for my boss, but I wasn't about to tell my cousin that. Already she was teasing me and enjoying it thoroughly. She hadn't stopped grinning.

She held up the *chania-choli*. "Definitely this."

I put the mascara back on the dresser and started to unbutton my shirt. I glanced at her after I'd pulled on the *choli*. "What brings you here today? You're always studying or working."

"I need your help with something. I'm on the newsletter committee this semester. You know I'm hopeless at that sort of thing." She pushed the cream dress aside and sat on the bed.

"Then why'd you agree to do it?"

"I had no choice. They pick people at random because no one wants to do it. Everyone who's enrolled in a medical program is too busy to edit some silly newsletter, let alone write something for it."

"It's exactly the kind of work I like doing."

Her eyes lit up. "So you'll do it?"

"No problem, kiddo." I stepped into the skirt and zipped up the side. "I'll help . . . if you promise to help me with this ensemble and do my hair."

"Deal." She jumped up, buttoned my *choli* in the back, then draped and pinned the *chunni* over my shoulder.

I put on my amethyst-studded silver necklace and matching earrings.

Amrita combed my hair, expertly pulled a section of it up, and fastened it with my silver-and-faux-amethyst barrette. The rest of my hair fell in smooth waves over my shoulders. I stepped into my black, high-heeled sandals with silver buckles.

I looked almost as tall as my cousin. My face glowed.

"Thanks, Amrita. I'm glad you showed up."

Amrita stood back and studied me. "You look beautiful. I think this Ajit guy is going to start drooling."

I sighed at the thought of Ajit. "I hope not."

"Why would you say that?" It took Amrita a moment to comprehend my words. "Oh . . . It's Nayak."

I shrugged and adjusted my *chunni*.

Amrita's eyes narrowed. "Is Ajit an instrument to make Prajay jealous?"

Clever girl. She'd figured it out in a split second. But then she'd had an almost perfect score on her SATs. "I'm not saying anything." I picked up my black-and-silver clutch.

Clucking like a mother hen, Amrita put her hands on her hips. "You better be careful when you start playing games like that with your dates, Meena."

"I'll try to be careful, Mother dear," I replied.

Amrita looked at the bedside clock. "What time are you leaving?"

"Ajit is supposed to pick me up around six."

"It's nearly that now."

She followed me down the stairs, and we went into the family room where I could keep my eye on the driveway. It was easier to let Amrita keep chattering about the newsletter than to carry on a conversation.

The prospect of meeting Prajay's new flame was giving me a mild headache. What Amrita had cautioned me about was bugging me, too. She was right, the wise little devil. I was playing dangerous games. Never having done this sort of thing before, I doubted if I was capable of dealing with the fallout.

Several minutes later, Ajit arrived. He looked good in black slacks, crisp white shirt, and a sports jacket. Under ordinary circumstances his brilliant smile should have made my heart flutter. These were no ordinary circumstances.

Amrita was right behind me, so I introduced Ajit to her. "Ajit, meet my cousin, Amrita."

They shook hands. "Nice to meet you," Amrita murmured.

I could have sworn she was blushing. The roses in her cheeks looked pinker.

"Likewise," said Ajit, and he gave her his most charming smile. "Are you the cousin that's in med school?"

"Yes." Amrita's blush deepened, rose turning to hot pink, making me wonder why she was so discombobulated at meeting someone as easygoing as Ajit.

"So how do you like med school?" Ajit put his hands in his pockets and tilted his head to one side, a gesture I'd come to realize meant he was paying close attention.

"Work, work, and more work," said Amrita with a resigned smile.

"I'm sure you'll survive." Ajit blinked a couple of times.

"Thank you." Amrita's voice was low and demure.

Mom and Dad stepped into the entry foyer to greet Ajit, and they started up a conversation.

After a minute of polite talk, Ajit and I left. Ajit turned to me as he started up the car. "You look fantastic this evening."

"Thanks. You look good yourself. I like your jacket."

"What, this old thing?" We both laughed at the cliché. As he pulled out of the driveway, he asked, "Is Amrita your cousin on your father's side or mother's?"

"Mother's." I glanced at him. "Why?"

"No reason," he said. "There isn't much resemblance between you two."

"None of the cousins look anything alike. Even my brothers are so different from each other, you'd never know they were siblings. Maneel is average height and weight, but Mahesh is tall and skinny. I'm the little runt in the middle, fairer in complexion and spunkier than those two."

Ajit laughed at my words, but didn't comment. We drove mostly in silence. Ajit seemed to be deep in thought. I glanced at him once or twice to see if I had inadvertently said something to offend him, but it didn't seem that way. He appeared to be thinking. Maybe he had other things on his mind.

The party was just getting started when we got to Akbar restaurant in Edison. What caught my eye as we stepped into the banquet hall was the delightful Christmas-Diwali display.

On a round table was a lovely golden statue of the goddess Lakshmi, resplendent in a red and gold sari as she posed imperiously inside a giant lotus blossom. She was surrounded by brass oil lamps. Next to her sat a miniature Christmas tree, about the same height as the goddess, beautifully decorated in red and gold ornaments and miniature lights.

A perfect Chri-wali exhibit. East meets West.

For a minute, Ajit and I marveled over the themes of Hinduism and Christianity blending in such seamless harmony. It was such a lovely sentiment.

The rest of the large banquet hall was set up with several round tables and a polished wood floor in the center for dancing. A DJ was already at his post at the far end of the floor. Hindi movie music played softly in the background. About twenty or more people were scattered around the room, talking.

With my luck, Gargi Bansal was the first person we ran into.

I had a feeling she'd seen us and deliberately decided to bump into us. Dressed in a silvery *salwar-kameez,* she put on a disarming smile, most likely for Ajit's benefit. "Hi, Meena."

"Hi, Gargi." Loath to seem ill-mannered, I introduced her to Ajit. Mercifully, a minute later we moved forward to chat with others.

I introduced Ajit to some other folks. My big surprise came when Deepak Iyer stopped by and wished us happy holidays. From the look in his eyes he'd already had a drink or two. But whatever it was that was making him amiable, I was grateful. I didn't want a scene with someone I'd dated once. He was even courteous to Ajit, despite knowing Ajit was my date for the evening.

A little later we saw Nishant, who, as always, had on a loud print shirt and khakis. He pumped Ajit's hand with great enthusiasm when I introduced the two. "Nice to meet you, Ajit. Stockbroker, huh? I got to talk to you, man. See, here's the thing . . ." He looked around cautiously and took Ajit aside to a safe, quiet corner and started whispering. Their heads were close together. I could see Ajit paying careful attention.

While I waited for Nishant and Ajit to finish their conversation, I felt a tap on my shoulder. Turning around, I came face-to-face with Prajay. My mouth turned dry. He was dressed in a dark suit and snow-white shirt—not a hair out of place. He looked bigger than usual, maybe because all the short guys in the company happened to be around us.

"Hi, Meena." His smile was warm and . . . platonic.

"Hi." I wasn't sure if I'd succeeded in covering up my breathlessness. My tongue was tied up in knots.

"Good to see you," he said.

"Hmm." My tongue was untied, but still felt stiff. "How . . . have you been?"

"Very busy. I've been working fourteen-hour days on a new project." He shrugged. "Other than that, doing fine." He studied me intently for a second, sending the blood soaring into my face. "I see you're doing brilliantly. Lovely as always."

I cast my eyes downward. "I don't know about brilliantly, but I'm okay. I'm busy, too."

"Paul says you're doing great. But I meant you're *looking* wonderful." His eyes had a speculative look. "I've never seen you in Indian clothes."

"Thanks. You're looking well yourself. Fourteen-hour workdays must suit you."

"Hard work has its pros, especially if you enjoy it." He inclined his head toward the bar. "Shouldn't you be drinking something, enjoying the party?"

"I will, as soon as my date finishes talking to Nishant," I said, glancing at the two men still deep in conversation.

"Ah, you brought a date." His bushy eyebrows lifted a notch. "Is that . . . uh . . . the guy you mentioned the other day?"

I nodded. "Ajit Baliga." I let my eyes rove over the room for a spectacularly tall woman. I didn't see any. "So where's *your* date? I assumed Alpana would be here this evening."

"Archana."

"So where is Archana? I was hoping to meet her. After all, I've played a small part in your meeting her. I—"

"She's not here."

"Why not? Aren't you two engaged, or at least going steady by now?" I wished I could keep the acid out of my voice, but it was hard under the circumstances—what with my skin tingling from his nearness and my heartbeat thundering in my chest.

"No, we're not engaged. She's . . . well . . . It's a long story. I'll tell you some other time."

He looked uncomfortable, making me wonder what was going on between him and the beanpole. A tiny spark of optimism went off in my brain, but died just as quickly. There were other women on that list. He'd go on to the next, and the next, until he found the right one. I'd never be in the running.

Just then Ajit returned to my side, and I made the introductions. The men shook hands, both seemingly cordial. If I'd been hoping for animosity or a hint of jealousy on Prajay's part, I saw none. Naturally Ajit had no reason to dislike Prajay.

"You look familiar, Ajit," said Prajay with a puzzled look.

"When Meena mentioned your name the other day, I told her it rang a bell. Have we met before?"

Ajit shook his head. "We may have. In our community that's not impossible. I wouldn't be surprised if we're related." A second later, he snapped his fingers. "Wait. Did you by any chance attend any of the New England area summer camps in your high school days?"

"I was a youth counselor at one in Connecticut in my junior year in high school." Prajay paused a moment. "I was trying to build up my resume for my college applications."

"That's where we met. I attended the camp two years in a row."

Prajay's brow creased. "You were a counselor?"

"Not a counselor, but a camper. I think you were our youth counselor during my first summer. I remember an exceptionally tall Konkani guy who taught us soccer. I couldn't remember the name, though."

"Ah . . . yes. That's why you look so familiar—but I couldn't place you. You were only a kid." Prajay gave himself a moment to recall some facts. "You were the guy who played the guitar?"

"That's me. I played that for a couple of years. Then I moved on to drums. By the way, I think your parents and mine are acquaintances."

Prajay laughed. "I bet they are. Like you said, we may even turn out to be distant cousins." He ushered both of us toward the bar. "Let's all get something to drink, shall we?"

After I got a glass of chardonnay and Ajit got himself some shiraz, we found a table. I was hoping Prajay could join us, but he couldn't. As the co-host he had to mingle with all the guests. These were all his people; this was his world.

Pinky and her husband joined us, necessitating further introductions. While Ajit and I talked to them and several other people who wandered over to sit at our table, my eyes followed Prajay around the room. The crowd had swelled in the past twenty minutes, and it was harder to seek him out, despite his height.

Meanwhile, waiters were bringing around trays of hot and

cold appetizers. The food was delicious. I hadn't realized how hungry I was until I smelled the meat and vegetable *samosas*. Deep-fried turnovers.

Paul and Jeremy stopped at our table for a chat. As usual Jeremy looked like he had stepped out of a page from *GQ*. His suit fit him like a dream.

After the two guys moved away, Ajit whispered to me, "Do I detect a special relationship between those two guys?"

"Very special." I didn't care to elaborate. I didn't want the others to think Ajit and I were whispering and behaving like lovesick adolescents.

Ajit, being an easygoing, friendly sort, got along well with the folks at our table. The good thing about working for a software company was that most everyone was young. We had plenty to talk about.

I must have been unusually quiet, because Ajit asked me, "Are you all right? You seem preoccupied."

"I'm fine. I guess the wine is going to my head."

"The wine or the host?" His eyes were looking directly into mine.

I stilled. "What do you mean?"

"Nothing." He gestured toward the dance floor. "How about a little dancing? You can get rid of the wine buzz—dance it off."

The DJ had just announced that the dance floor was open, and several couples were already shaking their bodies enthusiastically to *Bhangra* music. "Why not?" Ajit was right. Maybe I could dance some of that frustration off, if not the wine buzz.

Ajit took off his jacket and placed it on the back of his chair, then led me to the dance floor. I was in for a mild surprise. Come to think of it, not so mild. He turned out to be a great dancer, full of life. Other people were watching him with interest.

It was nice to have a spirited partner, but it also put the spotlight on me. I loved dancing, too, so it was a lot of fun. I unabashedly copied the bold but graceful moves Ajit was making.

I was discovering a lot of things about my date—first the guitar and drums, and now the skilled dancing. The guy had talent.

At one point, the rest of the dancers stopped and formed a circle around us, clapping to the sound of the latest Hindi movie song, pressing us to keep moving. For several minutes Ajit and I danced in sync. We made quite a team.

The mad, exotic, pulsating rhythm was both mind-numbing and exhilarating at the same time. I wasn't sure if it was the music, or the wine, or my super-talented partner that did it, but my body was on fire, almost on an erotic high. I felt like I could dance away the whole evening.

When it ended, Ajit stunned me by hoisting me up in his arms. He twirled me around once and put me back on my feet, leaving me breathless and giggling. Then he took my hand and forced me to take a low, theatrical bow alongside him. In the next instant he threw his arms around me and kissed my forehead, much to the crowd's delight. They whistled and stomped. The applause continued for several seconds.

Just like that, Ajit went from being my date to being the life of the party.

And when I finally found a moment to look around to check out our audience, I saw Prajay standing on the outer edge of the circle, arms folded across his middle, staring intensely at Ajit and me.

Chapter 30

Amidst a lot of cheering and compliments on our dance routine, Ajit and I pushed through the circle of spectators and walked back to our table. We were both out of breath. Ajit had sweat running down his face, and he grabbed several paper napkins to wipe it off.

Fortunately I didn't perspire as much, so a simple dabbing with a napkin was enough. Our table was empty, since our table-mates had been watching us dance and were now off somewhere.

I excused myself and hurried to the ladies' room to fix my face and hair. I saw Ajit heading toward the men's room.

A couple of other women were in the ladies' room, but I didn't know them very well, so I merely smiled and said hello. Just as I emerged from one of the stalls, I once again ran into Gargi. This time I knew she'd followed me.

"Fabulous dancing, Meena," she commented wryly. "I didn't know you were a regular Aishwarya." She was referring to the highly popular Bollywood movie star known for her exotic looks and dancing talent.

"Thanks." I started rummaging through my purse for my lipstick.

"Your boyfriend is quite a dancer, too," she said before disappearing into one of the stalls.

While Gargi took care of business, I quickly applied my lipstick, combed my hair, and rushed out. That woman set my teeth on edge, and I was in no mood to spar with her this evening. I had enough problems keeping my equilibrium around Prajay.

And what was that dark expression on Prajay's face earlier? I would have expected him to be smiling and clapping like the others while watching Ajit and me dancing.

We had made his party go from ho-hum to lively, and people were having a good time. Instead of being happy he'd looked like he was ticked off about something. Had he just received bad news? Or did he think our dancing was a bit too rowdy for a stuffy software company?

When I returned to the table I found Ajit back in his seat, his face dry and his hair neat. "Wasn't that a terrific workout?" he asked with a grin.

"I think I lost five pounds." I sat down and gulped down half a glass of water.

The rest of the folks at our table returned one by one with fresh drinks and appetizers, all of them excitedly congratulating us on our performance.

Pinky gave my shoulder a playful smack. "Hey, girl, I didn't know you could dance like that."

"I didn't know I could, either," I said. "It's my partner who got me started."

The dancing continued, and Ajit and I joined the crowd. We didn't do any repeats of the earlier exhibition dancing, but it was fun nonetheless. When the sumptuous buffet dinner was served, the DJ went back to playing slow, sentimental numbers.

Prajay and Nishant stopped by our table once to play the good hosts by inquiring about the quality of the food and drinks. They did some backslapping and general kidding with the guys. Prajay didn't say one word to me.

My heart ached, but I tried to keep a smile on my face by telling myself it was the holiday season. Time to be jolly. Ajit was turning out to be a popular guy, and that should have been enough to make me happy. Who wouldn't want to be seen with a guy all the other girls were eyeing with interest? And yet, I was hurting.

Thank goodness Archana hadn't shown. If she had, my heart would've been bleeding.

Sometime after dinner, I felt exhausted, and my ankle was beginning to feel a twinge or two, so I asked Ajit to find himself other dance partners. He was so full of bubbly energy that I didn't want to put a damper on it. "I had a sprained ankle not too long ago, and it's beginning to bother me a little. Why don't you ask one of those lovely girls to dance?" I suggested.

"Are you sure?" he said, eyeing my foot with genuine concern.

"I'm sure. Look at all those girls who've been casting melting glances at you."

He laughed. "No one's ever melted from looking at me, but it sounds romantic." Then he turned serious and whispered close to my ear, "I know it's none of my business, but what's going on with you and Prajay Nayak?"

"Nothing. Why?" I gave him my best puzzled look. The music and chatter were loud enough that people couldn't hear a word of our conversation.

"Your eyes have been following him all evening, except while we were dancing vigorously."

My cheeks warmed. "Oh boy."

"You have a serious crush on him or something?"

I shut my eyes and sighed. "Serious crush is an understatement. I'm in love with him. Big time."

"So why did you want to start seeing me?" His expression was solemn, but he didn't seem perturbed.

"I don't stand a chance with him, Ajit. He's in love with the idea of finding a tall wife to suit him. I'm not stupid enough to hang around waiting for him to notice me."

"So that's how I ended up here." Again, he seemed amazingly unaffected by my explanation.

"I have to get on with my life. I'd like to get married someday, have a kid or two . . . you know . . . seek out my own Indian-American dream."

"I see. But I noticed Prajay's expression when you and I were on the dance floor. He looked like he wanted to crush my skull."

"I didn't notice," I said quietly.

Ajit excused himself, got up from his chair, and approached a young woman sitting at the next table. In the next second he was leading her to the dance floor, and I watched them dance to the next two songs.

Wondering if I'd hurt his feelings after all, I nursed my glass of water and tried to carry on a conversation with the others at our table. The topic was something benign like new restaurants in the neighborhood, so it needed little attention.

When Ajit joined me later, he was perspiring all over again. He said, "I'm going to go wash my face. Meet me in the lobby in five minutes. I have something to discuss with you."

I frowned at him. "You mean we're going to step outside for the clichéd breath of fresh air and then kiss under the stars?"

"No." He grinned. "I promise not to make you swoon in my arms and kiss you under the midnight sky."

"Good. In that case I don't need to get my coat."

When I stepped into the lobby, Ajit was lounging comfortably on the sofa. The area was empty save for the two of us. I plopped beside him. "So what's this furtive rendezvous for?"

"I want to make a confession."

I put a hand to my chest and gasped. "You're a serial killer!"

"Interesting thought, but no."

"You work for the CIA and need to leave on a secret assignment right away?"

"I wish I had an exciting job like that," he admitted with a chuckle. "What I want to tell you is that I sort of . . . liked your cousin. The one I met at your house."

"Amrita?" I recalled the way he'd stared at my cousin, then blinked rapidly. "Why didn't you say something earlier?"

"I thought it was horrible of me to come to New Jersey to take you out on a date and then declare interest in your cousin."

"So why are you telling me now?"

"Because you seem to have your heart set on some other guy. I know you feel nothing for me, never have. Am I right?"

"I like you a lot. I think you're a great guy."

His laugh was soft and husky. "But you're sorry because there's no chemistry between us, and we can be good friends . . . yada, yada, yada."

He'd read my mind like a poster. How embarrassing. I shrugged. "I'm glad you told me anyway. And you know what? I think Amrita kind of took a liking to you, too."

The corners of his mouth tilted upward. "How'd you figure that?"

"Amrita and I are as close as sisters. She's a few years younger, but she doesn't usually blush and get tongue-tied like she did when she met you. I detected a definite undercurrent of awareness between you guys."

He made a face. "So you wouldn't mind if I like . . . asked her out or something?"

"Not at all." The relief I felt was immense. All this time, Akka's words of caution and even Amrita's solemn advice about playing dangerous games had been bothering me. I was using Ajit as a pawn. Only now, he didn't seem to mind one bit. "So you want me to put in a good word for you with my cousin and her parents?"

"You'd do that for me when I've been such an asshole?"

"Are you kidding? I thought *I* was being a bitch by using you to make Prajay jealous. Although, when I decided to meet you I was sincerely hoping something would click. When my parents got married there was no such thing as compatibility or any-thing. And yet, look at them now. They're happy as clams."

"So are my parents," he said.

"I'd hoped that would happen with you and me, and I could forget Prajay and get on with my life." Having said all that, I sighed and sank back against the backrest, feeling hopeless. "Only it didn't work. The two of us liked each other, but there was no spark. You like my cousin better than me. And Prajay was friendly with you but he ignored me."

"You're wrong. I just figured it out. I think he watched us do that dance routine and assumed that you and I may be getting serious. He didn't like that, especially when I picked you up in my arms and kissed you. I believe that's why he was giving me dirty looks."

My heart took a painful leap. "You think?"

He nodded. "You need some help in that department?"

"Serious help. But he's so damn stubborn about his stupid idea that I'm too tiny and delicate for his big and clumsy ways, I doubt anything's going to work. One way or the other he'll find a big woman, or he'll die trying." I let out an unladylike groan. "If I sit around waiting for him to notice me, I'll be eighty years old and forced to chew my rice with false teeth."

Ajit hooted with laughter. "I have an idea. A friend of mine owns an advertising agency in Los Angeles. I believe he's looking for someone with experience in advertising."

I pursed my lips. "So . . . what are you saying?"

"Maybe we should tell your Prajay that you're being considered for the job. That might open his eyes a bit."

"That's lying."

"Who said anything about lying? Give me a copy of your resume. I'll e-mail it to my friend right away, with a strong recommendation. Believe me, you'll at least get called for an interview."

"You'd do that for me, a virtual stranger?"

"You're not a stranger anymore. We've had three dates so far, and I can tell you're bright and good at your job, or you wouldn't be working for a company like Rathnaya. Nishant was filling me in on the company's plans for the future. Very promising. So you could be a viable candidate for that job in LA."

"How big is this agency?"

"It's not a tiny back-room operation. My friend Brian is smart and ambitious. He's got about a dozen employees, and he's expanding rapidly. His clients are upscale, including some from film and television. They do newspaper and glossy magazine ads, lots of Internet publicity. They're expanding into TV commercials. They also do some PR work for movie and rock stars."

I shut my eyes and pictured an office in sunny LA, with movie executives walking in and out. The weather in California could beat East Coast weather hands down any day. It wasn't an unattractive prospect. I opened my eyes and gave Ajit my most grateful smile. "Can you get me a copy of the job posting, so I can tailor my resume to it?"

"No problem. Except, what are you going to do if they actually offer you the job?"

I hadn't thought of that remote possibility. Taking another job or even applying for one hadn't entered my mind. Until now. I was happy at Rathnaya. "I honestly doubt it'll come to that. I'm sure they'll be inundated with applications."

"But very few come with solid references from a trusted friend," he assured me.

"And you're a *trusted* friend?"

He nodded. "Brian knows I wouldn't recommend just anyone."

This was happening so quickly, I had to catch my breath. California was the other side of the country. When I'd been away at college, I'd been close enough to visit my family often and spend my summers at home. The West Coast was too far. What if I hated it?

Surely my job at Rathnaya would be filled immediately after I left, and if I changed my mind about LA and wanted to come back east, I'd have nothing to come home to. It was a tough decision, but it was worth pondering, especially if it came with a higher salary.

"I'll give it some thought," I said to Ajit.

We sat for a few more minutes, talking about various things, mostly about Ajit's wanting to get to know Amrita. "Is she open to seeing someone or is she one of those med-school nerds with her nose buried in her anatomy book?" Ajit asked me.

"She's very studious, but I think she's okay with meeting the right guy. She claims she's too busy to think about it, but I have a feeling," I said with a sly smile, "she might be willing to see *you.*"

"Yeah?" Ajit's smile was equally wily. "You want to share her e-mail address with me?"

"After I talk to her about you. She's probably going to pretend disinterest and resist the idea. Give me a few days to work on her."

"Okay. Meanwhile, get that resume in shape."

"Yes, sir." I rose to my feet. "Time to get back to the party. You don't want to disappoint all those girls lining up to be your dance partners."

He got off the couch and reached for my hand. "Tomorrow I'm going to be so sore, I'll curse your holiday party. But tonight," he said, doing a quick jiggle with his hips, "I'm going to do some more dancing. Come on, baby," he said playfully and put his arm around my shoulder.

I had a feeling that third glass of wine was giving him a healthy buzz. But I had to admit he was a fun escort. He'd be good for my oh-so-serious cousin. In fact, he'd be perfect. Amrita could use some loosening up. Her life revolved around school and work and exams.

Laughing at Ajit's theatrics, I let him escort me back to the banquet room.

Halfway into the room, we came face-to-face with Prajay.

"Hi," he said, his eyes shifting from my face to Ajit's. He'd caught us laughing. Prajay's greeting to us was friendly enough, but his wide mouth was set in a grim line. Those heavy eyebrows were sitting rather low over the sockets.

I got the distinct feeling he didn't approve of Ajit's arm hooked around me.

Ajit patted my arm. "Let me tell you, Prajay. This lady is exceptionally bright. You have a gem working for you."

"I'm aware of that."

"I'm trying to talk her into going to work for a friend of mine," added Ajit. "He has a job opening that has her name written on it."

Prajay's scowl intensified. "Is that right?" Without another word he turned on his heel and headed for the bar.

My mouth was wide open as I faced Ajit. "Why'd you do that?"

"Do what?"

"It was in bad taste to mention the LA job to Prajay." I tossed him an indignant look, but secretly I had been pleased to note the dark expression on Prajay's face.

Ajit merely shrugged. "Did you see his reaction? For that alone you should pay me a fee."

Chapter 31

On Sunday afternoon, I settled in front of my computer to update my resume. Perhaps Ajit's crazy plan could work. I was willing to try anything. Within reason. In an hour I had the resume polished and e-mailed to Ajit, with a brief note to thank him for being such an entertaining date at the previous night's party.

And I meant it. Too bad we weren't meant for each other.

In my message I didn't mention anything about his getting together with Amrita, although I knew he was anxious. It was in some ways a bit humiliating that my date had become interested in my cousin; nonetheless it was a balm for my conscience.

Besides, in our culture it often worked that way: If a boy was deemed unsuitable for one girl or if things didn't work out as expected, he could always be considered for another girl in the family—a sister or cousin—or even a neighbor.

But first I had to discuss it with my mother. Naturally she'd be disappointed that it hadn't worked out between Ajit and me. I had seen that optimistic light in her eyes last evening. Better to nip her dreams in the bud, I reflected, and made my way downstairs.

I found Mom reading a mystery novel in the family room. Dressed in sweats and wool socks, she looked cozy and rapt. Her feet were tucked under her. She worked long and erratic hours and rarely found time for pleasure reading. I felt a little guilty about disturbing her hard-earned moment of leisure.

"You have a minute?" I asked her.

She looked up absently. Her mind was probably still immersed in the mystery.

"I need to talk to you," I said.

"Sure." She peered at me suspiciously before peeling off her reading glasses. "What's up?"

Taking a seat beside her, I cleared my throat. "Mom, I noticed the look on your face last evening, when Ajit and I left for the party."

"What look?" She wasn't a good actress.

"The look you get when you see me going out with an eligible Konkani guy." I gave her a second to ponder that. "The one that says you want to start making wedding plans?"

"I'm a mother," she retorted. "I'm allowed to dream a little about my children's futures."

"Well, you can forget the dream."

She gave a resigned sigh. "I suppose it has to do with what you call chemistry?"

"I guess."

"I should have known it was too good to be true."

"But it's not a lost cause." I patted her hand.

"What does *that* mean?"

"He liked Amrita a lot."

Her frown returned. "He comes to take you out on a date and hits on your cousin? What kind of nonsense is that?"

"Mom, it's not like he claimed to be in love with me or anything. It was our third date, and nothing was happening between us. We went out on a friendly date."

"Friendly date," Mom sniffed. "Right."

It was my turn to sigh. "It just didn't work for us, okay?"

"So if it never works with any guy, does that mean you'll remain single all your life?"

I laughed at her query, although deep down the possibility bothered me. A solitary spinster's life would very likely be my lot as long as I was in love with Prajay. "It's not a sin to be single, you know."

"No, but it would be a shame to give up the chance to have a more fulfilling life," she said, her eyes softening. "Marriage has so much to offer."

"I know, Mom. I'm not against it. It's just that I haven't found anyone who I want to spend my whole life with. Not yet," I added quickly. "But let's get back to Ajit and Amrita."

"Amrita's still a student. She's not ready to meet eligible boys yet."

"Wrong, Mom. Amrita's definitely ready. Did you notice how she blushed and went all goo-goo-eyed when she met him last evening?"

"She did?"

For a bright woman Mom was clueless about certain things. "Yep. I could sense the vibes between Ajit and her. I think you should talk to Shabari-pachi about him."

Mom stared at her book cover for a minute. "What kind of a boy is he?"

"Nice. He's really smart and a lot of fun. And he has a great job. He even owns a single-family house and drives a pricey car," I added for good measure. I was beginning to sound like a real yenta, a marriage-karma consultant.

"Hmm." Mom looked sufficiently impressed.

"Too bad there's no spark between him and me. But if Amrita and he hit it off, it'll be nice, don't you think?"

"But he's so much older than Amrita."

In my enthusiasm I hadn't thought about age. After all, I was in love with an older guy myself. "You think seven years is too big a gap?"

"That's not unusual for our generation. Madhuri's husband is ten years older than she." Shifting to a more comfortable position, Mom put her glasses back on. "I'll talk to Shabari about it. It's up to Amrita and her."

"Do it soon, then. Despite the age difference I have a hunch he and Amrita are well suited."

My mother pretended to get back to her book, but I could tell she was giving serious thought to what I'd said. I had a feeling she'd be picking up the phone any time now. An eligible bachelor was too precious a commodity to be allowed to go to waste.

I returned to my room. Now I'd sit back and let Mom take care of the rest. Poor Ajit was probably sitting on pins and needles, dreaming about getting together with my pretty cousin.

Meanwhile I'd have to wait and see if my resume would at least earn me an interview.

Ajit surprised me midmorning on Monday, when he called me on my cell phone. "Get prepared for an interview next week," he said on a cheerful note.

"You're not kidding, right?" I asked. I had had no idea Ajit was going to move at lightning speed. I'd been thinking in terms of weeks, not hours.

"I e-mailed your resume to Brian and talked to him yesterday. He's interested. He wants to know if you can fly out to LA for an interview sometime next week."

"That soon?" A frisson of unease ran up and down my arms. This crazy plan was moving too fast.

"He wants to hire someone soon. His employee who left to have a baby doesn't plan to return to work."

"So hers was a sudden decision?" What kind of an employer was this Brian, anyway?

"Apparently she's decided she wants to be a full-time mom for a while. Brian and his manager are interviewing some applicants next week and want to get you in during the same week."

"Can I . . . get back to you on this?"

"Getting cold feet?"

"A little," I admitted. "Look, I'm awfully grateful for all you're doing . . . but . . . ."

I heard his groan clearly. "But you're in love with the big guy and don't want to give up vying for his attention."

"It's not that. He's never going to notice me . . . unless I miraculously grow a foot taller overnight."

"What is it, then?"

"I like my job, Ajit. Making drastic changes because of my personal feelings for someone seems kind of juvenile."

With the high adrenaline level caused by the wine and dancing the night of the party, and seeing Prajay's cool attitude, it had seemed perfectly logical to look for another job, perhaps teach Prajay a lesson. But in the clear light of day, it was beginning to look a lot less attractive.

Cutting off the proverbial nose to spite my face wasn't a mature way of dealing with my problem.

Ajit went quiet for a beat. "It's up to you. Think about it, and let me know soon. I have to call Brian back. By the way, they'll pay for your travel."

"Thanks, Ajit. I'm sorry if I sounded ungrateful. I didn't mean to."

"No problem. We're helping each other." The implied message was that I'd be helping him get ahead with his personal life.

"Um-hmm." I thanked him again and ended the call. It wasn't the right time to tell him I'd already set the ball rolling on his behalf where Amrita was concerned. At this rate, my younger cousins would marry and become mothers twice over long before I could even dream of a bridal shower.

"Why California?" My father looked thoroughly puzzled. "Are you losing your job again?"

I fidgeted with the fringe on the chenille throw covering my legs. I'd kept my news to myself through dinner, but I had introduced the topic of my job application and potential interview after we settled in the family room.

With their bellies full and a cozy fire burning in the fireplace, I figured it would be easier to discuss something that was sure to upset my parents. Besides, I couldn't keep it a secret any longer.

"No, Dad, it's not a layoff," I assured him. This was more difficult to explain than I'd assumed. "I need a change."

"Change? But you've had this job only a short time," my mother reminded me. "I thought you liked your work at Rathnaya."

I glanced at Mom, comfortably settled on the other end of the couch, under her own fleece cover. I wondered if she and Dad would ever understand my rationale. But then, what did they know about falling in love and having one's heart broken?

At the moment I envied my parents' uncomplicated relation-ship. For the umpteenth time in recent weeks I wished I could settle for their kind of arranged love, where two parts of a whole fitted together perfectly, despite being designed by two unrelated craftsmen who each had no idea what the other had envisioned and molded.

Mom and Dad argued at times, disagreed often, but I'd never seen a serious rift between them. They were always a twosome.

"I like my job a lot, but Ajit mentioned this job with his friend's company in LA, and I sort of . . . thought it might be good to try something different—more exciting."

Dad clucked in frustration. "What is it with you kids and ex-citement?" He picked up the remote and shut off the TV, prob-ably because this was a more serious discussion than he'd previously thought. "You have a good job with a decent salary. And it's close to home."

"I know all that, Dad. But my generation isn't like yours. Most people my age change jobs several times before they hit their forties."

Mom, always the more insightful of my parents, had another tough question. "Does this have something to do with Ajit Baliga being interested in Amrita?" She paused to give me a wary look. "You're feeling rejected?"

I shook my head. "Nothing of the sort. Ajit and I have be-come friends. He thinks I have great promise in the advertising field, and the LA firm deals with movie producers and stars. He felt I might be interested in moving from a boring software com-pany to Hollywood." I switched glances between my frowning parents. "It's not the end of the world, you guys. It's a five-hour flight."

"If it's glitz and glamour you're looking for, then New York City has plenty of both," offered Mom. "Manhattan is the leader in the fashion and advertising industries."

"True, but the job market in those industries is tight at the moment."

"All the more reason to hang on to what you have in hand."

Dad got up from his recliner, shaking his head. "Looks like you have made up your mind. I suppose there's no point in voicing our opinions."

"That's not true, Dad. I value your opinion and Mom's."

Mom rose from her comfortable seat and folded the fleece coverlet. It was time for the twosome to go upstairs to their bedroom and discuss my announcement in private.

"Whenever you make up your mind about something, you won't budge, no matter what we say." Mom placed the throw over the back of the couch. "If excitement is what you crave, then it's best that you go to this interview. I don't want you to say later that we stopped you from pursuing your ambitions."

"Thanks. I may not even get the job. They're interviewing other candidates."

I watched them walk away, heard them climb the stairs together, and wished my relationship with them was the kind in which I could honestly tell them that excitement had nothing to do with my decision. I wished I could tell them I was only trying to escape from heartbreak. But I couldn't.

They were my parents, not my friends.

They'd be sure to discuss me and my inane plans as they got ready for bed. Their rebellious daughter was at it again—doing these wild, impulsive things that could only disappoint her and ruin her future. Mom might even blame Akka for my actions, since this was happening on the heels of her recent visit. Poor Akka.

One thing I knew for sure now that I hadn't quite known earlier: The conversation had somehow helped me make up my mind about going to LA for the interview. At first I'd been merely rolling around the idea with my parents, looking for their reactions—even hoping they'd talk me out of it. But the way the conversation had ended, with my getting defensive, they'd taken it for granted that I'd made up my mind about going. It had made me realize, too, that I was leaning in that direction.

It seemed inevitable. I couldn't stay any longer and watch the man I loved settling into holy matrimony with someone else. I'd torture myself every minute, imagining her in his life, in his arms, in his bed. I needed to get away.

I got to my feet, shut off the lights, and went upstairs to call Ajit about my decision.

Ajit sounded pleased. He promised to contact his friend right away and set up an appointment, then let me know about the date and time.

With some reluctance, I went to my computer and started looking up nonstop flights from Newark to Los Angeles. I'd never felt so uneasy and undecided about anything I'd done in my life. What if they offered me the job? Was I willing to leave everyone I loved, everything I valued, my secure lifestyle, and go off on my own?

I badly needed to talk to someone. Even as my eyes scanned the airlines' information on the screen, my hand reached for the phone. There was only one person in the whole world I could turn to. It was around seven o'clock on the West Coast. I hoped Akka was available to talk.

My cousin, Akka's grandson, answered my call, and I chatted with him for a minute before Akka came on the line.

"Are you in trouble, Meena?" asked Akka the moment she heard my voice. My forced cheerfulness hadn't fooled her.

"Yes." I let out a deep breath and stretched out on my bed. "I need your advice. Again."

"You know I'm never short on advice, *charda*," she replied dryly. I could almost picture the serene smile on her face.

"You have to promise not to tell anyone. Not a soul."

"Not a soul," she vowed.

We talked for nearly an hour.

Chapter 32

Restless. I was hopelessly restless, though I tried hard to keep my mind on work at the office.

My job interview was scheduled for the following Monday. I was going to fly out on Sunday afternoon.

I should have been excited. To be considered for a job that required talent, skill, and ambition should've been flattering. The lure of Hollywood and the weather and culture of southern California should have been compelling for a young, single woman.

And yet I felt no enthusiasm. Not even for Christmas. My heartache over Prajay had pretty much ruined my Christmas spirit this year.

The California job was a great opportunity, I tried to tell myself. And Brian Murphy sounded like a nice enough guy from the brief phone conversation I'd had with him. Any friend of Ajit's had to be amiable. Plus, Ajit had assured me that I didn't have to accept the job if I didn't think it was right for me, assuming there was a remote chance they might offer it to me. I didn't think it was plausible, considering I had limited experience.

"Why the grim expression?" Pinky asked when she came into my office at the end of the day.

"I look grim?" I pretended nonchalance.

"You've been looking like that all day. You've been very quiet, too." She gave me a speculative look. "Feeling okay?"

"Fine." I smiled brightly. "Still a little sore from all that dancing on Saturday night."

"Of course you're sore. You and your boyfriend danced nonstop for hours." She shrugged into her coat and pulled on her gloves. "He's cute, by the way."

"He is cute," I agreed.

"How did you meet him?"

"My aunt introduced us."

She wiggled her brows. "Do I hear wedding bells?"

"Hardly." I waved her away. "You're getting to be just like my mom. One date, and it's a straight path to the altar."

"Just wondering, that's all. You two make a nice-looking couple, you know."

"Doesn't mean we have to end up getting married."

"We'll see about that, missy," she said. Rummaging through her purse, she fished out her car keys. "Good night."

"Take care, Pinky." I returned to work, grateful for the peace and quiet. Paul had left a few minutes ago, so I was left all alone to finish my last memo. My eyes were tired from working at the computer all day.

It wasn't just my eyes. My whole body felt drained—not to mention my mind. I hadn't slept well the previous night. I needed to go home, eat a hot dinner, and get to bed early. At this rate I didn't know how I was going to last through the week.

Other than Ajit and my parents, I hadn't told anyone else about my interview. I'd told Paul and Pinky that I was going to California to visit my great-aunt and her family for a couple of days.

Holding on to a secret was exhausting.

I sent the memo to the printer and logged off my computer, then pressed my fingers over my eyes.

"You seem tired."

I nearly jumped out of my seat at hearing that deep, familiar voice. My heartbeat shot up instantly.

Prajay stood in the doorway, taking up the entire space.

"Y-you startled me," I murmured.

"Sorry. I thought you would have heard my footsteps." He looked a bit tired, too. Must be those fourteen-hour days he'd mentioned.

"Guess the printer drowned them," I replied. "How come you're still here? I thought you'd be gone after the party."

"I had some things to take care of here. I'm leaving tomorrow."

"I see." Rising from my chair, I went to pluck my coat off the coatrack.

"Are you in a rush?" he asked, sliding his hands into his pant pockets.

I put on my coat. "Not particularly."

"Do you have a minute to talk?"

"Sure." I'd noticed his uncertain tone. "Why? You have another secret project or something?"

He flicked his shirt cuff to look at his wristwatch. "I'd like to take you out to eat." He raised his brows. "That's if you don't have other plans?"

I glanced at him briefly. "No."

"Good. I thought you might have plans with Ajit."

"He lives in Connecticut." I retrieved my purse from my desk drawer. "He was here just for the weekend."

"So you'll go to dinner with me?"

"Sorry. Can't. I'm exhausted." I waited for him to move aside so I could step into the outer room—Pinky's domain. "I just want to go home, eat with my parents, and call it an evening." I gave him my best professional smile. "If there's something you need done, tell me. I promise I'll start working on the project first thing tomorrow morning."

"Are you mad at me, Meena?" He looked unsure of himself.

I'd never seen him look like this. "Why would I be mad?" I shifted closer to Pinky's desk and placed my purse on it, just in case I needed to hang on to something solid to maintain my balance.

"I don't know. You've been distant and cool since my last trip to New Jersey."

"You're my boss, Prajay."

"So?"

I cleared my throat. "So there's the conventional employee-employer distance between us," I replied, noticing the door leading out into the corridor was shut. Prajay had obviously closed it after he'd entered the suite.

But I wasn't worried about my safety. If anything, Prajay should've been worried about his. I was the one crazy in love with him, not the other way around.

"Don't be silly, Meena." His eyebrows clenched into a tight, annoyed knot.

"You implied a while ago that our relationship should be nothing short of professional," I reminded him, feeling just as annoyed as he looked. But I kept my best placid face on. Besides, I honestly wasn't in the mood to play his love manager any longer. I'd had enough of that.

I was secretly proud of my cool façade. Inside, however, my stomach was churning, nauseating me in the process. It was hunger. It must be.

"Oh, come on, we're more than colleagues. We're friends, too, aren't we?" he asked.

"We are?" I searched his face. "You're the one who said it was inappropriate for a boss to get too close to an employee."

"That's not what I meant, and you know it." His hands were out of his pockets. Now they were fidgeting with his car keys. "What I did to you that evening bordered on sexual harassment. *That* was inappropriate."

"I kept telling you it wasn't harassment. I asked for it."

"Doesn't mean it was right."

"Okay, then. Whatever you think is right shall be done. You're the boss; you set the rules." I pulled on my gloves. "Now, what was it you wanted me to do?"

"Nothing. I just want to talk to you." His scowl remained.

"Fine, let's talk." I faced him squarely, trying to ignore the electricity humming through me. "Everyone's gone home for the day. We can talk privately about anything you want."

He sighed. "Never mind. You seem to be in a difficult mood." He dismissed me with a wave. "Go home, Meena. You clearly need your rest."

"You said you wanted to talk." I folded my arms across my chest. "I'm ready to listen. Go ahead."

"I was thinking of a more relaxing atmosphere than this office for what I had in mind—maybe a bite to eat, where we could really talk. Like friends."

Picking up my purse again, I slipped the strap over my shoulder. "But you've made it crystal clear that we're *not* friends. I'm your paid consultant, remember?" I moved toward the door, leaving him behind. "If friendship is what you want, why don't you call your girlfriend?"

"I don't have a girlfriend."

My feet instantly stopped in their tracks. I pivoted around and faced him. "Your fiancée, then."

"I don't have a fiancée, either."

"Why not? What happened to your Amazon-in-a-sari?" Despite my sarcastic tone my heart fluttered a little. My lower lip started doing its usual trembling act. And I couldn't stop it in spite of biting hard on it. Any harder, and it would bleed.

"That's what I wanted to talk to you about."

The tears were gathering momentum. They were burning my eyelids. In a second they'd come gushing out. What in God's name was wrong with me lately? Why couldn't I control my weeping?

This man was ruining my life, even my attitude toward life. Everything.

I took a step backward, away from his disturbing presence. "Look, I have no interest in your love life." I swiped a gloved hand over the first traitorous tears that were pooling in my eyes. "Go find your own damn bride. Just leave me out of it."

All my attempts at self-control had failed. I hated crying in front of him. I hated crying, period.

"Damn it, Meena! Don't do this to me." In an instant he closed the space between us. He scooped me up in his arms, carried me back to my office, and shut the door with his foot. Depositing me on top of my desk, he kept his arms wrapped around me. "Don't cry. Please, baby, don't."

I buried my face in his chest. Instead of feeling better, I felt worse. He was making it difficult for me to hate him. He really was a nice guy, but I wanted to dislike him. I needed to dislike him, to make myself fall out of love with him. The only way I could do that was by keeping my distance. Instead, here I was, sniffling, carrying on in his giant octopus arms and ruining his beautiful shirt.

"I'm s-sorry," I hiccupped. "I d-don't usually cry like this."

"That's okay." He rubbed my back with long, gentle strokes. "You're tired and still recovering from an injured ankle."

I latched on to that remark. "It's that stupid ankle and all that medication. It's turned my emotions to mashed potatoes."

"I understand." His hand moved from my back to my head. He smoothed my hair with the same soft motion. "You've had a lot to deal with. You've been working too hard and not getting enough rest."

My weeping turned more bitter and noisy. Why was he being so kind and sweet? He was playing havoc with my equilibrium. If he'd been brusque and brutish, I'd have been fine.

I could stand up to a big bully. I could hold my own against any man, but I didn't know how to deal with this kind of warmth and tenderness. And all the while he held me and soothed me, like he would a child disturbed by a nightmare. He'd even called me *baby*.

The tears eventually stopped, and all that remained was the annoying hiccups. I pushed away from him, grabbed a bunch of tissues from my desk, and thoroughly blew my nose. I couldn't stay close to him anymore.

One more second of that and I was likely to embarrass both of us by confessing that I was in love with him.

"Sorry," I repeated. "I ruined both your shirt and your evening."

"Not at all," he assured me. "Anything to help a friend."

"Well, since you played friend so admirably, it's my turn to return the favor. You said you wanted to talk?"

"We can do that some other time." He studied my face with the same worried expression he'd worn the day I'd fallen outside his office. "You're in no shape to talk. You need to go home and rest."

"No, I'm fine. Honest." I slid off the desk, pulled off my gloves, and thrust them in my coat pocket before unbuttoning it. "Sit down, Prajay. Tell me what you came here to discuss." Taking off my coat, I went around the desk to sit in my own chair. Putting the desk between us was necessary.

After a moment's hesitation he sat down in the guest chair. "All right. This won't take long. I just wanted to tell you that Archana and I aren't seeing each other anymore."

A happy little note of satisfaction pinged in my brain. "Why?"

"She didn't like me." He made a face, but it wasn't an unhappy expression. In fact it was funny.

"Really?" I asked on a shaky laugh. "What didn't she like about you?" How could anyone dislike a gentle giant with a clever brain, a big heart, and a sense of humor?

He shrugged. "Guess I'm just not a likeable guy." He made that silly face again, wrinkled nose and all. "Isn't that obvious if I'm nearing forty and still single?"

"Means nothing," I assured him. "I'm sure you'll find the right woman soon enough." I thought about what my wise Akka would have said. "These things take time. When it happens, it happens very fast."

"You're so smart and practical, Meena," he said. "And wise beyond your years. That's exactly why I wanted to talk to you."

"Oh?"

"You understand me so well. You're the only one I can talk to. I mean really talk."

"Glad to be of help." I stood up once again and reached for my coat. Outside the window, it looked pitch dark. The forecast had promised snow at night. I hoped it hadn't started already. That's when it struck me that it was a blessing my office was on the sixth floor. No one could have seen me enfolded in Prajay's arms. There was no other tall building in the immediate vicinity.

He got to his feet, too. "Thanks for being a good listener."

"So, I guess you'll be contacting the next person on your matrimonial list?"

"No, I've decided to give up on that. I have something else in mind. I . . ." He shook his head when I gave him another questioning look. "Never mind, I'll tell you some other time, when you're not so tired."

Once again I pulled on my gloves and adjusted the wool scarf around my neck, wondering what his Plan B involved. Singles' bars? Going to India to find a suitable bride? Arranged marriage like his parents and my folks had?

It was none of my business, I reminded myself.

"If you lower your expectations substantially, there's no reason why you can't find the woman of your dreams," I said to him before opening the main door of the suite and stepping into the hallway.

"Meena, wait. I have to ask you something."

"What?"

He studied the keys in his hands for a beat, as if he were trying to figure out where each one fit. "Is it . . . is it true you're looking for a job on the West Coast?"

After a moment of silence I nodded. "I'm giving it serious consideration."

"Are you unhappy here?"

"No."

"You must be, if you're looking for other jobs."

"That's not it."

"Is it the salary? The kind of work?"

I shook my head. "It has nothing to do with my job or my work here."

"Then what is it?"

"Strictly personal reasons."

When I glanced at him to gauge his reaction, Prajay looked bemused, like he was seeing me for the first time. Then his eyes went wide. "I get it! Ajit must be moving to California, and you want to be near him."

"Good night, Prajay." I let him draw his own conclusions.

Let him think I was in love with Ajit and whatever else rode on that assumption. "Please pull the door shut when you leave, if you don't mind." I started striding toward the elevators. I knew he was staring at my back, so I fought the urge to turn around.

Outside, it definitely felt like snow in the air. Shivering, I got behind the wheel of my car and waited for the engine to warm up. He'd been so kind to me, so understanding. How could I even think of giving up my dream job at his company and walking away? Being with him, literally in his arms, had tempted me to call Brian Murphy's office and cancel my interview.

But now, sitting alone in my car, in a dark parking lot, the hopelessness of the situation caught up with me afresh. Prajay hadn't shown one iota of interest in me. Granted, his heartbeat while I had my face buried in his chest had sounded like drums beating furiously, and his hand moving over my back had been a little unsteady, but as long as he considered me a friend and nothing more, I had to walk away from him—sooner or later.

For the sake of my mental health, I preferred to make it sooner.

Chapter 33

I boarded the hotel shuttle bus outside the Los Angeles airport, gave the driver my name, and told him I had a reservation. I was the first passenger in.

"Welcome to LA," he said absently. It was probably a standard greeting required of him. He was an older African-American man with thick glasses and loads of unruly gray hair. He got up from his seat, grabbed my suitcase, and deposited it in the luggage area. I held on to my laptop and purse, my precious possessions.

"Thank you." I smiled at him. "My reservation was booked and paid for online."

"Yes, ma'am," he concurred.

"Roughly how long is the ride to the hotel?" I asked him. I was dead tired after the long coast-to-coast flight, and the prospect of sitting in a stiff seat for another hour or more wasn't appealing.

"About thirty minutes, depending on traffic."

"Thanks," I said, gratefully sinking into the single seat directly behind his. He kept the engine running for a while and waited till several other passengers came aboard.

Meanwhile I took off my jacket, settled back in my seat, and closed my eyes. But I couldn't relax. I'd had a difficult week. Ever since that unexpected visit from Prajay, and the odd, disturbing conversation we'd had, I'd been irritable.

Every night I'd tossed and turned, and every day I'd been second-guessing my decision to go to the job interview.

When the bus finally started to move and pulled out of the airport's concrete confines, I opened my eyes and delighted in the golden sunlight coming through the window. The warmth was welcome after the wintry weather in New Jersey. And despite my long flight, with the time difference it was still afternoon here in LA.

I still had a couple of hours of sunshine ahead of me. With a bit of my energy returning, I decided I wasn't going to waste them.

Once I got to the hotel and strode into the spacious lobby, I took a deep breath and looked around. It was a nice lobby, with subdued décor and lighting and a long, cherry reception desk.

A tastefully decorated Christmas tree sat next to the desk, reminding me once again that Christmas was two days away. Sadly, I had put away plenty of money in my Christmas fund this year, but hadn't shopped for any gifts.

The hotel wasn't fancy, but it was extremely generous of Brian Murphy to arrange this for me. A twinge of guilt stabbed me right between the ribs.

Nonetheless it was too late to go back to New Jersey, so I had to make the most of my trip. I approached the desk and the young blond woman standing behind it.

"Would you like a valet to take your luggage upstairs, Miss Shenoy?" she asked a few minutes later, handing me my key card after she'd finished registering me.

"That won't be necessary, thanks. I don't have much luggage," I explained. "But I would appreciate a map of the local area and a list of cab companies, please."

She produced both right away. I tucked them in my purse, thanked her again, and walked toward the bank of elevators, wheeling my suitcase beside me. As I waited for the elevator to arrive, I observed the street scene outside the floor-to-ceiling windows.

Maybe I could take a quick shower and head back out, check out some of the stores. Their display windows looked inviting, with elegant wreaths, twinkling lights, and gold and silver bows. I could stop at a neighborhood café and pick up some seafood for dinner. The brilliant sun was beckoning me.

I'd been to LA some years ago, but that was to attend a Konkani convention with my parents. We'd been surrounded by crowds of fellow Konkanis who had come together from every part of the U.S. and Canada, and some even from the Middle East and the U.K. It wasn't the same as having the freedom to discover the place alone.

A strong floral scent greeted me as I let myself into my room. Whatever they used to deodorize the rooms here was potent, I reflected, closing the door behind me. But I enjoyed perfumes, so it wasn't a problem.

And then I saw them—flame-colored roses arranged in a vase and a bottle of white wine chilling in a bucket of ice sitting on a table beside the window.

Sunshine poured in like liquid gold through the panes, making the glass vase look iridescent. Sweat had beaded on the outside of the stainless steel ice bucket.

What a marvelous welcome. These West Coast folks really knew how to treat a potential employee. I was being wooed like the next CEO of a major corporation.

But all this fuss was only adding to my guilt—I was being treated like royalty when I wasn't even serious about the job. Another troubling thought came on the heels of that one. Their magnanimity made me wonder what sort of job it was. Why were they trying so hard? What was the real reason the previous employee wasn't coming back to her position? Was this a job from hell? What exactly was I getting myself into?

Again, it was too late to turn back.

I dropped my luggage and purse on the floor and walked across the room to read the card propped against the bucket. The message was brief. And anonymous.

Meena, Wishing you lots of luck. Enjoy your surprise.

It was certainly a delightful surprise.

Frowning, I read the note again. Who could have sent me

flowers *and* wine? The message sounded too familiar and friendly to be from Brian Murphy. No one in my very down-to-earth family was the wine and roses type. Suddenly I knew.

"Ajit, you devil!" I said aloud with a chuckle. It was thoughtful of him to send me such lavish gifts just to wish me luck. But then again, I was his shortcut to Amrita.

I took an appreciative sniff of one fat rosebud. Lovely. The wine was a nice California chardonnay. "You have class, my friend. Amrita's a lucky girl," I said.

"Not all of it was his idea," said a voice behind me, making me jump.

With a squeal I turned around. The card slipped out of my hand.

Prajay stood halfway across the room, hands in his pockets.

"What the . . ." I stared at him.

He didn't say one word, but stood rooted to the spot, clearly enjoying my confusion. I blinked a couple of times.

I had to be hallucinating. I couldn't shake Prajay from my mind, no matter how far I ran from him. I blinked again, hoping to clear my vision. But the hologram wouldn't go away.

"Surprised?" he asked finally.

"More like cardiac arrest," I shot back, wondering how I still had a tongue in my mouth. And asking myself why I was talking to a computer-generated image. A technical genius like Prajay could probably create something spooky like a hologram quite easily.

"This is *your* surprise?" I asked nevertheless, gesturing toward the table.

He nodded. "Part of it. The flowers are from me. The wine's from Ajit."

"Gee, thanks. You must want me out of your life desperately if you're wishing me luck with a job interview at some other company."

"You've got it all wrong," he said.

"Anyway, what are *you* doing in *my* hotel room?"

"Welcoming you to LA," he said.

"Why? Making sure I go to the interview and take the damn

job?" The delusion was continuing too long and getting more bizarre by the second. I needed to snap out of it and face reality. Seeing his image like this was too upsetting.

"I wanted to be with you." His eyes looked warm in the bright light. His clothes had a few uncharacteristic creases in them. A shadow of a beard made his skin look darker on the cheeks and chin. He appeared a little travel-weary, just like me.

He was a figment of my imagination. He looked delectable all the same.

Unable to stand on my shaking legs any longer, I collapsed onto the sofa next to the bed and closed my eyes. "This is a dream, isn't it? I can't take this anymore. Please . . . tell me this is only a dream and you're not real." I opened my eyes.

"It's not a dream." Maybe to prove it, he finally began to move toward me. "It's real. *I'm* real."

"If it's not a dream, then what are you doing in LA? There's something wrong with this picture."

"Like what?"

"You should be in your office . . . or wining and dining some beanpole with a Mensa membership card."

He sat down beside me. "I was in my office until this morning. I flew in a little earlier than you."

"Really?" I wondered what in heaven's name was going on. He still hadn't revealed what he was doing here. In *my* hotel room.

"Because of the Christmas rush I had to do a lot of maneuvering to get a last-minute ticket from DC to LA."

I squinted up at him, still suspicious about my mental condition. "You mean you followed me here?"

He nodded and picked up my hand. No wonder he looked somewhat disheveled.

The warmth in that large hand was real enough. Just to make sure, I let my free hand glide over his, the long, square-tipped fingers, the texture of the skin, the short hair on the back of it, and the sturdy knuckles. His hand shook a little, just like mine.

There was satisfaction in knowing a tiny person like me could make a guy like him tremble.

Okay, I wasn't dreaming. "How did you know where to find me?"

"Thanks to two very nice people."

"My parents?" Unlikely, but not impossible.

He shook his head. "Akka and Ajit."

My eyes opened wide. "Akka?"

"Why are you so surprised?"

"Akka was sworn to secrecy. She promised not to rat on me. And Ajit had no business telling you any of this."

"Don't be mad at those two. After Akka called me, I called Ajit and forced him into telling me where you'd be staying in LA."

"I can see how you bullied Ajit, but why would Akka feel the need to call you?"

"She said she was breaking an oath, but she couldn't stand by and see you miserable, so she called me at my office yesterday. She was lucky to reach me on a Saturday, too. She told me you're in love with me."

My cheeks instantly warmed. How embarrassing. And dismaying. Akka had betrayed me. The one person I'd trusted and always held in high esteem had given away my deepest secret. How *could* she?

Prajay put a thumb under my chin and raised it so I could meet his inquiring gaze. "Is that true, Meena?"

I remained silent for a few beats. "Yes," I admitted finally. "And to think I trusted the old lady."

"She's a wonderful old lady. She went against her conscience for you and me. I'm very grateful to her for giving away your secret."

"Why?" I murmured.

"If it weren't for Akka, I'd never have known how you felt about me."

I'd been wearing my heart on my sleeve all this time, and he still hadn't known? But now he knew everything, thanks to Akka. This was humiliation to the max. My heart was wide open for an assault. "Why did you come all the way to LA?" I demanded.

"To take you home."

"Home?"

"I've been a big, blundering fool, Meena. I've fought my feelings for you since the day I met you."

"The day I fell down?"

"You were so small and pretty and in so much pain. I felt awful because I'd almost killed you with my clumsy ways. I was so damn relieved to learn that it was no more than a sprained ankle."

"It was partly my fault."

"Later, I wanted to tell you how I felt when you were in Virginia, but you were so stiff and professional—hard to approach. Besides, we didn't have a single private moment."

"You had plenty of other opportunities," I reminded him dryly.

"Last week, I stopped by your office and asked you out to dinner, so we could talk privately. I wanted to tell you then. But you gave me the cold shoulder—and the impression that you had something going on with Ajit Baliga."

"I never said anything."

"Precisely." He shook a finger at me. "When I asked you about the California job, you clammed up, again leading me to think it had something to do with Ajit."

"How could I have known what you had on your mind that evening? Why couldn't you just spit it out instead of beating around the bush? As far as I knew, you were obsessed with finding a tall woman," I retorted.

"At first yes, but not after I got to know you better. That's when I began to realize I had very strong feelings for you."

"Then why did you continue looking for an Amazon, for heaven's sake? I pretty much offered myself to you that night in your condo. But you rejected me."

"I thought you had a temporary crush on your boss. Why would someone as beautiful as you want a serious relationship with a guy with my looks?"

"Why not? You have so much going for you."

"Sure, my business is doing well. But just *look* at me, Meena."

"You underestimate your looks, Prajay," I scolded him. "I happen to think you have a great personality, and you look very distinguished."

"Thanks." He gave a helpless shrug. "What can I say? I'm an idiot. I was wrong on many counts."

Something struck me then. I narrowed my eyes at him. "Are you telling me this *now* because Archana turned you down?"

"No—"

"Since you can't have a tall woman, am I your last resort?"

"Listen, I—"

"Sort of like settling for a stale burger because that's all that's available when you'd rather have a juicy steak?"

He clamped a hand firmly over my mouth. "No, I lied a bit about Archana. On the two occasions she and I met, I was so preoccupied with thoughts of you that she came right out and asked me what my problem was. I decided to tell her the truth. Fortunately she had a sense of humor about it and advised me to go after you if you were single and available."

I yanked his hand off my mouth and rolled my eyes. "You've got to be kidding."

He made that same funny face he'd made the previous week. "She told me I was stupid for letting the perfect woman slip away from me because of some silly hang-up about height and weight."

"Smart woman." Suddenly Archana was taking on a golden glow.

"Damn right. That's why I decided to talk to you about my feelings."

Hope sparked inside my belly. "What kind of feelings? The kind you feel for all your consultants?"

"Hardly." He gave what sounded like a frustrated groan combined with an amused laugh. "What I feel for you has been torture to hold inside. I love you. I knew for sure when I kissed you that evening."

"Then why would you want to hide such fabulous feelings? That night in your condo, you hurt me badly when you pushed me away."

"I'm so sorry." He kissed my hand. "At the time, I felt I had to. I'm so much older than you. Besides, you're so tiny and delicate. Any kind of physical relationship with me would be the death of you."

"So how's it different now?"

"Now I know you feel the same way about me. *That* is the difference." He ran a caressing hand from the top of my arm all the way down to my wrist. "So fragile. Can you honestly see a man over two hundred pounds making love to a little doll like you?"

The spark inside me was slowly exploding into full-blown fireworks. "I can see it clearly. And it looks pretty good to me." I was still trying to get over the fact that Prajay was here, sitting next to me, telling me he cared about me, when I'd made myself miserable over him for weeks. Especially this past week. I'd been brooding during the entire flight from Newark to LA, too.

"Just *pretty* good?" he teased, with a hint of smugness.

"Very good," I replied, my mouth twitching in spite of my efforts to suppress the smile.

In the next instant he picked me up by the waist and hauled me into his lap. "Can't you do better than that, Miss PR and talented copywriter?" He drew me closer and touched his forehead to mine.

"All right. Getting physical with you sounds delicious," I said on a nervous giggle. Lord, even that was too tame to describe what I was feeling at the moment. It felt like heaven sitting so close to him, enclosed in a tight embrace. He smelled super, too—a combination of his signature cologne and clean sweat from a long day of work and travel.

"Much better," he murmured on a satisfied note. Then his hand cupped my face and his mouth captured mine—curious, achingly hungry, matching my own need.

I twined my arms around his neck and kissed him back, venting all my pent-up emotions from the past weeks. "Okay . . . so . . . how *are* we going to do it?" I asked him, finally coming up for air. "Get physical, that is."

"Exactly like this. I can pick you up with one hand very easily," he replied with a mocking grin. But the grin disappeared momentarily. "I'm still worried about you. You'd be making love with an elephant."

I pulled away to look into his eyes. "Does size really matter that much to you, Prajay?"

"Only in terms of your safety. Even if we're careful and all goes well in the love department, our children will be big, strapping infants. My dad's a giant of a man, and my mother apparently had difficulty giving birth to three large boys. And my mom's a lot bigger than you." He kissed the tip of my nose. "I'd worry myself sick over your health, baby."

Baby. I liked that. "If and when the time comes, I'll manage. Medical care has come a long way since your mom gave birth," I assured him, before he could dream up a few more excuses. I kissed him with renewed ardor.

"So, how did you magically appear in my room?" I demanded a while later.

He inclined his head in the direction behind my left shoulder. "See that door? I'm in the room that connects with this one."

I turned to look at the door. "So you planned all this in advance?"

He nodded. "Nice surprise?"

"Um-hmm," I purred, burying my face in his neck.

Speaking of rooms, I realized I was in this place for a reason. "Oh, no! I have the job interview tomorrow."

"Not anymore," he said with quiet confidence. "I'm not going to let you get away from me."

"It's unprofessional not to show up for a scheduled interview, Prajay," I argued. "Ajit's friend went to all this trouble to fit me in at the last minute and all."

"It's all taken care of. Ajit called his friend and canceled the interview." Prajay's hands slipped under my shirt—a bold, unexpected move that sent a tremor through me. His big hands were firm but gentle.

"And you guys let me think I had an interview and let me fly out here? How devious is that?"

He stroked my ribcage. "We didn't want you to guess what

was going on. Akka, Ajit, and I planned this together—down to your favorite roses and white wine."

I glanced at the roses. I should've known as soon as I saw them that something strange was afoot. I placed my palms around his face. I loved the raspy texture. "How did you know they were my favorite flowers? You sent me those when I sprained my ankle, too."

"When I was feeling guilty about your injury, I asked Pinky if she knew what kind of flowers you liked. She told me."

"Hmm." Pinky had never divulged that bit of information to me.

"I love your surprise, but poor Brian Murphy is paying for my expenses," I insisted weakly, giving in to the delightful sensation caused by Prajay's roving hands kneading the sides of my breasts.

"I've already reimbursed him for everything," Prajay assured me.

This was a pleasantly aggressive side of Prajay I'd never encountered before. And I liked it a whole lot. I liked strong, decisive men who went after what they wanted. And yet it was empowering to know he'd been uncertain of my feelings for him. I didn't want to be taken for granted. I took a shaky breath and basked in the wonder of it all.

This was what I'd been seeking all along.

"You took care of everything." I batted my eyelashes at him, savoring the moment. "You're so efficient."

"That's why I'm the CEO of my company," he said, none too modestly. His heated gaze held mine for a long moment. "Am I moving too fast for you?"

"No." He was moving at exactly the pace I wanted. Needed.

"Won't your parents get upset if they find out you're alone in LA with me?" he teased.

"They'll be ecstatic that their wayward brat has finally fallen in love with a suitable man." I didn't want to tell him I had no intention of telling my parents about certain things surrounding this trip. Of course I'd have to tell them a few things, including the canceled job interview. The rest was going to be my private, slightly guilty pleasure.

Before his wandering hands could shift again, I caught them in mine. "I have to ask you some questions before we go any further."

"Is this some kind of test?" His eyebrows were raised.

I gave it a moment's consideration. "You could call it that."

"Multiple choice?"

"Uh-uh. Right or wrong answers only."

"Damn."

"First of all, how long are we staying in LA? I have to let my family know."

"I thought we could make it a well-earned, week-long vacation—get to know each other without any interruptions. We've never had any time to ourselves. And we could spend Christmas together."

"Good answer." This could turn out to be my best Christmas ever. I squeezed his hands to show my approval. "Second, are we dating exclusively now, or are you going to start with that 'fragile piece of fluff' and once again go off on some wild quest for an Amazon in a sari?" I held my breath for his answer.

"Why would I want anyone else, now that I know you care about me? I've been crazy about you since the day I met you."

I let the joy of it settle around my heart before continuing. "Third, you're sure you won't regret your decision later?"

"The only decision I regret is not telling you earlier. I wasted a lot of time."

"You certainly did." I proceeded with my questioning. "Since this is clearly a conflict of interest, will I still be working for you?"

"Oh, that, yeah." He sighed. "Uh . . . I suppose I could make you a junior partner in the firm or something," he said. "That way you won't be working *for* me but *with* me." He gave me one of his rare grins. "How am I doing so far on the test?"

"You're *this* close to a perfect score." I held my thumb and forefinger very close together. "I have one more question. Is this a short-term or long-term relationship?"

"Neither." His mock frown was fierce enough to look like the real thing. "This relationship is permanent. You're going to marry me right away, Miss Shenoy."

I sent silent messages of thanks to Lord Ganesh and Akka, then threw my arms around Prajay's neck and smacked a noisy kiss on his mouth. "You aced the test, Mr. Nayak. You may now propose to me the old-fashioned way. Ask me nicely."

Author's Note

I have always been a strong believer in karma, and entirely fascinated by it, a mystical word that comes from my Indian-Hindu culture.

It is a complex term, used widely across the world in varied contexts, yet impossible to define precisely. It is loosely used to mean fate or destiny. But on a deeper level, it is closely related to reincarnation, the Hindu concept of the soul being reborn again and again, to pay for the sins of previous lives, until it has atoned for every ill and become perfect enough to achieve *moksha*. Immortality.

In my latest novel, *The Reluctant Matchmaker,* my heroine is anxious to seek her own destiny, to shape it to her vision and ideals. But little does she know that *karma* cannot be molded to one's way of thinking. It is a potent, mysterious, and unpredictable force that strikes in bizarre ways, and along the way teaches some valuable lessons in life.

I love to write stories that entertain and educate my readers, women's fiction with romantic elements and that reflect my ethnic Indian culture, what I call *"Bollywood in a Book."*

I sincerely hope you enjoy this refreshing new story with its karmic touch, which depicts the unique challenges faced by young, second-generation immigrants.

Happy reading.

Shobhan Bantwal

THE RELUCTANT MATCHMAKER

Shobhan Bantwal

ABOUT THIS GUIDE

The suggested questions are included
to enhance your group's
reading of this book.

DISCUSSION QUESTIONS

1. Despite growing up in a culture that places so much emphasis on arranged marriage, a practice that has worked well for so many in her family, why do you think Meena Shenoy firmly rejects the notion? Discuss the concept of arranged marriage.

2. Discuss the pros and cons of growing up in a mixed cultural environment like Meena and Prajay have. Does straddling two or more diverse cultures help or hinder personal growth?

3. Despite Prajay's remarks that he doesn't place emphasis on looks, he still wants to marry someone based on physical appearance. Discuss the contradictions and the implications of his statement.

4. Discuss Meena's relationship with Deepak Iyer. What does Deepak bring to her life and to the story?

5. Meena's mother is a successful career woman and a dominant matriarch. How does she influence her children's lives?

6. After admitting to herself that she's in love with Prajay, why is the intrepid Meena so afraid to confess that love to him?

7. What roles do Meena's brothers play in her life? How do they factor into her quest for the perfect man?

8. Discuss the scene that involves Prajay's young niece and nephew. How do they enhance the story?

9. Akka, Meena's elderly great-aunt, plays an influential part in Meena's story. How does Akka bring a whole new twist to the plot?

10. Another character who makes the story more complicated is Ajit Baliga. Discuss his role in the story.

17x